RISEN

THE SECOND SEAL OF
THE KRYPTEIA CONSPIRACY

MICHAEL KOOGLER, JED QUINN, & JAREN RILEY

Dedicated to Perseverance, and everything she continues to teach us.

Zephaniah 1: 14-15

14 The great day of the LORD is near, it is near, and hasteth greatly, even the voice of the day of the LORD: the mighty man shall cry there bitterly.
15 That day is a day of wrath, a day of trouble and distress, a day of wasteness and desolation, a day of darkness and gloominess, a day of clouds and thick darkness,

PROLOGUE

Ground Zero, London, England: Sirens continued to blare. People continued to die. The end of the world had come for them and, all things considered, they would be the lucky ones. They would avoid the plague that was bearing down upon the world, an emerging terror unlike anything the world had ever seen. They would avoid the risen. The rest of the world—those who lived—would experience a nightmare from which there would be no waking.

The figure walked slowly through the wreckage along a shattered London street, savoring the smell of death and the terror that permeated the air like a thick blanket. He was cloaked in black, and against the smoke-filled night sky, he was all but invisible. Even the flickering flames did little to illuminate his shape as he passed through the streets in complete silence. Occasionally, he would hear a desperate cry for help or the sobbing of some poor wretch who had given up all hope. But beyond the small smile these dying people elicited with him, he continued on, unseen and unheard.

In this particular part of the ruined city, some distance from the epicenter of the nuclear detonation, there were still a few buildings that attempted to remain standing amidst the incredible destruction. Of those that had not yet collapsed, windows were blown out and walls compromised. Most of them were still on fire. As he walked, he found it all to be absolutely perfect. The covering had been ripped from the whispered conversations that spanned decades, thrusting the horror of nuclear war back into the forefront. Accompanied by the apocalyptic tide of the risen that was about to break upon the world, the people would be more than ready for him to save them.

But for the moment, there was still much to do. There were many pieces to still move about the chess board. His companion had returned and would do his part in bringing the United States to its knees. More importantly, the kings were on the run. With the right help, they would survive…at least until the sacrifice. And of course, he had to attend to the vessel. There was still the matter of raising the general who would lay waste to Europe.

Stepping over and around rubble and debris and bodies, he found himself nodding in satisfaction. This was but the opening salvo in a gambit that had been thousands of years in the planning. Hade had orchestrated it, pushing Krypteia's cause to a new level. But in the end, it would be he who would reap the ultimate benefits, not his dark lieutenant. He would use the catastrophe to gather more power. He would use the coming plague of the risen to foment fear in the populace of the world and drive them to their knees, worshipping him and begging him to deliver them from the evil that surrounded them.

And he would gladly oblige them. He would be their savior. He would usher in the coming millennium with him at its head and as its ultimate ruler.

And God would be no more.

CHAPTER 1

Brighton, Utah: As dawn broke over the eastern horizon, Windy Covington sat alone on a large wooden chair on an outdoor deck at the Brighton Ski Resort high up in the Wasatch Mountains. From her vantage point, she could look out across the valley and see the flickering lights of many fires burning in and around Salt Lake City, at least where they weren't obscured by the thick haze of smoke that now covered much of the valley floor. The sky was steel gray, but the clouds were shot through with occasional streaks of brilliant white where the sun was still able to penetrate for a few brief moments. It could almost be considered inspiring, if one were removed from the current state of the world and able to view the sky purely for the beauty that it held. But Windy was not such a person. She had survived too much ugliness in her life to see any beauty in the world anymore. Instead, she viewed the world for what it was – cold and brutal.

She still didn't know exactly what had happened to send the world into a tailspin of chaos, only that it had broken out across the globe with a savage fury. After what she had experienced with her now ex-boyfriend, Cole Banyon, yesterday afternoon, a world suddenly in flames was oddly poetic to her and validated her world-view completely.

Having Cole nearly kill her had finally driven away the comforting numbness that she had cloaked herself in for years. It had caused her to take a cold, hard look at her life and at what she had supposedly accomplished. The conclusion was inescapable. Despite everything she had done for her handler and for Cole, she realized she had never done anything for herself. The beating Cole had delivered had driven that point painfully home.

Physically bruised and mentally reeling, she had slowly picked herself up off the floor, desperate to find a way to reclaim her freedom. Unfortunately, her cell phone's ring tone—R.E.M. singing about the end of the world—brought her handler back to her in all his hated glory and she quickly realized that freedom was just a dream that would never come to be.

The man's orders had been crystal clear, with the spoken understanding that if she thought not to comply, he would personally find and kill her. He had informed her that the hounds had been unleashed across the world and, if she had any hope of salvaging what was left of her life and surviving the storm, she was to leave town immediately and take refuge in a particular ski lodge. This ski lodge. He had promised her that it would be empty and she should spend the night and not leave for any reason. To do so would be extremely dangerous and, if she somehow survived disobeying him, she would not survive his punishment. He had then said he'd contact her the following morning, where he would have one final assignment for her and then she would finally be set free.

For a few moments, she had thought about simply telling the man to burn in hell. She wanted to run to Owen, to somehow find him in the growing maelstrom, and flee together to some island in the Caribbean where they could live happily ever after. But that was the stuff of fairy tales and she knew it. So she told her handler she would do exactly as he instructed. At the very least, it would buy her some time to consider her options, limited as they were. She did not believe that he would actually set her free—he had dangled that carrot before her far too often in the past. She knew that she could not simply run away, either. He would easily find her no matter where she hid. No, Windy knew that if she was going to free herself from his yoke, she would have to think it through. She would have to have a plan.

After he ended the call, she had grabbed an emergency bag she always kept packed, jumped into the Camry—Cole had taken her Jag—and sped out of town. It became quickly obvious to her as she drove, that she was leaving just in time. The city had gone wildly and wickedly berserk, its inhabitants, both alive and dead, rising up and turning on each other with catastrophic results. She'd had several close calls, but ultimately escaped the center of town, where the carnage was most pronounced. The road up the mountainside had been clear of other vehicles and, as promised, the resort itself was vacant, too. There was food in the pantries and a well-stocked refrigerator, so she had hunkered down with a hot meal and turned on the television, hoping to find out what had been happening in the valley.

Unfortunately, she had been met with nothing more than test patterns and static on the local stations. The few national news stations still operating all told her the same story. What was happening in Salt Lake City was not isolated. The world itself was suffering through the same brutal ordeal, and she spent the next several hours watching reports about worldwide mayhem on a scale never before seen. News anchors reported the horrors, columnists and talking heads decried the savagery, and most of the religious leaders the world over were hailing it as the beginning of the end.

The world had indeed gone stark raving mad.

Now here she sat, staring down at the smoke of destruction over Salt Lake City, alone in a resort that shouldn't be empty. She looked at her watch again, noting it was only two minutes later than the last time she had checked. Interestingly enough, her handler's instructions had failed to mention what time he would call her. An oversight, perhaps? Hardly. He'd never once, in all their years, forgotten to tell her what time he would call, so this was virgin territory for her. There had to be a reason behind it and she'd had a lot of time to consider what it could be. None of her conclusions had made her feel any better.

So, she had sat on the deck, her fully charged cell lying on the table and a powerful Glock-9 handgun, a long-ago gift from her handler, duct taped underneath the table within easy reach. In her years working for the man, she'd learned that she should always protect herself and take nothing for granted.

As the minutes crept forward and the light of the morning grew slightly brighter under the dark gray clouds, she looked out over the burning city, letting her thoughts drift back to her life and what it had become. Somewhere in all that smoke and haze, a lot of people had died and a whole lot more were about to. A normal person would be immensely relieved to be in her spot, safe and sound in a deserted ski resort with plenty of supplies and food. But all Windy could think about was that those who had died must certainly be in a better place now, while she was still living the nightmare that her life had become. "I wonder," she said quietly to herself as she sank back in her chair and curled her long legs up underneath her, "if there will ever be a better place for me."

"Of course there's a better place for you, my dear Windy," came the reply from directly behind her. It was a deep, husky voice that she knew all too well.

Windy's nightmare had come calling.

Fighting down the panic that rose within her, she remained calm and forced herself not to turn around, despite the burning desire to finally see the man who'd made her his puppet for so many years. "So, you decided to finally pay me a personal visit," she said softly.

"Indeed," he replied. She heard the sound of heavy boots on the deck as he made his way toward her.

Windy finally turned her head to see him and her eyes widened in fear. Over the years, she had pictured her handler a thousand different ways. But even the most frightening apparition she could have conjured had not prepared her for the reality of him. He was huge, easily one of the tallest men she had ever seen, if not the tallest. He wore all black, from his alligator skin boots to his pants to a black tee shirt stretched tightly over a powerfully muscled chest. Long black hair was pulled into a ponytail and black shades covered his eyes. Wherever his skin showed through it was covered in intricate tattoos depicting scenes of suffering and death. His trench coat hung open and she glimpsed a myriad of weapons and other devices tucked into numerous pockets and holsters.

"You said you'd call," she said quietly, keeping her voice even and her eyes on him as he approached. She wondered briefly whether she could get her gun in time or if it would even do any good against such a monster. She had prepared herself to be ready for battle, but this... this monstrosity before her was too much. Despite her best efforts, she was terrified of him.

"I apologize for that," he said with a laugh. "But in my defense, I thought it was finally time to formally meet." He raised both hands and then performed an exaggerated bow. "Allow me to introduce myself to you, Windy Covington. I am Hade." He did not wait for acknowledgement as he took a seat in a nearby chair across from her. He leaned back, laced his fingers behind his head, and kicked his huge black boots up on the table. "Beautiful morning, wouldn't you say?"

Windy looked up at the dark sky again and swallowed her fear. Even up here, it was difficult to tell if the sun was simply obscured behind clouds or if it was due to the smoke from the chaos below. She guessed it was both. "I suppose that depends on your taste," she answered carefully, turning her crystal blue eyes back to the burning valley. "But I would hardly call the city beautiful today."

"No? Well, I disagree," Hade replied with a huff. "The subtle flares of reds and oranges showing forth through streaks of grays and blacks. One could only imagine what the impressionist masters Monet, Cézanne, or Renoir could have done with such a landscape before them. I can't even imagine what music Mozart or Beethoven might write, standing before such a view as this."

"The view from high above any slaughter is never the same as if you were in the middle of it," Windy interjected. "Beauty from a distance often masks ugliness and pain up close."

"Well spoken," Hade said with a smile. "On an individual level, I suppose you're right. This is likely horrible for many who are currently experiencing it. But to get a true picture of the worth of the world's sacrifice, one has to stand above it. So for me, it's a masterpiece."

"So you did this?" For some reason, this didn't surprise her at all.

"Well, I had a small part," the huge man replied with a chuckle. "Okay, we both know false humility isn't my strong suit. Yes, I admit it. I'm behind it all, my dear girl. Just as I've controlled you over the years, I've controlled so many others preparing for this day."

"Like you've controlled Cole all these years?" she accused him, forgetting for a moment that she should be exercising extreme caution.

"Nothing like cutting to the chase," Hade laughed. "I have certainly trained you well, my dear girl."

"If you could call it that," she said, her beautiful eyes blazing with anger.

"Why, Windy," he chided. "By the way you're looking at me, I'd almost think you were angry."

"Don't mock me, Hade," she snapped bitterly. "After all I've done for you; after all that you've put me through, I don't deserve that."

Hade nodded slowly. "True," he agreed and then sighed. "You have a point. You have played your part remarkably well in all of this, to be sure. Frankly, I'm rather sad that it's coming to an end."

"Then why?" she pushed. "Why tell Cole about me? I spent years doing your bidding to save him, only to find out that he's known about it all along, laughing at me and despising me more and more every day."

"Well, I should think it would be obvious," Hade replied with a shrug.

"I wouldn't ask if it was obvious," she went on. "I know you're done with me, Hade. One last job, you said, and I'm dead. But I want to know why."

"Now, I never said that," Hade objected. "I do believe I even offered you your freedom."

"And I never believed you for a moment," she replied, not caring anymore whether she made him mad. "We both know you're not the caring type and, in this business, assets are not simply turned free when they're used up. I'm wise enough to understand how it works, Hade."

"Things change," he said, yawning as he looked out over the smoke-filled valley. Turning back to Windy, he smiled. "You wanted answers, I am happy to give them to you. You deserve that at least, I think."

She was silent for a moment, before voicing the one question she needed answered. "Then why Cole?" she asked angrily. "All this time I've been desperate to save him. But instead, you've been turning him into a monster. Why?"

Hade chuckled, a deep throaty sound, and Windy got the distinct impression that it was the devil who was laughing at her. "Now, now, Windy," he explained. "I thought I had always made things fairly clear about your role in my little play here. In hindsight, though, perhaps I haven't really given you enough information to see where you truly fit in, and for that I apologize."

"I don't understand."

"I was hoping we wouldn't have to discuss this today, because I knew you wouldn't like the answer. But you have earned an explanation," he said. "So an explanation I will give. You see, Windy, I've done many things to get to this point. Some I've enjoyed. Others? Not so much. But I've always done what I had to. Always. That's my role, to do what has to be done, Windy. And I've done that.

"Now I don't know if this will bring you great comfort, or great pain, but the truth is that this has never been about you. It's always been about Cole. I hate to put it in those terms because it sounds so harsh and cold, but it's true. Everything you've done for me has not been for your benefit or even for mine, but to turn Cole into a useful instrument for me. And thanks to your hard work, Cole has turned out beautifully."

"You wanted him like this?" she asked incredulously. "How could having Cole strung out and psychotic possibly be a good thing?" she asked, drawing in a heavy breath, already beginning to understand.

"I can tell that you've already answered your question," he answered with a smile. "The world we live in today is not even close to what it could or should be, Windy. In a perfect world, I wouldn't need to crush Cole's soul just so I could build him back up and make him my puppet. But this isn't a perfect world, and that's what I'm trying to fix. It pains me that I have to turn him into a cold-hearted killer, but it's only for a brief moment in history, enough to aid me in getting rid of those who would stand in my way. That's why I set this whole charade up. I supplied everything—the drugs, the drive to get cleaned up, the slide back into the depths, and all of his many reasons to hate you. Cole is now the perfect devotee, and I have his future all planned out for him. He's going to help me make over this world anew."

"No!" Windy broke down, tears finally welling up in her eyes, less for Cole and more for the lie that her life had been.

"Alas, it's true," Hade said with exaggerated sympathy. "I was the one who kept whispering in his ear that you were using him, telling him exactly what you were doing, who you were seducing, and why he must never speak of it to you. It nearly drove him insane, but you played it perfectly all those years. And then Owen came along and allowed me to push Cole right off the edge of the cliff and into a lifetime of servitude to me."

"No," she repeated, still reeling from the revelation. "I refuse to believe Cole could ever be your sycophant."

"That's a lie, and we both know it," Hade said politely. "The Cole you loved died in that hotel room a long time ago. The Cole you know today is a monster that you have helped me create. You saw it firsthand," he pointed to the bruises on her neck, "when he had his hands around your throat and was about to kill you. The only reason he didn't was because I told him not to and he's quite aware of what I do to those who disobey me. However, I have to admit, it was still touch and go. He truly hates you, Windy. I half expected him to kill you anyway, despite my dire warning."

"But this...this just isn't possible," she whispered, feeling the darkest despair rise up and drown her.

"Oh, but it is," Hade countered. "Cole has had a black heart for a long time, but he needed a lot of work, a lot of finishing, if you will. Now, the world I've created has allowed me to turn him from your average, ordinary junkie into a first-class psychotic killer on my payroll. Dedicated employees like that are not easy to come by, my dear."

"I don't believe it," she cried. "This can't be real." But it was real. Even as she said it, her mind raced back through the years, looking for bits of evidence to support this new reality, and she shuddered visibly as the pieces of the puzzle began to fall into place. Everything—from the small and the innocuous to the grand and terrifying—everything fit together perfectly. Too perfectly. In the end, Hade was right. It did all add up. She realized she'd been unwittingly led, thinking she was saving Cole when in reality she was destroying him. Her sacrifices had been for nothing. No, she thought, not for nothing. They'd all been for evil.

Hade recognized her misery and spoke, further illuminating the depth of her dizzying fall from grace. "Unfortunately for you, Windy, it is indeed real," he said softly. "But look on the brighter side. With Cole now fully mine, you're finally free. Well, almost free," he amended with a grin.

She whirled on him, her beautiful blue eyes filled with tears. "And I'm supposed to be happy about all of this now? You used me! You destroyed my life!"

"We all make our choices, Windy," he shrugged. "Cole made his. You made yours."

"And what choice was I ever given?" she spit out.

"Well, for starters, you could have let Cole hang himself in that hotel room," he answered smugly.

"You're a bastard," she snapped, tearing her eyes away from him, desperate to rid herself of his image. Her mind turned to the handgun she had hidden underneath the table. No, she thought. Not yet. She wasn't ready for that just yet. Whether she died today or not, she still had a chance to at least right some of the wrongs she'd committed by killing him. But before she did, she wanted more answers.

"That wasn't a very nice thing to say," Hade said, feigning mock indignation. "Still, you're probably right. But you really need to look at the bigger picture here, my dear. I'm the spider and you're the fly. When you saved Cole in that hotel room, you wandered right out into my web. Over the past years, I've allowed you the freedom to dance around my web having a grand old time, but all the while you were simply spinning yourself into your own tomb and you never even realized it. While I've enjoyed watching you work for me, you really didn't have a choice in the end. You gave that up when you saved him. Free will aside, no matter how far you've journeyed, you've never left my web."

Windy was silent for a bit, inwardly calming herself. The façade had been ripped away, exposing her life for what it truly was, and that wasn't an easy thing to accept. When she spoke, her voice was measured again. "So, everything I did made Cole into a monster, and now I'm assuming you have him out killing people you don't want around."

"Astute as always," he said, touching his nose.

"Who?"

"Now we're getting to the truly inspirational piece of this whole sordid puzzle," Hade answered with a perfectly sinful grin. "Cole isn't quite ready yet for the big time, so I had to dangle the right bait in front of him to get him excited about his first kill. It had to be someone he was passionate about. It had to be someone with meaning. The first one always has to have meaning. Obviously, you would have been the perfect choice, but I'm not done with you yet. So I had to come up with another suitable target. I didn't have to look far, you know," he finished, arching his eyebrows knowingly.

Windy felt her heart fall into a bottomless pit. She knew, but she still had to ask. "Who?" she asked again, her voice falling to a whisper.

"Do I really have to say it?" Hade laughed.

"You sent him after Owen!" Windy was moving before she realized it. Her hand shot underneath the table where she had stashed her pistol, her fingers closing in on...

...nothing.

Her eyes widened in shocked horror as she looked up at the man. Hade threw back his head and laughed while Windy could only stare, completely defeated.

The huge man finished laughing and looked at her, a glint of amusement in his eyes.

"How could you have known?" was all she managed to say, sinking back into her chair, entirely defeated.

"I've been around for a very long time, Windy," he said, reaching into his trench coat and pulling out her gun. "I haven't lived this long or been this successful by underestimating those who choose to pit themselves against me." He tossed the Glock-9 on the table in front of her.

"You've been here all along," she said quietly, shivering involuntarily, but making no move toward the gun that was now within easy reach.

"Since early this morning, actually," he admitted. "I removed your gun when you went to make yourself a cup of cocoa. I didn't think you needed it, to be honest. You're not a killer, Windy. A seductress, a nymph, a siren you are. A spy, an infiltrator, an intelligence collector, as well. But you care too deeply to ever kill anyone and be able get over it. Everyone in this world has their limits, and one of my special talents is using people up to and including their limits without pushing them so far that they break and become unusable."

"You don't believe I could kill you?" she asked, reaching out and picking up the weapon.

Hade shook his head, completely unconcerned. "It's not a matter of belief, my dear girl. I know you better than you know yourself. You care too much."

With a practiced hand, Windy popped the clip out of the gun and glanced at it. It was still loaded. She slid it back into the grip and jacked a bullet into the chamber. Pointing the gun at Hade's head, she said, "Maybe I don't care anymore."

Hade locked stares with her and never flinched. "If you feel the need to shoot, then shoot," he said calmly, letting a smile play at his mouth. "I don't believe you have it in you, but the ball is in your court to prove me wrong, Windy. Pull the trigger."

She kept the gun trained on the big man's forehead, her face unmoving. "You've used me for years to take Cole away from me, Hade," she said. "And now, when there's even the tiniest fleeting spark of hope of reclaiming my life and myself, you've taken Owen away as well."

"When did I ever say Owen was dead? I knew you had feelings for that mongrel from the start," he stated with a knowing smile. "He's nothing, sweetie, believe me. Sure he's cute, has charm and wit and everything else a girl could want, but his star is fading."

"But you said..."

Hade held up a finger and waved it in the air to stop her. "I said no such thing," he corrected. "Cole has his orders, but Owen isn't his target."

"So, Owen is still alive?" she asked, barely able to breathe.

"He is," Hade stated plainly, grinning at her sudden reaction. "At the moment, Owen is alive and well. Well, I don't think the word 'well' is the right word here, because he's in Vegas experiencing the same thing that's happening here. Now, whether he remains alive is going to hinge a great deal on what you're willing to do for me."

Windy barely heard him, but she understood the threat. Owen was alive. For now. Her heart raced and her mind focused on all the possibilities that could mean for her future, so she lowered the gun and tossed it on the table. "You win, Hade," she said softly.

"I always win, Windy," he stated matter-of-factly. "But that doesn't mean you still can't."

Hade went on, not waiting for her to speak. "I know you're still hoping and praying that Owen is your knight in shining armor and that he'll survive and win your fair hand. The problem here is that this isn't a little girl's fairy tale, and your fairy godmother happens to be a bastard—your word, not mine." He chuckled when he said that. "That does not preclude, however, that this can't all work out for you in the end."

"It was never more than a fool's hope," she admitted sadly. "Just a silly little girl's dream after years of having none."

"There's nothing wrong with being a silly little girl from time to time, even for someone like you," Hade countered. "And besides, you know what they say about the fat lady and all."

She looked at him again and glared, her anger returning. "She sang a long time ago for me, Hade. Why are you dangling this bait in front of me now? One last job, I suppose?"

"Well, now that you mention it, yes," he replied easily. "But it's not a job, per se. I'm actually going to grant you your wish."

"Meaning what?"

"Meaning I want you to go and meet Owen."

Windy fought to keep herself calm. "Meet Owen," she repeated, her voice quiet.

"Yes, meet Owen," the big man replied. "That's pretty clear, isn't it?" he said somewhat disdainfully.

"I told you earlier not to mock me, Hade," she snapped.

"And you know I don't like repeating myself," he growled back, his voice suddenly ice cold. He watched in satisfaction as she shrank back into her chair, her fear quickly evident. He could taste it, and he smiled. "Now, here's the deal, Windy. Are you ready to hear it?"

She looked at him, fighting down her terror. "Yes," she said meekly.

"Good," he said. "Owen is in the middle of quite the storm right now and it's about to get significantly worse in ways he can't even begin to imagine. At the moment, he's somewhat off the grid for me."

"Where do I come in?" she asked, a faint hope in her voice.

"If things go according to plan, and I very much hope they do, then Owen's going to need some guidance," Hade explained. "He's going to need a friend—someone who he knows isn't going to try to hurt him. One of the unexpected benefits of your last assignment was your budding feelings for the young man. He's going to need a little extra motivation to do what I need him to do, and you're the perfect girl to provide that for him."

Windy blanched. "What do you want him to do?" she asked carefully, every warning bell in her mind going off at the same time. She had a long and storied past with Hade and she knew that if he was involved, there was no way this was going to end well for Owen or herself.

"If you know Owen as well as you think you do, then you know he'd never do anything he didn't believe in his heart was right and honest. So, I don't want you to convince him of anything. I don't want you to manipulate him in any way, Windy, if you can believe that. I just need you to be there so he can feel that the decisions he's already made are justified and that he's on the right path for himself."

"You're not telling me everything," she accused.

"Of course I'm not," he laughed. "I've never given you the whole story, Windy. You know this. But what other choice do you have?"

She was silent, staring at him with a mixture of hatred and revulsion.

"Look, my dear," he went on, leaning forward. "I'm giving you a chance to get out of the life I've forced you to live. You can take this chance, use all the gifts I've given you to your advantage, and perhaps, just perhaps, things will work out the way you want them to."

"Long odds," Windy finally said quietly.

"One in a million," he agreed. "But your odds here are far better than winning the lottery and, as they always say, someone's got to win. Why can't it be you?"

For the longest time, she just stared at him, mulling his offer over in her mind. It was the same routine they had gone through a thousand times before, only this time they were face-to-face instead of on the phone. Finally, with a sigh, she agreed. "Very well."

Hade nodded in return and pulled a small box out of his trench coat, which he placed on the table. "This is a personal GPS. Keep it with you. As soon as I know where Owen is, I'll send the coordinates to the unit. It won't be until tomorrow, most likely, which gives you plenty of time to come up with a strategy."

"Then I'm just to go to him?" she asked doubtfully. "What's the catch?"

"The catch is that there is no catch," he answered with a shrug. "Just be honest with him. I can't promise this is going to work out well for you, but I can't say you will fail, either. There's a chance here that you and he may make it out of all this alive and, even better, together."

"One in a million, right?" she scoffed.

"Better than nothing," he answered. "I know you aren't going to believe me now, Windy, but the truth is that I've grown rather attached to you. You've done incredible work for me and there's no denying that. Yet all I have to offer you right now is a little bit of honesty and a small chance at something wonderful. It's not much, but it's something."

"Your word?" she asked, looking hard at him.

"Meaning?" Hade asked, his eyebrow arching up.

"I mean, I have your word that if I play this right, you'll actually let me live? You'll leave me alone? You'll leave us alone?"

"I give you my word that one way or another, Windy Covington, in less than forty-eight hours, you'll be free of me." He held his hand out toward her. "Your phone, please," he requested.

"Why?" She was trying her hardest to keep focused, but even the slightest chance of finding happiness had turned her whole world upside down. She didn't want to screw something up now, but all she kept thinking about was a bright future; a chance at happiness she had never had. And even though it was extremely doubtful she could attain it, it had never felt so close.

"Because your phone is your last connection to me," he explained, his hand still out. "Place it in my hand and you're free. When you receive the GPS coordinates, you may complete your task. Your life will then be yours. Fail me and I'll find and kill you without a word, if you are even still alive. Either way, you and I will never speak again."

Windy picked up her phone and looked at it. For years, it had been her chain to Hade, her link to a life she'd never wanted but had been forced to live. She dropped it in his outstretched hand, her eyes locked on his. With a smile, Hade closed his fist around it and his knuckles whitened as he tightened his grip. There were several cracking sounds and, when he opened his hand a moment later, the shattered pieces of her cell phone fell to the table.

The chain had been broken. She was free.

Without another word, Hade stood up, smiled and winked at her, and walked out of the resort. She had half-believed this meeting was going to signal the end of her life, and it very well might have, but the fact that she now had a chance to make things right sent shockwaves through her mind. It gave her a reprieve, brief as it was. But reality came crowding back, and with it came the black cloud of reality. If her handler was really responsible for what was happening throughout the world, she knew it was going to get significantly worse before it got better. The world was in flames, but for the first time in a very long time, hers was not. It would be up to her to figure out how to keep it that way.

CHAPTER 2

Salt Lake City, Utah: The world had gone absolutely insane and Alexis Kennedy knew she was right in the middle of a nightmare. Still dazed at the terrifying chaos that was engulfing the city, she sat on the tile floor next to Libby, holding her hand tightly as her best friend lay unconscious on an old army surplus stretcher at the makeshift triage center set up in the Road Home homeless shelter. Dr. Evan Hewson, a young intern from Primary Children's Medical Center, had been volunteering in the building when the chaos struck and was trapped as well. His medical skills had been put to use on the numerous injured who had taken refuge at the shelter. At the moment, he was working on Libby, doing his best to stop the bleeding from her head wound and get her stabilized. He'd constructed a makeshift splint for her broken leg, but had explained to Alexis that they needed to get her to a hospital as quickly as possible to deal with her head trauma. It wasn't the news she'd wanted to hear.

It had been over a half an hour since Gen and Todd had dropped them off on their way to rescue Todd's sister, and Alexis was growing nervous at their continued absence. They should have been back by now. As more time passed, she got angry with herself for separating from them in the first place. While the world continued to fall apart, she was stuck at the homeless shelter with no way of getting her critically injured friend to the hospital. For the moment, they were trapped. Gen's return with her car might solve that particular problem, but right now, Alexis could only worry and wonder.

As she looked around the shelter, she noticed for the first time that, while the shelter was a large building, with a capacity to house hundreds of people, there were perhaps only fifty to sixty people there. Usually when Alexis volunteered, there were three to four times as many and, with the insanity engulfing the city, she'd expected a long stream of refugees passing to safety under the giant stained-glass window created by children who'd stayed there over the years. And that was another thing that seemed odd: she saw no children. In fact, there was no one at the shelter she recognized at all. It was as if she was in the right place, but the right place wasn't right.

She tried to call Gen again, only to get the recording that all circuits were down. Even her texts wouldn't go through. She shoved her phone back into her pocket and pressed her hand to her forehead, trying hard to stay in control. Everything about her situation was wrong and she felt so alone. Tears of desperation began to well up in the corners of her eyes when she heard a voice behind her, causing her to look up.

"Lexy," a woman's voice called out, and Alexis turned toward her. The woman had a grim look on her ebony face as she approached. Catching sight of Libby's unconscious form, her already strained countenance fell even further. "Oh sweetie, I'm so sorry."

"Sally," Alexis said wearily, almost overwhelmed to see someone she recognized. A South Carolinian transplant from years past, Sally had never lost her southern drawl. Tall and big boned, as she called it, she was the driving force behind the shelter, and Alexis had always enjoyed their time together when she volunteered after class. While clearly worn by the events of the day, Sally was still a rock of strength. Alexis threw her arms around the woman, the tears now cascading down her cheeks. Almost as relieved to see Alexis, Sally grabbed her back, hugging her close.

"Oh, girl," Sally said loudly, "I'm so glad to see you're safe." She let go, stepped back and looked Alexis up and down, noting her bloodstained clothing and bedraggled appearance. "Well, as safe as anyone can hope for," she said quietly, shaking her head sadly. "Are you okay, honey?"

Alexis wiped the tears away from her face. "I'm okay, but I don't know about Libby. She got hit by a car. We were running from the... the..." She trailed off, more tears beginning to flow. Sally placed her hands on Alexis' shoulders and looked her in the eyes.

"Now just calm down a bit, Lexy," Sally said, her voice firm but kind. "We'll get through this and, as soon as we can, we'll get Libby to the hospital."

"Do you really think so?" Alexis almost pleaded.

"Of course, sweetie," came the reply. "That's why they call this a shelter. We'll be fine. How'd you end up here, anyway?"

Alexis wiped the tears away from her face. "We couldn't get to the hospital, so Gen dropped me off with Libby while she went with Todd. I'm worried about them, Sally. They've been gone for a long time."

"Well, all we can do is hope and pray your friends stay safe. But you did the right thing coming here. Libby's safe for now." She looked at the injured girl again. "How is she?"

Dr. Hewson, who had been sitting nearby, shook his head slightly. "She has a severe concussion and is unconscious right now," he explained. "She may have a skull fracture, but I have no idea if she has any bruising or bleeding on the brain. Without a CAT scan, it's too hard to tell. She could come out of it just fine with a few scars, or the problems could be much more severe. I just can't tell you without getting her to the hospital and right now, that's not possible."

At that moment, an older couple entered the main lobby, blood spattered all over the left arm and shoulder of the man. Doctor Hewson gave Sally and Alexis a quick nod and was off to help.

"Sally, if something happens to Libby..." Alexis began and then trailed off, her shoulders shaking with renewed sobs.

"Now Lexy, you can't think that way," Sally did her best to

reassure her, hugging the young woman again. As she pulled away, a group of nearly a dozen people, eyes wide with terror, staggered into the shelter. Sally patted Alexis on the shoulder and said, "You take a moment to calm yourself down and I'll be back in a minute. I have to get these people organized and I'm going to need your help. The best cure for any ill is helping those who have it worse then you."

Sally moved away, working among the people, helping the newcomers by directing and explaining things as best she could. Alexis noticed a few of the men in the shelter had started moving couches and anything else large they could get their hands on, intent on blocking the entrance from anyone, or anything, they didn't want to let in. Two other men took up positions on either side of the front doorways, one with a rifle and the other with a pistol. Alexis couldn't quite decide if that made her feel more or less safe.

She looked around slowly, taking in the gravity of the situation they were in. Several radios were on and, wherever they were, groups of people were gathered around, listening intently. No music played— none had played for a while now. All of the stations continued with the warning tones of the Emergency Broadcast System, punctuated often by official announcements and instructions. National Guard troops and local and state law enforcement were fighting battles with what the news reporters kept referring to "crazed rioters." A curfew was already in effect, and citywide martial law was also in effect. People were warned to stay indoors at all costs and not to use their phones so that lines would remain open for emergency personnel.

As if on cue, her cell phone rang and she quickly answered it, hoping beyond hope it was Gen calling to tell her they were safe or they were on their way back to the shelter. But the line immediately went dead and the monotonous announcement of "all lines are busy" started in again. It had been the same problem since everything had started—lines were jammed, calls could not get through, communication by phone was almost non-existent. Calling her parents' house in Pocatello, Idaho had gotten a busy signal, and the one time she had actually managed to get through to her brother in North Carolina, it had gone directly to voice mail. She'd been so dazed when she called she couldn't even remember if she'd left him a message.

The person she kept trying to get hold of, though, was Owen. Even in the best of times, Owen rarely had his cell with him or turned on, but she had hoped he would have it turned on now. It was driving her crazy not knowing if he was safe and just unable to get in contact, or if something worse had happened, so she kept calling over and over, hoping at some point he would pick up.

He never did.

As she sat there, leaning up against the wall, she allowed herself to cry softly while she slowly caressed her injured friend's hand. Hopelessness threatened to overwhelm her as she wondered what lay ahead for her, for Libby, for any of them. After some time, she felt as if someone was watching her and she looked up. Through her tears, she saw a little girl, her clothes in tatters and her hair matted with dried blood. She must have just arrived, as Alexis was sure she would have noticed her earlier.

"Hi there," Alexis said softly, quickly wiping the tears from her eyes.

The little girl looked at her solemnly.

"My name is Alexis," she went on, making a conscious effort to be strong. "What's your name?"

For a moment, the girl did not answer, but then, ever so softly came the reply. "Dakota."

"Dakota," Alexis repeated gently. "That's a pretty name. How old are you, Dakota?"

Another pause. "Seven."

"Wow," Alexis said, offering the little girl a warm smile. "That's pretty old. Are you in college, Dakota?"

The girl paused, still a bit unsure of Alexis, and then replied matter-of-factly, "No, ma'am."

"Well, you look very smart," Alexis said knowingly. She beckoned the little girl to come over and Dakota slowly walked around the cot and sat down next to Alexis, pulling her knees up to her face. "Are your parents here?"

Immediately, Dakota's bright blue eyes fled behind the safety of her knees and Alexis felt the girl's back begin to shake with sobs.

"Shhh," Alexis soothed softly, scooting over slightly to place her arm around the girl without letting go of Libby's hand. Dakota immediately latched on to the arm, burying her face against Alexis' shoulder and crying harder. Alexis just held her close, letting her cry it out. "Want to tell me about it?" she finally asked gently.

Dakota raised her head and looked squarely at Alexis, trying her hardest to be brave. She was a beautiful little girl, red curls framing her pixie face and trailing down her back. She was dressed in a short-sleeve white tee shirt and a yellow jumper, with white tennis shoes. "I'm waiting for my mom," Dakota said stoically, trying to act as grown up as possible.

"Where is she right now?" Alexis asked.

"Out there," she answered. "We were coming home from Andy's birthday party..." she trailed off and Alexis knew she was probably fighting a running battle within herself just to talk about it.

"Is Andy your brother?" Alexis guessed.

Dakota nodded. "We were in the car and it crashed when all the bad people came," she explained as only a seven-year-old could. "Mom told me to run to the shelter." She looked up at Alexis, showing a truly angelic face now completely overtaken by grief. "Do you think it will take her a long time to come get me?"

Alexis did her best to keep upbeat. "Well, sweetie, if your mother told you to come here, then you'd better wait right here for her. I'm sure she'll be here soon." As she said this, she saw a glimmer of hope on the little girl's face. Alexis smiled at her and, for the first time in hours, felt like she was doing something purposeful besides just running for her life. She vowed silently she would make sure this little girl got out of this in one piece, both physically and mentally. With newfound strength, Alexis' whole demeanor changed. She put her arm around Dakota and started a new, happier conversation. "I have an idea. What if we went and got you cleaned up and found something to eat?"

Dakota nodded, and after a quick check to make sure Libby was okay, the two headed off to the restroom. Alexis was glad to see there was still running water, and after a thorough rinse, she had Dakota's hair looking better. She was also glad to see the blood had not been hers, but she silently worried whose it actually was. Forcing herself to be strong for the little girl, she worked quickly to remove the dirt from Dakota's face and in a few minutes, the young girl looked like a child should once again. Alexis cleaned herself up as much as she could, as well, and after a quick trip to the kitchen where they secured a box of Pop Tarts and two bottles of water, the two were back sitting beside Libby, nibbling at the toaster treats and feeling a little better about their situation.

As Alexis finished the last of her pastry, she almost jumped as her cell phone rang. "Hello?" she answered it excitedly.

"Alexis?" came a female voice on the other end. "Are you okay?"

"Rebekkah?" How in the world had her Israeli friend gotten through to her? "Rebekkah! I can't believe it's you!"

"Are you okay?" the Israeli asked again, concern in her voice.

"Yes...well, no," stammered Alexis, aware of the little girl nestled close to her. "It's really bad over here. There are... they're calling them rioters and they're everywhere. I'm so glad you're okay!"

"I was so worried something had happened to you. It's bad just about everywhere," Rebekkah said. "That's all there is on the news right now. That and London."

"What happened in London?"

"Someone set off a nuke," Rebekkah replied in a tone filled with horrified awe. "Right in the heart of the city! Can you believe it?"

"Oh, no," Alexis whispered, completely stunned. It was suddenly clear to her that the world was completely falling apart. "What about you? What's happening in Israel?"

"I'm fine. It doesn't look like any of this is hitting Israel like it is everywhere else, which is really a surprise when you think about it. What about you, though? Are you safe?"

"For now," Alexis answered slowly. "I'm at a shelter. Libby is here, too, but she's hurt and we can't get her to a hospital because of what's happening." She looked down at the little girl curled up under her arm and smiled. "I'm looking after a little girl named Dakota, too, who's waiting for her mother to come pick her up."

"I'm so glad you're safe. Any word from Owen?"

"No. I wish he was here," she answered with a shiver. "He's supposed to be in Vegas on that stupid trip of his, but I can't get a hold of him."

"Is there anyone else you can call?"

"I've tried just about everyone," Alexis said, thinking through all the different people she'd tried to call since arriving at the shelter. She frowned as she quickly realized there was someone she hadn't, who was nearby and would probably come help her if she could get through to him. "I haven't tried Petr," she went on, more to herself than her friend.

"Petr?" Rebekkah asked, a hint of mischievousness in her voice. "Does Owen have some competition?"

'No, he's just a friend," Alexis sighed. "How can you even talk about that at a time like this!"

"Okay, fine. But could he fill in for your knight in shining armor right now? It sounds like you could use one."

"He's not a knight...at least he's not my knight," she answered truthfully. "He's a classmate of mine from Russia. His name's Petr Zhugravinsky." There was silence on the other end of the line and Alexis froze, thinking she'd been disconnected. "Hello?" she asked after a long silent pause.

A few moments passed before Rebekkah finally answered, her demeanor dramatically changed. "You said Zhugravinsky?"

"Yeah."

"Alexis," Rebekkah warned quietly. "That's Russian mafia. Some of the worst. You don't mess with those guys. Ever."

Alexis just sighed. "Owen told me the same thing, Rebekkah. Sorry, but I just don't buy it."

"Owen knows, and that isn't good enough for you?" Rebekkah pressed, shocked at the statement. "Look, just promise me you won't call him, no matter how desperate you are. I saw an online story a few hours ago describing how almost the entire Zhugravinsky family was found dead. Brutal murders, Lex. That's who these people are! Stay where you are and wait for Owen, but don't go near this guy."

Alexis was about to respond when her phone beeped telling her she had another call. She looked down at the number. "I've got to go! Gen's on the other line. Stay safe."

"You too, Alexis. I'll try to call soon. Bye!"

The call disconnected and Alexis switched over to Gen. When the call went through she was completely unprepared for what she heard. The scream on the other end cut through her like a knife, startling her so badly she almost dropped the phone. A moment later, she heard Gen's terror-filled voice. "Alex! Help me! They've killed Todd!"

"Gen!" was all Alexis could get out before her friend screamed again. She heard Gen's phone drop to the pavement along with a scuffling sound. Gen shrieked a final time before her voice choked off into a gurgle, followed by the wet thumping sound of something hard striking flesh and bone over and over again.

A loud burst of static signaled someone had smashed the phone, ending the call. The staccato disconnected sound went on and on as Alexis realized numbly that she had just heard her friend's voice for the last time. She sank to her knees in grief and shock, tears flowing more freely than ever before. Gen was dead. Libby lay unconscious nearby, maybe dying. She felt like the world was going to collapse on her right then and there, when a small, quiet voice reached into her soul and helped bring her back from the brink.

"Alexis?" Dakota said, placing her tiny hand on her arm. "Are you okay?"

Alexis struggled to regain control. She opened her eyes and, through her tears, she saw the girl's innocent face. "Oh, Dakota," she whispered. "I'm so sorry. It's just…" she looked at the girl and pulled herself up a bit. "It's just my friend called and she had an accident. I'm very worried about her."

"It's okay," the little girl replied softly. "I'm worried, too. But when I get worried or scared I always sing my favorite song from The Wizard of Oz, 'Somewhere Over the Rainbow'."

Alexis looked at the little girl in silence and then wrapped her arms tightly around her. Holding her close, Alexis buried her face in the little girl's still damp hair and cried again. But this time, she cried for what Dakota had just given her. She felt strength once again flow through her and her resolve tightened. Gen was dead, but she still had Libby and she still had Dakota. She would push the insanity of what was happening out of her mind and focus on taking care of those she still could save. "Thanks," she said quietly to Dakota, pulling away and looking deeply into the little girl's blue eyes.

"For what?" Dakota asked, truly confused.

"For being so smart," Alexis replied and then kissed her on the forehead. "You're a pretty special little girl, you know that?"

Dakota just smiled and hugged her back.

Even as she felt renewed, Alexis realized just how tired she was. If she was to be strong for Dakota and get Libby to the hospital, she was going to need to recharge. The weight of the day was still heavy on her, but for the moment the shelter was a quiet haven from the madness outside. "What do you say we take a little nap, Dakota? I think we could both use it."

"I don't take naps anymore," Dakota began to object, yet added quickly, "but I'm really tired."

"Me, too," Alexis said, standing up and helping the little girl to her feet. A few minutes later, she'd managed to get her hands on a couch cushion and the two of them were snuggled together, their heads resting comfortably on the thick pad just feet from Libby's stretcher. Moments later, they were fast asleep, exhaustion pushing them deep into welcome slumber.

RISEN

CHAPTER 3

Salt Lake City, Utah: All eyes turned toward Father Michael Dalacourt as his phone rang loudly for a second time. For a moment, he had no clue why they were looking at him, before remembering he was carrying the phone Archbishop De Solei had given him before leaving. He had been meant to use it to keep in touch with his mentor in the Vatican, but the past 24 hours had rendered the phone practically useless.

"Are you going to answer that or would you rather wait for a bunch of walking dead to mosey on over here and answer it for you?" Tom McCain, a New York police detective, asked.

"I'm…I'm sorry," the young priest stammered, reaching into his pocket and pulling it out. "I completely forgot I had it!" He answered it a bit sharply, "Yes?"

"Is that the proper way to answer a call, Father Dalacourt?" Francis De Solei's patronizing voice immediately came over the other end.

"I'm sorry, Father," Dalacourt replied, trying to convey the proper sense of meekness in his voice without compromising exactly what he was thinking. "We're just a bit preoccupied right now and this is really the first that it's worked since everything began happening."

McCain held up a hand in warning. "Keep it down, Father," he said quietly. "We have no idea who or what is anywhere near us right now."

"Archbishop," Dalacourt went on, lowering his voice. "This isn't a good time."

"I would disagree," De Solei replied, sounding happy. "We're in the final days, Michael. Before us, we're beginning to see God's hand bringing about the millennial reign of Christ."

Dalacourt shook his head sadly. His mentor simply did not understand, and perhaps he never would. "I'm not so sure," he countered, regretting his words even as he said them.

"I have cautioned you before on blasphemy, Michael," De Solei said, his voice suddenly icy. "Should you insist on continuing along this soul-damning path, I will no longer stop with a simple rebuke."

"Listen to me," Dalacourt continued, feeling somewhat empowered in the presence of the old Indian and his other companions. "People are dying over here."

"The wicked are dying everywhere."

Dalacourt shook his head emphatically. "No, you're wrong. Good people are dying, too." There was a pause on the other end and Dalacourt soldiered on, unwilling to kowtow to his mentor on this. "I have watched several good people die most horribly."

"Then they cannot have been good."

"With all due respect, these were not wicked people. One of them was a sweet little old lady, terrified beyond belief and reciting prayers just before she was beaten to death!"

"And your point is?"

"She came back."

Another pause.

"She came back," Dalacourt repeated, "with the very people who had killed her."

"To do what?"

"They were trying to kill us," he answered in near exasperation. "There are only four of us left from the bus. The rest are dead."

"Where are you now?" De Solei pressed.

Again, Dalacourt was shocked by the uncaring disregard that De Solei had for others. "We are outside Salt Lake City," he answered with some hesitation. "One of the survivors says he knows of a safe place within the city." He was suddenly struck by an odd feeling. De Solei did not appear to be worried at all about what was happening in the world. He actually seemed to be taking some sort of perverse joy in it, and that left the young Father feeling extremely uneasy. "Your Excellency, are you not experiencing the same thing in Los Angeles?"

"We are to an extent," De Solei answered evenly. "But there are soldiers patrolling the streets here and things are relatively quiet. I have been watching the local news and it appears the occurrences here are still happening. However, they are isolated and are being contained, not that the same thing can be said for the rest of the world. Other than that, much appears to be continuing as normal here in Los Angeles, although I would add that we had a full house of worshippers today."

"I do not doubt that," said Dalacourt quietly. "But what about the rest of the world?"

"The sinners are being punished," De Solei maintained. "We are seeing the beginning of the end, and I require your presence here in Los Angeles as quickly as possible. How soon will you arrive?"

"My presence?" Dalacourt repeated, trying hard not to let his absolute disbelief show through. He was smart enough to know that, in the grand scheme of things, he was nothing to De Solei and his mentor certainly did not need him.

"Yes, yours," came the curt answer. "Do you have a problem with my request?"

"Perhaps you didn't hear me," Dalacourt replied.

"Oh, I heard you quite clearly," De Solei interrupted, his voice sharp. "That does not excuse you from your duties to the church or to me. I assume you are aware of the tragedy in Rome?"

"I am," the young priest answered somberly, fighting back the urge to ask his mentor if he thought His Holiness was being punished, too. "I heard the news while on the bus."

"Many men of God were called home," De Solei continued, "and until the conclave is called, an emergency meeting of the surviving cardinals has given me the authority to lead God's Church in America. I expect you here post haste to help me in this endeavor."

There was a click on the other end. Dalacourt stared at the phone in stunned disbelief.

"Problems on the home front?" McCain asked, cocking an eyebrow.

"Leave him be, Tom," the old Native American, John, said softly and then turned to face the priest. "Remember what I told you concerning the archbishop, Michael. Consider well those words, my young friend, for they were not spoken lightly."

Dalacourt thought back to the bizarre dream he had in Belle Plaine, when the young girl had laid bare De Solei's own grievous sins to him and demanded his obedience. Could it be true? Could the Francis De Solei who had taken him under his wing and mentored him at the Vatican, be someone else entirely? He looked at the cell phone, his features thoughtful, and came to a difficult conclusion.

He tossed the phone into the bushes and walked away.

John watched the priest move ahead, his features sad as he picked his way through the brush behind him. He knew the young man was dealing with an incredible amount of pressure. He knew Dalacourt felt loyalty and dedication to his church and to his mentor, and it was not something he took lightly. Therein lay the problem, and John hoped for everyone's sake that Michael Dalacourt would follow the right path. He could not know how important it was to the entire world that he do so.

They were on the outskirts of Salt Lake City, having stayed within patches of trees or in the shadows as much as possible throughout their trek. They had seen a few figures in the distance during their march, but all indications were that they were like the other killers they had encountered since the world had turned upside down. So they had moved as quickly and quietly as possible, always heading in the general direction John had indicated. The craggy old Indian had said their destination was a homeless shelter where he hoped to find others that he knew, adding only that there was strength in numbers. For the moment, though, they stood just inside the shadows of a number of trees, staring down a street lined with new houses, the outermost ones still under various stages of construction. But they saw no one and the street was eerily quiet, though in the distance toward the center of the city, they could hear the sporadic pop of gunfire.

"Fighting in the city," McCain said, echoing everyone's thoughts.

"Archbishop De Solei said that in Los Angeles, soldiers are patrolling the streets, keeping everything under control," Dalacourt added.

"They may be attempting to do it here, too," McCain replied. "That's automatic gunfire, and a lot of it. Chances are the National Guard is staying busy, especially if the uprising is concentrated in the city center."

"Well, we aren't going to the city center," John cut in. "The shelter is on this side of the city, maybe three or four miles from here."

"Then let's get a move on," McCain said, stepping from the shelter of the trees and looking around. "I don't like being out in the open."

"What if your friends aren't there?" Stacia asked John as they moved out. Stacia McCain was Tom's daughter, a young woman of considerable fighting and survival skill, which had been on display several times during the uprising of the dead.

The old man laid a reassuring hand on her shoulder, but did not smile. "I'm certain we'll find some allies," he replied. "But even if we don't, it's a chance we must take."

With that, the four jogged quickly across the street, ducking into the shadows between the houses as soon as they could. Behind them and out of the trees, numerous other figures emerged and began to follow.

Less than fifteen minutes later, as the four companions continued on at a quick pace, John looked worriedly at McCain. The detective's determined look told him that he, too, was well aware of their pursuers.

"How far?" McCain asked quietly, without even looking at John. He was too busy scanning their path, seeing shadows and movement where he wished he didn't. He'd been pretty sure a number of the beasts had been shadowing them for some time. Now he was certain of it.

"Far enough," John answered grimly, also understanding how dire their predicament was quickly becoming. "We are going to have to stand and fight."

"There are too many and you know it," McCain replied. "We wouldn't survive it."

"We might if we run while we fight."

McCain shrugged. "Hard to say, but we might have a better chance if we narrow the arena somewhat."

"What do you mean?"

"Follow me," he said loudly and then turned abruptly from the street, heading toward a nearby house at a dead run. "Go!" he shouted as their pursuers finally abandoned their stealth and began detaching themselves from the shadows and coming on as fast as they were able to guide their stolen bodies.

McCain took the steps up to the front door three at a time and, without slowing, slammed his foot into the door, shattering the door jamb as the door exploded inward. "Into the house," he bellowed, then turned and pointed the shotgun at the closest creature lumbering up the driveway, a length of electrical wire trailing from one of its hands. The shotgun boomed and the figure lurched to the side and collapsed, a huge hole blown in its gut. McCain ratcheted another shell into the chamber and shot the next one in the head before following his three companions inside. He slammed the door back into its damaged frame and turned to look at them. All three were watching him uncertainly.

"We're trapping ourselves," John said quietly.

"Don't be so pessimistic," McCain countered and pointed behind him. "Up the stairs, everyone! We'll have cover, and the only way they can get to us is up the same stairs." There was the sound of glass breaking from somewhere in the house. Their enemies were all around them. "Now!" he roared, pushing them toward the stairs.

One of the living dead lurched around the corner and into the hall, having come through the double doors in the kitchen. It was brandishing a claw hammer and drove past the startled priest, swinging the hammer with deadly force at the old Indian. John caught the dead man's arm, but the creature's strength was incredible and John wondered if he could hold it back. The monster might have overwhelmed him, had McCain not put the barrel of the shotgun in the creature's face and pulled the trigger.

The others were already going up the stairs as two more of the creatures burst through the front door. McCain blew the nearest one away and then spun and shattered the jaw of the second one with a blow from the butt of the shotgun, knocking it backward. Then he quickly followed the gore-spattered Indian up the stairs, turning around and blowing a hole in the chest of yet another creature as it attempted to follow. Backing his way slowly up the stairs, he kept the gun trained on the hallway below, ready to dispatch the next enemy that showed its head. But the spirits that inhabited the dead bodies were intelligent enough to stay out of his sight now, congregating on both sides of the stairwell in the hall. He knew they were there as much as they knew they had their prey trapped.

"While they hate us with more vile energy than you can imagine, they're not just mindless killing machines," John said quietly from behind the detective. "They're intelligent and won't willingly show themselves to be shot down. They've worked too hard to get these bodies."

"All the better for us," McCain growled. "Saves ammo."

"Perhaps," was John's reply. "But they'll find another way to get to us if they can't come up the stairway."

"Then we need a diversion."

"What about this?" Stacia called to him as she opened up a set of closet doors in the hallway.

McCain, not daring to look away from the stairs, called over his shoulder. "What is it?"

"It's a washer and dryer," John replied, looking into the utility room.

"Is the dryer on a gas line?"

A moment later, Stacia's voice called out. "Yes!"

"We might be in business then," McCain said grimly, motioning John over. "Here, take the shotgun," he said, shoving it into the old man's hands. "Shoot anything that moves downstairs."

"What can I do?" Dalacourt asked from his position near Stacia.

"Get a window open in one of those rooms," McCain ordered,

leaning close and keeping his voice down. "Make sure it leads onto the roof, somewhere we'll be able to jump down from. Keep your eyes peeled, too, Father. We don't want any of them climbing up to meet us."

Dalacourt dashed off down the hall, followed closely by McCain's daughter.

The New York City detective ducked into the utility room, silently grateful so many new houses had the washer and dryer located upstairs with the bedrooms. With a grunt, he pulled the new Maytag dryer away from the wall and looked down at the couplings. The natural gas line ran up through the floor and into the unit. He glanced around and could not believe his good fortune when he found a hammer on an upper shelf. "Good thing I said my prayers last night," he muttered with a determined smile.

As he picked it up and hefted it in his hand, he heard the shotgun go off. He stepped out of the closet and looked at John, who was still aiming down the barrel of the gun. At the bottom of the stairs, a zombie lay sprawled on the landing, half its head blown away.

"Looks like he peeked," McCain stated matter-of-factly. "Nice shot."

"We do what we must," John said quietly. "What's the plan?"

"We're going to blow the house up," McCain whispered. "Get out on the roof and stay low while I watch the stairs. I'm going to disconnect the gas line and when the gas gets strong enough, I'll join you and blow the house."

"That sounds extremely dangerous."

"And what would you call being trapped in a house by an army of zombies?" McCain said darkly as he headed back into the utility room. He yanked the dryer out further, stretching the flex-steel gas line. Kneeling down, he raised the hammer. "Please God, don't let it spark," he prayed aloud and then brought it down as hard as he could. The hammer struck the coupling solidly, bending it, and a soft hissing filled the air. McCain smelled the gas immediately. Picking up a towel, he draped it over the leaking coupling and then slammed the hammer down on it once more. This time, the coupling broke off completely and the gas flowed into the room. Leaping up, he tucked the handle of the hammer into his pants and grabbed the towel, before turning and running back to the stairs.

"Done?" John asked.

"Done," McCain replied quickly, taking the shotgun from him and draping the towel over his shoulder. "Get out on the roof and be ready to jump when I tell you. Stay in the shadows. If they see you on the roof, they'll be waiting to catch you."

"Understood," John said and then joined Dalacourt and Stacia.

McCain pointed the shotgun down the stairs with one hand and reached into his pocket with the other, pulling out a battered silver lighter. It was a gift from an old cop friend of his, felled nearly ten years ago by a drug dealer's bullet. He hadn't smoked in years, but had never given up the memento. Now, he was profoundly glad he'd kept it. Holding the lighter tightly in his hand, he grabbed the towel and pressed it to his face, the gas already thick around him. At the bottom of the stairs, he heard low unintelligible murmurs, and while he had no idea how many were downstairs waiting for them, he knew he was overwhelmingly outnumbered.

As he watched the downstairs hall, he had a sudden thought. What if these abominations could smell and got wind of their plan? Thinking fast, he took the towel from his mouth and shouted down the stairs, hoping the taunt would keep the monsters in the house. "Let's see another one of you deadbeats stick your head around the corner!"

More murmuring and movement, but none dared approach the

stairs. They were not stupid. The gas got thicker and still he waited. Finally, when his eyes were watering and he could stand no more, he slipped the lighter back into his pocket and set the shotgun down. He took the hammer from his belt and, grasping it by the handle, he flung it down the stairs, where it crashed into the wall with a loud crash and imbedded itself deeply into the drywall. One of the creatures immediately stuck its head out and looked up the stairs at McCain with flat, dead eyes. McCain grabbed the shotgun and pointed it at the undead creature. He did not pull the trigger, though, and the thing ducked back out of sight. His ruse complete, the detective immediately whirled around and dashed down the hall and into the room where the others had gone. The window was open, but the gas was all about him and he doubted he would have any problems igniting it. Stepping through the window and onto the roof, he tossed the shotgun to John.

"You guys get going," he coughed, trying to clear his lungs as he pointed to the edge of the roof. "Jump down and start running."

"What about you?" Dalacourt asked.

"Just get on the ground, Padre," McCain snapped angrily. "This isn't open for debate."

Dalacourt moved to the edge of the roof. It was a normal one-story drop to the ground and, swallowing his fear, he jumped off, tucking his legs to absorb the impact and rolling when he hit the ground. He was on his feet in a moment, looking around in the deepening darkness. When he looked up, the young woman was on her way down. She hit the ground rolling, too, but came up with a wince and favoring one leg. She stoically remained silent, refusing to acknowledge it.

John stood on the edge of the roof and looked down to Dalacourt. "Catch the gun," he said in a low voice, dropping it into the priest's waiting hands. A moment later, he had joined them on the ground, leaping rather gracefully for a man as old as he appeared. Without a word, he took the shotgun back and pointed the way, then set off at a dead run across the back yard, the other two close behind.

From the roof, Tom McCain watched them disappear between two houses and then smiled grimly. For the moment, he saw no one following them. "Well, this is another fine mess you've gotten yourself into, Tom," he grumbled, taking out his lighter again and thumbing the flint. As it flared to life, he pulled one of the curtains through the open window and held the flame to the cloth, letting it catch and grow brighter. When he was certain it was not going to go out, he released it and then practically threw himself off the roof.

He hit the ground and rolled to his feet, already running, his legs pumping hard to get him to the safety of the next house. That was when the burning curtain ignited the gas. The explosion was tremendous, the force of it flinging him forward like a ragdoll. Luck was with him, though, and he missed several small trees, the blast knocking him between them and their support stakes before hammering him to the ground.

After lying there just long enough to assess whether he'd lost any body parts, he rolled over onto his hands and knees. Groaning in pain, he slowly climbed to his feet and looked behind him, as small pieces of the burning house began to rain down around him. Both floors of the house had been obliterated, although there were a few burning pieces of wooden framework still standing. Through the smoke and the haze, he saw nothing moving except for the flickering flames. With a look of satisfaction, he turned away and limped toward his three companions who were hiding in the shadows between two houses.

"You're hurt," Dalacourt said immediately as the wounded detective walked slowly up to them.

"It's just a flesh wound," McCain said with a crooked grin. He was bruised and bloodied and he was fairly certain he had cracked a rib or two. But as long as his ribs remained in place and were not free-floating, he was pretty sure he could stick it out. "Let's get moving," he went on wearily. "That bought us a temporary reprieve, but I'm sure there's more of those things looking for us."

"Agreed," John replied, then turned and pointed west.

"Lead on," the detective said.

With that, the foursome made their way quickly down the street, heading toward what they hoped would be safety.

RISEN

CHAPTER 4

Salt Lake City, Utah: Petr could see the Red Lion Hotel ahead of him. Situated in the heart of downtown Salt Lake City, the area around the hotel was usually teeming with people. Today was no exception, except the people were in full insurrection. From the back seat, Rene screamed as Petr slammed on the brakes to keep from hitting several people who seemed to be stumbling across the street. He quickly realized his mistake as the small group turned their dead faces toward the car. Hands clenching metal pipes, rocks, and boards, the rioters began hammering down on his car, denting the metal and shattering the windows. As a pair of hands reached through a shattered back window to grasp at Rene, Petr did the only thing he could think of. He floored it. The car shot forward, sending several of the attackers over the top of the car or under the wheels. Petr was beyond caring at this point.

"The hotel is down there!" David shouted, pointing ahead.

Getting there, however, was going to prove a difficult trick. While the drive to the hotel had been relatively easy, with only small pockets of chaos along the way, West 6th, where the Red Lion was located, was a true warzone. The streets were swollen with the living dead, most of them sporting purple faces and bruised necks, though some had more obvious wounds. Police officers could be seen in small pockets around doorways and barricaded behind vehicles, or inside buildings with shattered store windows. They were blasting away at the mob with service pistols and shotguns. Propped up against the wall of the nearby convention center, a S.W.A.T. truck had been wrecked and was lying on its side. A pair of fully geared officers were squeezing off bursts from their automatic rifles.

Bodies were everywhere, lying in the streets and sidewalks. Most were average citizens, complete with gunshot wounds to head or chest or both. Others were police officers and other officials, having been overwhelmed by sheer numbers. Not all the bodies scattered about were staying down, though. Some were getting back up.

Petr swore in Russian as gunfire ripped through the front tire of his car as a nearby police officer opened up on them. Petr saw the man briefly as he wrenched the wheel to the side and sent the car into a skid, slamming down several combatants in the middle of the road. His disabled Intrepid came to an abrupt stop, facing the officer directly, and Petr watched the man stand up, not more than ten feet in front of him. He saw in the man's eyes a complete and terrifying madness. The officer had snapped and was simply killing to kill. As the gun came up, taking aim at Petr's head, the Russian waited for the bullet he knew would be the end of him.

It never came.

A powerfully built man stepped out from behind a nearby car and wrapped an arm around the officer's waist. The gunshot went high as the attacker lifted the officer in the air and then slammed him viciously to the ground. Several other attackers joined in, hands reaching for the now screaming officer.

As the scream ended suddenly in death, the Russian cast a desperate look at David and then back to Rene, who was white with terror and bleeding from a head wound she'd gotten when hands were trying to pull her out of the car. "We have to run for it!" he yelled, kicking open his door. He looked back to make sure his companions were joining him and, seeing they were both out of the car, leapt forward into the fray.

He was moving on pure adrenaline now, and as the nearest attacker—a middle-aged man wearing a blood-stained green polo shirt—reached for him, Petr grabbed him and violently threw him into the side of the car. The man stumbled and went down, before slowly trying to regain his footing as if the spirit guiding the body was having trouble making all the parts work correctly.

Making sure David and Renee were close, he whirled around only to see a couple of young women in matching sorority sweaters had peeled away from the main mob and were advancing toward him. One of them dragged her right leg, her ankle obviously broken as it flopped around, but she was armed with a blood-streaked hammer. The other did not appear handicapped at all, but was unarmed. Both had angry purple bruises on their necks and blood-flecked spittle was still visible on their chins where they had been savagely strangled.

With an angry shout, Petr met the reaching hands of the first one by throwing her arms out wide and purposefully slamming his forehead into her face. Bone cracked, yet the undead girl would not go down. The second girl reached for him, swinging the hammer toward his head. He easily ducked it and hooked his arm up under hers, catching her in a half nelson. He spun her around, turning the hold into a headlock and then violently jerked upward, breaking her neck. Grabbing the hammer from her hand as she fell, he turned and buried the claw end in the other assailant's head. She, too, slumped to the ground.

Petr took a deep breath, but the first attacker he'd slammed into the side of the car was already back on his feet and coming for him. Before Petr could react, David was there swinging his walking stick like a martial artist. A pair of sharp blows to the midsection of the creature slammed it back into the side of the car, before David snapped the walking stick completely around, catching the thing in the side of the head with a resounding crack of wood on bone. It slumped to the ground, unmoving.

Petr grabbed Rene by the hand and started off at a dead run

toward the hotel. David hurried behind him, all indications of age and weariness gone. All three hoped they would survive the short run for their lives. Luck was with them, though, and in a few seconds they broke out of the main melee and made their way around several police cars blocking the road near the hotel entrance. The officers behind the makeshift barricades gave them only a cursory glance, before continuing with the wholesale gunning down of more of the walking dead. Apparently, they were satisfied that David, Petr and Rene were simply trying to escape the carnage. The three of them probably were not the first.

As they ran toward the hotel, another officer in full riot gear stepped in front of them and grabbed Petr by the arm. "Your name," he demanded, bringing his sidearm up to the ready position.

Petr stumbled and almost tried to jerk away from the officer, before David laid a reassuring hand on his shoulder to calm him down. "This is Petr," David explained evenly. "He's from Russia and doesn't speak English very well."

The officer cast a suspicious glance at Petr before turning his attention to the older man. "Not being able to speak the language isn't a very good attribute right now," he stated, jerking his head in the direction of the fighting. "Seems to be a trait shared by our friends out there."

Petr blanched, but quickly spoke up. "Nothing to worry about, sir," he said in a much more heavily accented Russian dialect than normal. "I was just startled, that's all."

The officer seemed to relax slightly and then looked at the girl.

"Rene," she answered quickly as she held up one of her bloody hands, understanding the officer's meaning all too well. "My name is Rene," she said, pressing her hand back to her wounded forehead.

Satisfied, the man released his hold on Petr's arm and pointed at the hotel. "Safest place for now is the Red Lion, although we've got people holed up in just about every building in the area, and we've got officers holding the front doors."

"Thank you," David said and led the other two toward the front doors of the hotel. A pair of grim-looking police officers armed with shotguns flanked either side of the entrance and watched them as they approached.

"Get on inside with the others," one of the men commanded, all business and not at all friendly.

The second officer glanced harder at David and a look of recognition crossed his face, causing his features to soften. "I know you," he said quietly and then added. "Sorry about your son, sir."

"You knew my son?" David asked more out of reflex than anything else.

"Not personally, but he was a heckuva basketball player. Nice kid, too. He signed a ball for my son last year at the children's hospital. It's a shame when we lose the good ones," he said sincerely.

David forced a smile. In his few days here in the States, he had learned a great deal about his son as a person, things Gideon had not told him in any letters or phone calls back home. Gideon had never spoken of his visits to hospitals and charity events or of his desire to give back. "Thank you for your kind words," David replied, feeling the tears just below the surface. He pushed quickly through the entry and into the hotel lobby, fighting back a fresh wave of grief over his missing son.

"Do you think you'll ever find him?" Rene asked gently, as she followed him in.

"I hope so," he answered sadly, not needing to say more.

Inside the lobby, the gunfire outside was muted somewhat but still loud enough that one would have to be crazy to think they were truly safe. There were perhaps fifty people in the lobby, many sitting in chairs or on the floor staring vacantly in shock or talking amongst themselves in hurried conversations, trying to make sense of the absolute insanity that had gripped the world. Some were vainly trying to use their phones while others were trying to follow the news on the large screen television at the far end of the lobby, which was at the moment only showing the emergency broadcast pattern. The refugees ranged from mid-level business executives to vacationing families to some of the hotel staff.

Petr pulled out his phone, saw zero bars, and swore under his breath in Russian. He was about to try Alexis again anyway when he heard someone behind him.

"You guys all right?" said a voice, causing them all to turn. A young man, likely in his mid-twenties, was approaching them, tucking a phone back into his pocket. He appeared to be a hotel bellhop, though he had long since lost his hat. He ran a nervous hand through a thick mop of blond hair as he approached, and his blue eyes were locked on them somewhat anxiously.

"We're fine," Petr said, his voice rather cold as he quickly took in the measure of the man. He was immediately on his guard, the Zhugravinsky blood in him taking control.

"Name's Donovan," the bellhop said as he stuck out his hand in greeting, ignoring Petr's icy demeanor. "Can you believe what's happening out there? Man, this is nuts!"

"It is indeed disturbing," David said, leaning heavily on his walking stick as he accepted the young man's handshake. He was exhausted—the spryness and agility that had helped lead them through the fighting outside was gone. "My name is David. This is Petr and this young woman is Rene," he went on, introducing the other two. "It's good to make your acquaintance, Donovan."

"So, how'd you end up in here?" Donovan asked, but suddenly slapped himself in the forehead as if he'd just remembered something. "Man, I'm sorry for the fifth degree," he explained sheepishly. "It's kind of my job right now. I'm supposed to be going around making sure everyone's okay. You're the last ones to make it in, I guess. How'd you get to the Lion, anyway?"

"What's the situation here at the hotel?" Petr asked abruptly ignoring the question.

Donovan looked around and shrugged. "People are camping out here for now, while the police deal with the riot. It's safe here for the moment and there are cops all over the place." Turning back to face them, his features were almost excited as he went on. "You know, some people are saying they're not even alive! It's like *Night of the Living Dead* or something! And you should hear the religious nuts going off about it! People are crazy, man!"

David and Petr exchanged looks, before David decided to limit their conversation. "I'm a guest of this hotel, visiting from Africa," he said. "Is it safe to go up to my room, Donovan?"

"Well, yes and no," he answered. "Management shut down the elevators and stairwells to keep people in the lobby. Some guests are locked in their rooms, but the cops said if they had to evacuate the hotel, they wanted as many down here in the lobby as possible."

David turned to look out the front door. The two officers were still crouched on either side of it, their shotguns at the ready. It was getting dark outside as the afternoon headed toward evening. The gunfire was already growing more sporadic as the killers were either gunned down or disappeared into the deepening gloom. "So we're trapped here for the moment?"

"They certainly won't let you back out," Donovan replied with a crooked grin. "Not that I'd want to even try. I thought they were going to shoot one guy who tried to leave a little bit ago. Other doors are all covered, too," he went on. "They seem to think that at least in here, we're safe."

"Or easy targets," Petr added uneasily. "I don't like this one bit," he spoke directly to David. "It severely limits our options."

"Nevertheless, we appear to have no choice in the matter," the older man replied with a sigh, looking around for somewhere to sit.

At that moment, Rene's eyes fluttered and she collapsed to the floor. Petr and David both quickly knelt beside her, and after a tense moment she opened her eyes and smiled weakly. "I'm sorry I fainted," she whispered as the two men helped get her to a couch.

"She has lost a bit of blood," David said to Donovan.

"And I'm so hungry," Rene said. "Can we get any food?"

Donovan thought for a moment and then leaned forward, whispering. "You know, they closed down Cafe Olympus a couple hours ago, but there's the Sky Bar on the top floor. You'd have to take the stairs and it's thirteen flights up. If we're careful, I can sneak you up the back way. They probably still have the buffet set up if you're hungry. Doubtful anyone has thought to take it down."

"What about the rest of these people?" David questioned, looking around at the others in the lobby.

"What about 'em?" Donovan replied casually. "None of them are fainting. Besides, if I let everybody upstairs, there wouldn't be any food left for us."

David turned to the young Russian. "What are your thoughts, Petr?"

Petr was busy looking around as he listened to Donovan's offer. Something about the whole thing had him feeling uneasy. He'd learned long ago to trust his instincts and right now, they were warning him that something wasn't right. He looked down at Rene and saw that she was getting paler, a wad of bloody Kleenex pressed to her head. "Rene needs to get that cut cleaned up. Do you have anything?" he asked, holding his growing uneasiness at bay for the moment.

"There's a first aid kit at the bar," Donovan assured them.

"We don't appear to have many options, Petr," David said, noticing the look of unease still on the Russian's face. "Let's go upstairs and take care of Rene. We'll consider what comes next at that point." He looked at the girl. "Do you think you can make it upstairs?"

"Yes," she nodded slowly. "I can make it."

"Okay," Petr agreed reluctantly. "At least if those things bring the fight to the hotel, we'll have some kind of warning." He hadn't said it to the others, but he had also realized that the higher they were, the better chance he would have of getting phone service and connecting with Alexis.

"Then it's settled," Donovan said with a smile. "Let me clear the way. Management is watching the stairwells to make sure people don't start spreading out all over the hotel, but one of the guys on duty is a buddy of mine. He'll let us through and we'll head upstairs. Wait right here. I'll be back." Without waiting for their answer, the bellhop scooted through the crowd and disappeared down one of the hallways.

"You seem a little troubled," David remarked to Petr as he watched Donovan leave. "Our bellhop seems to be friendly enough."

"Yeah," agreed Petr thoughtfully. "He's almost too friendly."

"Perhaps you are reading too much into this?"

"Perhaps," Petr agreed unconvincingly as he resumed looking around, trying to discover the source of his growing apprehension.

David turned his attention to Rene. "How are you feeling, my dear?" he asked, looking at her forehead.

Rene pulled the bloody tissue from the wound. It was superficial and the bleeding had slowed to a small ooze. "I've been better," she replied shakily, shifting the Kleenex to a cleaner spot and then pressing it back against the cut. "But I'll be okay once I get something to eat," she went on and then changed the subject. "What's happening out there, David?"

The old African leaned heavily on his walking stick and rested his head against the smooth wood. "I honestly don't know, Rene." He closed his eyes and shook his head as he sighed deeply.

"Do you really think it might all be biblical prophecy?" she pressed.

David offered her a helpless shrug. "I suppose it could be," he answered her with a small smile. "But I'm far from certain."

"It seems to be quieting down," Petr broke in. "Maybe they've got things under control."

David craned his neck to look out the window. Darkness was moving in, but he could see the two officers still in their positions on either side of the entrance. Several other officers had joined them, and that provided him with a small amount of reassurance. "You may be right," he said.

A moment later, Donovan rejoined them. "Perfect," the bellhop said as he sidled up, casting a furtive look at the manager who was near the front desk, arguing with a couple of college-aged men. "That should keep the boss man busy for a few minutes. This is our chance. We can head up the back stairs."

"Are you certain this is okay?" Rene asked worriedly.

"We'll be fine," Donovan reassured her. "We'll get your forehead cleaned up and grab a bite from the buffet."

"We could do the same down here," Rene pointed out, still not ready to leave the perceived safety of numbers.

"Well sure, if you want cold bologna sandwiches," Donovan said, screwing up his face in a grimace. "Personally, I'd like a few hot-wings and a beer myself. What about you, Pete?" he asked the Russian.

Petr was silent and looked around. He wasn't ready to trust the bellhop yet, but he liked isolation in situations like this and in the end, that feeling won out. "Fine," he agreed curtly. "Let's go."

"Great," Donovan said and then led them through the crowd of people and into the hall toward the stairwell. A quick peek to make sure no one was taking too much notice of them, and they were through the door and up the stairs. Petr soon found himself almost a full flight behind Donovan and David as he helped Rene along.

"You don't seem to trust the bellhop," Rene said quietly when they were out of earshot.

"I don't know," Petr shrugged. "I'm just not feeling right about this."

Rene stopped and looked at Petr. "If you're really worried, we can go back downstairs."

A shout came from above from Donovan. "Are you guys coming or not?"

Petr stood, quietly pondering. Everything in him was telling him to trust his instincts, but David had agreed that going to the bar was a good idea and obviously Rene needed some help. Shaking his head, he reached out a hand to help Rene. "Yes, we're coming!"

"So how long have you been in the States anyway?" Rene asked after a few moments.

"Not long," Petr answered. "Just long enough to get situated and get into some classes at the university."

"Your English is superb," she pointed out. "I mean, anyone can tell you're from Russia, but you sound like you've been here a long time."

Petr allowed himself to smile. "Thanks," he answered awkwardly. He was going to have to get used to American girls, he thought to himself. First Alexis, now Rene. Much more outgoing than the girls he knew back home. He concentrated on the stairs, his mind wandering.

"You're thinking of that girl again," Rene said gently, still smiling.

He looked at her with surprise. "How do you know?"

"Woman's intuition," she answered. "Besides, I've seen how you attacked your phone a couple times, trying to call someone. Had to be a girlfriend. How'd you two meet?"

"I met her in a couple of classes," he replied with a weary sigh. "Her name is Alexis."

"Well, I know you're worried about her, Petr," she said with genuine concern. "But she'll be okay. You have to think the best in a situation like this."

He nodded, thinking about how quickly his fortune had changed. When the day began, the prospect of life in the United States was practically limitless. Twelve hours later, his prospect for even basic survival was in question and he had no idea how Alexis was faring. For all he knew, she could already be dead. Gritting his teeth against that morbid thought, he trudged on in silence.

Thirteen flights of stairs will add up on a person and, by the time they reached the top, all of them were winded. Rene was struggling, her face extremely pale, and Petr had spent a lot of the climb helping her slowly along. At one point, David had asked if it would be possible to return to his room to grab a quick change of clothes, but Donovan pointed out that the fire doors were all locked from the stairwells. Only someone coming from the other way could open it and he doubted anyone would be hanging out in the halls to hear them banging on it.

They finally arrived at the Sky Bar, breathing heavily and grateful to be done with the climb. There were several other people in the bar, hotel employees by the looks of them, and Donovan greeted them heartily. Two of them were seated in the dining area, feet kicked up casually on a table as they chatted and ate from heaping plates of buffet food. A third man, wearing a tie-dyed shirt and with long thick dreadlocks, was behind the bar, busy mixing up some drinks. It was obvious they were friends of Donovan's.

"Hey, Juke," the bellhop called out with a wave as Petr moved to help Rene into a nearby chair. "Do you have a first aid kit? Girl over here got cut pretty bad."

"Sure, mon," the bartender replied in a thick Jamaican accent as he disappeared behind the bar and then popped back up with a standard white plastic kit and tossed it to him.

Donovan caught it, talking as he did so. "I brought these three up with me, guys. Rene here needs some medical attention and some food. And this gentleman here," he paused to point to David, "is Mr. Sumbawanga, here in Salt Lake City looking for his son Gideon. I recognized him from the news reports, so figured I'd sneak him up here and give him the VIP treatment." Donovan pointed to the two seated employees. "These two lazy bums here are Cappy and Miguel. They work maintenance. And that's Juke, the worst bartender money can buy."

Petr relaxed and some of the uneasiness he felt about the young man began to fade. He pulled out his phone, saw he had one bar and tapped on Alexis' name to call her. It took an eternity as the phone searched and searched for a signal, but in the end the "all circuits are busy" recording came on and Petr slid his phone back in his pocket, doing his best to mask his frustration.

"Da boss see ya?" Juke asked Donovan with a frown.

"Naw, he was too busy looking official," Donovan replied, handing the first aid case to Petr.

"I heard about your son," Cappy said between bites of a chicken wing. "Great 'baller'."

"I appreciate your sentiments," David answered politely.

"Yeah," Donovan chimed in. "That dude was going number one in the draft, no doubt. Can't believe he disappeared."

David nodded, not quite certain how to react to the sudden talk of his missing son.

"Eat up, guys," Donovan went on, walking over and picking up a plate. "If we don't eat it, someone else will, so you might as well make good use of it."

Miguel held up a stripped chicken bone, his eyes watering. "Watch out for the wings," he added. "They've got a pretty good kick to them."

Petr, David, and Rene began to relax visibly and, after Petr had dressed Rene's head wound, the seven people passed the next hour eating and talking about what had been happening in the world. Donovan and his friends didn't appear to have much interest in the affairs of the world beyond that they were living in a real life zombie movie. They were more interested in having a room full of free food and drinks, while talking about the upcoming basketball draft, as if it would happen normally despite the world's sudden plunge into insanity.

After a while, Petr, David, and Rene moved over to one corner of the bar and let the four hotel employees talk amongst themselves. Rene looked much better with her forehead cleaned up and bandaged and some food in her, and Petr had to admit that it had been good for all of them to eat. They decided to get a little sleep and see what the morning would bring. Settling themselves into their chairs, they drifted off one by one, Petr being the last.

A short while later, Petr woke with a start, his heart racing. Something was wrong.

"Wake up, Pete," Donovan whispered, shaking him again.

"I'm awake," Petr replied, coming out of his chair and looking around. The bar was empty. Only Donovan remained. "What's going on? How long have we been sleeping?"

"Couple hours, I guess," Donovan said as he shook his head. "But something's going down," he went on nervously. "Juke and the others went downstairs to see what was up and I just heard someone scream."

"Your friends?" the Russian asked, reaching over and gently shaking Rene awake.

"No idea," he replied gravely. "But I think those things are coming."

At this point, David was awake, having heard the conversation. "What do you suggest?"

Donovan turned and pointed to the exit sign. "The rooftop," was his answer. "There's one door out and we can block it closed—lock it or something. If there's anybody coming, we can keep them from getting to us."

"The rooftop?" Petr asked, narrowing his eyes in suspicion. His internal alarms were all going off again. "Not a chance. We'd be trapped."

"Have it your way," Donovan said, sounding somewhat angry. "But we either go up top and fight them as they come up or you can try fighting your way down a stairwell that might have them coming after you from both sides." He lifted up an icepick he'd found behind the bar. "Me? I prefer the defensive high ground if we've gotta fight."

"Our friend is correct," David pointed out quickly. "We've little choice at this point. If we can barricade ourselves on the rooftop, we can hold a single door until help arrives."

"So they're in the hotel now?" Rene asked, her voice strained with fright.

"It would appear so," David answered, casting a look around.

Donovan slipped the ice pick into his belt and started toward the exit. "Come on, while we still have time."

Donovan led them quickly through the bar and out the door. He turned down a hallway and pushed open a door that said "Employees Only." "Hurry," he said, letting them move past him and up the stairs. They ascended the short flight and Petr pushed open the door. He took a single step out onto the rooftop into the night air when something heavy slammed into the back of his shoulder. He pitched forward to the gravel, trying to roll with the blow even as Rene screamed from behind him. Bodies pressed down on him and hands were grasping at his throat.

At that moment, Petr Zhugravinsky snapped and the beast took control once again. With a roar of fury, he threw off several of the attackers and scrambled to his feet to face the ambush. There was no telling exactly how many there were in the darkness and, through the haze of red rage that enveloped him, he didn't care. Several older men dressed in bathrobes and one in just his boxer shorts were closing in on him, outlined by the dim glow of the rooftop lights. They looked as if they had been guests of the hotel. Now they were on the roof, trying to kill him.

The man in the boxer shorts had a severely bruised face and one of his ears looked as if it had been nearly ripped off. He was armed with a towel rack torn from a bathroom wall. The rack came swinging in and Petr ducked the blow, letting his attacker's momentum carry him past. The young Russian threw a back kick at the nearest bathrobe-wearing man, sending him crashing back into the doorway they had just emerged from. He caught a fleeting glimpse of Donovan moving out of the way, before turning his sights back to the man armed with the towel rack. The man was trying to recover, but Petr lowered his shoulder and drilled him in the lower back, sending him sprawling. He pulled up sharply, though, not allowing himself to be taken to the ground again, and stomped down hard on the back of the man's neck. Bones popped and the thing went still.

Petr scooped up the towel rack and turned and swung, denting the side of another attacker's head, a middle-aged woman. He swung again and the bar hit her in the same part of her skull with a loud crack. This time she dropped to the gravel-covered rooftop, out of the fight. Still armed, Petr whirled around, gauging the threat. As he caught sight of Donovan pulling Rene away from the melee, an arm encircled his throat from behind. Still in a rage, he stepped backward and grabbed the arm, then flipped his attacker over his shoulder. Before his enemy could recover, Petr slammed the towel bar into the thing's face, finishing it.

A blow caught Petr across the jaw and he nearly stumbled. Somewhere in the darkness, he thought he heard David shout for help, but he had his hands full as he faced his assailant. It was one of the bathrobe-wearing men who had punched him and Petr went low, slamming the bar into the man's side. The man barely staggered, though, and came on again. Petr caught the next blow and threw the man's arm out wide, then slammed the end of the bar into his chest. The rod shattered bone and penetrated flesh. The man's hands clamped feebly around the metal bar that was now protruding from his chest before he stumbled and fell.

Petr continued to move in a fighting circle, his vision focused on the next closest enemy. Two of them moved in on him and in a matter of seconds, both were finished, one with a broken neck and the other with an upper leg that had been savagely broken by a kick from the enraged Russian. It writhed on the ground for a few moments before going still. Petr continued moving, driven by the murderous rage that consumed him. A young lady fell to his blows, her once-pretty face broken where he'd driven his elbow into the bridge of her nose. A teenage boy ended up with his back broken over Petr's knee. Tossing that corpse aside, the Russian noticed only three attackers remained, shuffling silently toward him and intent only on his death.

But Petr's mind was back in his own country, where the violence associated with his life was as common as dinner with the family. One by one, they were beaten down in a savage fury until finally, it was over and all was quiet. His breathing ragged and his body nearly spent, Petr bent over with his hands on his knees, gulping air. He had done it and they were safe. He'd killed them all and it filled him with a feeling of power he'd never experienced before, even living in Russia as a Zhugravinsky.

"Hey, Superman!" a familiar voice called out and Petr turned his head wearily toward it. "You forget something?"

Petr went cold, his blood freezing in his veins. Donovan stood near the edge of the roof, still holding Rene. But Rene's eyes were wide open in terror and her mouth worked soundlessly, blood dribbling from her lips. The handle of Donovan's icepick protruded from her chest in the middle of a growing stain of crimson. Petr realized with sickening dread that it had been driven into her heart.

"You don't have a lot of luck with women, do ya?" Donovan spit viciously and in one move, flung Rene backward over the edge of the roof. Rene's final scream ended abruptly—thirteen floors below.

Petr never moved. So shocked at what he'd just witnessed, he failed to see the towering figure loom up behind him. The falling blow was severe, catching him in the back of the neck just below his skull. He slumped to the rooftop as blackness quickly took him.

CHAPTER 5

Highway 15, Mesquite, Nevada: The four young men had been driving for almost an hour, following the interstate signs back toward the little town of Mesquite, Nevada. The road had been surprisingly barren, which was a plus for them. They saw only a handful of cars traveling toward Vegas—people who had no clue what awaited them when they got there—and had not passed a single vehicle going in their direction. It was as if the interstate had just closed down and, for the moment, that suited them just fine. The drive had given them time to sort things out and, although they had made little progress on figuring out the "why," they had at least been able to get a firmer grasp on the "what."

Because they had no cell phone service, Clint had tried to keep the radio tuned to stations that kept an update on the chaos in Las Vegas, but as they were in the middle of nowhere, there had been long stretches where he'd searched in vain for any radio stations still on the air. They found several simply broadcasting the emergency broadcast signal and only one actually broadcasting live. That one had been faint and lasted only a few minutes before fading into static, but in those short minutes, they'd learned a lot.

The violence was apparently widespread, random, and not the least bit centralized. It was happening all over the world: Beijing, Hong Kong, Moscow, Nairobi, Barcelona, Santiago, Mexico City, Berlin, and numerous other large cities were under siege by crazed rioters in various degrees. Yet in other places, including Mecca, Sao Paulo, Jerusalem and the American West Coast, all seemed to be rather quiet, with little more than minor flare-ups here and there—easily quelled. While no one knew why the world had gone mad, the potential causes being considered for these bizarre attacks ranged from plague, to terrorism, to the outright supernatural. The last one at least lent credibility to what the four friends had gone through in Vegas. They even caught an excerpt of a speech by some archbishop in the Catholic church, claiming the dead were rising and that this was the beginning of the end, heralding the Second Coming of Christ. Moments after that piece had played, the radio station had faded to static and they had been unable to get it back or find any other to take its place.

They drove on, knowing if they had tried to find a worse place in the world to be at the moment, they would have been hard pressed to do so. They might as well have been on a deserted island in the Pacific. Luke's car was laboring more and more as each mile passed beneath them. It had taken quite a beating in Vegas and did not seem to have much left in it now, leaving all of them to fervently hope it would at least get them to Mesquite. If it died in the middle of nowhere, they knew Luke was finished.

Unfortunately, Luke was getting much worse. Whatever it was that had afflicted him when Gideon had attacked him a couple hours before, was beginning to spread. The desiccated area that had at first only affected his face had now moved down his neck. A recent examination by Chad had shown the effect had spread to Luke's chest and back and was also moving down his arms, leaving the skin as dry and cracked as old leather. It was as if all the moisture was being sucked out of his body, leaving him in an almost mummified condition. His breathing was ragged and shallow, and his tongue was beginning to swell and push out of his mouth.

"I don't know how much time he has left," Chad finally spoke up from the back seat after a long silence. "I can't even begin to figure out what's happening to him."

"Just a little further," Clint answered, trying to coax a little more out of the car. He dared not open the engine up fully for fear the stress would push the car over the edge. He'd been cruising along as close to sixty-miles-per-hour as he could without pushing the damaged car beyond its diminishing capabilities. "We just passed a sign that said Mesquite is seven miles ahead."

"Then we just have to find a hospital," Chad answered back gravely.

"If the town hasn't gone through the same thing as Vegas, we'll find it," Clint answered matter-of-factly. His voice trailed off, not wanting say the words they all knew came next. If Mesquite had indeed been hit like Las Vegas, Luke was as good as dead.

Less than two minutes later, they saw a miracle.

"I see a blue sign!" Owen shouted out, pointing through the shattered windshield. "Right there! Hospital, exit 120!"

"We're close," Clint breathed a sigh of relief and managed a tight smile. "Two or three miles and we'll be there."

The engine coughed.

Clint looked at Owen and the two locked stares.

It coughed again.

"This is not happening," Clint said in disbelief, easing off the accelerator. The engine coughed a third time and then smoothed out a little as he slowed. "Come on, baby," he coaxed the car as they dipped under fifty miles-per-hour. "Just get us there." Amazingly, it did. After a few heart-pounding minutes, Clint eased the battered vehicle onto the exit ramp leading to the hospital.

Being an hour out of Las Vegas, it was a small miracle a place like Mesquite had ever grown large enough to have a hospital. But, as the only real town between Las Vegas and St. George, Utah, signs made sure anyone coming to town could find the Mesa View Regional Hospital quickly and easily. As hope surged in all of them, Clint turned left and drove across the interstate and onto Dump Road. Just past the end of the overpass, what they saw caused their renewed hope to quickly die and the icy tendrils of fear and doubt began to gnaw at them again.

The image was haunting. Two cars were mashed together off the exit ramp intersection, dimly lit by the street lamp shining down. Someone had tried to crawl out of one of the damaged vehicles. His body lay in the middle of the road, one leg bent at a forty-five degree angle halfway between his knee and his ankle. There was not an emergency vehicle in sight.

"Oh, no," Owen said softly, his eyes scanning the wreckage.

Before he could say another word, their own car's engine coughed twice, sputtered, and then finally died completely. It had rolled its last mile. Clint turned the key in vain several times, but the engine only turned over weakly before going forever silent. Cursing under his breath, he slammed the gearshift into park.

"Hey, we're close," Chad said as calmly as he could from the back seat, unbuckling his belt. "The car got us here. The rest of it we can do on foot."

They all quickly got out, but it was Clint who brought them back to reality. "Come on, guys," he said angrily, standing up on his side of the car and slamming his hands down on the battered roof in frustration. "Do you really think if there was anyone at the hospital who could help Luke, that guy over there would still be lying in the middle of the road?" He finished heatedly, pointing at the corpse lying in the intersection. "That's what waits for us if we screw around here!" he exclaimed. "Let's face reality, guys! It's no different here than it was in Vegas!"

Both Owen and Chad cast their glances back to the accident scene and then back to Clint. "Look, we have to try," Chad finally said, his voice shaking. "We can't just leave him to die." He reached back into the car and unsnapped Luke's seat belt. Putting his hands underneath his friend's arms, he pulled Luke out of the car and gently laid him on the concrete.

A sharp intake of breath startled them and all three of them looked down. Luke was going into convulsions. His body went rigid and his teeth clamped down and sliced through his swollen tongue. His arms and legs shook forcefully and his body literally bounced on the road. All three of them dropped to the ground beside him, desperate to help their friend.

"Hold his arms!" Owen shouted as he grabbed hold of Luke's legs and tried to stop the violent shaking. Chad and Clint each had an arm, trying in vain to hold them down, both of them horrified at what was happening. Black blood poured from Luke's butchered tongue and the damaged skin and tissue on his face cracked and sloughed away, showing white bone underneath. Then, as quickly as it had started, it was over. Luke gave out one final rasping breath, then his body relaxed and he went still.

Luke Jorbo was dead.

For a long minute, the three men did not move as tears coursed silently down their cheeks.

"He's gone," Chad finally said, rolling away from Luke's body into a sitting position. Burying his face between his knees, he let the tears flow, his body wracked with quiet sobs.

Clint and Owen both sat down heavily near Luke's body, words failing them. Both of them cried—neither had any reason to try to hide it. Heads buried in hands, overcome with grief, they never saw Luke's eyes snap open, their milky whiteness almost glowing in the darkness.

Sensing something, Clint looked over just as Luke sat up, his hands grasping for Clint's throat. Owen bolted to his feet and fell back, while Chad crab-walked backward as fast as he could, yelling at the top of his lungs.

Luke grabbed hold of Clint and bore him to the ground with renewed strength, pinning him down and strangling the life out of him. Clint struggled mightily, finally throwing Luke off his body and breaking the hold long enough to suck in several panicked gulps of air. Luke was back on him in a moment, bony hands stretching for his throat again. Again, Clint fought for his life as the reanimated Luke got his fingers around his throat once more. The hands began to squeeze, choking off his air. This time, Luke slammed his head forward, smashing his forehead into Clint's face. Stunned, the fight went out of Clint and he slumped back, allowing Luke to get a death grip on his throat. The blackness came quickly and Clint sank into oblivion.

Regaining his wits, Owen jumped forward to save one friend at the expense of another. Standing over the unbelievable nightmare that was once his good friend, Owen swung the tire iron he'd grabbed from the car trunk with all his strength and shattered the side of Luke's skull, knocking him off Clint. Luke rolled to the ground and tried to feebly rise, half his head caved in. Owen stood over him for a moment, tears still streaming down his face. He raised the crowbar high and then brought it down quickly, slamming the heavy metal bar into Luke's upturned face. Luke's body shivered once and then fell back to the pavement to lie still. There was surprisingly little blood, and what there was of it was as black as tar.

Owen tossed the tire iron aside and turned to look at Clint, who was up on his elbows, coughing and sucking in air to his starved lungs. He managed to look up at Owen through watery eyes and could only nod gratefully.

"What in God's name was that?" Chad asked, walking slowly back toward them, his face white as a sheet as he looked down at Luke's body.

"That," Owen said softly, looking up into the star-filled sky, "is the end of the world."

"That wasn't real, was it?" Chad asked, still disbelieving. "I mean, it can't be!" He was on the verge of hysteria.

"Maybe it is now," Clint said weakly, prompting both his friends to look down at him still sprawled on the concrete. "Look." He was pointing down the road and their eyes tracked in that direction. Several figures could be seen shambling into the dim glow of a street light, moving toward them. Several were wearing hospital gowns and a couple were clad in white lab coats. At least one appeared to be in full surgical garb, complete with mask.

"I don't think they're here for the accident victim," Clint went on with difficulty, struggling painfully to his feet. Owen moved quickly to help him, but Chad remained rooted to the spot in shock and terror.

"We need to move," Owen said quickly.

Clint leaned up against the car, rubbing his throat. "Where?" he rasped, his eyes still on the approaching figures. They were not that far away and slowly closing the distance.

"Anywhere but here," Owen went on, pulling his friend away from the car. "Back across the bridge. Let's go."

They started to run, but suddenly stopped, eyes going wide in terror. In the middle of the bridge was a familiar figure, tall and clad in long robes of black. His hood had been pulled back up over his head and hid his face, but there was no mistaking who it was.

Gideon had found them.

"You rotten son of a..." Clint snarled, taking a shaky step forward.

Owen grabbed him by the shoulder, stopping him. "No, Clint! Remember what happened to Luke. We can't take him! We need to get out of here or we're all dead!"

Clint stood for just a moment, staring at Gideon with hate in his eyes. Then common sense won out and he turned with his friends.

Owen looked back at the approaching mob and hesitated. Behind them, he could see the lights of a truck moving slowly up the road behind the mob, the first vehicle they had seen in quite some time.

"Think we can make it?" Chad asked, reading his mind as he, too, watched the truck approach.

"There's no way to get around them," Owen replied and then pointed in a northeasterly direction that would take them at a forty-five degree angle away from the approaching mob. More importantly, it would take them almost directly away from Gideon. "There's some lights over there," he said quickly. "Maybe we can find help."

"Or maybe we run into more of those things," Chad said quietly, his eyes shifting back to the shambling figures as they continued to draw closer.

"Doesn't matter right now," Owen snapped, turning to look at Gideon again. Their former friend had not moved. He just stood on the bridge, watching them, his presence all but overpowering. "We have to get out of here. Whatever is over there can't be worse than this." With that, the three of them started off at a run, leaving the pavement and pounding across desert sand toward the lights. Off to the side, some of the approaching creatures shifted course in pursuit. But they were much slower and the men easily outdistanced them, leaving them behind.

As the three remaining friends disappeared into the darkness, the driver of the eighteen-wheeler coming up the road slowed his rig as he came upon the wandering creatures. Most had stopped now and were simply facing in the direction the men had run, but they made no further effort to pursue. The driver took a moment to survey the situation, then opened the door and hopped out of the cab. Showing absolutely no fear, he walked down the road and right through the group of undead. They paid him no mind and simply stood where they were. Some looked at him with dead eyes, while others continued to look in the direction of their departed prey.

The man passed unmolested through the small mob and walked purposefully up to the car. Noting the damage to it, he chuckled and then walked around to where Luke's body lay crumpled on the ground. He looked at it for a moment and then pulled out a photograph, matching what remained of the dead young man to one of the faces in the picture.

Satisfied, he looked up and across the barren overpass, wondering briefly why the men hadn't run back across the bridge to get away. He preferred to have them on or near the interstate where they would be easier to track, but he would make do with the situation as it was. They would quickly find out Mesquite was not going to be the friendliest of places. He had only a moment to consider it before his phone started playing "It's the End of the World As We Know It," a rude tribute to his former girlfriend.

Smiling, Cole Banyon slid his finger across the screen. "Yeah," he answered, "they made it to Mesquite." A pause. "Right, I have the truck." Another pause. "Yeah, I know where it is. I passed it on the way in." Pause. "Right. Oh, and one more thing. They're down to three." A pause. "Yeah, one of them is dead. I just checked the body. Looks like he took a couple of blows to the head." Pause. "No, it's not him." Pause. "Yes, sir," he finished. "I'll see to it."

He turned his phone off and pocketed it. Then, taking one last satisfied look at Luke's body, he returned to the truck.

Behind him in the darkness, Gideon watched him go.

CHAPTER 6

Salt Lake City, Utah: Alexis awoke, disoriented and unsure how long she'd been asleep. She didn't know what it was, but she knew something was dreadfully wrong. Rolling over, careful not to wake the small child sleeping next to her, she leaned over and checked on Libby. Her friend was still unconscious, her condition unchanged. Confused as to what was bringing on the sense of alarm, she looked out across the common room. It only took her a moment to understand what was wrong—the lights were out. All of them.

As she adjusted to the dark, she realized that even more furniture had been wedged up against the windows and doors and, between the spaces, she saw only darkness. Faint light streamed in through the giant stained-glass window above the doors, making it clear to Alexis that it was nearly night. She and Dakota had slept for some time. The voices of those in the shelter were hushed whispers—even the radios had been turned off.

Alexis checked her phone, the glow from the screen emitting a ghostly light in the near darkness. No calls from her mother, no calls from friends and family, no calls from Owen. She quickly pocketed it and looked at Dakota. She lightly stroked the little girl's forehead, waking her. Dakota's eyes snapped open and instinctively, Alexis placed a finger to her lips. "Shhh," she whispered.

Dakota whispered back. "What's wrong?"

Alexis shook her head. "I don't know," she said, taking hold of the little girl's hand and helping her up. "I want you to stay with me," she went on. "Can you do that?"

"Yes," Dakota replied in a whisper, her voice trembling.

"Good girl," she replied and then looked around. There was very little light in the shelter, but there was enough to make out some features of the people around her. A few moments of searching and she saw Sally toward the front of the main room, talking quietly but urgently with several others around her. Taking hold of Dakota's hand, Alexis hurried toward her, working her way through the knots of people. "Sally," she said quietly as they drew nearer. "What's happening?"

Sally looked hard at the young woman, then at the little girl who was now holding tightly to her leg. For a moment, a wave of despair seemed to wash over her face, but she mastered it just as quickly. "The lights went out a while ago, so we barricaded the windows with the furniture," she said quietly. "Phil, over there in the corner, went out to check on things just a few minutes ago and saw a large group of people moving in this direction."

"Do they know we're here?" Alexis asked, fighting to keep the growing panic out of her voice.

"No idea, girl," Sally answered. "But I'm not one for taking chances. We're keeping our heads down and our mouths shut and maybe they'll move right on past us."

Alexis looked back at Libby, knowing she couldn't leave her friend behind. "What are we going to do if they find us?"

"Honey, look around this room," Sally replied sadly. "Tell me what you see."

Alexis scanned the room, her eyes taking everyone in. There were old couples from the nearby neighborhood who didn't want to be alone, homeless men and women with nowhere else to be, volunteers who had come to help, and people who had come, like Alexis and Libby, because they needed care for injuries. Many of the people at the shelter were old, weak, or tired. Most would not survive long in any kind of a fight and all of them would die if they were pinned in the shelter and a mob attacked them.

"We can't survive if we stay and fight, Sally!" Alexis objected. "I saw what's out there! We need to get help."

"Lexy, darling," Sally said quietly, placing both hands on the young woman's shoulders. "If there was any help to be gotten, we'd have been out of here a long time ago. Fact is, even if we did get word out that we needed help, no one would get to us in time. You see who's here—who's taken shelter. Think what'll happen to them if we scatter out into the streets. No, honey, our only chance is to stay quiet and hope this passes us by."

"But if we stay..." Alexis began, but Sally shook her head and stopped her.

"I like our chances better here," Sally said, a note of sad acceptance in her voice. "Besides," she went on, "if they come after us here, maybe we can use it as a diversion to get any little ones to safety." Sally looked down at Dakota with a motherly smile and then looked back at Alexis, telling her what she would need to do without speaking the words.

Alexis understood immediately what her friend was offering and was aghast. "We can't leave you," she protested. "I won't leave Libby."

"You can and you will, girl, if it comes to that," Sally replied, her voice stern. "We have to be ready for any and all possibilities. If this is our Alamo and we have to stand and fight, then so be it. But I'd rather my sacrifice meant something."

Alexis was speechless. She couldn't believe what she was hearing, but she also knew she couldn't argue with Sally. The woman was right. Alexis' shoulders slumped and she lowered her eyes to Dakota and gently squeezed her hand.

"For the time being, we sit tight," Sally went on. "Maybe we get lucky and they move on. Maybe they come after us here. Either way, we wait."

There was an urgent whisper from a man near one of the windows. "Sally! Come here!"

The woman hurried toward him, Alexis right behind her with the little girl in tow. "What is it?" Sally asked.

The man was silent, only pointing around the big couch sitting in front of the window. In the darkness down the street, there was movement—lots of movement. It took only a few seconds for them to realize it was indeed a large group of people moving up the street toward the shelter. They moved slowly, awkwardly, and many were carrying items in one or both hands. The wait had not lasted long at all.

Sally turned away, raising her voice. The time for silence was obviously over. "All right, everybody," she said with surprising calmness. "Our secret is out and we're gonna have some company. If you're here, you knew this was a possibility and you know they ain't coming to share dinner with us."

There were murmurs among the group and one man nearby muttered, "This isn't real!"

"Honey, I hate to tell you this, but this is as real as real gets," Sally replied, then turned to look at Alexis. "You take the girl with you and get into the kitchen near the back fire door," she said. "There's still a chance they'll move by us, but I don't think so. Hopefully, what's coming up the street is all we have to deal with." Turning to address the rest of them, she went on. "Anybody else here with children, take them and follow Lexy here. If things go badly, get out the back door and run. Run and you don't stop until you find help."

"What about the rest of us?" an elderly man asked, his voice laced with fear.

"You're here with me, dear," she replied almost sadly. "If you wanted to leave, you had your chance a while ago. Now you stand and fight. Maybe we can hold them off. Maybe all we can do is buy some time for the little ones to escape."

"We're all going to die," another woman said through desperate tears.

"If we die, then it was meant to be," Sally replied evenly. "My momma always told me, when it's time to go, it's time to go. God will take you home when he wants you home and not a minute sooner." Turning back to Alexis, she pointed toward the kitchen. "That fire door opens out to the rear parking lot. Go say good-bye to Libby and then get moving, child. If it looks like things are going south, get out and run for all you're worth."

Alexis started to protest, her thoughts entirely on her injured friend. "Sally, I can't leave Libby!" she stammered.

"Honey," Sally said with resigned sadness. "You have to think about the little girl, now. There's nothing you can do for Libby. If we make it through this, she'll make it through with us. We'll get her to the hospital and you can find her there. If we don't..." she trailed off, leaving the almost certain outcome unspoken.

"I can't do it," Alexis whispered desperately. "I can't."

"Yes, you can. You can and you will. You've got more strength than you know of, girl. I've seen that for a long time." Sally reached out and touched Alexis' cheek tenderly, motherly. "Now get going!" With that, she fairly shoved Alexis toward the kitchen. "Listen and wait. If it goes bad, you run, girl, and you don't look back, you hear me?"

Alexis spared a final desperate look at the kindly woman and then walked quickly over to Libby. She knelt at her friend's stretcher and took both of Libby's hands in her own.

"Libby," she said between sobs. "I'm so sorry. Sally's right. I can't stay here. I'm going to take Dakota and try to get help. I'll come back for you. I don't know if you can hear this, but you stay alive. I'll see you again." She stood up, wiped the tears from her eyes, reached down, grasped Dakota's hand, and walked toward the back.

She glanced at the barricades one last time and saw almost everyone in the shelter preparing for battle. There were the two men with their guns, along with others armed with lead pipes pulled from the plumbing, pots and pans, lamps, broken off pieces of door trim, and even an old blender. Dr. Hewson was in the middle of the make-shift army by the front door, standing next to Sally, an old hammer held tightly in his right hand. Heroes all. Martyrs all.

Alexis looked at Sally one last time and then headed for the back. There was one other woman already there, holding a young child of perhaps three. Alexis looked through the drawers for a weapon and found one last steak knife. Touching the blade she realized it had probably not been sharpened for over a decade, but she still felt better holding something she could use as a weapon if needed. She crouched down with Dakota behind the counter in the kitchen, taking refuge by the fire door to await the unknown.

Dakota pulled on Alexis' sleeve, tears in her eyes. "Alexis, I don't want to leave. What if my mom comes here to find me?" the little girl asked plaintively. "She won't know where I've gone if I'm not here."

"Oh, sweetheart," Alexis soothed her as best she could. "When things settle down, we'll come back and look for your mom." She smiled and smoothed the little girl's hair away from her eyes. "We might not even have to leave, but I promise if we do, we'll come back as soon as we can."

"Pinkie swear?" Dakota said, holding up the last finger on her right hand.

"Pinkie swear," Alexis answered, curling her little finger around Dakota's. "Now let's be quiet and see if the bad people just walk on by and leave us alone, okay?" She could feel her heart pounding nearly out of her chest as they waited silently to find out their fate.

80

They didn't have to wait long.

Minutes later, a long drawn out scream from the front of the shelter told them the siege had begun.

They came at the shelter in a group, silent and with purpose, the dead seeking the living. They pressed up against the building entrance, were thwarted at first, and then began prying their way past blocked windows and doors. Sally led her beleaguered band of refugees in beating back the onslaught, and at first, the little group of defenders seemed to hold their own. For a brief moment it looked as if they might even beat back the surge.

But the number of attackers was far greater than those defending the shelter and, little by little, they began breaking through. The living were pulled down by sheer numbers, screaming as they were mercilessly beaten or strangled to death. What made the war unwinnable, though, was that most members of Sally's army who died lay still for a few moments and then rose up to join the growing legion of undead—malevolent spirits seeking even more vessels for the countless evil souls still awaiting their chance to unleash their eternal hatred of the living.

In the kitchen, Alexis Kennedy held her hands tightly over Dakota's ears, as did the young mother with her child, hoping to block out the terrible screams in the main room. They could not yet escape the shelter as more of the attackers milled around outside the building, looking for ways in. Several times, they had flinched in terror when something had banged up against the outside of the metal fire door, but as more of the creatures forced their way into the building from other points, the assault on the outside of the fire door lessened. The screams and wails of the dying went on in the main room until Sally's voice rang out one final time.

"Run, Lexy!" the woman yelled before a final scream was torn from her throat.

"Good-bye, Sally. Good-bye, Libby," Alexis whispered sorrowfully. Then, tightening her resolve, she pushed open the door and fled into the deepening evening, one hand holding tightly to Dakota's little hand, the other brandishing the steak knife. The other woman followed mutely, holding her small child close to her.

"Come on," Alexis whispered and cut along the side of the building. She paused for a moment to listen and then quickly looked northward. In that direction, she heard the muffled sound of gunfire. It was not intermittent, but regular, indicating an organized response to the madness. That made her decision an easy one. "Dakota, stay with me," she said to the little girl.

Staying low and in the shadows as much as possible, the two women and their charges made it almost two blocks before the attack happened. Running hard, Alexis only caught the moving figures in the darkness with her peripheral vision, but she still reacted enough to pull Dakota away from the outstretched hands reaching for them. The movement sent her and the little girl tumbling off the edge of the curb and sprawling onto the road. Cut and scraped, they were the lucky ones. The woman and her child never had a chance.

Hands from numerous killers grasped at the woman, pulling her screaming child from her arms. Alexis cried out in desperation as the abrupt popping and cracking of bones silenced the child and the mother was beaten viciously to the ground with pipes, boards, and hammers. Dakota was wailing in terror as Alexis jumped to her feet and grabbed the little girl. One of the creatures lurched forward, a middle-aged man in a bloodied and torn suit. He held a length of steel cable in his hand. The creature swung the makeshift whip hard and all

Alexis could do was to turn quickly to shield Dakota. The cable tore through the fabric of her shirt, opening up a bloody gash in her back. Screaming in pain, anger, and outright terror, Alexis pushed Dakota away from her and spun around, throwing herself at her would-be assassin. The knife in her hand sunk deep into its chest. It was not enough to stop it, but it staggered back, giving Alexis the opening she needed.

Grabbing Dakota on the move, she swung the girl up to her chest and started running. "Hold on tight to me!" she shouted, trying to put the moans of the dying mother out of her mind. Dakota, for her part, wrapped her arms tightly around Alexis' neck, her legs around Alexis' waist, and buried her head against the young woman's shoulder. There, she held on for dear life as Alexis ran for all she was worth.

Alexis ran harder and faster than she'd ever run in her life. Her mind was empty of everything except survival, and even the weight of the little girl clinging tightly to her could not slow her down. Legs pumping, arms wrapped securely around her precious passenger, she would not be stopped until she'd found safety. As blocks raced by, the occasional figure detached itself from the deepening shadows and moved after her. Alexis paid them no mind and, when a pair of things that had once been living humans rose up in the street before her, she simply cut to the side and through someone's yard, never slowing, leaving them far behind.

Terror beyond anything she had ever known, and the fervent desire to save the little girl whose life was now totally in her hands, drove her beyond her endurance. On she ran and, as her energy drained away and she felt she could go no further, she came upon the end of a pitched battle in the middle of the road. Several undead killers lay on the ground unmoving, while a small group of living humans finished off three others. One of those had to be a priest, his collar quite visible in the darkness as she approached. A young woman about Alexis' age and an older man fought side-by-side, efficiently re-killing the animated bodies, the woman attacking with a wooden pole that she wielded like a trained martial artist and the man with an empty shotgun that he was using as a club. The fourth, she recognized immediately, having seen him many times before.

"John!" she screamed, even as he spun his opponent around, cupped a weathered and sun-browned hand at its chin and ruthlessly broke its neck.

He flung the body to the ground and looked up. "Alexis?" John asked in complete shock and amazement as the woman charged toward them.

Alexis, relief flooding through her, finally stumbled, her strength spent. John and the unknown priest caught her as she fell, John supporting Alexis and the priest holding the terrified child. She had no words and was unable to speak. All she could do was cry, her breath heaving in great gasps, as John swept her up in his aged but strong arms and held her close.

"Our little band grows," John said quietly, looking meaningfully at the others as he held the sobbing young woman tightly, with a strength that belied his aged features. "We need to find someplace to hole up quickly. We aren't going to reach the shelter tonight. There are too many of them."

"Agreed," McCain said, then pointed back the way they had come. "We'll backtrack and head south into the commercial district. There was a strip mall not too far back there. We ought to find something defensible."

"We should be able to find something to eat and resupply, too," Stacia added, leaning on the wooden pole. At one time, it had been a garden hoe, but she'd broken off the metal end in a zombie skull earlier and had been wielding it as a staff with deadly accuracy ever since.

McCain held up his battered and gore-streaked shotgun. "It'd be nice if we could find an ammo store," he sighed, having run out of shells quite some time ago. "I'd really like to be able to use this the right way."

"Do you know her?" Dalacourt asked John, shifting the little girl in his arms, so she could more comfortably cling to him. She held on to him tightly, not daring to let go.

"Her name is Alexis," the little girl spoke up softly, her face still pressed against the priest's shoulder and her voice muffled. "She saved me and promised she would help me find my mommy."

John smiled warmly and then looked down at Alexis' sweaty and tear-stained face. The young woman had passed out from her exertion and now hung limply in his arms. "She's a good one, this one is," he said quietly. "And she's one of the people I've been looking for."

"Are you kidding me?" Tom McCain asked, looking at the unconscious woman.

"Not one bit," John answered. "Let's find someplace safe, so we can talk."

Immediately, the four of them started back the way they had come, John and the priest carrying their burdens, while McCain and his daughter walked point, ready for anything. Fifteen minutes later, John was laying Alexis down on her side behind the counter of an abandoned Payless Shoe Store. He immediately began tending the deep gash on her back from where she had been whipped with the steel cable only an hour earlier. The store itself was empty and they had not seen any living person for quite some time. People were now keeping low and hidden as the marauding mobs continued to seek more victims.

The young priest had settled into a sitting position against the wall, the little girl curled up tightly in his lap, while the New York cop and his daughter searched the store. "Who is she, John?" Dalacourt asked, nodding toward the still form of Alexis.

"Someone who befriended me in the past," John answered quietly, relieved that the wound was not too serious. He grabbed a roll of paper towels he found behind the counter and fashioned a pad of sorts, placing it against the bloody gash and rolling her gently to her back. "She's someone vital to everything happening today and everything that will happen tomorrow."

Before Dalacourt could question that cryptic statement, Stacia returned with a half bottle of water and a small hand towel she had found in the back room. "Here," she offered the items to John. "There's a dead fridge in the back," she motioned toward the rear of the store. "Nothing in it but this. It's still cool."

"Thanks," John answered, taking the water and the towel from her. He opened it up and dumped some on the towel, then began to dab at the young girl's face, wiping off sweat, dirt, blood, and tears. A minute later, she opened her eyes. "Good to see you again, Alexis," John said with a warm smile as he dabbed at a spot of grime on her forehead.

Alexis quickly sat bolt upright, panic showing on her face. "Dakota!"

"Shhh," John hushed her, placing a strong hand on her shoulder to calm her. "The little girl is fine. She's snuggled up with Father Dalacourt."

Alexis breathed a deep sigh of relief and sank back to the floor with a wince, just as the other man came into view. Looking down at her, he smiled. "Evenin', ma'am," he said with a wink, offering a grin and tipping an imaginary hat. "Tom McCain," he went on, introducing himself. "The girl over there is my daughter, Stacia."

"Stacia?" Alexis repeated in somewhat of a fog. She was still trying to come to grips with the sudden appearance of her rescuers.

McCain rolled his eyes. "Yeah, cute name, eh?" he said, mistaking her question for one aimed at his daughter's odd name. "Her mother thought of it."

"You'd have named me Sam," the young woman retorted, poking her father in the arm.

"And what's wrong with Sam?" he asked, throwing up his hands in mock exasperation. "Good solid name."

"Whatever, Pops," she said, rolling her eyes and turning away to hide her grin, a moment of levity in a nightmare that didn't seem to have an end.

McCain shrugged and turned back to John, who was slowly helping Alexis into a sitting position. "Back to more serious matters, we need to get out of here fairly quickly, John. This store isn't very secure, and having the entire front of it as one big plate glass window doesn't give me a lot of confidence."

"It's dark now," John pointed out, looking outside. Without electricity and streetlights, though, there was little chance to see much.

"Yeah, it is," agreed McCain. "And because of that, we need something that will better protect us. You know these things are roaming around and they don't seem to have much trouble finding us."

John nodded in agreement. They'd been fighting a running battle since McCain had blown up the house. "It's the spirits," John answered almost absently. "They guide those that have already possessed bodies."

"All the more reason to move," McCain replied matter-of-factly. "I saw what looked like a department store just down the road. Much bigger and probably has an upstairs office. We should be okay there."

"Shall we all go now?" John asked, starting to stand.

"Not yet," McCain answered. "Let me go check it out. If it's okay, I'll come back and get everyone and we'll relocate."

John nodded, even as the man quickly slipped out the front door and into the darkness.

"I can't believe it's you, John," Alexis finally said as he turned back to face her. She took a grateful sip from the bottle of water. "How on earth did you end up here and who are these people with you?"

John smiled. "How I got here is a very long story and one I'll tell soon enough," he replied softly. "As far as these people with me, they're friends. That's Father Michael Dalacourt over there where your little friend is curled up."

The priest offered a nod of greeting and a small wave, taking care not to jostle the now sleeping child.

"Tom McCain is a New York City detective," John went on. "We're lucky to have him and his daughter with us. They're very capable, and we owe our survival to them several times over."

"I'm so glad to have run into you when I did," Alexis said softly, wincing in pain and also at the memory of her terrifying run. "I couldn't have gone any further."

"You're safe for the moment," John said and then nodded toward the little girl in Dalacourt's arms. "Do you mind me asking who the little girl is?"

"She was alone at the shelter," Alexis explained. "She lost her family somewhere on the way. Somehow, she made it to the shelter alone. She's been with me ever since."

"Why not stay at the shelter?" John questioned.

A look of anguish crossed her face. "The shelter was attacked. A couple of us got out the back while the others fought them off. They didn't make it, John," she choked. "None of them made it."

John reached out and gently stroked her hair. "We'll see this through, Alexis," he said.

"Where will we go?" Alexis asked. "The whole city has gone crazy."

He looked up and into the darkness outside. "I'll have to give it some thought," he answered. "My plan was for us to eventually make it to the shelter, but after what you've just told me, we'll have to find something else."

"Why is this happening?" Alexis was on the verge of breaking down, her voice strained. "I don't understand any of this."

"That's another long story, my dear girl," the old man replied, offering her a sad smile. "Let's get settled in somewhere safer for the night and get some sleep. There'll be time enough for stories tomorrow."

Alexis closed her eyes and leaned back against the counter, trying to gather her thoughts around the events of the day and evening. It had been nothing short of a nightmare, but the appearance of John was a godsend. She'd met the old man several times as an occasional visitor to the shelter. He'd always come to help and seemed to have a way with some of the transient people who showed up at the shelter. Alexis had come to like the old man in the few times she'd seen him, so running into him now could not have happened at a better time. She didn't know the other three, but she did know they made her feel much safer.

A sound at the front of the store startled her and her eyes flew open in panic, but it was Tom, returning from his reconnaissance of the department store down the street. He knelt down beside John, who was still seated on the floor near Alexis.

"The store should work for us," he said quietly. "Unfortunately, it looks like they had some problems there earlier."

"Dead bodies?"

"A few," McCain answered somberly. "Old and young. They're pretty bad, too. Whoever did it was acting out of anger and not looking to gather up more troops."

"I'm afraid we're going to see more and more of that as we move forward."

"The office is fine, though," McCain went on. "It's up at the top of the stairs in the back and it's defendable."

"Is it escapable?"

"Yeah," he answered. "There's a window in the office that we could easily get out of and onto the lower roof, if needed. From there, it wouldn't be any worse than jumping off the roof of that house."

"Don't forget we have a little girl with us," Alexis interjected, having listened to the conversation. "She's been through so much already."

"Not to worry," McCain answered, reassuring her. "The office is clean—no bodies. And with the power out, it's dark in the store, so even from the office, she wouldn't be able to see the bodies on the store floor. There's also a couple vending machines in there. The power hasn't been off too long, so the sodas should still be cold. Lots of candy and chips, too, so we can at least get a bite to eat, even if it's just junk food."

John rose slowly to his feet. "Then we go," he said, reaching a hand down to help Alexis to her feet. "Quickly and quietly."

McCain helped Father Dalacourt up as well, the little girl still snuggled in deep and sound asleep. Without another word, the group made their way out into the night. They silently travelled the two blocks without incident. A few minutes later, they were through the brutal death scene in the department store and up the stairs, barricading themselves in the office. McCain quietly closed the office door as everyone began to settle in and, with John's help, he moved a small file cabinet in front of the door. It wouldn't keep out anyone who really wanted to get in, but it would slow them down a little.

There was little talk as they were all near exhaustion. There was a battered couch in the office and Alexis immediately laid down on it with Dakota. John sat down on the floor, leaned up against the far wall, and closed his eyes. McCain went to work on the vending machines as quietly as he could, while Stacia looked out the interior window into the darkened store below, idly rolling the wooden pole between her hands. Dalacourt sat down on the floor near the couch and smiled at Alexis.

"Not tired, Father?" Alexis asked quietly, returning his genuine smile.

"Actually, I don't think I've ever been this tired," he answered honestly. "But sleep has been a hard thing coming for me these past few days."

"It's all been so unreal," Alexis agreed, her eyes taking on a distant look as she thought back over the horrors of the day and the deaths of so many people—people she knew. It was hard to believe that just a short time ago, she had been at the mall with a couple of her best friends—friends she would never see again.

"I apologize for the abrupt introductions earlier," he went on, stretching out his hand. "My name is Michael Dalacourt...Father Dalacourt, I suppose," he corrected, a sad look on his face.

"You don't look very happy about that, Father," she pointed out, her vision refocusing as she accepted his handshake. It was firm, warm, and gave her comfort.

"I don't know what to think anymore," he answered, leaning back. "Much of it is my own doing, I suppose, but there are some things I simply don't understand—many things, to be honest with you."

"Well, you're not alone in that," she agreed. "My name is Alexis

Kennedy," she continued. "What brings you to Utah?"

"I was actually on my way to Los Angeles," he answered slowly, staring at a spot on the floor as a pained look crossed his face. "I was supposed to report there as part of my reassignment from the church. It's part of something I don't understand right now and perhaps I never will. John seems to understand it more than I do."

"John, huh?" Alexis repeated, smiling. "I still can't figure that one out. I always thought he was local here."

Dalacourt chuckled softly. "I think John is local everywhere. I actually met him at a cemetery in a little town in Iowa, if you can believe that."

"A cemetery?"

"It was almost like he was waiting for me."

"Was he?"

"It certainly felt like it," he answered thoughtfully. He was silent for a few moments and looked over at the old man, whose eyes were closed in sleep. "We had a long bus ride together and he told me a great many things that were quite simply unbelievable."

"What did you talk about?"

"Mostly about what is happening in the world right now," he answered. "I find there's a ring of truth to much of what he imparted to me. He seemed to know we were going to end up here. For that matter, he even seemed to know we would meet up with you."

"Me?" Alexis asked, her eyes widening in surprise.

"Yes, you," Dalacourt nodded, "much like he seemed to know he would find me in a cemetery in Iowa." He shook his head and sighed. "I don't know what to make of it, to be honest. But he's aware of a great many things and, while much of what he has said to me I'm still struggling with, for some reason I trust him more than I've ever trusted anyone else in my life."

"I've always liked him, myself," Alexis replied thoughtfully. "From the moment he first came into the shelter, I suppose. I really don't know him that well and I've certainly never had any earth-shaking conversations with him, but I do trust him. I mean, I'm here, hiding with him from almost certain death. I guess that takes a lot of trust, doesn't it?"

Michael Dalacourt smiled. "Yes, I suppose it does. The past twenty-four hours have certainly done nothing to shake my own trust in him. He predicted that all of this would happen, although he hasn't told me anything about what happens next," he said quietly. "What about you, Alexis?" he continued, changing the subject. "If you'll pardon my saying so, you look like you've been through the ringer."

"That's one way of putting it," she answered softly, her eyes fixing on a distant point. "When I woke up this morning, all was well with the world. But instead of a normal day, I find myself fighting to keep from being killed. I have listened to one of my friends die over the phone, I left another to die at the shelter, and I've watched so many other people die—I don't know that I could take much more."

"To say we live in perilous times would be an understatement," the priest said thoughtfully.

"It's all so surreal," she said quietly. "I could never in my wildest nightmares have imagined that I'd be living through something like this. It's what Hollywood movies are made of."

"The Lord says that in the final days, we will see many great and wondrous things, many terrible and impossible things," Dalacourt explained. "We study these things daily; we say we are prepared for the final days. And yet when they finally come, we are terrified and wonder how it came to this."

"Do you believe these are the final days then?" she asked, looking hard at the priest.

"In a sense, I believe what we are experiencing is the beginning of the end, but I believe that it is a journey that is far from over and perhaps only beginning."

"Do you think we'll survive it?"

"Humanity will survive," came the straight answer. "Individually, though, is a question I cannot answer. None of us know what God's plans are for us personally."

"I've seen so much death already," Alexis lamented, leaning back and closing her eyes as she cuddled the sleeping child closer. "I'm just not sure I can handle any more."

"I know it's cliché, but God knows what you're capable of handling and it's usually much more than you give yourself credit for," Dalacourt replied. "Always remember that, even in your darkest hour."

"I don't know," she replied with a weary sigh. "Just getting Dakota to safety was almost more than I could deal with."

"Dakota—such a pretty name," the priest said, looking warmly at the sleeping child beside her. "Such innocence, too. It's so sad that one so young has to experience this."

Alexis nodded her head and yawned as she absently ran her hand through the sleeping child's long curls. "It's terrible," she whispered. "I just want to keep her safe." She closed her eyes again and sighed deeply, trying to let the stress and terror of the past day seep away. It did, if only a little, and in a few moments, Alexis was sound asleep.

Michael Dalacourt watched the young woman and the child for some time, before McCain crouched down beside him and thrust a couple of Snickers candy bars into his hand, as well as a plastic bottle of Coke.

"Grab yourself a bite and a drink if you want, but try and get some sleep," the detective said, before looking down at the junk food he was offering. He chuckled and added, "I know, I know. Let me give you a bunch of sugar and caffeine, but go to sleep anyway."

"Thanks, Tom," Dalacourt said, gratefully accepting the snacks. As the cop stood and took a position near the window with his daughter, he opened one of the candy bars. He took a bite and chewed slowly, thinking back on the past few days and how much his life had changed in such a short time. Moments later, he, too, had drifted off to sleep.

It seemed like he had barely slept when Tom McCain was urgently shaking them all awake.

"Hurry," he whispered in the darkness. "They've found us."

RISEN

CHAPTER 7

Salt Lake City, Utah: Petr awoke to a throbbing pain in the back of his head. It took several moments for him to remember what had happened. He opened his eyes and then quickly shut them as light painfully attacked his senses. A sharp slap to his face brought him back again, but when he tried to move, he realized he couldn't. His hands and arms had been immobilized, and that was enough for him to slowly force his eyes open, despite the glare. When he did, he was staring right into the grinning face of Donovan, who slapped him again just for spite.

"Mornin', sleepyhead," the bellhop said with a chuckle, reaching out to shove the Russian's head back.

As Donovan moved aside, the bright light once again seared Petr's eyes, forcing them closed. Eyes closed again, he experimented with moving his arms and legs a little, testing his bonds for weaknesses. He found none. Unable to visualize where he was, he strained his mind to search his last conscious thought to see if his memory would tell him what his eyes could not. At first, his brain rebelled, casting everything into a gray haze. But as Petr mastered his will, the events of the last few hours fell correctly into place and he remembered everything. Even more, he knew what it all meant.

They had been set up.

He felt his rage build as he realized the painful truth. From the moment they had arrived in the hotel lobby, it had been an elaborate ruse. What made the entire situation worse was that it had been right there in front of him. He had suspected it. He had known! And he had allowed himself to be talked into ignoring his feelings.

Now he was caught, Rene had been murdered, and David was…where was David?

As the helplessness and rage threatened to overwhelm him, he took a deep, shuddering breath and tried to steady his nerves. He calmed considerably. First things first, he thought. He had to take stock of his situation. He tried opening his eyes once more, but the light was still there, shining directly in his face. It was close enough he could feel the heat from the source. Forcing himself to remain calm, he focused his attention on the senses still available to him: sound, smell, and touch.

Sirens filled the air and the smell of smoke was heavy. Above the wailing of the sirens, he could hear the occasional crack of gunfire. So the battle for Salt Lake still raged on. There was gravel underneath his feet, so he assumed he was still on the rooftop of the Red Lion and, judging by his position, he was seated on a cushioned wooden chair. His feet had been tied to the front legs of the chair and his hands were bound behind it, likely tied off to the rear legs. It was obvious he was not going anywhere soon. With a better idea of his situation, he asked quietly, "Can you turn the light off?"

There was a short hesitation, before another familiar voice answered. "Yeah, sure." It was one of the men he had seen in the Sky Bar. Cappy, he thought.

The light was snapped off and Petr opened his eyes and took in his surroundings. The first thing he saw was David, sitting upright on a nearby red sofa, unbound. His eyes were closed and his face was pinched and looked ashen. He held onto his mango tree walking stick, his blood-covered hand gripping it so tightly his knuckles were bone white.

The other man from the bar, Miguel, was seated on the arm of the sofa, holding what looked like a police officer's service pistol. Cappy joined him, walking over and standing off to the side. He was similarly armed. The Jamaican bartender, Juke, was there, too, pacing back and forth, his eyes haunted as he clutched a small case the size of a notebook in his hands.

"What's this all about?" Petr asked, his eyes locking on David. "What'd you do to him?"

Donovan laughed—cold and remorseless—and walked over to David. He placed a hand on the older man's shoulder and then shoved him roughly forward. Petr saw a white hotel towel, blood-soaked, pressed against his back. Donovan allowed him a moment and then pushed David back into a sitting position. A soft moan of pain from David told Petr he was alive.

"Why?" Petr snapped, utterly unable to comprehend the depravity displayed by Donovan. "He did nothing to you!"

"Dude, for the cash we were paid to get you up here, I would have sold out my own mother," the bellhop replied. There was nervous laughter from the others and Donovan smirked at his captive.

"Who paid you?" Petr demanded, but his blood immediately turned to ice as the answer came to him. Only one person would have gone to these lengths to set him up.

Nikolai.

But the voice that spoke behind him was not his brother's. It was a deep baritone, one he had never heard before. "I paid them," the voice said, and Petr turned his head toward the door they had come through earlier. A huge man, dressed all in black, stepped out of the darkness of the doorway and onto the rooftop. He wore a long leather trench coat that nearly swept the ground. It was hard to distinguish it from his black pants, boots, and tee shirt. Even in the dark of night, a pair of black shades completed the outfit, hiding the man's eyes. Black hair hung down his back, pulled into a tight ponytail, and a long black beard covered his face. "I'm the one who wanted you and I'm quite accustomed to getting what I want," the newcomer finished easily, walking toward him with long strides, black alligator skin boots crunching heavily on the gravel rooftop.

"Who are you?" Petr asked quietly, watching the man carefully. Thoughts of Nikolai were quickly forgotten. He knew instinctively that the man standing before him was the more dangerous of the two.

Instead of answering, the man reached into his trench coat and withdrew a cloth-wrapped object. "Please give our esteemed guest something for his pain," he said casually to Donovan as he tossed it to him. Petr watched as the bellhop-turned-killer unwrapped the cloth, revealing a small syringe. Without a word, he bent down and stuck the needle into David's arm, then depressed the plunger.

"What are you doing?" Petr demanded angrily, rage once again coursing through him. If he could only get loose, he would kill them all.

The huge man turned back to face him, an amused look on his scarred face. "I'm repaying a debt," he replied easily.

Petr turned hate-filled eyes on the man, but forced himself to calm down once more, leaving the beast within shaking with rage. "Who are you?" he snarled.

"Who am I?" the man repeated as if it was the most ridiculous question ever asked. He gazed at Petr with a look of pity and then answered. "Why, I am Hade."

"Hade," Petr repeated, glaring at the man.

"Exactly," he replied, giving the Russian a little congratulatory golf clap. "Personally, I think a lot can be derived from a name. I like the name Hade, to be honest. It sounds rather menacing. It instills so much more fear than say, the Ferryman, wouldn't you agree?" While the other four men snickered among themselves, Petr continued to stare, his eyes saying plainly what he would do if he was freed. "Well, mull it around in your mind a bit," Hade went on, ignoring the Russian's look.

"Trust me when I say that Hade is a name you will become infinitely familiar with as time goes on."

The huge man walked over and stood in front of David, looking down at him. David's features seemed to have relaxed and his eyes were open. The old African seemed alert enough to be taking in what was being said. Hade placed his hand on the side of David's face and looked closer into the man's eyes. Finally, looking satisfied, he straightened and turned back to Petr. "Now, as for who Hade actually is, well, there's so much about me that makes up the whole picture. I love haiku poetry, a glass of warm milk on a cold night, and long walks in the rain with that special someone." He finished deadpan and looked expectantly at the Russian, before throwing back his head and laughing loudly.

Petr's murderous expression didn't change.

"Rough crowd," Donovan remarked off-handedly.

Hade instantly stopped laughing and cast the bellhop a baleful look. "This is a one-man show, Donovan," he warned. "If you speak again without being spoken to, I'll kill you. Can you comprehend that?"

"Yeah," the bellhop replied sullenly, looking away, unable to meet the man's gaze.

Hade turned back to Petr. "You know," he went on, "the more I think about it, the less interesting I am to other people. You don't want to know what ice cream flavors I like or who my favorite gladiator was from the reign of Hadrian. I'd be willing to bet you could care less that I have a pet Dalmatian puppy named Terry who'll chew up a left shoe but never a right. No, none of that matters to you, nor should it. Correct?" Without waiting for an answer, he continued. "No, you would much rather know why you are up here on the roof of the Red Lion Hotel. You want to know why Rene is dead, why David lies here mortally wounded, and why I'm answering irrelevant questions when the world is undergoing such a wondrous transformation."

"What do you want with us?" Petr demanded.

"Now, that is the million dollar question, is it not?" Hade asked with a smile. "Are you aware, Petr Zhugravinsky—yes, I know precisely who you are—that I'm the sixth richest man in the world? Are you also aware that, riches aside, I'm perhaps the most powerful man in the world at this very moment, simply for what I have at my command?" Hade waited expectantly and when he received no answer, he leaned down, his face coming very close to the Russian. "Those are 'yes' or 'no' questions, Petr, requiring a vocalization or a visual indication of an answer on your part."

Hade moved quickly and his huge hand grabbed the top of the young Russian's head. His nose was inches from Petr's and Petr thought Hade's fingers were going to drive right through his skull and into his brain. "Yes or no, Petr," Hade said quietly. "Were you or were you not aware of these things?" Hade twisted his hand back and forth, painfully forcing Petr to shake his head in the negative. "No? Well now you are." Hade released him and stood straight again, his voice once again light and easy-going.

Hade smiled, flashing brilliant white teeth. "So, knowing who I am and the power I have at my fingertips, you now might be wondering why two people as insignificant as a Russian kid with unattainable dreams and an African father pointlessly searching for his lost son, are so important to someone of my caliber and pedigree." He paused for effect and walked around to stand in front of David. "The answer might surprise you."

Hade knelt down in front of David and looked closely into his eyes. "How are you feeling, old man?" he asked with what sounded like genuine concern.

David swallowed thickly before answering. His voice was weak, but steady. "I am still alive," he said quietly.

"Good," Hade answered as he stood straight again, a pleased look on his face. "The morphine will take the edge off. It's not much, because I want you to remain lucid for what's coming, but it should suffice."

"What happened to Rene?" David asked slowly, his eyes scanning around the rooftop for her.

Petr looked up at the older man in confusion. Had he not seen what happened?

Hade, for his part, was looking knowingly at Petr. "I'm sure our Russian superman could tell you," he said patronizingly. "While he was so devastatingly effective against the raging horde, he was just not quite up to the task of saving young Rene's innocent life. Or yours, for that matter," he finished knowingly, nodding toward David.

David looked at Petr, a questioning look on his face.

"There was nothing I could do," Petr stammered, suddenly uncertain. "Donovan killed her. He stabbed her in the heart with an ice pick and then threw her off the rooftop. I watched him do it."

Hade put it in perspective. "I'm certain David wishes to hear the entire truth, not just your version of it, Petr." Hade turned his gaze back to David and continued. "The truth, David, is that Petr got carried away in the fight. He was enjoying himself, single-handedly taking down the bad guys!" he said with a flourish. "It's too bad there was no camera about. It was pure Hollywood and I'm certain I could have sold Petr as the next big action star."

Hade grew somber and continued. "Yet, as grand as it was, poor Rene, so young and so full of promise, was cut down." Hade looked hard at Petr. "Rene died because you were too busy playing action hero to make sure she was safe, Petr," he accused. "You had a choice between protecting Rene or giving in to your base instincts, and you chose the latter. You might as well have tossed her off the roof yourself."

Donovan, apparently forgetting Hade's dire warning from earlier, turned and snickered as if about to say something. Hade moved with blinding speed, stepping forward and driving the edge of his huge hand into Donovan's throat with a stomach-turning pop. The bellhop staggered backward, his eyes going wide as his hands went to his crushed throat. Hade snapped a hand back up, grabbing hold of Donovan by the back of the neck and pulling the choking young man close so he could look in his eyes. "Your comprehension is lacking," he growled and then shoved the dying man to the ground. "More's the pity."

Donovan writhed on the rooftop, eyes wide in terrified panic as he died a slow death. Hade turned away, his eyes going to the other three hotel employees who had obviously not expected this. Hade simply shrugged as if answering an unspoken question. "Donovan will no longer need his share of the payout," he said casually. The men continued to stare in shock and fear. "It really is simple math," he went on. "Three is less than four. That means more for you."

Without waiting to see their reaction, he looked at Petr, who was once again straining against his bonds, determined to free himself. "Oh, stop that," Hade admonished him as a parent would scold an unruly child. "You're going to wind up giving yourself a rope burn and those things hurt like the devil," he said, cuffing him on the side of the head hard enough to snap his head back.

"I didn't kill her," Petr gasped.

"Well, you certainly didn't save her, and from where I come from that's sort of the same thing" Hade added with a smile. "As a matter of fact, had you not picked her up in the street, she might still be alive right now."

"She was being attacked!" Petr snapped viciously. "I couldn't let her die! It was your hired goon that killed her!"

"Technicalities," Hade shrugged indifferently. "So you gave her a few more precious hours of life. You should be commended. My hired goon, as you so eloquently stated, spared her from the horrors yet to come, so I should be commended, too." Hade smiled and held out his hands. "See, we're all in the business of making lives better."

"We won't parlay with murderers," David said weakly from his seat on the couch.

"Really?" Hade asked, folding his massive arms across his chest. "Not even when, in doing so, you would find the answers to those questions that vex your soul?"

"You have nothing for me," David replied with a grimace of pain. "I demand that you untie Petr. Release us."

Hade chuckled. "No, I can't do that, David," he answered. "At least not yet. You see, while you are ruled by logic, Petr is ruled by passion. Sure, he has moments of clarity, but at times like this, he's more like his brother, Nikolai, than he would ever care to admit. He hasn't accepted his complicity in Rene's death or your injury, so I think he'd likely just get himself hurt if I release him now."

Petr stared daggers into Hade and the big man just smiled again.

"When I'm confident he's regained control of himself, I'll release him." He stepped over in front of the older man. "You, however, being ruled by logic and not a slave to your passions, will want to remain in order for me to repay my debt to you."

"Your debt isn't to me," David said quietly. "Your debt is to all of those you've hurt or killed."

"Then we're in agreement," the huge man said easily, kneeling down again in front of David and looking at him earnestly, "because I've hurt you and killed someone you care deeply about. I took something from you, David Livingston Sumbawanga," he went on. "Just a few short days ago—yes, I know it seems like ages—I reached across the world to your cozy little home in Africa and I ripped out your heart."

David froze, his eyes locking with Hade's.

The big man spoke softly. "I see you know what I speak of." He held his right hand in the air and snapped his fingers loudly. Immediately, Juke hurried over and thrust the case he was holding into Hade's outstretched hand. "I believe in paying my debts, David," Hade went on, unzipping the case and then laying an iPad on the man's knees. "I believe in ensuring that I don't forget those who make sacrifices, even if your friend does."

"What do you mean?" David asked hollowly, looking at the tablet as a cold feeling of dread began to creep over him, making him forget the dulled pain deep inside him.

"You know exactly what I mean," Hade replied knowingly, tapping the screen. A video immediately filled the display, the white triangle play button in the middle. "Your answer is there, David. Just press play and all will be made clear. Your search will come to an end and you'll be able to go to your grave in peace."

David's eyes were drawn slowly to the tablet screen. His hand shook considerably as he reached out, wanting desperately to activate the video.

"That's right," Hade urged. "You want the truth."

David did. A moment later, the video clip was playing what appeared to be a home movie. It was somewhat grainy and jerky and the light was not the best, but there was no mistaking what it was about.

"I apologize for the lack of clarity," Hade said. "I wasn't going for style."

David put his hand to his mouth in silent horror and watched as the camera panned over the naked torso and face of his son, who appeared to be lying dead on a table of some kind. The camera moved, focusing in tighter on Gideon Sumbawanga's peaceful face, and Hade's voice came through the speaker as he narrated.

"This is for posterity, Mr. Sumbawanga," he was saying. "I hope you'll find the closure I'm certain you're seeking. I may be driven, but I still believe in recognizing those who donate to the cause, even when they don't realize they've done so."

The camera zoomed in—Gideon's face filled the screen, peaceful and serene in death.

And then it happened.

A shadow seemed to settle down over Gideon's body and then slowly sink into it. It only took a moment for Gideon's eyes to snap open and, as David watched, those eyes turned completely black. His face stretched and his skin began to dry to the consistency of parchment. His mouth opened and closed as if he was attempting to say something, but only silence came forth. The camera pulled back, taking in Gideon's upper body. The skin of his chest and arms quickly took on the same look as his face, turning the once finely honed muscles into something akin to mummified remains. Slowly, Gideon sat up and then turned as he positioned his long legs so he could stand. He did so, drawing himself to his full towering height.

"Behold," Hade's voice sounded on the home movie, pulling back enough so several other figures could be seen on the screen. Two men dressed in white lab coats were dragging a terrified looking young man wearing a University of Utah tee shirt, his hands bound behind his back. His eyes were wide with horror as he saw the thing that was Gideon standing before him.

"No!" the doomed young man shouted. "What are you doing?"

No one answered him. Instead, the two unknown men simply shoved the young college student at Gideon, whose hands snapped up with incredible speed and fastened themselves to the student's head. Immediately, where Gideon's hands grasped him, his victim's skin started withering. As the agony coursed through him, and the realization of what was happening struck him, the young man opened his mouth to scream one last time. His lips cracked, blackened blood began to drip, but just as quickly seemed to dry up. The effect rapidly covered the dying student's face and moved down his arms. The skin withered and cracked and then sloughed away. There was one last dying gurgle before the thing that was once Gideon shoved the now desiccated corpse to the floor. A moment later, the camera went dead.

David never moved.

Petr, who had not been able to see the video from his angle, but had heard the chilling audio, paled in horror.

"My son, my son," David finally whispered, tears rolling down his cheeks. "What have you done to my beautiful son?"

"Your son is dead, David," Hade replied in a low voice. "He has given his life so that what you just witnessed can live." Hade bent down and retrieved the tablet and placed it on the sofa next to the wounded man. "I would have shown him to you personally, David, but he has business to attend to in Nevada tonight, so you were given the home video version."

"What have you done?" David asked again hollowly.

"Look around you," Hade replied, becoming animated. "Isn't it obvious? Do you remember what you went through to get to the hotel, David? You saw the people—everyday people—doing the unthinkable to each other. Do you really think an executive would drop his make-or-break deal of a lifetime to join a riot in the street? Do you really believe a mother of three would stalk the streets with a lead pipe, looking to club anyone who didn't exhibit the same homicidal tendencies she was now filled with? Consider the streets out front. Consider the rooftop up here," he went on, indicating the corpses still strewn about, dead where Petr had killed them. "Think of the dead bodies. Think of those who you saw fall. Think of those you saw rise right up again!"

"But how?" It was Petr asking, still shocked at everything he had witnessed and now heard. "Why?"

"The 'how' is a bit technical," Hade replied, turning his focus on the young Russian. "The explanation is long and involved and quite frankly, I'm due to another appointment. On the other hand, the 'why' is pretty simple," Hade continued, walking over to stand before the bound Russian again. "The answer is they come back and they work for me."

"You speak of the living dead," David said softly, wincing as a wave of pain stabbed through him. The morphine was not enough to completely erase the agony and he was feeling it.

"I do," the big man answered.

"But how could you do this to my son?" David went on. His face said it all. Utterly despondent, his spirit broken and his body dying, David was the picture of a man ready for the end.

"Your son is a special case, David," Hade answered, turning back to him. "Frankly, I could not care any less about your average everyday citizen, the ones you see dying in the street. In a nutshell, they die, their bodies are possessed by particularly hateful spirits, and voilà—perfect shock troops. They're short term creations, to be sure," he went on. "They are not altogether talented and it doesn't take much to bring one down, but they are quite effective in sowing absolute chaos all over the world.

"Then there's Gideon," Hade continued, stepping over to stand in front of David again. "There's no denying that what you witnessed on the tablet is the physical manifestation of your son. You saw his face. You saw his hands, his physique. It's his body, indeed, David. You saw how it flowed and moved. It was like watching a great cat."

"How did he become a monster?" David asked, his voice nearly breaking.

"I made him," Hade replied. "Or rather, I prepared the body for what he has become today." He placed his hands behind his back and began pacing as he went on. "I killed your son, David. I admit it completely. I knew of his heart condition. As a matter of fact, you might say that it was I who designed his heart condition. And I knew just how to end his young, vibrant life."

David shook his head, not wanting to believe what he was hearing. "How could you have known?"

"He's a magnificent specimen, David," Hade answered. "You should be proud. But as I said, none of this has been by chance. I've been following him, you and your wife, even his grand and great-grandparents, for some time, helping the process along as best I could. When the time came to harvest him, I did so with no regrets." Hade stopped his pacing in front of David again. "I must tell you, though, that it wasn't personal. It was nothing more than a business decision, and when my business is reshaping the world, some sacrifices are required. But if it's any consolation, his last thoughts turned to you as his life force faded away. He looked to you for guidance, for strength, and for peace, and I think he found it. I suppose there's some solace in that."

David closed his eyes, grief overwhelming him, uncaring about the pain that was burning more fiercely in his lower back. The shock of seeing his son dead and then coming back to life as a brutal killer was almost too much to bear. He had wanted closure in his search. He had wanted to know. But now that knowledge had become a terrible burden. His son—his only son—a monster. It was simply too much to bear. He had not wanted this.

"Why are you doing this to him?" Petr finally broke the silence, his voice angry. "He's done nothing to deserve this!"

The huge man turned back to the Russian. "There's so much to it, young Petr," Hade answered. "I really couldn't do it justice in the few short minutes we have left. That said, Lord Byron, one of the greatest of the romantic poets, once said, 'All who joy would win must share it, happiness was born a twin.' In other words, it's no fun at all if you accomplish something no one has ever done before and no one knows you did it."

"You're insane," Petr said, shaking his head.

Hade just laughed at him. "All the great people of history have been called insane. In my view, that's the greatest compliment you could possibly give me," he said and then leaned closer, his voice dropping. "I've studied you for some time, Petr. You might even say it's been kind of a part-time job for me over the last few years, and I feel you alone have the ability to appreciate what I've accomplished." Hade quickly stood up, once more towering over Petr.

"You still haven't answered my question," Petr asked again, looking up at Hade. "What does this have to do with David or me?"

"Why, it has everything to do with you, Petr," Hade remarked. "For David, I only wished to provide him with the answers he sought before he died. I have done that and our business is concluded. In truth, though, all of this is really about you." He reached down and placed his hand on the back of Petr's chair. "It's all about this."

At that, Hade effortlessly tipped the chair onto one leg and spun it around so Petr was facing in the opposite direction. There, Petr's eyes locked with the dead eyes of Donovan the bellhop as the formerly dead man was just climbing to his feet. Petr's heart caught in his chest.

"It's a new age, Petr," Hade went on, kneeling down and effortlessly snapping the ropes that bound Petr's legs to the chair. "There are new rules," he continued, breaking the rope that tied his hands. "Everything is possible again," Hade finished and stood up. He looked at Donovan and said two words.

"Kill him."

CHAPTER 8

Mesquite, Nevada: Owen, Clint, and Chad raced across the desert, each of them falling more than once in their haste to escape. They were not as worried about getting caught by the marauding group of undead killers as they were each terrified of Gideon showing up again. None of them spoke—they simply ran for all they were worth, heading toward the not-so-distant lights. They crossed a four-lane road, ignoring the few shattered cars they passed, and continued on, only stopping when the ground beneath their feet turned from desert to grass.

"Where are we?" Clint panted, coming to a halt and looking around in the darkness, trying to make out any possible landmarks. A few nearby streetlights did little more than throw deep shadows across what appeared to be lush grass, but it was Chad who had the answer.

"We're on a golf course green," he said after a few moments, holding up a flag he had just pulled out of a hole in the green a few yards away.

"That figures," Owen said, looking around. "The only places in Nevada that aren't still desert are golf courses. At least we're near houses—there are lights over there," he finished, pointing across the golf course.

"There's a golf cart over here," Clint called out, walking into the shadows toward the overturned conveyance. "Looks like the owners left in a hurry." He bent down and picked up a club, hefting it in his hand. "This might come in handy."

"You really think this will help?" Chad asked worriedly.

It was Owen that replied. "I can't see how it won't," he replied grimly, walking over to Clint. His friend tossed him a five iron. "I feel better armed, anyway."

Chad walked over, accepting a four iron from Clint. "What are we doing, guys?" he asked, clearly at a breaking point. "I mean, what on earth is going on? First Vegas, now this? Gideon is some kind of nightmare. Luke gets killed and what...he comes back and tries to kill us? Now we're picking up golf clubs, expecting to use them against people? People that are already dead? This isn't possible!"

Clint scowled, his face almost invisible in the darkness. "All that matters right now is staying alive. The only way we're going to make it through this is if we stay together."

"Clint's right," Owen agreed. "Think about what we've seen. Think about the hotel."

"I don't want to believe it," Chad whispered.

"I don't want to, either," Owen went on, his voice rising. "I don't want to believe the Luke is gone and that Gideon killed him. I don't want to believe our families and friends back home might very well be dead, too. I don't want to believe any of it!" He paused, before finishing. "But I have to, Chad. I also have to believe there's something I can do; something we can do. We're still alive—we're alive for a reason."

Chad sighed deeply, his breath quivering as he fought to keep the tears from flowing. "I know," he answered, looking down and absent-mindedly digging his golf club into the green. "It's just..." he trailed off, unable to finish.

"I know," Owen repeated, knowing the fear and uncertainty that his friend was obviously feeling. "It's a nightmare." He patted Chad on the shoulder. "But we're together. We can do this."

Chad looked up and for a moment he was silent. "Let's go home," he finally said quietly.

With nods of agreement and encouragement, the three friends turned in the direction of the lights they had been following and set out. The attack came almost immediately and without warning. An older man dressed in running sweats lurched out of the darkness, snaking an arm around Chad's throat before they even knew what was happening. Chad let out a strangled yell before the arm tightened against his throat, cutting off his air.

"Here they come!" Clint yelled, whirling around as several more shapes lunged out of the darkness. He neatly sidestepped the first one, spun and swung the golf club hard and low. The head of the iron struck one directly on the kneecap, shattering it and dropping the thing to the ground. He was not as quick on the second one and a younger woman of maybe twenty raked her long nails across his face, scratching his left cheek deeply. Clint swung the club high, burying it into her right eye.

Nearby, Owen watched as three more attackers appeared out of the shadows, but went right by him, intent on his friends. Confused, he whirled around and nailed a middle-aged man in the back of the head with a hard shot from his golf club, dropping him to the green. The other two had split, one going for Clint and the other going for Chad, who was still dealing with the first assailant. Chad had taken advantage of his first foe overbalancing in his attempt to choke him and stepped back, neatly flipping the old man over his shoulder. A moment later, he dropped an overhand hatchet strike with his club right into the killer's forehead.

"Chad, look out!" Owen yelled, even as the next assailant went low, tackling him around the lower legs. Chad went down in a heap, his legs tangled up by a man who was holding on tightly. A moment later, he knew why. Four more attackers came out of the darkness, hands reaching for him. A teenager dressed in a Boy Scout shirt hefted a large rock over his head. Chad saw it and had only a moment to shout before it descended.

Instead of crushing his face, the rock fell harmlessly from his hands as Clint hacked at the teenager with his own bloody golf club, snapping the scout's right arm above the elbow. Off balance, the boy began to fall and Clint finished him off by cracking his club against the boy's chest and knocking him to the ground.

Screaming and kicking for all he was worth, Chad managed to free himself from several other attackers, but took several hard blows in doing so. One fist to his face caught him in the eye and it immediately started to swell. Another attacker punched him in the gut, driving the wind out of him. The zombies renewed their attack, and he might have died at that moment had Clint and Owen not cleared the rest away with several well-placed club swings.

Clint quickly pulled the terrified Chad to his feet. "Never leave a man behind," he yelled as he thrust Chad's club back into his hands even as a fresh surge of attackers came out of the darkness at them. This time, though, the three friends were prepared and they went to work with vicious swings and hacks, clearing the green. In a few minutes, it was over. A dozen of the undead lay on the grass, beaten down, not to rise again.

"We can't stay here," Owen panted. "There's bound to be more."

"Where to?" Clint asked, wiping the blood from his cheek where the woman had scratched him. "In case you didn't notice, these guys weren't from the hospital. These things are everywhere."

Owen realized Clint was right. None of their assailants were wearing hospital gowns or doctor's lab coats. They were normally-dressed family types—fathers, sons, mothers, and daughters. In the dim light bathing the green, he could see a number of them bore bruises around their throats, attesting to the causes of their deaths. A shocking and sudden realization hit him, nearly making him sick. "You guys," he said softly in a horrified voice. "I know what they're doing."

"What are you talking about?" Chad pressed, visibly shaken from the fight. Adrenaline only took one so far, before sobering realization brought one back to reality.

Owen didn't say anything, just looked from body to body. Clint had already figured it out as well. "Oh, man," he said in a whisper of realization. "They're recruiting."

"They're what?"

"They're adding to their ranks," Owen explained. "Look at these people. They were probably alive a few hours ago. Looks like more than a few of them have been strangled."

"What's that got to do with anything?" Chad asked, clearly growing angry. He wasn't sure how much more he could take.

"The dead don't need to breathe," Clint replied evenly and then pointed toward the lights. "Think about it. One walking dead guy strangles a healthy person and then there are two. Those two each get one and then there are four. Then there's eight. Then sixteen." He stopped and looked at both of them before finishing. "Man, we're on the wrong side of this math equation. I highly suggest we find a car and get out of here."

"Agreed," Owen replied as an overpowering dread of what they were facing threatened to overwhelm him. He grabbed Chad by the arm, but as they turned to run, a towering figure glided out of the gloom in front of them.

It was Gideon.

His face hidden deep within his cowl, Gideon was a wraith, moving silently and with purpose. He was much more agile than those who had attacked first, and he went straight for Chad. Owen saved his friend's life by shoving him hard to the ground, just as Gideon's hands were reaching for him. Owen, too, dove to the side and out of the specter's reach.

"You!" Clint shouted, masking his fright with as much bravado as he could muster. "You killed Luke! Now you're gonna pay!" He stepped forward, swinging his club as hard as he could, wanting to strike down the murderer of his friend. The impact caught Gideon dead in the chest with a dull thump and Clint's eyes immediately went wide in shock. The golf club dropped from nerveless fingers as icy vibrations rang through his hands and up his arms. Gideon's hooded cowl turned to face him, black eyes glittering like chips of obsidian. "No," Clint breathed in a sudden realization that he was a dead man. He backpedaled away even as Gideon advanced on him.

A hand reached out, thin and bony, wasted away. But its grip was like iron as it clamped down on Clint's right wrist. Clint screamed in agony as fire flared through his hand and up his arm. He sank to his knees, paralyzed with fear and pain. But Gideon didn't get the chance to press the attack. Instead, Owen came at him, swinging his club and drawing Gideon's attention. Gideon raised an arm to block the brutal swing, and Owen expected the club to snap the frail arm in half. Instead, he felt like he'd just struck an iron pole. His hands stung terribly, but he advanced and swung again, desperate to save his friend. Gideon ducked the next swing and spun away to avoid the third. Owen screamed out his rage and swung a fourth time for all he was worth. The head of the club caught the edge of Gideon's cowl, ripping it back from his face and, for a moment, time stopped.

For the first time, they all saw Gideon clearly, and what he had become was truly terrifying. It was the face of Gideon, but it had changed horribly. Skin was tattered and desiccated, stretched taut over pronounced facial bones. His eyes were black and had sunk deep into their sockets, but shone with an unholy red light. Lips, dried to the point of almost disappearing, were stretched tightly over blackened teeth in a perpetually horrifying sneer, turning the whole of his face into a living skull. For a moment, those eyes burned into Owen, showing him a depth of evil no living person before had ever witnessed. Owen expected the apparition to finish his work then and there, but instead, Gideon offered him a nightmarish smile and then was gone, melting back into the blackness of the night.

Owen stood in shock, his club held loosely in his hands. He had just stared into the face of death and he felt himself falling into a bottomless pit of hopelessness. How could they go on? How could they face these things that kept coming at them? Worse yet, how could they escape from the thing Gideon had become? Owen had never felt so trapped and desperate in all his life.

"Owen," Chad's soft voice tried to penetrate the shroud of darkness covering his soul. Getting no response, he was more insistent. "Owen," he repeated a bit more forcefully.

Finally, Owen turned slowly to face Chad, his eyes haunted. He tried to speak, but had no words.

"I know," Chad said quietly. "I saw it, too. But we need to focus here." He pointed to Clint, sitting on the golf green, his club lying beside him. "Clint's hurt," he went on gravely.

That was enough to shake Owen out of his paralysis. Turning quickly, he dropped to his knees beside Clint, who was sitting and holding his right wrist tightly in his left hand, his face bone-white.

"How bad is it?" Owen asked, trying to lift Clint's arm up.

Clint pulled it away quickly and snapped a glare at his friend. "Don't touch it," he replied, teeth clenched and face white with pain. "I'll be okay."

"What happened?" Owen pressed.

"I said I'll be okay," Clint snapped, rolling to his feet. His face was lined with pain and his eyes were dark and haunted, but determined. Turning away from them, he took hold of his shirt and began ripping a long strip from the bottom.

Owen grabbed his friend by the shoulder and whirled him back around. "Clint, what happened?" His eyes fell on Clint's injured wrist and he gasped. Where Gideon had grabbed it, the skin had turned to paper, dry and brown. It was the same horrible affliction that had killed Luke. "Oh no..."

Clint's face blazed in fury. "I said I'll be okay," he snarled.

"Your wrist..." Owen began, his voice shaking.

"I'm not going out like Luke," Clint cut him off, wrapping his wounded wrist tightly with the strip of torn shirt. Leaning close, he looked Owen directly in the eye. "I won't be what he became."

Owen nodded numbly. Nearby, Chad could only look on in revulsion.

Clint finished tying the cloth and bent down to retrieve his golf club with his good hand. When he stood up, his face was solid stone and his eyes shone with an inner fury. "Let's move," he commanded, breaking into a trot and heading toward the lights on the other side of the course. Without a word, his two friends followed him, both of them trying to process the horror of what they had just seen.

They moved silently across the dark golf course, each of them praying they wouldn't meet up with any more of the things roaming about. Owen quickly took the lead, heading toward what he hoped was a house or garage where they might find a car they could escape with. As he jogged in silence with his friends, his mind was flooded with the many thoughts he'd kept suppressed, just simply to survive. He imagined Clint and Chad were considering the same things. He thought of everyone he knew, trying hard to judge their survival chances if Salt Lake City was indeed going through the same nightmare everyone else was experiencing.

He thought of his family and managed a small smile. His father would take care of his family, having been preparing for some kind of worldwide calamity for the better part of a decade. A full food storage, weapons and ammunition, and a reinforced basement would afford them plenty of protection from anything short of heavy artillery. Yes, his mother, brother, and sisters would be safe under his father's care.

From there, Owen's thoughts turned to his friends, and heavy tendrils of sorrow crept over him as he thought of the danger they would all be in. Most of his friends were athletic and strong-willed. He was sure they would be able to survive. However, Luke had been one of those capable friends and now Luke was dead. He could only hope that, besides Chad and Clint, his other friends would somehow find their way to safety.

Briefly, Owen thought of Windy. He hardly knew the young woman, but his compassion and concern for her was no less. To him, she certainly seemed capable. He was again perplexed at the effect she had on him, but he pushed it aside and thought of how she carried herself, how she interacted with others. She was as strong a person as he knew, in just the short time he had known her. She should be fine, he thought to himself.

And then, his mind turned to Alexis. She was the one person who needed him the most, of that he was certain. Her family was scattered, and her friends? Well, they were just a couple of flighty girls. Other than Owen, Alexis had no one else to take care of her. He knew her resolve, her willpower, her ability to make do in any situation. She had led a tough life and it had made her a fighter. But, could she handle something like this? Could she handle the world turning into an absolute nightmare? Time would tell, but if Owen had anything to say about it, he would be by her side in a few hours. She needed him and he realized he needed her, too. That was what drove him now.

Lost in their own individual thoughts as they approached what appeared to be the golf course clubhouse, the trio did not see the small group of zombies moving across the parking lot toward them until it was nearly too late. There were only four of them and the lights of the parking lot showed them fairly clearly. Unlike the others they had dealt with, these were horribly mutilated and covered in blood and all four of them appeared to be in an advanced state of decomposition. One younger man had a hatchet lodged deeply in his skull and another had a bullet hole in his forehead and several in his torso. A woman looked as if the police had just dragged her body out of a lake after a very long time under water and the fourth, an older man from what they could tell, had been hideously burned.

"This will be cake," Clint said, his voice icy calm as he gripped his golf club in his good hand. If he had been harboring any reservations about crushing the skulls of things that were once human, Gideon's attack on him had driven all doubt from him.

"Any way we can just bypass them?" Chad asked, looking around nervously. "It could be a trap and we still have no idea what we're up against."

"Let it be a trap," Clint said through clenched teeth. "Let Gideon show up again. If I'm going out, I'm going out with a bang!" With a yell of cold fury, he exploded forward, brandishing the gore-spattered golf club high above his head. Charging forward, he had no doubt about the outcome. He was dictating the terms this time and nothing would stop him. As he charged ahead, Owen and Chad ran right behind him.

Their enemies, however, did something none of the young men expected them to do. Up to this point, the undead had been relentless in their pursuit and single-minded in their purpose. They seemed to exist solely to kill and had never wavered in their dedication to mete out death, nor to push forward even when such a move proved disastrous to them. Retreat did not seem to be programmed into their mentality.

And yet, this bunch did just that. As soon as they saw Clint bearing down on them with murderous intent, followed by his two friends, all four of the creatures turned as one and began running in the opposite direction. Despite the last few hours of wear and tear, the three young men were still much faster. As Clint bore down on the young drowned woman, she tripped and lurched forward, rolling to the side. In the same motion, she pulled her legs in, covered her head in a fetal position, and began to scream. Clint reached her, his shadow throwing her form into darkness. He raised the club, prepared to deliver the killing blow, but suddenly Owen was there, placing a restraining hand on his arm.

"Clint! Stop!"

Clint turned on him, eyes blazing. "I'll never stop, Owen!" he snapped. "I'll kill every last one of them!"

"No," Chad joined in quietly. "Look at her, Clint."

When he did, what he saw nearly caused him to fall backward in dismay. The drowned woman was looking up at him, tears in her eyes, pleading for her life. "Please, don't kill me," she sobbed. "Please..."

Clint staggered backward, letting the club fall from shaking hands, suddenly unsure of himself. The woman lying before him was not dead. Somehow, miraculously, she was still alive.

"We're all alive," the man with the hatchet in his brain said softly as if reading his thoughts. The other three of them were walking slowly and cautiously back toward them, watching the young men fearfully, ready to flee at the first sign of aggression. "We're as alive as you guys."

"How's that possible?" Owen finally found the strength to ask. He still held tight to his club, remembering Chad's warning about it possibly being a trap. If they were alive, they'd be the first people they'd seen since Vegas. If it was a trap, Owen meant to end things quickly.

"Well, we haven't died yet," the older man replied through his horribly burnt lips and then stuck out a mangled hand. "I'm X, by the way."

"X?" Owen asked skeptically, slowly accepting the handshake.

"Yeah, it's kind of a gaming thing," he replied, sounding somewhat embarrassed. "Picked it up when my wife became my ex, if you will." He turned and pointed to each of his companions in turn. "That's Tin," he said, indicating the man with the bullet holes, "Narn has the hatchet in his head and the girl is Gru."

"So what's with the get-up?" Chad asked in confusion.

"That's the ironic thing," was his reply. "We were heading to Salt Lake City for a horror convention when all hell broke loose. We were attacked a few miles outside of Mesquite and ended up walking all the way back here, hoping to score a ride back to California, where civilization is pleasantly nutty but not trying to kill us."

"What convention are you talking about?" Owen pressed, trying to put it all together.

"The big horror convention," the young woman answered, slowly getting to her feet but watching them carefully. "It was supposed to run all night tonight and through tomorrow, but obviously, we didn't make it."

"Yeah," Tin continued. "We holed up in Vegas for a couple of days, played some slots, then got into costume and headed out yesterday morning. Figured we'd hit Salt Lake in plenty of time to make a flashy entrance. Fate, it seems, had a different idea," he finished almost wistfully.

"How far out of town did you get?" Owen asked, mentally trying to picture how much further they would get if they managed to get out of town. If the roads were plugged up, they might get out of town only to find themselves stuck in a worse position than ever.

"A ways," X replied. "It was a long walk back, I'll tell you that."

"So why did you come back here?" Chad asked.

The man shrugged. "What else is there? It's Mesquite. Twenty thousand people and twenty thousand golf courses. We figured it would be easy to find a ride and get back home. Then we started hearing about everything that was happening and figured we'd have to boost a car instead. Up until a few minutes ago, we'd struck out."

"Did you find something?" Owen asked hopefully.

"Yeah," he replied, hooking a thumb behind him. "There's a Hummer and a Lexus on the other side in the parking lot. We were just about ready to break into the clubhouse to see if they had a valet box with the keys. That's when we saw you guys."

Chad brightened at that and started toward the building. "Well, let's not waste any time," he said. "The quicker we're on the road, the better off we'll be."

X nodded his head in agreement. "If you guys are heading back to Salt Lake, you'll want to take the Hummer. You'll need to go off-road to get around the traffic jam that stopped us. We'll take the Lexus. It'll fit the four of us nicely and we can fly in it."

"You better go around Vegas," Owen pointed out. "Not much is left of the place after the army got through with it."

"Not a problem there, friend," X replied.

The clubhouse was unlocked and still had electricity, so they found the box quickly. Inside, there were exactly two sets of keys. Owen took the one for the Hummer and tossed the other to X. "Thanks," the man replied, grabbing them out of the air. "Be careful."

"You, too," Owen replied and then retreated outside. Holding the keys up for Chad and Clint to see, all seven of them started around the building to the parking lot. They found the two cars parked side-by-side in the corner of the lot. As the four horror convention goers piled into the Lexus, the three friends got into the Hummer. It was painted black and was probably the sharpest vehicle any of them would ever drive, and they knew it.

"Well, if you're gonna steal a car, you might as well do it in style, I suppose," Chad said with a sigh.

Owen slid into the driver's seat and fumbled with the key. A short good-bye beep of a horn had them all looking up and they watched the Lexus pull out of the parking lot and head down the lane away from them. Owen turned the key, and the engine roared to life. Unfortunately, the inside of the Hummer remained dark.

"Where's the dash?" Owen finally asked after looking around and playing with as many controls as he could find in the dark. The only thing he managed to do was turn on the headlights. "Aren't these things supposed to be digital?"

"Who cares," Clint finally said, closing his eyes as fatigue burned at him. The injury to his wrist was getting worse and he could feel it spreading. It hurt in a way he couldn't explain. Touching the skin elicited no reaction—it was as dead as could be. But his bones hurt and his muscles throbbed, growing tighter and tighter in his arm and working up toward his chest. "Just get us out of here," he finished.

Owen needed no extra urging. He put the big vehicle in gear and they put the horror of the golf course behind them. They exited the lane and headed west on Pioneer Boulevard, looking to hook back up with the interstate. "We're going home, fellas," Owen said, trying in vain to feel upbeat. Beside him, Clint's breathing seemed labored, and in the seat behind him, Chad was silent. There were no words to describe what they had faced that night. They had to simply hope they could get home.

The Lexus was parked in the dark on the west side of Country Club Lane, lights and engine off. All four of the horror fans got out of the car, each of them silently watching the taillights of the Hummer shrink into the night. As the lights disappeared, X reached into a pocket and pulled out a smart phone, opening up the contacts. There was exactly one number. He ran his finger across it and the phone was picked up immediately on the other end.

"They're on their way," he said coldly.

CHAPTER 9

Salt Lake City, Utah: Alexis rubbed her eyes, blinking in the darkness as McCain shook her awake. "How long have we been asleep?" she mumbled.

"Not long," he answered urgently. "Maybe a couple hours."

At that moment, Stacia hurried through the door and into the office. The file cabinet had been pulled off to the side. "They're a few blocks down and coming this way. Lots of them," she went on breathlessly. "They have to be coming for us."

"They are," John agreed grimly, pulling himself to his feet. "They won't stop until they have us, either." He turned abruptly toward Alexis. "Listen to me. If these are part of the group that attacked the shelter, it's likely you'll see some familiar faces among them."

"What do you mean?"

"It's a long story," he answered, "but the short of it is that these are the bodies of the dead, inhabited by malevolent spirits."

"Zombies," Alexis stated, not at all surprised at the revelation. She had already half-believed the news stories and rumors she had heard and, listening to John talk about it as he did, it only affirmed it in her mind.

"That's a crude term for them, yes," John replied. "However, these aren't what you usually think of when you think of zombies, though. People think zombies are created by a virus, radiation, toxic waste, or as a result of hell being overcrowded. They're usually depicted as mindless, flesh-eating animated corpses with no purpose other than their own need to feed."

"Isn't that what these are?" she asked.

"No," he answered. "These are different. These particular creatures are filled with evil spirits fully capable of thought, and they have a purpose beyond simple death and destruction."

"Of course, it's always a pleasant thought to know that the monsters of your nightmares are capable of thinking about how to best kill you," McCain put in with a shake of his head.

"So, be warned," John added gravely. "If you see someone you think you know, it's not really them. Run or fight or do whatever you need to do to survive, but you must get away."

"Is this really the end of the world?" Alexis asked.

"None of this is happening without a reason and there is much that you do not know yet, Alexis," John replied. "But for now, you simply have to trust me. The end of the world is not yet upon us, but it is much closer today."

"So where do we go?" Alexis asked, fighting to keep her growing desperation in check as she gathered a sleeping Dakota up in her arms. "They'll see us if we run, won't they?"

"Leave that to me," McCain cut in. "I'll draw this group inside and take care of them. The rest of you need to get out through the window. But don't jump down until I tell you."

"You have a plan?" John asked.

McCain smiled as he pulled out the handgun he had taken back from Stacia earlier. He popped the clip out and checked it for the few bullets that remained. "Let's just say I haven't been sleeping for the last couple hours."

"You don't have enough bullets," John cautioned, watching him slide the clip back into the gun.

"I only need one, old man," the detective replied. "Now get to the window and be ready." Grabbing his daughter by the arm, he pulled her close and pointed back to the window. "Stay with them," he said, his voice low and serious. "You know what's at stake here."

"I know, Dad. Just don't do anything stupid, okay?"

"Me? Have I ever done anything stupid before?" he asked innocently.

Stacia could only shake her head and smile.

"Yeah, best not answer that one," McCain said, giving her a quick hug. "Now get going." He turned and bolted through the office door and down the stairs into the darkened store. A few seconds later, his voice rang out loud and clear and very off-key as he began belting out "The Star Spangled Banner" at the top of his lungs.

"Good thing he doesn't do baseball games," Stacia sighed and turned to help the others through the window and out onto the roof. "We hold on the roof and wait for his signal. John and Michael go first. We'll drop Dakota to you and then Alexis and I will follow."

"Off the roof?" Alexis answered almost angrily, unable to believe they were simply going to jump down with a young child in their care.

"Short drop," Stacia replied quickly. "She'll be fine. The alternative is not so pleasant."

"Don't worry," Dalacourt added wryly, patting Alexis on the arm. "We've done this before."

"Alexis, where are we going?" Dakota asked sleepily, raising her head from the young woman's shoulder. "And who's singing?"

"We're going to leave, honey," Alexis answered the first question and ignored the second. "We need to go somewhere else."

"But I'm so tired," Dakota continued. "And he's a really bad singer."

"I know, sweetie," she replied, unable to suppress a smile. "But we just have to go."

"Are we going to find my mommy?"

"We will," Alexis promised.

McCain's singing turned to shouts of "Hey, you!" and Stacia urged them on. "Let's move," she said. "We'll have to be quick."

As Stacia followed the last one through the window, McCain's voice carried up to them again along with the sounds of large items being thrown through the plate glass windows of the store. "Move out!" they heard him yell.

"Quickly now, before they surround the store," Stacia ordered and both men dropped the short distance to the ground. Stacia pulled out a small but powerful pocket flashlight, switched it on, and dropped it to Dalacourt, who promptly shone it upward. A few moments later, Dakota landed safely in John's arms, followed by the two women. On the ground, Stacia took the flashlight back and switched it off. "We move east," she said quietly, laying her makeshift quarterstaff across her shoulders. "National Guard troops are going to be doing their best to clear the city tonight, so we need to get out of town and away from them."

"Shouldn't we go toward them?" Alexis countered.

Stacia shook her head. "It's dark and complete chaos. Trust me, they'll shoot first and ask questions never, Alexis." She looked ahead into the darkness. "No, the safest thing will be to get out of town and wait this thing out. So stick close to me."

She took off at a jog and the others fell quickly in line, running silently and keeping their eyes on her shape in the darkness. They had only traveled a few blocks when Tom McCain made good on his promise. Behind them, an enormous fireball illuminated the night sky and the accompanying explosion rattled the windows in the buildings around them. Stacia skidded to a stop and turned to look as the ball of flame shot skyward. As she watched the flames light up the night sky, she whispered softly, "Good job, Dad." Then she turned around and resumed her trek, putting the inferno further behind them.

"What happened?" Alexis asked as she ran near the young woman.

"Hard to tell with my father," the girl answered, keeping her eyes straight ahead. "But that ought to put off some of the pursuit. Still, we keep moving," she went on. "We've got a few hours before daybreak and I don't want to get caught in the open by these things."

"What about your father?" Alexis challenged. "Shouldn't we wait for him?"

"If he's okay, he'll be along," Stacia replied quietly. "If not, then he did what he had to do."

"We can't just leave him!" the young woman said incredulously.

Stacia stopped and whirled around on Alexis. "Listen to me," she said firmly, shooting a worried glance at John who stood silently off to the side, holding Dakota. "My dad and I have been in this thing for a long time. We've known what the stakes were since the beginning and both of us have been long prepared to do what was necessary to see things through." She paused before finishing, her voice measurably softer and, despite her sternness, her concern shone through. "So just do what I tell you and we'll get through this alive."

Without another word, Stacia turned and switched on the flashlight. She started off again at a brisk jog, her flashlight beam sweeping the road in front of them as they went. The others followed silently, all of them absorbed in their own thoughts. Even Dakota, now riding piggyback on John's strong back, was quiet. They saw nothing as they ran, quickly leaving the glow of the burning store behind them. Eventually, the stores gave way to houses and in the darkness, they saw no signs of life. Every house was dark. They were alone with just the sounds of the night—until the sound of breaking glass off to the side startled them all.

Stacia reacted immediately, tossing the flashlight to John, who quickly trained it in the direction of the sound. Two figures were moving across the lawn toward them and none of the little band had any doubt as to their intents. Stacia met them head-on, the wiry young woman swinging her makeshift staff with deadly precision. She caught the lead creature in the head with several rapid back-and-forth shots, shattering its facial bones. As the other one moved in, she went into a spin and dropped low, sweeping the zombie's legs out from under it. She was back to her center before the second creature even hit the ground, spinning and driving the end of her pole into the first monster's eye. The creature twitched once on its feet as she yanked the pole free, then it fell to the ground as she brought the pole down viciously against the face of the second zombie, stilling it as well. The whole fight had lasted less than ten seconds.

"Wow," Alexis could not help but say aloud.

"She was trained well," another voice added evenly and everyone turned to see Tom McCain approaching them from out of the gloom, a tired grin on his face. Aside from his clothes being singed and darkened with soot, he seemed relatively unscathed and was sporting a brand new, bulging backpack that was slung over one shoulder.

"Good to see you again, my friend," John said with a smile, clapping the man on the shoulder with one hand, while holding on to Dakota with the other.

"Hi, Dad," Stacia said, her relief evident as she stepped into her father's embrace and hugged him.

"What happened back there?" Dalacourt asked, looking back toward the glow of the fire that still lit the horizon behind them.

McCain shrugged. "Just the usual," he answered. "Big department store. Sporting goods. Gas grills. Lots of propane tanks."

"So you blew them up again?" the priest said, shaking his head in amazement, but managing to smile nonetheless.

"Hey, those that fail to learn from history are destined to repeat it," McCain shrugged, but quickly grew serious. "Still, there's a whole lot of those things coming," he went on. "I didn't get them all. There's no doubt they're coming after us."

John straightened and said quietly. "They're being led. They sense the end of their existence and they're driven beyond anything you can imagine to seek out and kill the living in what little time they have left."

"So this is going to end?" Alexis asked hopefully, hardly daring to believe what she just heard.

"Oh, most assuredly, Alexis, and then we'll be faced with a new crisis," he answered gravely. "This is but the first salvo in what will be a very long, a very bitter, and a very final conflict." Turning to McCain, he asked, "Any ideas on where we should go?"

"We keep heading out of town," the man answered plainly. "As long as we keep them behind us, we should be fine."

"That would be acceptable, but they're not behind us anymore, Tom," John said, his voice dropping to a whisper as he pointed the flashlight up the road in the direction they had been heading. In the light, they could see more figures emerging out of the darkness and moving slowly toward them.

"Look," Stacia added, pointing as even more of the creatures begin filtering between the houses, effectively hemming them in.

"We're trapped," Dalacourt said fearfully, seeing movement all around them.

"No, we're not," McCain cut in sternly, reaching behind and grabbing several long cylindrical tubes he had tucked in his belt. "But we'll need to fight." In one quick motion, he dropped his backpack and slammed the ends of the objects against the concrete. The cylinders flared to life with red fire. "Picked up some extra road flares from the department store," he explained, quickly tossing each of the three to the ground, forming a rough triangle around them and giving them sufficient light to move around in. "Spread out and keep the little girl in the middle," he commanded.

John thrust Dakota into Alexis' arms, ignoring the overwhelmed look on the young woman's face. "Stay between us," he stated before moving to a position in the circle even as the creatures moved in.

"Remember what you're fighting!" Stacia shouted, stepping forward and cracking the pole against the side of the nearest creature's head. It was down in seconds and the young woman was moving quickly and fluidly into the oncoming mob, her graceful movements akin to those of a dancer as she took down the creatures around her with brutal efficiency.

Her father was more direct, stepping into a lead pipe swing by one of the attackers and taking the blow high on his side. He grunted with the blow, but dropped his arm over the pipe as he turned violently to the side, wrenching it from the zombie's grasp. A moment later, Tom McCain nearly took its jaw off with a vicious swing of his new weapon.

The fight was desperate, the four companions struggling for their own lives, as well as to protect Alexis and the child, who huddled between them holding tightly to each other. In the beginning, it appeared the little band would beat back the onslaught, but that all changed in one terrifying moment. Michael Dalacourt, untrained and unprepared for events such as this, overextended himself when shoving a zombie away from him. Before he could back up and regain his position, the fallen creature had reached out and hooked his leg, pulling him to the ground. In moments, others were crawling all over him. Undead hands clamped on to his arms and to his throat. He would have been killed had John not intervened, throwing zombies aside with a fury no one had seen before. Unfortunately, this action caused an equal and more terrifying reaction and, like a long line of dominoes, the repercussions spread forth until the end was upon them.

With the circle broken, the creatures surged forward, hands reaching for Alexis and the little girl. Surprised, Alexis did the only thing she could think of. Grabbing up one of the flares, she jammed it into the face of the nearest monster. Without a sound, it fell back, hands clawing at its burning face. Two more took its place, hands reaching for the little girl. Before they could get her, though, McCain was there, clearing them out with his lead pipe.

Alexis struggled to her feet and watched several more of the zombies move into the light of the flares as she pushed Dakota behind her. She froze as she recognized one moving toward her, limping heavily on a broken leg, a bloody bandage still wrapped around her head. John had tried to prepare her for this, but nothing could have steeled her for the shock of seeing her dead friend stumbling toward her. She knew Libby was already gone, but the fear and revulsion of seeing her friend and the blank look in her dead eyes was enough to root her to the spot.

A moment later, Dakota was gone.

"Mommy!" the little girl shouted with joy as a battered woman appeared in the glowing light of the flares, staggering toward them on an obviously broken ankle. Oblivious to the danger around them and blindly overjoyed at finally finding her mother, Dakota ran toward the woman.

Alexis tore her eyes from Libby in time to watch as the little girl ran toward her "mother" and practically leaped into her arms. Alexis screamed a long and utterly heart-wrenching wail as the reanimated woman calmly turned and lurched back into the darkness, the child held tightly in her arms. In the darkness, Dakota's excited chattering turned to a shriek of terror and a moment later, the scream was abruptly ended.

Alexis screamed and started to run forward, only to have her long hair grabbed from behind. Pain roared through her head as she was pulled roughly to the pavement and suddenly, Libby's face was leering over her. Alexis watched her friend raise a brick high in the air.

Something inside Alexis snapped. She shifted to the side and the brick struck the concrete, sending shards of rock slicing into her cheek. Blood welling from the wounds in her face, she twisted violently, coming to her knees even as Libby swung the brick at her a second time. Alexis ducked and Libby's momentum took her around too far, allowing Alexis to get her in a headlock and drag her to the ground. Grabbing her attacker's wrist with her other hand, she slammed her former friend's hand to the pavement. Fingers broken, the brick came free. Still holding the thing that was once Libby in a headlock, Alexis scooped up the brick and crashed it into the side of her friend's bandaged head. Libby's body went limp and Alexis twisted again until she was straddling her friend. With a scream of primal fury, she slammed the brick down and through her dead friend's face.

A moment later, she was up, her bloody features contorted into an unrecognizable frenzy of anger. The others were fighting for their lives against several attackers at a time, but Alexis did not care. All she cared about was Dakota and she shoved past John, laying her bloody brick into the side of one zombie's head as she charged toward the spot where Dakota had disappeared.

"Alexis! No!" John shouted, starting after her, but finding himself beset again as several of the creatures pushed toward him.

Alexis never heard him. She was aware of only a loud buzzing in her ears as she beat back several of the creatures and nearly stumbled into Dakota's mother. The dead woman was bent low, hands fastened tightly around her daughter's throat. One look at the little girl's features and Alexis knew Dakota was already dead. With a cry of anguish, she brought the brick down against the back of the woman's head with all her might. Bone shattered, and the woman pitched forward as death claimed her a second time. More of the undead moved toward her, but

Alexis stood over the little girl's body and swung her weapon. Several more went down until a board slammed against her arm, jarring the gore-covered brick loose from her hands. Alexis simply fought on with her fists, swinging blindly, sometimes connecting and other times missing completely. A piece of pipe hit her in the back, driving the wind from her, but still she fought. Another board glanced across her shoulders, knocking her off balance, but she never noticed. All she felt was grief and rage. She struggled to right herself, but a heavy blow caught her in the temple, buckling her knees. She snarled and tried to stay upright, but there were just too many. Hands grabbed at her and rained blows down on top of her. Alexis finally fell, her last conscious thought to shield Dakota from the murderous creatures.

Finally, sprawled across the body of the little girl, Alexis Kennedy knew no more.

CHAPTER 10

Salt Lake City, Utah: "Kill him."

It was unclear whether Hade was talking to Donovan or Petr, but the thing that was once Donovan immediately lurched forward, hands outstretched. Petr dove off the chair to the gravel-covered rooftop, ignoring the pain of the rocks grinding into his knees. His legs and arms were tingling from where he had been tightly bound.

Donovan struck immediately, clubbing him on the shoulder with his fist and driving him back to his knees again. The Russian lashed out, punching the walking corpse in the stomach as it advanced on him, but it had no effect. Donovan swung down again, clumsy but brutal. This time Petr was ready. From his knees, he caught the arm with one hand and swung up with his other, catching the bellhop in a fireman's cradle wrestling move. Using his opponent's momentum, he threw Donovan over his back. His attacker down, Petr got back to his feet quickly and picked up the chair he'd been tied to. Turning around, he watched as Donovan rolled over and slowly climbed to his feet. With a roar of fury, Petr brought the chair down across his back, shattering it into pieces of wood and fabric and driving the killer back down.

Off to the side, one of Hade's helpers raised his gun and pointed it at Petr, but Hade held up a hand. "If you pull the trigger, Miguel, I'll personally remove each and every one of your appendages while you watch," he said in warning, eyes flashing angrily. The man immediately lowered his weapon, knowing the huge man meant every word.

Petr paid them no attention, though. Donovan was slowly climbing back to his feet again as Petr picked up one of the broken legs from the chair. As Donovan stood straight, Petr drove the makeshift stake directly into the man's left eye socket. His other eye remained expressionless as his hands closed on the wood as if he was going to pull it out, but Petr never gave him the chance. Grabbing hold of his end of the weapon, he yanked it out himself and then drove the gore-spattered shard into his attacker's chest, straight through his heart. Donovan went slack and fell to the rooftop. His body twitched once before going still.

Petr turned on Hade, his gaze saying he intended to kill the huge man or die trying. He took two steps before Hade pulled a Glock 17 Semi-Automatic from beneath his coat and pointed it right at Petr's chest. Petr stopped in his tracks. Wincing as if he half expected the man to fire, he was instead surprised to see Hade smile.

"Bravo, dear Petr, bravo," Hade said with the air of a major movie director. Looking down at the wood stake piercing Donovan's torso, Hade shook his head and laughed. "Wooden stakes not only work for vampires, they work for zombies, too, apparently." His countenance transformed instantly as he cast a dark gaze on the three remaining thugs. The gun remained leveled at Petr's heart. "Leave us," he commanded. "Wait for me in the Sky Bar."

"What about the money?" Miguel asked, causing his companions to fidget uncomfortably.

"We'll finalize our deal shortly," Hade said coldly. "Now leave or I'll arrange an express elevator to the pavement for you."

Without another word, the men hurried through the door. Juke pulled it shut behind them.

"So now we're alone, we three," Hade said as they disappeared. "As it should be." He switched his gaze from Petr to David, who was still seated on the couch in an agonized daze. Looking back at Petr, Hade continued. "Your brother Nikolai would have been proud of you tonight, Petr. He's long waited to see you as your true self."

"You don't know my true self," the Russian snarled, still breathing heavily.

Hade merely smiled. "Sure I do. You're a killer. Look around and tell me I'm wrong."

Petr scanned the rooftop and was shocked at the carnage, almost all of it from his own hand, but he shook off the misgivings and glared at Hade. "Killing those things means nothing to me; they're possessed by evil spirits. You told me this yourself."

"It's nice to know you were listening," Hade said, still smiling, "but were you paying attention? We know you can kill my creations, but I wonder how you are at killing the living?" He flipped the Glock around in his hand and tossed it to Petr.

Petr caught the gun and in one fluid motion had it pointed back at Hade. His finger tightened around the trigger, but he didn't squeeze it yet. "You think I won't shoot you?" he spit, taking a step forward. "After all you've done?"

"To be honest," Hade sighed, "I'm a bit surprised you haven't fired yet."

"Give me one reason why I shouldn't," Petr barked.

"I could give you fifteen," Hade said, holding up an extra clip for the gun in his thick hand.

Petr paused. He'd held a Glock many times before—it was one of Nikolai's favorite guns—and he knew how the gun felt loaded and completely empty. This one felt loaded, but...

"Exactly," Hade said, reading his thoughts and turning the clip over in his hands. "Right now you are wondering why I gave you the gun and whether the gun is filled with dummy bullets or live ammunition. As Dirty Harry once said, 'You've got to ask yourself one question: do I feel lucky?' Well, do you, Petr? Is it worth risking my wrath? If you try to shoot me and the gun is filled with blanks, what happens to you? Or more importantly, if the gun is loaded with live bullets, are you sure you really want to shoot me at all?"

Petr kept the gun still but his heart and head were pounding.

"Come on, Petr," Hade goaded him. "Are you ready to go all in?"

Petr wavered. "What are you up to, Hade?" Every warning system he had was overloaded and it was becoming difficult to think straight.

"I'm hoping you haven't fired at me yet because you like me, but I think there's another reason why and that's what I want to talk to you about," Hade said with a smile. "Now, are you going to lower the weapon so we can have a discussion—man to man—about your future, or are we going to stand here all night staring at each other? The choice is yours, Petr," he challenged.

"Let's play it out, Hade," Petr replied angrily, keeping the weapon leveled at the monster. "Then I'll decide whether I'm going to shoot you or not."

"I suppose that will have to do for civility," Hade sighed and sat down on a nearby bench. He waved Petr over to sit next to the semi-conscious David. Petr, the gun still pointed in Hade's direction, sat down and checked David's pulse and the blood-soaked towels pressed to his back.

"There's still time," Petr said, his voice full of anger. "Let me get him to a hospital. They can save him!"

"No, I'm afraid it's too late for that," Hade insisted. "It was always too late for this one. To tell you the truth, I'm going to miss the old bird." He paused thoughtfully before going on. "It's ironic, you know? If Mr. Sumbawanga had returned to Africa after his son's memorial, he would have likely lived out the rest of his days there in relative peace. Well, at least as peaceful as the world today would leave him. But now, here he is, dying on a rooftop because he could not let go of his son. In my experience, Petr, parents tend to love their children too much or not enough. This one, I think, loved too much. It certainly blinded him to the consequences of his actions."

"He knew what he was doing," Petr said defiantly. "He knew what he had to do."

"Oh, I'm quite certain he did," Hade agreed. "But did he stop to think what would happen to his daughter, Chuike, after he passed through this mortal veil?" Hade shook his head in mock sadness. "Now what's going to happen to her?"

Petr's eyes widened as the full implications of what Hade was saying hit him. "If you hurt his daughter..." he began, but Hade interrupted him.

"You'll what?" the huge man chided, leaning forward dangerously. "Will you shoot me? Come, come, Petr. You know better than that. I am Hade. It will take far more than an angry young man with an overdeveloped sense of vengeance to take me down. And you must understand that, while I have no interest in David's daughter, I'm not the only thing that goes bump in the night."

"Hade is correct," David's gasped, choking slightly as his lungs slowly filled with fluid. "I'm dying, Petr," he continued. "I beg of you to please...find my daughter. Find her and keep her safe." He closed his eyes again, the pain nearly overwhelming him.

From his bench, Hade spoke softly. "Yes, this one certainly loved too much."

Petr ignored him and took hold of David's hand. "I'll protect your daughter, David," he said. "I swear it."

"Noble," Hade said. "Noble indeed. You know, I've always been fascinated by how people react to the death of a loved one. I think David knew this would happen someday, and that knowledge made it easier on him. I wonder how you would react to such news."

"What do you mean?" Petr asked slowly.

"Well, there's your brother, for instance," Hade explained.

"What about him?" Petr could feel the hairs rising on the back of his neck.

"Oh, haven't you heard?"

"Heard what?" Now he was growing nervous.

"Your family is dead," the huge man replied easily, leaning back on the bench. "Nikolai killed them. He killed them all. How does that make you feel?"

"You're lying," was all Petr could reply.

"Am I now?" Hade asked and then rubbed his chin thoughtfully. He reached into his coat and pulled out a smartphone, then tossed it to Petr, who caught it in spite of himself.

"It's unlocked," Hade said easily, "and the pictures are loaded up."

"What is this?" the Russian asked, his eyes still on Hade.

"Show and tell," Hade grinned. "Have a look."

Petr laid the Glock on the seat beside him and pressed the ON button. He let his eyes go to the screen. The bodies of two of his cousins—Aleksandr and Iosef—were lying on a sidewalk in pools of blood, one shot each to the back of their heads.

"Executed by Nikolai," Hade said coldly, knowing exactly which picture was first. "No pleading for their lives; no suffering. They were given a soldier's death, honorable indeed."

Petr looked at Hade in shock.

"There's more," Hade said. "Go on."

Petr silently scrolled the screen to the next picture. There were his two uncles, Ivan and Boris, splayed across a small table in front of a bistro with numerous bullet wounds to their bodies. "Anton did that. Not as honorable as your cousins, but then they were not as honorable as your cousins, were they? And in case you were wondering how your brother repaid Anton for helping him..." Hade motioned for Petr to go to the next picture, which turned out to be a photo of Anton lying on a forest path, his throat slit and his tongue forced out of his neck. "The old Sicilian necktie," Hade said with a touch of nostalgia. "That always was one of my favorites."

"My family is murdered and you mock them?" Petr said, the rage rising within him.

"Oh, no," Hade replied, "You mistake me. I'm just admiring your brother's work. He's a true artist. Next," Hade said casually.

Petr was afraid to scroll across, but he couldn't help himself. He had to know who else his brother had killed. The next picture was of Petr's grandfather, Vladimir, his face and body horribly covered in bruises and cuts.

"No!" Petr yelled out. "This man was a hero of Stalingrad! He didn't raise his entire family to greatness just to be killed like a common dog!"

"Alas, you are correct," Hade shook his head in disappointment. "I'll have a word with Vanya about that one. I knew Vladimir well, and a senseless beating is simply not acceptable."

"This can't be," Petr gasped.

"I'm afraid it is," Hade countered. "The next one, please?"

"I can't."

"The next one," Hade repeated, his voice holding a steely edge.

Petr slid his finger across the screen to reveal a picture of a burned out car. Nearby, laying on the road under white sheets were the charred remains of four bodies. "Your mother; her father, Mikhael; and, two more of your cousins," Hade narrated. "Vanya is much better with explosives, you have to admit. That one is a nice piece of work. Very quick."

Petr could barely breathe. Almost his entire family, gone. He looked at the screen and saw that there was one picture left to see. Not wanting to look but knowing he had to, he scrolled forward. His heart stopped as he saw his father, Lavrenti, with a single bullet wound to the heart. Lying across his chest was a single red rose, the Russian sign of respect for the assassinated.

"Nikolai pulled the trigger himself," Hade said with a polite nod. "He told me your father's last words were of you. Touching, I think."

"Why?" was all Petr could say as he dropped the phone to the gravel rooftop.

"Who am I to say?" Hade said with a shrug. "Epicurus said, 'As death is concerned, we men live in a city without walls'."

"But what of Sergei?" Petr stammered, wondering if his nightmare could get any worse.

"Sergei yet lives," Hade replied, "for the moment, anyway. All that remain are the brothers three: Nikolai, Petr, and Sergei Zhugravinsky, alone atop the Russian world of high crime and, quite soon, Russia itself."

"How could this happen?" Petr was reeling. "How could my brother do such a thing?"

"You can't expect me to believe you're that naïve," Hade admonished. "You know better than anyone that your brother is an animal. He's a fox, and when you left, you let him loose in the hen house. The resulting slaughter of your family was foreordained the moment you got on that plane to America." Hade snapped his fingers as he finished. "No more hens, Petr."

A soft moan of pain from David brought Petr's attention back to the rooftop.

"He's dying," Hade reminded him dispassionately. "For the moment, though, you need to detach yourself from that little drama and listen closely to what I'm about to tell you."

Petr couldn't take it anymore, and with a savage shout, he lunged off the sofa, swinging wildly at Hade. But the big man was quicker.

Without standing up, he caught Petr's outstretched arm with his free hand. Yanking it downward, he reversed the Russian's momentum and thrust his other hand forward, his open palm slamming against Petr's upper chest. Petr was stopped cold and sank to his knees, pain exploding in his chest as his breath was driven from his lungs.

"A little reckless, don't you think?" Hade asked in a bored tone, making a show of examining the fingernails on one of his hands.

Petr couldn't speak as he fought to get the air back into his lungs.

"What's done is done, Petr," Hade went on. "There's nothing you can do to change it, but you're still alive and that's important. I know you won't believe me when I say this, but I'm here quite literally to ensure you fulfill your destiny. You see, you're special. Unique. You have a gift to see the world around you and instantly know everything about it. You can see problems before they arise; you can hear in your mind what a person is going to say before he says it. I don't think you realize just how special you are, and that's why I'm here, Petr. I'm here to help you understand."

"Understand what?"

"Let's start with a question, shall we? It's sort of like a mental Rorschach test, so stick with me. When you saw me, what was your first impression? Did you think, 'Here is a man who has come to kill me?' Were you filled with fear? Was it revulsion? Or perhaps, it was something different. Perhaps you saw an opportunity?"

Petr couldn't answer. If he'd felt fear, it was for David's death and his inability to help him. Revulsion was reserved for his murdering brother. But an opportunity? That was something he hadn't considered.

But Hade had and he smiled. "That's why you didn't shoot me," Hade pointed out. "You knew I was someone who could be very useful to you."

"What are you getting at?"

"The clip in your Glock is full of blanks," Hade answered evasively. "But the round in the chamber is live. You could have shot me, Petr, but you didn't. You knew shooting me would be a mistake and you were smart enough to follow your instincts. Can we at least agree on that?"

Petr could only nod his head.

"Now let's get a bit academic," Hade went on. "This is important, so pay attention. I recently read the book *Blink*, by Malcolm Gladwell. Fascinating stuff, really. One of my favorite parts is how he demonstrates that companies tend to hire tall men as their CEOs because society looks to tall men as leaders."

Hade stood up to his full height, towering over Petr. "Makes sense to me. Anyway," he continued as he placed his hands behind his back, "the premise of his book is that more often than not, the decisions we make in the first two seconds when thinking about a problem are the correct ones. We like to think we make better decisions when given lots of time to think through a problem and really study it, but actually haste not only does not make waste, often it might just save your life.

"Now, he gives lots of examples of this, but my favorite is an experiment at the University of Iowa where they had people pick playing cards from four decks, two blue and two red. The cards had values of money, either positive or negative, and the goal was to try to choose which decks would increase your wealth. The two red piles had cards that won them great rewards, but also cards that cost them a great deal. The two blue decks had smaller positive and negative amounts, but over the long term it became clear that the more blue cards were picked, the more money one accumulated. Are you with me?"

"We don't have time for this," Petr said impatiently. "David is dying."

"I'll take that as a yes, but let's try to focus on the task at hand," Hade replied. "Now with this card experiment, practically everyone understood the pattern by eighty cards, realizing if they chose the blue cards repeatedly, in the end, they would end up with more money. A good portion of the group understood it within fifty cards. But the truly interesting thing is that these would-be gamblers were hooked up to a polygraph machine to gauge their stress levels during the experiment. The results showed that subjects became nervous as early as the tenth card. So while our conscious minds are unable to put together a pattern fully until much later—somewhere around the fiftieth to eightieth cards—our subconscious minds actually have it figured out much sooner than that, usually by around the tenth card."

"And?"

"The point is pretty simple," Hade answered. "Human beings think they need tons of data or information or proof to know things, yet nothing could be further from the truth. Most people don't realize this. But for you, Petr, it's essential to your makeup."

"So I can think through problems quickly and come to answers faster than others. That isn't so special."

"On the contrary, you have no idea how special that is. You have something referred to as 'the power of thin-slicing.' You can look at a very small amount of information or focus your attention on a very small amount of physical stimuli, and know what is happening and what to do with that information. All humans have this, but you're able to discern what's happening around you to a level few people can ever hope to achieve. You don't need all the information. In fact, you're at your best when you are making decisions literally in the blink of an eye."

"What are you getting at, Hade?" Petr fumed.

Hade smiled and then began pacing, hands behind his back as a professor delivering a lecture. "History is as important a subject as a person can study, and no history is more important than our own," he continued. "So let's examine some of your recent decisions. Let's see how you first reacted, using your intuition, or 'rapid cognition' as Gladwell prefers. Then let's compare it to the decisions you made when you had more information."

"Such as?"

"Let's start with a decision you made back in Russia," Hade answered. "Before you left for America, you returned to the meat-packing district to help your brother—and did so against your better judgment, I might add. In doing so, you made him angry enough to ultimately plan and carry out the slaughter of your family. Did you know this was going to happen? No. But did you know you should not have gone to help him? Of course, you did. You knew it the moment you heard about the problems he was having. You knew then that you should have let him deal with his problem on his own."

Petr was stunned. Hade was right. Petr had known bad things would happen if he went to the district, but he had gone anyway. Had that decision really led to the deaths of his family? He tried to convince himself that this was impossible, but his mind told him differently. Hade had connected all the dots for him, and it left him with a picture that was difficult to ignore.

"Personally, I believe we should not be judged by one wrong choice, Petr," Hade went on. "But honestly, it's almost as if you have decided to go against your better judgment whenever and wherever you can these past several weeks.

"Another perfect example would be your decision to meet with David after the debacle in the tunnel where Gideon died. Your first thought was to say no, correct? You knew the old man no longer had anything left to offer you, but you went anyway. And look what happened. All hell broke loose, and you've been stuck watching after him instead of going after what you really want—Alexis."

Petr froze. "How do you know about Alexis?"

"I am Hade, I know everything," he said. "Two decisions made, both seemingly simple and with hard-to-foresee repercussions, and both out of a courtesy to other, elder figures instead of going with your first instinct. You knew better, Petr, and now others suffer for your failure to go with what you knew was right in the first place."

The Russian could say nothing as the implications of what Hade said cut deeply into his very soul.

"There are other examples as well, Petr," Hade continued. "How about the decision to come to the rooftop? How about the instant you first laid eyes on Donovan? Did you trust him? No, there is no way a Zhugravinsky, not even Sergei, would have trusted such a man. Your instincts were right, yet you deferred to David. Now Rene is dead and David is dying because you knew, you KNEW, not to follow that man up those stairs."

Petr lowered his head in grief and shame. Hade was right. Damn him to hell, the man was right.

"You have a gift, Petr," Hade went on, his voice softer now. "With minimal amounts of information, you can size up a situation and act immediately and correctly. You're hard wired to think and act faster than anyone else around you, and that is perhaps one of the greatest gifts a man can have. Alexander the Great had it, Caesar had it, Constantine, Charlemagne, William the Conqueror, Peter the Great, Napoleon—they all had this ability, and so do you. And because of that, you can have what they had. Power, wealth, and more," Hade finished. "Much more."

Petr's mind reeled as he saw the pattern Hade was laying out before him. Did he truly have such a gift? Had his failure to use it cost the lives of innocent people? Countless examples of other times he'd known better but chose poorly when given more information flooded through his mind. It was all true. He'd always told himself he didn't want power, but was it just that he didn't want power the way his family had gained power? It was an intriguing possibility, and he was acutely aware that something new had awakened in him.

He raised his eyes and looked directly at Hade. "Let's say you're correct," Petr began.

"I'm always correct," the big man interrupted. "A few minutes ago you debated shooting me, and I wouldn't have blamed you for trying. I've killed your friends, helped your brother kill your family, and even now I'm refusing to let you save the one man who has tried to understand and help you. I've led you along a dark path and put you in impossible situations." Hade paused and smiled. "Despite all that, what does your intuition tell you about me?"

"It tells me to listen," Petr said evenly. "Whether I put that information to use, remains to be seen."

"Then we're almost there, but not quite, I think. We have one more hurdle to clear and then we're home free," he continued. "One last question. Why did you leave your family?"

"Because that's not the life for me," Petr answered forcefully. "I wanted nothing to do with the path my family was on."

Hade laughed deeply. "That's a nice little fairy tale, Petr, but I'm not interested in what the eightieth card told you. What did the tenth card tell you?"

Petr thought hard, trying to go back to the first moment he knew he had to leave. He had told himself he was different from his family for so long that he had come to truly believe it, but in his heart he had always known, and ignored, the truth. And there it was before him, plain as day. "I left," he began, "because I knew this would happen." He paused before finishing. "I knew Nikolai would be the death of us all, and I knew if I stayed, I would die as well."

"So, you willingly sacrificed your entire family in order to live another day," Hade reiterated plainly. "Is that correct?"

Petr wanted so badly to say no, but knew it would be a lie. "Yes," he finally admitted, "that's exactly what happened."

"I should be charging for this. We're really getting somewhere," Hade smiled. "So you accept that your decisions on a very deep level have led to the deaths in your family. I'm wondering, then, if you could tell me about Alexis? Specifically, what were your initial thoughts, your rapid cognition if you will, the first time you laid eyes on her in your English class?"

Petr debated asking Hade how he knew they had an English class together, but realized the more important question was the one Hade had asked. He focused his thoughts and mentally pictured Alexis walking into the classroom, sitting down, and looking into her bag as if she was alone in the room. It was a clear sign she was uninterested in Petr, that they had no future together, but he saw something different as he watched her. "I thought," Petr spoke as if in confession, "that I had to have her. I had to make her mine."

"Nothing about love? Nothing about growing old together?" Hade smiled. "You see Alexis as a trophy, a work of art, something to possess, don't you?"

Petr wanted to respond, to shout out this wasn't true, but he knew Hade was right again. He was not in love with Alexis, at least not in the way the bards of old wrote of love. She was a centerpiece and he had to have her.

"I know this is hard, Petr, but trust me, a bit of psychoanalysis is always helpful for the soul," Hade said. "Now tell me about Sergei. Tell me why Nikolai has spared him."

The answer came immediately. "It was because of me," he answered quietly. "He expects me to return, and needs something to hold over me. Sergei is that leverage."

"Congratulations," Hade said with a clap of his hands, "you got it on the first card. Despite Nikolai's savagery, he still loves you, Petr. I don't think he even understands why, but he does. It's his one weakness and his one strength. He's torn between both his love for you and his hatred of you. Because of that, he's stayed his hand." Hade paused, before finishing. "For now."

"So where does that leave me?" Petr asked.

"In the grand scheme of things, Nikolai is a very important piece of the puzzle for me. But that doesn't mean he's irreplaceable." Hade stopped, looking hard at Petr as if willing him to understand where he was going with his explanation.

Petr did.

"You would have me kill Nikolai as he killed the rest of our family?" Petr closed his eyes. There it was—the reason for all of it.

"In time, yes," Hade replied. "I want you to return to your country, return to your brother's side, and prove you didn't betray him," he said. "Stand beside him in his rise to power, knowing the true power rests with you. And when I'm no longer in need of him..."

"I'm to kill him," Petr finished.

Hade nodded.

"And then I become your puppet," Petr added, knowing exactly where he stood.

"That is not entirely true," Hade corrected. "Until you replace your brother, you would be his puppet master. It will be you who actually pulls the strings. You'll advise your brother, guide him, and once again be the rudder he so desperately needs. And in the end, when the time is right, you'll put him beneath your feet and the glory will be yours. You and your Alexis will rule Russia as Tsar and Tsarina."

"With your guidance, of course."

"I prefer to think of my role as your own personal genie in a bottle," Hade answered with a grin. "Only I get to pick your wishes."

"And if I say no?" Petr countered.

"If you were planning on saying no, you would have shot me when you had the chance," Hade replied.

This time, there was no hesitation. "You win," was all Petr could say.

"I always win, Petr. Never forget that," Hade stated with absolute finality.

"My father taught me at a young age that favors and gifts are never given freely. So what is it you would have me do?"

"The devil is in the details," Hade replied with a smile, "and in this case, the details are extremely complex. But your task is an easy one, and one I think you can certainly get behind."

"And that is?"

"It's about Alexis," Hade answered with a knowing smile. "At the moment, she's in grave danger. She's with a group of people she mistakenly trusts. They'll soon head to a place in the mountains that Alexis has been told will be a safe haven from what's been unleashed on the world. Sadly, the man who leads them is wrong," he finished. "Dead wrong."

"Who is this man?" Petr asked, his mind already working.

"He's been a nemesis of mine for a good many more years than you can imagine," he answered thoughtfully. "But the important thing, is that he cares little for Alexis beyond what she can do for his cause. They'll reach the mountain tomorrow and I will have quite a surprise for him. Perhaps I'll finally rid myself of this thorn in my side. But what should concern you is that he's using Alexis, and that puts her in great danger."

"Just as you are using me," Petr countered.

"Perhaps, but as they say in your homeland, 'Better an open enemy than a false friend.' At least you know what is at stake if you fail. Alexis does not."

"So what would you have me do?"

"I would have you rescue her," Hade replied plainly. "Now, that doesn't mean she'll rush into your arms and the two of you will ride off into the sunset to live happily ever after. We all have our free agency, Alexis included. She may be so grateful you've come to save her that she would accompany you to Moscow and become your queen. She might be grateful, yet still spurn you for Owen DiConte, whom she clearly has feelings for. Or she might even just shoot you," he added, walking over to stand directly in front of the Russian. "Regardless of her choice, if you do what I say, when you go to sleep at night you'll know that, despite failing so many people, you didn't fail her. That is, if you can save her."

Petr was again silent, turning things over in his mind. The more he thought about it, the more he realized just how perfectly Hade had planned everything. He knew where he stood with the man and knew what was expected. He understood it even before the tenth card. "Where is this mountain?" he asked firmly.

Hade smiled. "That will be made clear in the morning," he said, reaching into his coat and pulling out an object wrapped in cloth. He slowly unwound the material, revealing a hypodermic needle, the reservoir filled with a deep blue liquid. Before Petr could react, Hade jammed it into Petr's neck.

"What the hell was that?" Petr snarled, his hand going instantly to his neck. His skin felt warm where the needle had entered and he felt a crawling sensation creeping through his body.

"Relax, dear boy. It will not hurt you," Hade explained. "I have an appointment down the road and I honestly don't trust you enough to believe you'll spend the rest of this fine evening on the roof. So I injected you with a specialized sleeping agent. It's really quite sophisticated—one of the perks of having Legio Securities in my portfolio."

Petr's eyes narrowed in anger. "I don't understand."

"The injection contains a set of nanites that will trigger a chemical agent that will put you to sleep," he answered. "The wonderful thing about this little baby is that I can program the nanites to put you in and bring you out of sleep at specific times." Hade pulled out an antique pocket watch, checked the time, flipped it shut and placed it back in his coat. "You now have thirteen minutes before you go under. When you awake tomorrow morning, you'll feel refreshed and ready for what awaits. That should give you plenty of time to take care of one last detail."

"And what's that?" Petr said impatiently, beyond angry at what Hade had done to him.

"David," Hade replied flatly.

Petr knew immediately what Hade meant. "You can't ask that of me. I might be many things, but I'm not that."

"A single live bullet is chambered in your gun," Hade continued. "That bullet is for David."

"I can't kill him, Hade," Petr implored. "I won't."

"David is going to die," Hade explained. "The hospitals have all been cleared out and most of the former doctors are now walking around downtown Salt Lake City, performing unnecessary surgery on the innocent."

"There has to be something I can do!"

"There isn't, Petr," Hade replied evenly. "You need to square with that quickly. David will die and then it wouldn't be long before he un-dies, if you follow me. You can either shoot him before he dies or you can shoot him after he dies. Of course, if you take too long deciding and go to the eightieth card, you might be asleep when David reanimates, and that won't end well for either of you."

"I don't want this, Hade," Petr continued.

"Neither do I, but when did this world ever start giving us everything we want? Don't worry about David. If ever there was a man who deserved to go to heaven it's him. Seneca said, 'The day which we fear as our last is but the birthday of eternity,' and I think there's something to that. This isn't good-bye, really."

Hade walked toward the door that led down to the Sky Bar, before pausing to face Petr one last time. "You have less than ten minutes, Petr," he said. "Kill him within that time and then enjoy your slumber. When you awaken, I'll have a car waiting for you out in front of the hotel. The driver already has his instructions to take you to your appointed date with Alexis. Once you get there, the rest will be up to you."

Petr snarled. "You're a monster, Hade."

"Of that, my young friend, there can be no doubt," Hade replied easily and then disappeared through the door and back into the Sky Bar.

Petr was trapped. Over the years, he'd seen death numerous times. But this was different. How could he possibly end the life of a man he valued and respected, even in the situation he now found himself in?

He paced back and forth for several minutes, cursing loudly and trying to find any solution to this problem that didn't involve doing what he knew he must do. In the end, he calmed his breathing, gripped the gun tightly in his hand, and leveled the gun at David's chest. He was about to pull the trigger when the old man coughed weakly and opened his eyes. Petr was startled, having thought David was too far gone, and he pulled the Glock back. David's eyes settled on the weapon. It was clear by the look on his face he knew what Petr was going to do.

"He's right you know, Petr," David gasped, his breath nearly gone. "My time is up and I do not wish..." he broke off as he coughed. Blood flecked his lips and dribbled out of the side of his mouth, but when he looked up, his eyes had regained some of their luster. "I do not wish to come back as one of those," he finally said. "I hold you blameless."

Petr squeezed his eyes shut against the tears and the absolute helplessness that threatened to overwhelm him. David might not blame him, but Petr certainly blamed himself.

"Find my daughter," David finished slowly. "Protect her."

"I will," Petr said through his tears. "I promise." And with that, he placed the barrel against the old man's chest and pulled the trigger.

CHAPTER 11

Highway 15, Nevada: Owen and his friends had only put a handful of miles between them and Mesquite when the Hummer's engine started sputtering and missing.

"You've got to be kidding me," Owen growled, feathering the gas pedal in an attempt to get the engine to smooth out. It did not. If anything, it made it worse.

"What's happening?" Clint asked tightly, fighting against the growing agony in his arm but knowing he was losing the battle. He was running on fumes.

"I have no idea," Owen snapped, pounding the dashboard in frustration as the engine faltered and their speed slowed. "Freakin' thing is all digital and I don't have any dash lights, so I don't have a clue what's going on with it!"

The engine sputtered again and then died.

Owen growled angrily through clenched teeth as he eased the car off to the side of the road. "You'd think we could catch just one break," he sighed tiredly. Once the vehicle came to a stop, he tried cranking it a few times. The starter was strong, but he got nothing out of the engine. Finally, he slammed his hands on the steering wheel and closed his eyes in frustration. He was not sure how much more he could take.

"So now what?" Clint asked softly and in pain as he looked out the window and into darkness that was black as pitch. They were out in the middle of the desert and the headlights from the Hummer illuminated nothing in the distance.

"I'm not going back to Mesquite," Chad said quietly from the back seat.

Owen shook his head in irritation. "Well, we can't go forward, either. At least if we go back, we can look for another car to get us out of here."

"There was a diner a mile or so back," Chad went on. "I don't remember any lights on, but there were some cars and trucks out front. Maybe we could take one of those."

"Yeah, I remember passing it," Owen agreed, brightening a little. "We should be able to find something there." He opened the door and got out of the Hummer, then looked back in at Clint. His friend sat rigid in his seat, one hand gripping his injured wrist tightly. "Can you make it, Clint?"

Clint turned to look at him, his face drawn with pain. "I'll manage," he answered and got out as Chad exited the vehicle as well. A few moments later, all three of them were jogging back the way they came.

About ten minutes later, they found it.

The little diner was a tiny, run-down place with a single gas pump next to it and a double set of diesel pumps in front, just off the highway. It was built for truckers and there were several of the big rigs parked around the side of the building, as well as a couple of cars. In the inky darkness, they could barely make out the faded brown and white sign on the roof that identified the diner as the Tumbleweed. Their hopes for finding a vehicle to get them to Salt Lake City took an immediate dive when the door slammed open and a man stepped out, aiming a double-barreled shotgun at them.

"Whoa!" Owen shouted in alarm, skidding to a halt in the gravel and quickly throwing up his hands. "Don't shoot!" he pleaded. He was aware Chad had his arms raised, too, but Clint stood there, silently holding his wounded wrist.

The man didn't answer. Instead, he stepped forward and moved the barrel of his weapon up to center directly on Owen's forehead. He was big and burly, with a white tee shirt stretched over a powerful torso and a grease-stained apron wrapped around his large waist. He had a meat cleaver shoved into his belt and he looked quite capable of using it.

"I swear," Owen went on shakily, "we're not what you think. We just need to find a car to get us home."

"You plannin' on stealin' one of these, then?" the man finally spoke, his voice deep and angry. "I don't think any of the owners would be too happy with that."

"No," Owen tried explaining, suddenly realizing just how bad it probably looked to the man. "Our car broke down just up the road. We didn't think anyone was here. We're just trying to get home to Salt Lake City."

"Long way to go," the man said matter-of-factly. "I'm wonderin' how you plan on getting there without a car."

"Look," Clint finally spoke up, his voice ragged. The fact that the shotgun swung over to train on him didn't seem to bother him at all. He had seen too much—had been through too much. He was beyond caring anymore. "Cut us some slack. All we're doing is trying to survive the night. So, either shoot us now and be done with it, or let us on our way."

The man was silent for a few moments before he finally nodded and lowered the shot gun. "Had to be sure," he said quietly, offering them an almost sad smile. "You best get inside with the others. There's no tellin' what's out and about right now."

"Any chance of getting out of here?" Chad piped up, looking around hopefully. He was still entertaining thoughts of heading home in someone else's vehicle.

The man shook his head, his face hardening again. "We're holed up in the diner for safety," he said with finality. "Stay if you want or leave if you want. But if you leave, you'll do it on foot. Ain't no one going to give up their car, since they all probably want to make sure they can leave themselves when this thing blows over."

"We don't want any trouble," Owen said, lowering his hands. He looked at Clint, who could barely stand at this point, and then looked across the desert landscape, dark and foreboding. If they were attacked out in that, they wouldn't last five minutes. Hiding in some forgotten road-side gas station in the middle of nowhere was far from ideal, he knew, but they didn't have any other choice. It was this or almost certain death. He turned back to the man and said, "We appreciate you letting us stay for a while until we can get some help."

"Don't mention it," the man replied, standing aside. "Name's Chuck," he went on as they filed inside, ducking past a large blanket that had been nailed over the doorway. "I own the place."

They each mumbled their names to him as they went inside. Several dim lights were on and there were a number of people gathered within. The two front windows, as well as the smaller side windows, had all been carefully hung with blankets and each had a couple of tables stacked up against them, making it impossible for anyone passing by to see any light.

Owen had only taken two steps into the little restaurant but he could almost smell the fear. Everything that had happened that night had done so with frightening speed; the men and women taking refuge in the diner were struggling to cope with it. They had apparently been listening to the news and, judging by the state of the restaurant, had prepared for an attack as best they could.

There were about two dozen people in the diner, most of them truckers. Owen took note of a younger couple, a husband and wife by the looks of them, huddled together in a booth and holding tightly to the sleeping bundle of a little baby. At that moment, Owen was struck with the futility of everything, and his heart was in his throat as he thought of what might become of the little family if the murderous chaos found them here.

"Owen," Chad said quietly, grabbing his friend's arm and stopping him before he took a step toward the little family. "You can't save the world," he said softly, correctly reading his anguished friend's eyes.

"Someone needs to," he snapped bitterly and turned away, more to hide the tears threatening to flow than out of fury. The unfairness of everything that had happened was overwhelming.

One of the truckers, cowboy'd up to the nines, looked up from the counter. A small portable radio was in front of him and he and several others were clustered around it, listening to news reports. "You boys lost?" he asked, taking off his cowboy hat and putting it on the counter as he looked at them. "You're obviously not any of them that the news reports are talking about."

"Well, if they were, they'd already be dead," someone else piped up humorlessly.

Owen was grateful for the distraction and cleared his throat and replied. "We're just as alive as the rest of you," he said softly.

"Looks like it's been a harrowing ride," the cowboy continued.

Owen nodded. "You could say that," he said distantly.

"There was another one with us," Chad explained as he helped Clint to a bar stool nearby. "He...well..." he trailed off, his own voice suddenly choking off.

The trucker nodded his head in sad understanding. "Didn't make it," he said quietly. "But you three did. There's hope in that."

"Hope for what?" Owen asked bitterly.

"Well, you're alive," the man said, a sad smile on his face. "Take it from someone who's been out there a long time and seen many things, both good and bad—while there's still life, there's still hope."

"So what are we going to do with this hope?" another patron asked—a trucker clad in jeans, boots, and a flannel shirt. He had bright red hair and drummed his fingers nervously on the counter as he spoke. "Judging by the news reports, this is happening everywhere. We heard about Vegas, but there ain't nothing local on the radio to know how bad it got around here."

"It's bad," Clint spoke up, his face tight against the pain. "From what we saw, if anyone is still alive in Mesquite, they're probably bunkered down and armed to the teeth. Those things are everywhere."

"They get to you?" Chuck the owner spoke up, nodding at Clint's injured wrist.

Clint winced. "In a matter of speaking, yeah," he answered hollowly.

"So what are we going to do?" the red-haired trucker spoke up.

"We're going to survive," Chuck answered grimly, as he came back around the counter. "We've already had this talk, Red. I don't know what's going on any more than anyone else does. But I don't aim to go down without a fight." He tapped his shotgun with his free hand as he finished. "If they come for us, we'll be ready."

Another man at the counter, his feet kicked up on a nearby stool, snorted derisively. Incredibly, he didn't seem to be at all upset about what was happening and what they might be facing before morning. "It's the media, Chuck," he said with a wave of his hand. "You don't even know if half of what they're saying is true."

"You want to go get in your truck and move on out then?" the owner snapped angrily. "This ain't make-believe, Bill."

The other blanched and pulled his feet off the stool, turning quickly back to a half-eaten piece of pie before him. "I just think we're jumping to conclusions, that's all," he muttered. "I've never known the media to tell it straight anyway."

Chuck shook his head, his demeanor softening. "I hope you're right, Bill. I truly do. But I doubt it. This time, I think they're spot on."

"Everything you hear is true," Owen said, pulling himself together. "We were in Vegas when it all happened. We woke up and the National Guard was already all over the city."

"The whole city?" Bill asked skeptically.

"Just about everything was in flames. When we got out, they were letting people leave, but no one was getting in." Owen shrugged and sat down heavily on another stool. "We made it to Mesquite and found out the same thing had happened there, only no National Guard."

"You didn't lead any of them here, did ya?" a female trucker said, giving the three newcomers a dark look.

"Now, now," Chuck quickly cut in, laying the cleaver on the counter. "We don't need any accusations makin' things worse. This diner might not look like much, but it's pretty solid. We're in here together and we're armed. If'n these things aim to make a run on us, they'd do it with or without these three boys showing up. And frankly, if they do come, I'll be grateful for a few extra hands." Turning to the three young men, he continued. "I'm not much for small talk, boys, so let's break it down. We know what the media is saying, but what have you seen?"

"I don't really know I can believe it myself," Owen stammered.

"Just say it, boy," another patron cut in. "It's zombies. Radio's sayin' they're reanimated corpses."

Bill spoke up again, having regained a bit of his bluster. "I'm sorry, but I just ain't buyin' it," he objected. "How's anyone going to bring a dead person back to life? It doesn't make any sense at all. Can't be done."

"I don't know how," Owen answered quietly, "but the radio's right. They really are zombies. The dead are coming back to life."

"Did you see it happen?" Bill scoffed.

Before Chuck could cut him off, Clint was up out of his chair and glaring at the man.

"Yeah, I saw it happen," he growled through the pain. "I watched one of my best friends die on the road and then a minute later, he was trying to kill me!" He took a step closer to the man and pointed at him with his good hand, his face livid with anger. "Let me tell you something else. There's a reason behind all this. We've seen it. We know what they're up to. They're running around strangling the living so they can raise them up, too. One becomes two, two to four, then eight, then sixteen. You getting the picture yet?"

Owen stepped forward, placing a hand on his friend's shoulder. "Ease up, Clint," he said softly. "It'll be all right."

Clint whirled on his friend. "No, it's not going to be all right, Owen!" he fairly shouted, then turned back to Bill. "How many people have you seen die tonight, pal?" he raged. "I've seen hundreds in the last few hours. I've seen them die and we've had to kill them all over again." He grabbed the cloth bandage and ripped it off his wounded wrist, then held it up for everyone to see. The desiccation of his tissue had spread and his entire forearm looked mummified. The sight of it caused more than a few of the people in the diner to inhale sharply in shock. "You see that?" he snapped. "That's reality. That's what happened to my friend, only he got it in the face."

Bill was suddenly on his feet and backing away from him. "You stay away from me with that, boy."

"Does it shock you? Does it make you afraid?" Clint pressed. "Well, good! You should be afraid. We all should." He turned and walked back to his stool, paying no attention to several of the diner patrons moving away from him. "We're all gonna die," he finished bitterly and sat down heavily, turning away from everyone.

There was some murmuring among the patrons, most all of it aimed at the three newcomers, and it seemed as if they might force the three young men back outside and away from the relative safety of the diner. However, Chuck quickly recognized what was happening and spoke up. "Listen up," he said softly, but firmly. "This is my diner. Before you put the lynch mob together, you better understand that he didn't do anything to deserve what has happened to him and we ain't gonna pile on, either."

Bill started to say something, but Chuck silenced him with a glare. "I ain't kiddin', Bill," he went on. "My diner, my rules. If anyone gets kicked out, it'll be because I said so. You understand that?"

Bill was silent for a moment before finally nodding. "Sure, Chuck. I hear you."

"Good. Now that we've settled that, let's get down to business. Here's what we..."

He was cut off by a shout from one of the men standing by the barricaded window, peeking around the black-out blanket. "Big rig comin' in, Chuck!"

"Whatcha got, Les?" the diner owner asked, looking up in alarm.

"Bull hauler, judgin' by the chicken lights," the other replied. "He's coming in fast, too."

Chuck turned around and pointed to Bill. "Reach under the register and get them pumps turned off."

Without a word, Bill jumped across the counter and thumbed the switches underneath the register that controlled the fuel pumps out front. "Off," he shouted out, looking up.

"Oh my Lord..." It was Les' voice, full of terror. "He ain't stoppin'!"

"Everybody away from the windows!" Chuck yelled, turning away and leaping back toward the counter. He almost made it. With a roar and a resounding crash of wood, mortar, glass, and steel, the front wall blew inward as the oncoming truck plowed through the gas pumps out front and into the diner.

Owen shouted in horror as the booth holding the little family of three was suddenly buried under the twisted metal hood and tires of the huge Peterbilt. Then, the force of the impact threw him mercifully over the counter and into a silverware rack, so he did not see their last moments of life. He lay stunned for a few moments, dimly aware of the screams of the diner patrons that suddenly turned from pain to terror. His vision cleared and he realized someone was lying beside him. Looking, he saw that it was the man called Les. His head was twisted to the side at an odd angle and his unseeing eyes were staring straight at Owen. Les was dead, his neck broken from where the impact of the truck had thrown him across the restaurant. Owen leapt to his feet.

The scene before him was pure chaos. The cab of the truck was halfway into the diner, a mangled wreck of twisted metal. The impact had killed several of the diner patrons, including the young family. Through the huge hole in the wall, creatures were crawling in, seeking the living. Many were dressed in hospital gowns and others were in the white smocks and lab coats of doctors and nurses. Most were unarmed, but others were wielding scalpels and other blunt or sharp stainless steel hospital instruments. Owen realized with numb horror that the killers were the same ones they had encountered near the hospital in Mesquite. Somehow, they'd found them.

For the moment, attackers and patrons were about equal in number, but that began to change quickly as the undead poured into the ruined building, slashing and beating down everyone who was still alive. They were not adding to their ranks this time—they were brutally killing the living in the most horrific ways possible.

Nearby, Chuck buried his meat cleaver into the chest of a scalpel-wielding man in a hospital robe, only to watch in shock as the man just stood there looking at it. Swearing loudly, Chuck leveled his shotgun and blew a plate-sized hole in the man's stomach. The body crashed backward into the wreckage and fell to the rubble-covered floor, not to move again, while Chuck aimed and took down another.

As he moved to blast a third, there was an answering crack of a handgun and Chuck staggered backward, slumping against the counter. The shotgun dropped from his fingers and he slowly looked down at the blood welling from the hole that had just been drilled into the left side of his chest. Then his eyes rolled back in his head and Owen watched in dread as death claimed the kindly diner owner.

Owen had only a moment to see Chuck's killer calmly step from the wrecked cab of the truck. The man was different from the rest of the killers in one specific way: he was very much alive. Owen had the sudden notion he had seen him before, but the chaos of the moment kept him from spending any time on the thought. The look on the man's face was that of a cold-blooded murderer as he shoved a handgun into the waistband of his pants and pulled a long hunting knife from a leather sheath at his belt.

He stepped up behind Chad, who was desperately locked in a struggle with a doctor still dressed in bloody surgical garb. Chad never saw his killer and Owen never had time to yell a warning. The man reached around, grabbing Chad's head in a vice-like grip. A moment later, the hunting knife slashed viciously across the young man's exposed throat. Chad's eyes went wide and his hands went to his ruined throat. Blood poured from the fatal wound and Chad fell to the floor, his life flowing quickly out of him.

"No!" screamed Owen as a zombie lurched toward him, slamming a length of two-by-four into Owen's side. Pain shot through him as he stumbled and fell to the floor. He looked up only to see Chad's killer calmly pick up Chuck's fallen shotgun and aim it at Clint, who was leaning heavily against the bar, too weary to fight. He saw Clint's pleading look, saw the blast from the shotgun, and saw Clint's body fall to the floor, his heart blown through his back.

Owen struggled desperately to regain his feet, his eyes tracking his friends' killer. The man was looking at him, ignoring the fighting that raged around them. As Owen stood up, the man offered him a smile and casually tossed the shotgun to the rubble-strewn floor. At that moment, Owen realized where he'd seen him. He was the photographer at the charity basketball game who had taken their group picture. Unnerved and confused, Owen tried to get to the man and prevent him from escaping, but several more of the creatures moved toward him, barring the way. He fought desperately to get past them, but there were too many of them and the killer turned and disappeared into the night.

Desperation, frustration, and pure terror surged through Owen as he fought his attackers, despite being pulled inexorably down into the fathomless depths of grief. He realized then that it would be so easy just to give up. So much death; so much sorrow. What would it even matter if he just gave in? He thought about accepting his fate. How much preferable was that to living without his friends? He could join them on the other side; he could find peace and happiness there.

But the image of the man who had murdered Chad and Clint kept flashing through his mind and Owen knew he couldn't quit. Somewhere in this, his darkest hour, he found the strength he needed to go on. His friends would not die in vain. He would avenge them. He would find their killer and destroy him. He had to.

With one last surge, he picked up a lead pipe and gripped it tightly. He faced the oncoming killers with the fierce determination of a man who would not accept death without a savage fight.

Owen waded into the fray, shouting with fury and swinging the pipe with deadly precision, but it was a fight he could not win. There were just too many and, whenever he took down one, two more appeared to take their place. Eventually, only he and two other diner patrons remained alive, fighting desperately to survive. He knew then that there was no way they could outlast the crawling horde. They were going to die.

It was at that very moment of utter hopelessness that a new figure stepped into the diner through the shattered window. Huge and imposing and dressed in a long black trench coat, the newcomer brought the entire diner to a standstill. Wrap-around black shades covered his eyes and his long black hair was pulled back into a tight ponytail.

He jumped up onto a nearby table as his right hand disappeared into his coat and pulled out a wicked looking short-barreled shotgun. He smiled, teeth gleaming white, and muttered, "Time to earn my paycheck," before opening fire on the creatures. Emptying the gun's chambers, the man tossed the smoking weapon to the floor and pulled a long machete from underneath his trench coat as he jumped down from the table. He then began to slash his way through the undead, dispatching the creatures right and left. One of the undead rose up in front of him, hands grasping for his throat. Before the creature could grab him, the man kicked his foot forward and sent it flying across the diner where it slammed into the wall, its body broken and unmoving.

The man never stopped moving. In the time it took for the thing to fly through the diner and hit the wall, he had dropped the machete and pulled out a smaller handgun, firing eight rounds in succession. Each explosion of gunfire dropped one of the creatures, holes blasted through their heads.

In a matter of minutes, few of the undead remained. But still they moved toward the huge man. He met them all. Dropping the gun, he caught the closest one and drove his elbow into the creature's head. The zombie dropped to the floor, but not before the man had yanked a length of barbed wire out of its hand. The next advancing zombie suddenly found the wire wound tightly about its neck. With incredible strength, the man ripped the wire from the undead creature's neck, the metal barbs tearing into dead flesh and nearly decapitating it.

Grabbing the next nearest one, the warrior flung it out of the way. Another found its head nearly torn off as the big man savagely yanked its head sideways. "Game over, man," he said with a sneer as he waded through the last two remaining zombies, quickly disposing of them.

And just like that, it was over.

Silence descended on the diner and the giant turned slowly to face the three surviving patrons who stood spellbound and paralyzed behind the counter. Before anyone could utter a word, he reached back into his coat and pulled out a pair of enormous handguns—chrome-plated Desert Eagles. He pointed them directly at Owen's chest.

Owen closed his eyes in resignation as the man fired.

CHAPTER 12

Salt Lake City, Utah: Alexis' return to consciousness was difficult. It was the pain that woke her, thrumming from multiple points in her battered body. She tried to open her eyes, but realized that the task was beyond her for the moment, so she just lay there, trying to work through the pain. As she did, she heard the quiet voices of her companions and suddenly realized that, except for their voices, there was no other sound.

"She's coming to," Stacia said softly, dabbing the young woman's forehead again with a cool damp cloth. She had been tending to her since they had escaped the attacking undead.

Alexis felt the coolness of the cloth, but kept her eyes closed and tried to speak. "Where are we?" she finally managed to rasp.

John's voice answered, calm and soothing. "We are in the basement of a house, some distance from the fight," he answered quietly. "For the moment, we're safe, but that will not likely last for very long."

"How..." she began but ended in a cough, her lungs aching. "How'd we get here?"

There was sadness in John's voice as he answered. "Believe it or not, you saved us, my dear girl," he answered. "You drew them to you, scattering their ranks and making it easier for us to take them down and escape. You should have died, but other than a few bruises you seem to have come out of that surprisingly well."

"You're lucky," Stacia added, continuing to dab at the woman's face with the washcloth, wiping away blood and grime. "No broken bones, at least that I can find, but I can't imagine how sore you're going to be in a couple of days."

"Dakota?" Alexis asked, terrified of the reply she was sure she would get.

A long drawn-out silence was all the answer she needed and Alexis felt the tears come freely. Grief washed over her and, for a moment, she saw no point in it anymore. Dakota was dead. Her friends were dead. Her family was probably dead. And then there was Owen; out of reach and probably dead, too. Her grief was nearly overwhelming and her body was wracked with shuddering sobs that continued unabated until she felt a warm hand replace the cool cloth on her forehead. John's voice accompanied his hand, speaking in a strange language she didn't understand. As his words went on, she felt her grief begin to lessen and a feeling of peace flowed through her. She slipped toward pleasant oblivion, silently grateful for the release from her pain.

"What was that all about?" Michael Dalacourt asked quietly, having witnessed the sudden transformation in the girl lying before them. One moment, Alexis had been in silent hysterics and the next, she was still and peaceful.

John removed his hand as Alexis' body relaxed and the crying ceased. "Just an old Indian chant," John said dismissively and then knelt down beside the young woman. "Alexis," he went spoke softly near her ear. "Come back, child. Everything's going to be all right."

Alexis stirred and opened her eyes. Pain and sadness were evident on her face, but she held herself in control, buoyed up by something new that pulsed deep within her. It was a peaceful feeling of strength, and she anchored her mind and heart to it. "I don't know, John," she finally said in almost a whisper. "I don't know that it will ever be all right. So much death..."

"I know," John soothed, stroking her forehead. "I know. But all of this has been foreordained, my dear. We must persevere and see this through."

Alexis tried to sit up, but pain washed through her body again and she fell back to the couch she was lying on. "Why?" she asked breathlessly, feeling a touch of anger creep into her emotions. Her newly discovered inner foundation held firm, but she wasn't sure she wanted to see anything else through. She was tired of running, tired of fighting, and tired of seeing her loved ones die. "Why do I have to see this through?"

"You've been through a lot, I know," John went on.

"No, you don't know," Alexis replied quickly, forcing herself into a sitting position against her body's will. Closing her eyes tightly against the dizziness that suddenly assailed her, she stubbornly remained upright, holding fast to the anchor within her. "You have no idea what I've been through, John."

John rested his hand on her shoulder again. "I do understand, Alexis," he interrupted gently. "I understand more than you can know." He went from a kneeling position to a sitting position at the foot of the couch, his old bones creaking, before continuing. "You were right, my child," he went on with a sigh. "There has been so much death. But unfortunately, more will come. I wish I could tell you differently, but I cannot. The road of life is difficult and there are times when it becomes almost unmanageable. But that does not give us permission to stop along the way and perhaps turn back. Where would we turn back to, anyway? We must always move forward in the belief that where we are going is better than where we are today."

"You act like you know something about all of this."

"I do," he admitted softly. "And sometimes, like you, it's more than I believe I can deal with."

"So what's really going on here?" Alexis asked, throwing up her hands and wincing as the sudden movement shot pain through her body again. "I..." She trailed off, having no clue what to ask or where to even begin searching for the answers.

"We've reached the crossroads," he said quietly. "The enemy has mustered its army and is pressing its advantage. Dawn will break in a very short while and, before the sun sets on this day, much will come to pass to define the future of God's children."

"What do you mean?" she asked.

It was Michael Dalacourt who answered. "'In the age of the last dispensation, shall the anointed of the Beast arise from the shadows and come forth upon the earth, and Death shall be his name. And he shall bear before him the sword of War, and Famine shall be his chariot and Pestilence shall be his shield. And war shall be brought to the lands all around and death brought to the people,'" the young priest quoted the ancient and long-hidden scriptures from memory. "'And the earth shall give up her dead, insomuch that the dead shall stand with the Beast. And they shall march forth upon the earth and shall slay the living and shall rend the ground from whence they came.'"

John nodded solemnly and spoke to Alexis. "What he just quoted are long-lost scriptural passages, speaking specifically of the events of today. But there is more, my dear child."

"So all of this is prophecy coming to pass? The death, the dying, the undead?"

"In the final days, prophecy happens with frightening speed. What is happening right now is just the first salvo in what will be the final battle. We are in the last days."

"I'm sorry, but I just don't understand," she said, wincing from the pain.

"What if I were to tell you no one has the full knowledge of the scriptures as they lay out the final days, Alexis," John's voice was low, almost a whisper. "The Bible tells us that Christ will return in the end and Satan will be bound for a thousand years. But what mankind doesn't know is that the opposite can be true as well, if things happen in a certain way."

"What are you talking about?" she asked, disbelief in her voice.

The answer came from Father Dalacourt. "It means mankind has a choice," the priest replied after an uncomfortable pause, his words lending support to the old man's statement. "At least that's what John told me. Outside of that, I know little more."

"You've been wanting to know more, Michael," John said to the priest, handing him an ancient piece of parchment he had been holding. "Now is the time. Read what is penned, please."

Dalacourt locked his eyes on the spidery script of the lost scriptures and began to read:

"'And man shall strive against the anointed of the Beast and the days shall be bitter and there shall be much wailing and despair. And three kings shall rise up and stand upon the mountaintop. And they shall make war, one upon the other, and the blood of their brother shall be spilled and they shall serve the anointed of the Beast, lest they humble themselves before God. Victory will be sour in their stomachs and darkness shall cover the land for a thousand years and the presence of the Lord shall be withdrawn from all the land and the Beast shall reign.'" Dalacourt finished reading and looked up, his face white.

"What you've just read, Michael, is the alternative to what is written in Revelation," John said quietly.

"That's not possible," Alexis interrupted.

"But it is," John replied. "If the Book of Revelation stated the world could end up plunged into evil darkness for a thousand years, what hope would anyone have? What would drive people to do good if they knew there was no reason to do it?"

"I don't understand," the priest said, holding the paper before him, his gaze alternating between the hand-written script and the face of the old man. "How can this be truth?"

"It might be truth," John answered matter-of-factly. "But only a possible truth."

"Are you saying Revelation is a lie?" Alexis asked.

"Not a lie," John corrected, "only a part of the greater story. What mankind has in the Bible is ninety-nine percent of the whole. What I possess is the other one percent God forbade John the Revelator to reveal. It's the one percent God commanded be sealed up and not shown to man, for to do so would cause many of His children to dwindle into unbelief."

"But that's not possible," she argued.

"Unfortunately, it's as real as it gets," John replied.

"You said mankind had a choice," Dalacourt spoke up after a few moments.

"The choice is in the scripture, vague as it is," John answered.

"The three kings that were spoken of," Dalacourt mused quietly after considering the words again.

John pointedly ignored the guess and went on. "Remember, nothing is certain. As I stated earlier, we are at a crossroads and the actions of a few on this very day will portend the fate of all mankind for a thousand years."

For a while, no one spoke as everyone in the room tried to digest John's words. Finally, it was Stacia McCain, sitting quietly off to the side, who broke the silence. Her words were quiet and thoughtful and directed more at Alexis than anyone else. "We've come a very long way and we've survived much," she said. "I have no doubt there's a reason for all of this."

"All I see is death and destruction," Alexis said, shaking her head. "Evil is winning everywhere I turn and I am now being told that evil will probably win out in the end, too."

"That begs the question—what are they winning at, Alexis?" John said. "It's a struggle that's gone on since the dawn of time, a struggle in which one side or the other will emerge victorious in the end. But this isn't the end. Not yet, anyway. Not if we stand firm."

Alexis sighed and leaned back on the couch again, aware of her aches and pains. She was so very tired. "I don't understand something," she said. "I thought God was all-powerful? If He is, then how come this is happening?"

"God is all-powerful, Alexis," Michael Dalacourt put in. "And in His infinite wisdom, He gave us the choices that are today set before all of us."

"Michael is correct," John added. "The most beautiful thing about mortal life is the freedom to choose. We can choose to do evil or we can choose to do good. It was God's greatest gift to all of us, and it extends to all things. The second coming of Christ is our choice to make as God's children, as much as any other thing we do is our choice."

"And these things were never printed in the Bible because mankind, being what it is, would not have had the resolve to make the right choices if they knew it was going to be so difficult," Dalacourt added.

John nodded.

"So where do we fit into this whole thing?" Alexis asked.

"We're the peanut gallery," Tom McCain spoke up from his seat against the basement door. "And it's time to heckle the players."

"What?" both Dalacourt and Alexis asked simultaneously, turning to look at him.

McCain didn't answer, but looked hard at John. John nodded knowingly at the man and then answered the question himself. "Choices," he began, "can be affected by outside sources. Temptation to do good or bad will sometimes swing the balance in a person's mind.

When someone says the devil made him do it, chances are that some external force or pressure acted upon the person's mind to bring about that conclusion."

"Have you heard of the Illuminati?" McCain asked quietly.

Dalacourt scoffed, clearly knowledgeable about the phantom organization. "A conspiracy theory, spun to entertain the weak-minded."

"Spoken like someone who doesn't like Dan Brown novels," McCain answered with a smile, but immediately turned serious again. "It's a conspiracy theory, true—but it's one steeped in truth, Father. Be it the Illuminati, the Bilderberg Group, the Trilateral Commission, the Materese Circle, or whatever the conspiracy flavor of the day is—there is an element of truth to it," he explained. "Since the dawn of civilization, there has always been a power broker behind the scenes— someone working hard to effect changes they want to see happen. What's happening today is no different, except the power broker is nearly ready to reveal himself."

"You mean the Illuminati *is* behind this?" Dalacourt snorted. "Come on, Tom. You can't be serious."

"The Illuminati is a smoke screen, just like every other conspiracy theory you've ever heard," McCain explained. "These theories are nothing more than bizarre tales propagated publically to hide the fact that there is, indeed, an organization thousands of years old and dedicated to a single cause." McCain looked hard at the priest. "Truth be told, it's been around since the time of Adam."

Dalacourt shoot his head. "I find this impossible to believe."

"Is it harder to believe than the living dead walking around trying to kill you?"

Dalacourt paled.

"Krypteia is very real, Father Dalacourt," the detective said quietly.

"That's the true name of this organization and ultimately, it's behind all of those organizations I mentioned. They're the man behind the curtain, ominous and all-seeing, but unlike the Wizard of Oz, they're actually a very real threat and extremely dangerous. Make no mistake, they're the driving force behind what's been happening here the last few days."

"And they have the same scriptural passages we have," John added. "They've spent thousands of years reading the signs, searching the planet for clues, prying at the seams of prophecy until they think they understand exactly what it means. Everything that's happened is simply part of their opening move in what will be a final game between good and evil. They're confident they can begin something none of us can undo that will result in a thousand years of Satan's dominion over the earth and God's children."

"If this is true, it must go back to the three kings in the passages I read," Dalacourt said, his brow furrowing as he tried to grasp the ramifications of everything he'd heard.

"It does," John agreed. "This organization will try to influence those kings to make the choices that need to be made to eliminate Christ's Second Coming. If they can do that, they win. If they cannot, the battle will continue. This is a bold move this early in the game, but one I doubt would have been made lightly. They aim to end this war before it even begins."

"It's a huge roll of the dice," McCain added, "but they wouldn't make it if they weren't fairly sure they could succeed."

Dalacourt turned to look at McCain. He'd spent the last couple days with the man, but hadn't really tried to understand who the man actually was. Now, the questions loomed large in his mind. "You said you were a police officer from New York," he stated almost skeptically.

"I am."

"So how do you know about all of this?"

The man smiled and climbed to his feet, picking up a shotgun that had been leaning against the wall. "I said I was a cop, but that isn't all I am. Trust me when I tell you that I'm on your side as much as any person could be." McCain offered the priest a knowing wink, then turned and exited through the basement door and headed upstairs.

Dalacourt turned a questioning look at the old Indian, but John just smiled. "Tom McCain may be unconventional, my young friend, but he's as trustworthy an individual as you'll find in these trying times."

"So what do we do?" Alexis asked, clearly exhausted by everything that had happened and everything she'd been told. She wasn't sure she believed what she'd heard, but she had to admit there was a frightening logic to it all, and that was extremely unsettling to her.

"We survive," Stacia answered her question. "It's as simple as that. It will be light in a few hours, so we'll stick with our plan and get out of the city. When things have settled down, we'll plan our next move."

"How do we get out of town?" Dalacourt asked. "Those things are still out there."

"There's an Expedition in the garage. Dad found the keys in the house. We'll take a little rest if we can and then we'll leave at first light. These things might be killers, but they can't drive." She finished and smiled, putting both Dalacourt and Alexis somewhat at ease. "Relax," she added. "The worst is behind us in the city. We'll get through this."

"We will," John agreed, stretching out on the floor. "But for now, we should get a little sleep. The sun will be up shortly and we will need to be on the road."

"To where?" Dalacourt asked.

John did not answer, but the young priest had the distinct impression that the old Indian knew exactly where they were going.

John closed his eyes and was quickly asleep.

Everyone was quiet for the longest time, the silence broken only by John's heavy breathing as he slept soundly on the floor. Stacia sat in the corner, her legs drawn up and her face resting on her knees, her eyes closed. Dalacourt sat on the floor and Alexis laid back down on the couch, hoping to alleviate some of her aches and pains.

"What do you make of all this?" she finally asked quietly.

Dalacourt was silent for a few moments before answering. "I believe him, if that's what you mean," he answered.

"I guess I do, too," she said softly. "It's scary, though. I don't know if I'm ready for this."

"Ready or not, we're already in it," he pointed out. "We've survived this far and the sun will be up shortly. John seems to think this will end soon."

"That's just it, Father," she said worriedly. "What will end?"

"I suppose that's the big question, isn't it? When I was younger, I always wondered what the future would hold for me. As I became more in touch with my spirituality and with God, I began to temper those questions about the future by saying that everything is in God's hands. And truly, everything is. God has brought us together for a purpose, Alexis. Now, I don't have the foggiest idea what that purpose is, but I take comfort in knowing that God knows all. And even with everything John told us about what may happen, I still feel at peace. Maybe John's optimism is contagious, but I just feel that in the end, everything will be all right."

"I hope you're right," Alexis said and then was suddenly aware of her hunger. "Have you had anything to eat?"

Dalacourt chuckled and quickly stood up. "There's enough food in this house to last a long time," he answered as he went through a doorway into what had to be a storage room. A moment later, he was back and handing Alexis a dark green wrapped bundle.

She winced as she took it, recognizing it immediately. "M.R.E.," she sighed. "Nothing else?"

"Not unless you want to build a fire to cook something."

With another sigh, she tore it open and began sorting through the food inside. "Can I ask you something, Father?"

"Certainly," he answered, sitting back down against the far wall.

"Do you think we've been breaking God's commandments? I mean, we've been killing people, right?"

"I'll be the first to admit there is little I'm certain of right now, Alexis, but this is something I have no question about. Killing those abominations isn't the same as breaking the commandment of 'Thou shalt not kill'. What we're doing is no different than what a soldier does when he goes into battle, and I'm certain God gives absolution in situations like that."

Alexis nibbled on a dry cracker, her eyes distant. "When Dakota ran away," she began, her voice dropping to a sad whisper, "all I could think about was killing the person who was hurting her. Even if that person was still alive, I would have wanted to do the same thing." Her eyes focused on Dalacourt. "I was ready to end the life of another human being."

"I understand your concern, Alexis, but these aren't real people. They're nothing more than shells housing evil spirits," he consoled her. "As far as whether that person was alive or not, your intentions were noble. You wanted to save the child. I can't see how God would condemn you for that."

"But the rage I felt..." she started, but trailed off.

"...was little more than your desire to protect the child," Dalacourt finished for her.

"But I couldn't protect her," she said, closing her eyes. "I promised her and I failed."

The priest moved across the floor until he was next to the sofa. "You mustn't punish yourself like this, Alexis," he said gently. "You did everything you could do and truthfully, there was nothing more anyone could have done to prevent what happened. Dakota is in a better place. She's joined her mother and the rest of her family in God's presence. She's no longer here to witness the terrible plight of the world."

"What about us? Do you think we'll survive?" she asked the question point-blank.

Dalacourt never hesitated. "I do."

Alexis felt a tear slide down her cheek and she pushed her uneaten M.R.E. away. After a few minutes, she worked her aching body into a more comfortable position on the sofa. "I'm glad you're with us, Father," she said quietly and then closed her eyes.

Michael Dalacourt watched her drift off to sleep and then allowed himself to smile. For the first time in a long time, he truly felt he was where God intended him to be.

CHAPTER 13

Highway 15, Nevada: Owen was dead. He closed his eyes as the giant in front of him leveled the two enormous handguns at his chest. He heard the click of each trigger, felt the blast of pressure from each of the wide barrels, and smelled the gunpowder explode. He was dead.

Only… he wasn't.

Rather than the searing pain of a bullet through his skull, he felt only a sticky mist of blood and heard the strangled screams of the people standing to his right and left. Opening his eyes in disbelief, he saw what had happened. The bullets had torn into the other two patrons, slamming their bodies up against the blood-spattered kitchen wall behind them. That he was still alive was of little consolation, though, as he was staring down the barrels of two massive Desert Eagles. His reprieve would be short-lived.

For the longest moment, the two of them stared at each other in silence, before the huge man stepped toward him as he slid the massive firearms back into the shoulder holsters underneath his coat. "You know, it's like shooting fish in a barrel. But I suppose there's nothing wrong with that if you get your supper," he said as he reached down to pick up a bloody barstool. Setting it right, he settled down onto it and let out a sigh. Reaching behind him he snapped the rubber band from his ponytail, letting the dark coifs cascade over his shoulders and cover much of his face. Finally, he looked at Owen and smiled. "You know, I've always loved doing the whole Neo bit," he added with a flourish. "You've seen *The Matrix*, right?"

Owen could only stand and stare. Despite everything he had already gone through, what had just happened defied anything his mind could process. He knew only that he was alive and that, above anything else, was a miracle.

"No?" the man went on, answering the question himself and obviously displeased at Owen's lack of speech. "I suppose it doesn't matter anyway." He shifted gears. "I'm parched. Do you have anything to drink back there? A Monster Energy Drink, perhaps."

Owen was silent, his mind completely unable to process what was happening.

"No?" the man answered again, shaking his head in annoyance. "You know, a sure sign that society has regressed past the point of being salvageable is a total lack of civility in the service industry. Used to be a time you could get a drink if you asked nicely."

Owen felt like he was about to lose consciousness, black motes spinning before his eyes. He gripped the counter tightly, holding on to steady himself.

The man shook his head again. "Do you even speak English, boy?"

Owen stared at him for a lengthy time until he finally found the ability to break his silence. "Who are you?" he managed to stutter.

The man put his hand up and brushed his hair away from his eyes. "I'm really getting tired of that question tonight," he said impatiently. "I really am. It's fun to have a coming out party like this, but it really means no one knew who you were before. I find that rather disconcerting, Owen." He sighed and shook his head.

"How...," Owen began, swallowing fearfully. "How do you know my name?"

The man shrugged. "I know. Is that not enough?" he replied in a tone that suggested it would be futile to ask the question again. "Let's just dispense with the pleasantries and move on to more important matters, like getting me a drink."

"Who are you?" Own pressed again, trying desperately to get the words out.

"Again with the introductions," the man sighed, his irritation seeming to grow. "But since it's obvious we won't be able to move beyond this, then I'll tell you. I am Hade." He gave a mock bow from his stool. "What's more important than who I am, though, is who I can be. I can be your best friend, Owen DiConte. I can give you everything you ever wanted, if you really want it." There was an extended pause, as the man let those words sink in. "Isn't it nice," he finished, his voice syrupy, "to have a friend like that?"

Owen was still confused, but the word "friend" pulled him slightly out of his stupor. "My friend?" he asked and then looked over at the bloody bodies of his two friends. He felt the tears well up in his eyes. "My friends are dead," he said softly, fighting hard to control himself.

The huge man shook his head in exasperation and then walked around the counter, stepping on bodies or kicking them out of his way. Stopping in front of the cooler, he pulled out a tall black can with green writing, popped it open, and drained it. "Unleash the beast," he chuckled, wiping his mouth with the back of his hand and tossing the empty Monster can to the floor. Reaching back into the cooler, he withdrew two more. He tossed one to Owen, who caught it despite himself, then made his way back around the bar and sat back down on his stool. "I told you I was parched," he finished, opening the second can and taking a sip.

"Why are you doing this?" Owen finally stammered, setting his unopened drink on the bar. "If you're going to shoot me, why don't you just do it now?"

"I'm not going to shoot you, Owen," came the steady reply. "Not yet anyway." Hade offered a knowing grin, but it was gone in a second. He cocked his head to the side as a thought crossed his mind. "Then again, do you really want me to shoot you? Do you know what it's like when the bullet impacts your flesh, shatters bones, and makes mincemeat of your internal organs?"

"What does it matter? It's not like I have anything left."

"My question is, are you certain you want that? Dying by gunshot is a pretty rough way to go, boy."

"I'm ready for it, if that's what you mean," Owen replied, a touch of desperate anger in his voice.

"So confident in your place in the afterlife, are you?" Hade laughed. "Spoken with the true folly of youth. Descartes would have a field day with that, you know."

"What's your point?" Owen hated being mocked by anyone, especially by a stranger who was about to kill him.

"My point is, you haven't lost everything yet, so there's no need to play the suicide card. You still have yourself, don't you? You are thinking, therefore you are, which means you have something. Of course, if you think things through—a trait that seems to be lacking in today's youth, I might add—you will find that you have much more than that. You have a future, Owen, which is more than you can say for anyone else here in this God-forsaken dive tonight," he finished as he surveyed the bloody carnage with a derisive snort.

Owen's anger grew. He had been skating on thin ice for some time already and he felt that he was nearly ready to break through and plunge into the icy depths of insanity. "So you're not going to shoot me. Great. So you're a philosopher. Even better. What do you want from me, man?" Owen felt the grief falling away, replaced by a simmering fury. He feared for his life, to be sure, but he was done being talked to like a child.

"Finally, a question I can answer," Hade answered, ignoring the young man's anger. "It isn't what I want from you, but what you want from me. I'm here to save you."

"Save me? Why would you want to save me?" Owen retorted.

"You didn't save them!" he yelled, pointing behind him to the bodies of the two dinners Hade had just shot.

Hade frowned and made a small tsk-tsking sound. "I'm constantly perplexed at how far comprehension of the English language has dropped off in the past generation," the big man replied, adopting his professor-like tone. "I'm here to save *you*, Owen, not them. The fact that I shot them should be proof enough of that."

"But why kill them? What threat were they to you?!"

Hade shrugged. "They would have been distractions," he answered plainly. "You can tell just by looking at them and, in all honesty, I can't have any of those types around tonight. I've got a full plate, if you will, and I've got to be moving on shortly. So, 'bang bang' goes the gun." Hade mimicked the shooting with his finger. "No distractions, Owen. Trust me, the world won't miss them—not tonight, anyway. But you, Owen? Oh, the world would miss you greatly. That's why I'm here to save you."

"Why couldn't you have saved my friends?" Owen worked on fanning the flames of his anger. It was the only thing keeping him sane. "Would they have been distractions, too?"

"Owen, I try my hardest not to deal with 'what if' situations," Hade explained, sounding weary of the questions. "The world is what it is. Maybe I would have shot your friends, maybe I wouldn't have. But we'll never know because they were both dead already. Living in a world of 'what if's' will get you nowhere, boy. You become a distraction, if you know what I mean."

"I want to know," Owen stood his ground, refusing to acknowledge the veiled threat. "Would you have killed them?"

"Well, I can see this is going to take a while," Hade sighed. "Fine, we'll go with the pointless question-and-answer routine. Your friends are dead because these are the times we live in, Owen," he explained.

"These are violent times—important times, times that the entire world will turn on."

"Answer my question."

"I'm getting to that, Owen," he said firmly. "Granted, we need to hash this out fairly quickly, but I would caution you about interrupting me and becoming a distraction." At that, Hade reached into his coat and pulled out one of the Desert Eagles and laid it on the counter. "You know how I hate distractions," he menaced, looking at the young man knowingly. "This is one is my favorite guns," he went on. "You've already seen that it makes a really big hole in anything it hits."

Owen felt his blood turn to ice and he knew that the man was not kidding. But he held on to his anger, and continued to glare at him.

"Now, as I was saying, these are very important times we live in and there simply isn't room for everyone to have a lead role in the play. Would I have killed your friends? Probably, for the simple reason they aren't important to the greater good. However," he added, raising a finger to make his point, "I will say that I may have decided to spare them if I thought killing them would adversely affect the relationship that you and I are forging."

"We're not forging a relationship," Owen snapped.

"Oh, but we are, my dear boy," Hade countered. "Consider the situation. I'm in complete control here. I can decide on a whim to let you live or break every bone in your body or just shoot you for the fun of it. Any of those things are completely within my power. You know that, right?"

Owen refused to answer.

"Right?" Hade repeated dangerously, placing his hand on the Eagle.

"Right," Owen responded grudgingly.

"You see? You can be reasonable," the huge man said,

withdrawing his hand. "Now, our relationship might be forced, but it's still a relationship nevertheless."

"A relationship that involves you saving me by threatening my life every time I say something you don't like."

"Now you're getting it," Hade answered with a grin. He ran a hand through his tangled hair, peeling it away from his eyes again and then locked his gaze with Owen's. "Let's talk about your place in the world, Owen," he went on. "The world right now is a rough place and it has only gotten rougher as the years have passed. Today, we have larger weapons, bigger armies, more sophisticated ways of getting what we want, easier ways of killing the enemy. But with all of our increased capacity for slaughter, the age-old choice is still the same, Owen. You can choose: act or be acted upon. Give everything or take everything. Now me, I choose to take. You have chosen to give. Don't you think it's time for you to take something back?"

"I haven't given anything away!"

"No?" Hade replied, raising a skeptical eyebrow. "What about Luke?"

The question was so direct, so biting, that it took Owen a few seconds to recognize the full implications of what Hade was saying.

"Didn't you give his life away to save your own, or at least that of your dear departed friend Clint?" Hade pressed.

"How do you know…," Owen began, but faltered, before changing direction and snapping back. "I didn't have any other option! He wasn't Luke anymore!"

"Fine, fine, fine," Hade replied, holding up both hands in mock surrender. "Do settle down, though. Remember, the world is changing and will never again be the same. Where do you think you're going to fit in with this new world order: in the penthouse or as the doormat? Continue to be a giver and the world will wipe its feet on you. Step forward and be a taker and you can look down on the pitiful refuse that remains."

"I'll go where I'm needed and can do the most good," Owen replied icily, "and I'll do it on my own terms. I don't know what you want from me, but I'll tell you this. You're not going to get it."

"Very brave indeed," Hade said, softly clapping his hands together, pantomiming a golf clap. "But before you can be so certain, you must wait until you've heard my full proposition to make such a statement. In the meantime, let's switch conversational topics for a moment, shall we? Can I ask you a question, Owen?"

"What?" It was a statement of acceptance and Owen folded his arms resolutely, knowing he really had no choice in the matter. Hade held all the cards and if he had any hope of surviving the night, he knew he had to play the man's game, confusing as it was.

"It's a simple one, really," Hade replied, then swept his arms out in an all-encompassing motion. "Do you fear my creatures?"

"Your…creatures?" Owen asked dubiously, looking around. "What are you talking about?"

"I am speaking of what is before you," was the reply. "Do you fear these things that have hunted you, attacked you, and killed your friends? Do you fear what I have unleashed upon the world?"

"These things that attacked us are your creatures?" Owen could not quite believe what he was hearing.

"Yes, they are," Hade replied, looking positively elated. "Now, you're probably wondering why I took down my own creations in that amazing display of violence s few minutes ago, but since it looked like you weren't doing very well, I made the decision to come to your rescue. If I knew you would have made it out alive, I would have let this little clash continue. However, since my little beasties didn't quite follow orders here in the diner, it was necessary to intervene. Spirits can be so temperamental when you give them a little freedom."

"Wait...you made them?" Owen asked, trying to wrap his mind around the admission.

"The short answer would be yes, I am responsible for their existence in the world," Hade nodded. "Did I actually create them, though? I'm afraid that the art of creation itself is a bit beyond the scope of my abilities. I am many things, Owen, but alas, I am no creator. Other beings have that power, not I. However, I do have other talents. I can rearrange things. I can motivate people. I can pull strings and move governments. I can have people killed and I can have people saved. I can bring the earth to the brink of chaos and pull it back again. Do not be mistaken, dear boy. My powers are almost limitless, but I am no creator. Perhaps the best word to use to describe me would be...a re-assembler. I have disassembled what others have created and now I will reassemble the world in my own way to serve my purposes. Not as fancy as a creator, but just as powerful in the end, not at all unlike a project manager, if you will." Hade finished with a laugh.

"So you didn't create them," Owen slowly reasoned, trying to follow the man's dizzying conversational path. "But you were responsible for them. And then you had to kill them."

"They were a threat to you and it became necessary to remove that threat."

"But...why?" Owen asked, truly perplexed.

"Ah, now that is a difficult question," Hade answered. "Unfortunately, many of them seem to be slightly upset with me. Of course, I might have slightly exaggerated the amount of control they would have over these bodies and I might have embellished the amount of power they would have over the world when we had completed our task of reshaping it. Truthfully, though, I think the smart ones have figured out that they are merely pawns in a bigger picture and are therefore using their newfound abilities to their advantage. The rest," Hade went on, motioning to the bodies scattered around the little restaurant, "are merely shock troops—cannon fodder, if you will."

"So you had them attack the diner? All these people in here are dead because of you? A little baby is dead because of you!" Owen shouted the last accusation.

"I had them attack the diner to bring about a specific result," Hade replied evenly. "Present company excluded, everyone else who died in here was of no consequence to me."

"But why me? What's so special about me?" Owen still seethed with fury.

"Everything and nothing, which is what makes this so rich! The world is turning, Owen," Hade continued. "Events long since prophesied are coming to pass. Normal people are being called upon to do extraordinary things. Extraordinary people are being called upon to change the world. It's positively exhilarating to be alive on a day like today."

"I don't understand," Owen replied, very much confused now.

"It's the end of the world, my dear boy," Hade went on excitedly. "The dead are rising and this little diner is but a tiny piece of a very large puzzle. You, Owen, are an important piece of that puzzle. Alas, your friends were not, so they aren't here to partake in this conversation."

Owen shook his head, confusion still ruling his brain. "So this is all your doing?"

Hade nodded and smiled.

"All over the world?"

"Yes," the huge man answered. "And it's all been done so you and I could have this little conversation."

"I don't believe you," Owen said, so overwhelmed he felt dizzy. "You unleashed an army of the dead people on the world just to talk to me? This is crazy!"

"Crazy is as crazy does," Hade answered with a nod. "But this is more like sticking with the plan. I had to stop you before you got to California. There's just not enough action out west to accomplish what I needed to have accomplished. So, I blew up Vegas to turn you around. Now, that was fun."

"You destroyed Las Vegas because of me?" Owen asked in disbelief.

"Well, yes," Hade replied as if it was the most obvious thing in the world. "Flattered?"

"No," Owen stammered. "No…"

"Well, you should be. Why else would I destroy it? You don't think the National Guard would have been all over Circus Circus so quickly without some serious inside maneuvering, do you? I have pretty high connections in the military, Owen. Getting them to work over the casino was rather easy. Making sure they didn't kill you was a bit more difficult, but we managed."

"So Clint was right," Owen breathed deeply at the sudden revelation. "They were after us."

Hade nodded. "And under specific orders, I might add."

"And Gideon?" he asked, looking back up at Hade expectantly.

Hade smiled. "Gideon is a special case," the man replied. "But yes, Gideon, too."

"So you're telling me that you set all of this up?"

"I did."

"Just to get me here?"

"Correct."

"Prove it, then," Owen barked.

Hade sighed. "Oh, very well, if you insist," he answered. "First of all, how about the lack of vehicles on the highway to Mesquite? I had the highway closed after you were let through the checkpoint, in order to make sure you had a lonely drive and plenty of time to consider that Mesquite was your best destination. Anyone who was ahead of you, we had taken off the road. Anyone coming the other way was of no concern."

"That hardly proves anything."

Hade ignored him. "Then there was the particular timing of the welcoming committee from the hospital that forced you into town. My timetable, Owen," he pointed out, tapping a finger to his forehead. "I knew the only place you could run would be toward town, which would take you directly to the golf course. Once there, I made sure a few of my little pets were given a crack at your friends to whet their appetite. Then, there was the foursome heading to the horror convention in Salt Lake City, a rather ironic twist to the whole night, if I do say so myself."

That startled Owen. "What about them?"

"Isn't it obvious? They were plants, Owen," Hade said, seemingly annoyed again. "Their job was to get you into the Hummer and heading out of town."

"But they weren't like the others," Owen protested. "They weren't zombies!"

"Of course they weren't," Hade agreed. "I have as many associates among the living as I do among the dead. I did think the whole horror convention cover story and the Hollywood make-up was a nice touch, considering the circumstances." He smiled, obviously enjoying himself. "And then there was the coincidence of having only those two vehicles available at the country club. You, of course, were given the Hummer with the digital dashboard disabled, so you couldn't see that you had only a gallon of gas. Just enough to get you near the diner."

Owen shook his head. "No way," he blurted out. "That's all just too perfect."

"Perfect?" Now it was Hade's turn to sound incredulous. "No, it was far from perfect," he scoffed. "There was a bit of luck involved, to be sure, particularly in Vegas."

"All this," Owen said slowly. "All this to get me here..." he trailed off, unable to finish. It was simply too incredible to believe; too crushing to think that everything that had happened, the incredible loss of life—all because of him.

"In my world, Owen," Hade said, smiling at the look of defeat on the young man's face, "the end always justifies the means. Always. I needed you here so you and I could have our little chat. Everything else was just the details of making that happen."

"But all the killing?" Owen stumbled, nearly heartbroken. "I mean, why couldn't you just spare these people and find me?"

"Because you wouldn't believe what I've told you and still have to tell you," Hade answered. "Consider it a demonstration of my abilities."

"But what about the rest of the world?" Owen felt so utterly overwhelmed that he thought he would collapse. "All of this because of me?"

Hade just chuckled. "Owen, my dear lad, you do have a high opinion of yourself," he chided. "Of course, I can accept that and can even relate to it. There's a lot going on out there, to be sure. In the space of one day and night, I'll have completely changed the geopolitical state of the world. No living person on the face of the world today is unaffected by what I have done. But it hasn't all been just to have a chance to talk with you. That's part of it, to be sure, but there are things at stake here beyond your wildest imagination."

"What are you talking about?"

"I'm talking about history, Owen, and how that history is affecting us today. I'm talking about the fulfillment of the promises made at the end of the war in heaven so very long ago. I'm guessing you're familiar with this war?"

"I know the story," Owen responded. "Before the earth was created, there was a war in heaven. God planned to send us to earth for our spirits to inherit bodies, and to test our faithfulness to Him. Christ supported the plan and even offered to be our Savior. Satan opposed it and offered an alternative. He said there was no need for a Savior, he could save all of God's children automatically if He simply took away our ability to choose."

"And God would lose none of His children," Hade agreed, an odd look on his face.

"But it was a foolish plan." Owen found the courage to continue. "We would have been mindless slaves. Mindless slaves can't exercise faith. They can't make choices, overcome adversity, learn from mistakes, or progress. In the end, Christ won and cast Lucifer and his followers out of heaven."

"Accurate, concise, and passionate, but unbearably lacking in eloquence," Hade pointed out. "Still, you got it right. I'm compelled to ask, though—do you realize the real implications of this story?"

Owen shook his head, confused.

"Did you think about the fact that I chose to fight alongside Christ and earned the right to be here just like you? Did you really let it sink in that Christ and Lucifer are brothers, as are you? Staggering!" He threw his hands dramatically in the air for effect. "I often wonder about our choice, Owen. Did we unite with the right plan? Is it too late to implement the alternative? But I'm off on a tangent. Since we are Christ's supporters in that war and are now here, tell me, dear brother, where do you think Lucifer's followers went?"

Owen shrugged. "To hell?" he answered simply.

"So simplistic," Hade sighed. "God cast them out, not down, Owen. He cast them to earth and they've been here ever since."

"What do you mean?"

"I mean that they're spirits, existing among the living since the time of the original transgressor. They torment their brothers and sisters who opposed them in the war. They consider us traitors who robbed them of their chance to become like God. You know them as poltergeists, whispers in the dark, and the feeling of being watched. They're the boogeyman in your closet!" Hade's eyes shone with terrible intensity. "They need no rest. Their mission is singular. And worst of all, they know you, Owen. Oh yes, they've known you longer than you can remember yourself. Taking advantage of that knowledge, they will prey upon your weakness and expose your secrets until you can endure it no longer."

"And now they have bodies," Owen added, thinking about what he had seen that night.

"In a manner of speaking," Hade answered with a non-committal shrug. "As spirits, they're no different than you. Your spirit inhabits that shell you call a body; the same body you were given when you were born. Their spirits have no such shell, but certainly could if given the opportunity. Without a body, though, they're capable of nothing more than making the hair stand up on the back of your neck. And because of that, they hate you, Owen. They hate the living with such a passion that it even gives *me* the willies. For thousands of years, they've endured the torture of seeing what they'll never have." Hade paused, before finishing dramatically. "Until now."

"But why now?" Owen asked, still very much confused. "Why not in the past?"

"Now that's the sixty-four thousand dollar question, isn't it?" Hade said, smiling widely. "Let me set the stage for you, Owen. When a person dies, what happens?"

"Well…a person…ceases to exist, I guess," Owen stammered. "The body shuts down."

"Correct," Hade said. "The brain ceases to function, body fluids coagulate, and decomposition begins immediately. Rigor mortis sets in and the whole thing becomes a biological mess. A spirit could flit in and out of the body—they do that now, by the way—but couldn't make it run. You need fuel to run a car, right Owen?"

Owen only nodded.

"Well, like a car with an empty tank, a dead body is anoxic; it doesn't have the oxygen necessary to function. The heart arrests and the spirit vacates the body. Brain activity ceases, but its capacity remains viable for several minutes. In other words, the battery will still run the stereo, provided someone can turn the key and refill the tank. And as you've witnessed tonight, there are plenty of eager spirits willing to turn that key."

"So you figured out how to create a bunch of zombies out of a whole lot of pissed off spirits?" Owen asked, still stunned at what he was hearing.

"Well, the word 'zombies' is so Hollywood, these days," Hade replied with a smile. "When you watch a movie about zombies, do not the zombies always look desiccated, moldy, barely keeping it together? I mean, you always see them dragging themselves down the middle of the street with body parts falling off them. Take *Dawn of the Dead*, for instance. Brutal movie and not much of a plot, but the special effects were outstanding and the living dead actually looked like terrible monsters."

Owen did not even know how to answer.

Hade continued. "Yet, when you look around at the reality of my beasties, you see no such Hollywood damage or special effects. For the most part, you see bodies that are relatively young, relatively fit, and can move around fairly well. They are capable of wielding weapons. They are even capable of rudimentary thought processes."

"Luke came back," Owen stammered, remembering the horror of the attack on Clint. "He wasn't fit. He couldn't move very well."

"True, but he moved well enough to accomplish the task I wanted completed at that moment," Hade answered slyly.

"And what task was that?"

"To keep you on the move," Hade answered as if he was disappointed that Owen had not come to that realization himself. "Why else?"

Owen stared at him blankly.

Hade shook his head again. "You're not getting it, are you, Owen?" he said. "And here I thought you were smart enough to put it together a little quicker."

"Don't patronize me," Owen snapped. "What does Luke coming back have to do with anything?"

"He got you here, didn't he?" Hade answered with a smirk. "Beyond the fact that it wasn't a pristine body at that moment, didn't change the fact that a spirit was still able to inhabit his body to accomplish the task I needed completed."

"So all you needed was the gas," Owen said, beginning to understand. "That and a recently dead body."

"Very good," Hade smiled and then pointed over the counter. "Be a good lad and reach down there and fetch me a bottle of water out of that fridge." Owen hesitated, but the look Hade gave him had him scrambling to comply. He handed the bottle to the man, who quickly tossed the Monster can behind him and held the clear plastic bottle up.

"Years ago, I took a fledgling company and a somewhat gullible CEO and turned it into one of the most powerful corporations in the world and him into one of the richest men in the world," Hade explained. "And by putting together that conglomerate, I enabled their battalions of scientists, researchers, and think-tankers to solve the biggest problem of reanimation—to come up with the formula that ensured the body could find an alternative fuel source once the spirit had fled the building. And do you want to hear the best part?" Hade asked, but didn't wait for an answer. "The new fuel is actually created by the very waste products the body produces when it dies. It's absolutely genius! The synthesis of that enzyme made this grand scheme of mine possible. Oh, it's not a perfect science, to be sure, and it'll never grace the pages of any of the medical journals of today, but it does the job, even if for just a short while."

Hade smiled at Owen's speechless expression and shook the water bottle, then twisted off the cap and took a long drink, sucking down the entire bottle in just a few seconds.

"It's in the water?" Owen guessed, eyes suddenly widening in surprise.

"Just about everyone's," came the answer, followed by a loud belch. "Getting the formula into water supplies in the United States, Russia, China, and other large countries was extremely easy. A country like Israel, with their blasted Mossad, was a different story. Difficult, but not altogether impossible. But the answer to your question is, yes, most everyone's water supply was affected, including yours." Hade flipped his now empty bottle of water in the air and caught it, spinning it around on his finger like a basketball. "The proof is in the plastic."

"So I have it in me?" Owen asked, blanching.

Hade nodded as he set the empty bottle down. "Just like most everyone else, dear boy. Even now, there are spirits swirling all around you, just waiting for you to kick off so they can have a crack at your body. But don't worry," he soothed. "The chemical compound in the water is harmless to the living and becomes inert in a matter of twenty-four to forty-eight hours after the body is dead. The compound is pretty unstable, after all, just as it was designed to be."

"So what about the people in here?" Owen asked, looking around nervously. "Why aren't they reanimated?"

"You cover all the bases fairly well, but you're not thinking it through to the logical conclusions." Hade stated. "The body runs on electrical impulses from the brain, Owen. Biology 101. Therefore, a body with half its head caved in is hardly going to be worth inhabiting if the brain can't make those legs and arms move correctly. Of course, if the body has serious damage to any of it, or if the body has been dead for some time and decomposition has set in, it's not going to be a viable vehicle for a spirit to possess, either. In the same vein, it isn't worth inhabiting a body that is very old or very young, either, unless it serves a greater purpose. They're looking for high performance models, Owen. This makes them perfect killing machines, expendable to the last, and they require no upkeep. They lurch around a bit because they haven't had time to learn how to control their bodies like we have, but they are still very dangerous. And when all this is over, which should happen very soon, most of these little beasties will already be dead again, their multifold purpose fulfilled. The few that remain? Well, I like you Owen, but that will remain my little secret."

"So this is almost over?" Owen dared to hope.

"Almost," Hade nodded with a knowing grin, "but not quite. I've set a great deal in motion and so much is and has been dependent on timing. That's why I'm here, actually. I've got a job for you to do, and it has to be done soon."

"You killed my friends," Owen snapped, his eyes narrowing

angrily. "What gives you the ridiculous idea that I'd consider helping you?"

"Oh, Owen," Hade sighed. "I thought we were through with that bit already. I told you it really wasn't my fault, but you still seem to want to blame me. I know they were your friends and you've had a long day—trust me, I know—but you've still got some very important choices to make. So you'd best strip away the emotions and try to think straight for a bit longer."

"Easier said than done," Owen replied angrily.

Hade pursed his lips and then nodded. "Touché," he said. "Your point. But that doesn't change the fact that you've still got work to do." He reached into his coat and pulled out a battered looking pocket watch. "We're still on schedule," he said, glancing at the time, "but we really should hurry this up a bit. Let's get back to our discussion, shall we? So tell me, Owen, what do you think about good and evil?"

"What kind of question is that?"

"Work with me here, Owen," Hade said impatiently. "Good and evil—are they mutually exclusive or can they work together?"

Owen felt like he was in a boxing match and he kept getting blindsided by punches he didn't see coming. Still, he felt he could answer this one. "Wickedness never was happiness," he answered. "Evil cannot be good."

"Clever response, lad. The perfect Sunday School answer—and yet, not entirely true. You see, absolutes are never really absolutes. Can I give you an example? Answer me this—is it wrong to kill?"

Owen's mind fumbled with this. Of course it was wrong, he thought, but how much death had he handed out this very night on the golf course and now here in the ruined diner? He'd destroyed creatures that were technically already dead, but if what Hade had said was true, were they truly dead? "I'd say it's wrong to kill," he finally answered, nowhere near certain he was answering correctly.

"You're certain?" Hade smiled.

"I guess."

"I can see from your face that you're anything but certain," Hade countered. "What if a deranged lunatic who'd already killed scores of children and was bent on killing more, broke into your house and was on his way into your young daughter's bedroom. You knew beyond a shadow of a doubt that this was the evil villain responsible for so much death. Would you hesitate to pull the trigger on such a man? Would you flinch at all to protect your young daughter and the children of so many other good parents?"

"If it came down to that, then I'd kill him," Owen said slowly.

"Now you're getting it," Hade said. "You see, there is a good in this world, Owen, and then there is a greater good. And you would be wise to learn that often what the world calls evil must be used at the expense of good to promote the greater good. As I said, the end does justify the means. Always. And so this is where you come in. You're here to protect the greater good. It might require a little evil, as the world would call it, but in the end, it will be worth it. And if you let me, I can help you."

"Help me?" Owen said exasperated. "You're not what I'd call a white knight riding in to save the day."

"An astute observation, my dear boy," the huge man replied with a laugh. "I'm more like the red knight on a red horse. So perhaps I'm not here to save the day for everyone. But you? You can save the day, Owen. You can be the hero of the hour. Is that not your province?"

"Mine?"

"Yes," Hade agreed. "You're the dreamer, aren't you? Don't you aspire to heights unheard of by the mere mortals who surround you? Don't you dream of carving out a name for yourself among the echelon of this world's heroes? Don't you want to be remembered with monuments scattered across the globe as one of the greats? I can help you do that."

Owen was silent, his mouth tightening in defiance. "You can't help me," the young man proclaimed. "Evil has never been in the business of helping good."

Hade merely shrugged. "Once again, you're using a word without knowing what it truly means. What is evil? Now that's a question worthy of Socrates himself." Hade looked down at his watch again and smiled. "We still have time, so let's briefly switch gears for a moment. Answer me this: What is the opposite of heat?"

Owen stood waiting, expecting Hade to continue. Realizing eventually that the man in front of him was seriously waiting for an answer, he finally said, "Cold."

"Wrong. Back to Descartes again, we live in a world where we're taught from an early age that everything has a polar opposite. White and black, light and dark, Republican and Democrat, body and spirit, paper or plastic, life and death, good and evil. We're told that in everything there must be opposition. For good to exist, evil must stand opposed to it. For you to feel joy, you must also feel sorrow. To experience love, you must also hate. Do you not agree?"

"That sounds right," Owen answered carefully, not quite following the big man's logic.

"Wrong again," Hade pressed on. "The belief that in all things there must be opposition is one of the greatest fallacies of Western civilization. Is it really impossible to truly love unless you have truly hated? It seems absurd! Can you not fully enjoy the birth of a child until you have witnessed the death of a parent? Can you not create unless you can destroy as well? It seems almost farcical when put it in those terms."

Owen shook his head in confusion.

"The truth is that, while you've been told all your life that everything has an opposite, in reality, almost nothing does. What is the opposite of gray? What's the opposite of iron, or Algebra, or a poem? What's the opposite of a cardinal or a lion? There are things that aren't those things, but they aren't opposites, either. Heat, in particular, is even more vexing. People think the opposite of heat is cold, but what is cold? Can you make something more cold? Can you add cold to the world? No!" Hade pounded the counter at this, sending cracks spider-webbing across the Formica countertop. "You can only remove heat, Owen. You see, cold is merely the absence of heat. It's not anything in and of its own right. Thus, temperature is simply a sliding scale of how much heat you have."

"So what does that have to do with good and evil?"

Hade smiled. "Evil can be explained in exactly the same way. There is no evil, Owen. There's only a lack of good. The less good you have, the more people think you're evil, when in fact, you aren't evil—you are merely less good. Simply identifying something that is less good as evil, does a great disservice to society and blinds people into making small, safe decisions that eventually result in larger, bad consequences. I'm not beholden to those archaic and inane dualistic concepts about the world. They don't stop me from doing what must be done. I know what I want and I move up and down the goodness scale to make sure I get it. What could be more good than that?"

"Sounds like you have it all figured out, Hade," Owen replied as he considered the historical comparisons of what he was hearing. "You would make Machiavelli proud."

"Machiavelli was a fool and an ignoramus of the worst sort," Hade snapped back. "He showed his weakness by writing, 'It is better to be feared than loved, if you cannot be both.' That one should even care to be loved by people is one of the most ludicrous lines of reasoning of all time. He was completely beholden to the ridiculous notion that the world cares. The world doesn't care, Owen. It never has and it never will. Men want their wives to love them, their families to respect them, their bosses to give them raises, their churches to soothe them, their neighbors to leave them alone, and their governments to kill anyone who threatens to mess up the before-mentioned needs. None of this has anything to do with good and evil. It has to do with getting things done; with victory over your enemies. That is what people want, and those who are too afraid to go after it themselves want to follow someone who will.

"When tonight is over, no one will fault me for killing their loved ones. Instead, they'll love me for making the world over. They'll worship me for all the good that comes from this alleged 'evil'. That's not Machiavelli. I don't have to fawn over the affection of the people or create a public persona for the media. I am Hade and that is enough. That is more than enough."

"So you're telling me none of this is evil?" the young man asked, too confused and exhausted to even argue anymore. His injuries from the fight were throbbing and he wanted this conversation over.

"I'm telling you that all of this is simply a greater lack of good, in order to bring about the greater good. There are cycles to this world, Owen, and we're caught in the midst of one right now—you especially. I know you think I have nothing to offer you, but you're wrong. Dead wrong. I can offer you the world if you merely make the right choice tonight. Not the good choice, not the evil choice, not the prudent, easy, difficult, thoughtful, moral or proper choice. The right choice. But I warn you not to discount the supreme importance of this choice. What you choose now will have lasting reverberations for hundreds of generations in the future."

"What's this choice then?"

"Now we come to the most important part of all of this," Hade answered, looking hard at the young man. "Simply put, I seek an alliance, even if it's just a temporary one. I can give you everything you want, and all you need to do is help me with one little thorn in my side."

"How do you even know what I want?"

"For starters," Hade said more than a little smugly, "I know you want Alexis."

Owen went cold again. The fact that this stranger was mentioning Alexis should have thrown him completely off-guard, but something told him there was probably precious little that Hade did not know "Okay, I'll bite. What do you know about her?" he stammered after a long pause.

"I know that for the moment, she's alive and well in Salt Lake City. She's with friends, even an acquaintance of mine, and she's done quite well for herself up until now. But mortal danger still hangs over her head, and it comes from a source she does not even remotely suspect. And it will kill her, Owen. Of that, there is no doubt."

"Is this more of your doing?" Owen seethed, feeling himself tense.

"No, Owen," Hade replied. "The danger threatening Alexis right now is not of my doing. She has survived several attacks already and, with those who protect her, she will survive this night. But it's tomorrow that should concern you. If you help me, I can help you rescue her. You can save the day and be her knight in shining armor. You can ride off into the sunset with her and live happily ever after."

"I don't believe you."

"Owen, just because I follow a darker path, doesn't mean I can't still have a soft spot for true love," Hade almost pleaded with the young man. "It would thrill me if I could remove a problem and help a young lad reunite with his tender sweetheart in the same stroke. Power is emotion, my young friend, not the lack of it, and I feed on the entire spectrum."

"How do you know she's all right?" The question came out too quickly and Hade preyed upon it.

"I have been keeping an eye on her, just like I've been doing with you, and you'll have to trust me when I say she is fine at the moment. I have no reason to lie to you. Alexis has certainly had her problems, much as you've had, and like you, she's also seen her friends killed. But she's keeping it together. I had half expected her to have a nervous breakdown by this point, but she's a trooper. I can see why you care for her so much. She's one in a million. Well, one in seven billion, actually," Hade finished with a soft laugh.

"You would help me find her?" Owen asked carefully.

"As I mentioned, all is fair in love and war," came the reply. "I would deliver her to you on a plate, if I could. The bigger question is, will you do what is needed to reclaim your bonny lass?"

Owen never hesitated. "Tell me what you want."

"Well, let's look at the big picture for a moment," Hade answered. "We've determined you want Alexis and I can't say I blame you there, lad. I'm also pretty sure you want revenge for your losses tonight."

"True," Owen answered, his voice bitter. "But according to your logic, that's not likely to happen. After all, their deaths are not directly your fault, right? And the man who actually killed my friends is long gone and I have no idea where he went. That ship has sailed, Hade."

"Maybe. Maybe not. Let me shift gears one more time and let's head off to the theoretical world. Let us suppose, theoretically, that I know who is behind their killing. Would that be of interest to you?"

"You know who it was?"

Hade ignored him. "Let's suppose that this man is dangerous to me because he is not one of my followers and would, in fact, supplant me if given the chance. Furthermore, he is dangerous to you because he cares greatly about ensuring your demise and taking your leading lady for his very own."

"Who?" Owen demanded.

"Let us also say that this man is responsible for the death of his own family, that he has ties to organized crime, and that if given the chance, he could do more damage to this world than I could ever hope to," Hade explained. "While I simply want to rearrange the world for my benefit, this hypothetical man is bent on destroying it."

"So why not kill him yourself?" Owen fumed, not at all happy at the big man's evasiveness.

"What if I said I had tried, but he has proven difficult for me to reach? What if I said that in helping me, I could deliver both the man who shot your friends and the one who paid him to do so, all in one neat little package? And in doing what I ask, you could ensure the safe return of your true love?" Hade leaned back and smiled, having played his cards perfectly.

"Theoretically, I would turn you down," Owen answered after a few tense moments. "I'm not some assassin."

"Ah, but you are wrong on both counts, my dear boy," Hade answered. "First, none of this is theoretical. Of course, I suppose you suspected that anyway. Second, you could easily be an assassin if it served the greater good. We've already established that. So, if I made you this very real offer, you wouldn't take me up on it? After you've witnessed so much death? After you've meted out so much death yourself? In all the carnage that has already happened, would removing one very bad man really go against your own morality code?"

Owen straightened his back and stood as tall as he could. This man, with his twisted logic, could do much to confuse him. But here, on this ground, Owen was firm. "I will not be your assassin, Hade. I will find him on my own and take care of what I need to do without your help. Now if you have nothing more for me, I need to get back on the road." At that, Owen moved around the counter, intending to pick his way through the wreckage of the diner and leave through the shattered window. He had had enough of this evil man trying to convince him to do something he would never do. It felt too wrong to be the right path to choose. He had to get to Alexis and he could see that Hade was not going to help him unless he agreed to the big man's nefarious plan. That was not something he thought he could do.

His face expressionless, Hade picked up the Desert Eagle from the counter and held it up, staring at the shining metal. Owen caught the unmistakable intentions of the action and stopped cold. "You presume much, my young friend," Hade said matter-of-factly. "Do you really think that if you turn me down, I will let you simply walk out of this diner alive? I had honestly hoped it would not have to come down to threats, but there it is on the table, Owen. So let's not dwell on it, all right? I think we can still come to an agreement."

Owen watched as Hade leveled the huge handgun at his chest. One trigger pull and he would be as dead as everyone else in the diner. With the cold realization that he did not have any choice, he righted an overturned chair, then sat down and looked at Hade with eyes that blazed with hatred.

"Thank you for staying, Owen," Hade said with a smile as he laid the weapon back on the counter in front of him again. "It touches me deeply. Really. Now to be honest with you, I don't blame you for wanting to turn me down flat and leave at this point. I think what we've had so far is a failure to communicate properly and, I have to admit, that problem lies with me. You see, Owen, I have only given you some of the information you need to help you make your decision.

Suppose I told you the name of this person I wanted you to eliminate. Would that help?"

"I'm not going to kill anyone for you," Owen stated flatly. "So forget it. You can do what you want with me, but I won't be your assassin."

"Really?" Hade remarked smugly. "What if I was to tell you that the man behind the killing of your friends was none other than Petr Zhugravinsky."

There was another long pause before Owen finally whispered in shock, "What did you say?" Owen's mind filled instantly with images of the Russian he had met once and who he had grave concerns about regarding Alexis. His mind tried to fill in what Hade had said earlier about this person and he suddenly realized that his worst fears about Petr were now confirmed.

"It does appear that I've piqued your interest, Owen," Hade said with a perfectly wicked smile. "And since I have, let me fill you in on a couple more details. He's in Salt Lake City right now. He thinks you're finished, so fears nothing from you. He has killed Gideon's father, David. And even now, he plots how to win the hand of your fair Alexis."

"No," Owen whispered, shell-shocked.

"Actually, the correct word is 'yes,' Owen," Hade replied. "Trust me when I tell you there is little Petr won't do. He'll stop at nothing to get Alexis and, with you out of the way, there'll be nothing to stop him. And I dare say, if she rebuffs him, he'll outright force her to join him if he doesn't just kill her. Petr is not a man who accepts no for an answer, if you know what I mean. He is a Zhugravinsky and they are a family who gets exactly what they want, whenever they want it. Now, are you still certain we cannot come to an agreement?"

Owen sat there, his head spinning. The events of the night still weighed heavily on him, the stench of death heavy in his head; Hade's declaration of everything that had happened; and now this. Owen put his head in his hands, concentrating every ounce of his mental capacity to try and make sense of the situation. He ran through every option, every choice. Was this the only way? If he said yes, he knew he could do it to save Alexis, but at what price? If he said no, he had little doubt that Hade would simply mow him down. And if he let Hade kill him, there would be no one to save Alexis.

But in the confusion, a spark of logic showed itself and Owen grasped at it, hoping it might be the way out he so desperately sought. "Why can't you kill him yourself?" Owen finally asked, looking Hade up and down. Hade was certainly a capable killer and should have no problems with Petr, despite the Mafia connection. "Why do you need me?"

The huge man looked at Owen as if he had been expecting that question all along. "Petr knows me, so he would expect me to come after him and will be ready for it. You? He thinks you are finished. He would never suspect you, and that gives you the advantage of surprise."

Owen shook his head in confusion and bitter frustration. "I don't like being trapped into doing something like this," he lamented. "But you have me, and it seems as if I don't have much of a choice in the matter, do I?"

"Well, you do," Hade countered and placed his hand lightly back on the Eagle. "But the repercussions of not accepting my proposal are all profoundly negative."

"I've never liked Petr, that's no secret," Owen said, ignoring the threat. "If he's half the things you say he is, then I want him nowhere near Alexis. If he really killed Gideon's father, after all he'd been through, then I'd say he deserves death. I just want to know why it has to be me? You've gone through a lot of trouble to get me here. How can I be the one to do this and no one else can?"

"Ah, in your last few words you've announced your ignorance of the full ramifications of this series of events," the big man replied. "You're certainly not the only one who could do this; you are simply the most logical one at this point. However, if you fail, I will swiftly go to Plan B. So don't flatter yourself into thinking that you're utterly necessary to the greater good. In the end, while you are the best choice for this at the moment, whether it's you or someone else who pulls the trigger, the only thing that matters to me is the end result."

Owen started to object, but Hade raised a hand to silence him and continued. "But you, my dear boy, do not have the luxury that I do. You could refuse me outright, but the knowledge that you were afraid to save your loved one would be too much to bear. And in the unlikely event that I would even allow you to live after refusing me, the mere thought of your failure would utterly destroy you." Hade paused and offered Owen a condescending smile. "You already know this to be true, Owen. So you've already accepted in your mind that you will do as I ask. In the end, you can be of some use to me and I can be of great use to you."

"How do I know what you're telling me is true?" Owen challenged, still looking for an out, but knowing he had indeed already made his decision.

"You simply accept that it's true," Hade answered. "I have no reason to lie to you, Owen. Search your immediate past. Who else knew you were going to Vegas? I mean, who else besides a homicidal maniac who would want you dead so he could take your girl?"

Owen thought for a second. "No one," he answered softly.

"And who else has access to the kind of resources to make what has happened occur?"

"No one."

"And who else could have set in motion the events that gave my associate that?" Hade asked, pointing toward the dead body of Clint.

Owen followed the direction the man was pointing and froze. He saw it immediately, a blood-spattered photograph lying next to his dead friend's bloody body. He did not even need to pick it up to know what it was. His stomach churned as he saw the photograph of him and his three road companions. The photograph taken by the killer himself at the charity basketball game. "What's this?" he asked, his voice drained.

"A token perhaps?" Hade answered with a shrug. "Perhaps carelessly dropped by someone playing both sides of the game. You see, my truck driving associate, Cole Banyon, was to bring his truckload of beasties to the diner and let them attack. That was the extent of his orders, as I certainly didn't want him showing himself to you or your friends and jeopardizing what I had put into place. The fact that he had the photograph—something I did not supply him with—and the fact that he chose to crash through the diner and enter the fray of his own volition and kill your two friends, tells me that he is taking orders from someone else. That someone else is Petr." He paused to watch Owen carefully, before finishing. "Cole was an associate of Petr's long before he was an associate of mine, Owen. There can be no other explanation."

"He had the picture because he was there," Owen said hollowly. "He was at the game. He took the picture."

"More proof that he was working for another," Hade said with a shrug. "Those orders never came from me."

"But why?" Owen finally asked in desperation. "What did I ever do to him? Would Petr really have me killed because of Alexis?"

"He recently had his entire family killed," Hade replied nonchalantly. "And what are you to him? It seems there is always a girl involved in these things, and jealousy has bred murder more times than you'll ever know. As far as Petr is concerned now, you're either dead or, if not, there's at least no way he can be implicated. He's covered all his bases. There's no way for Alexis to tie him to this or to even think he's involved. As far as she knows, you will simply be one of the many who disappeared in the chaos. So, she's as good as his."

As Owen sat in a maelstrom of thoughts, one kept nagging at him and he latched onto it. Looking up at Hade, he set his jaw with determination. "So, if Petr wanted to get rid of me, why did his goon kill my friends and not me? Why didn't he shoot me as well?"

"For someone who is still alive, you sure are quizzical as to why no one has put an end to your life," Hade replied with a sigh. "While I can't answer that question with one hundred percent certainty, it might be because when I gave Cole his original orders, they were to ensure that he remained hidden and that you survived. Had he blatantly disobeyed my orders and killed you outright, even Petr could not protect him from my retribution. So his fear of me likely ensured your survival tonight. Like I said earlier, I'm your best friend."

"My best friend?" Owen spit out. "My best friends are dead, largely because of you, Hade. None of this would have happened without your involvement."

"You're confusing a few things here, lad, so let me set the record straight. I did not know for certain that your friends would die tonight. Sure, I thought it was a very real possibility, but what was to stop one of them from turning the tables and killing their would-be killer? What was to stop them from escaping the attack? You would be amazed how many would-be assassins never see their plans come to fruition."

"What would have happened if Franz Ferdinand's driver had followed the correct parade route?" Hade went on. "The world would never have heard of Gustov Ivoan, and perhaps World War I would never have happened. What if the man who rushed at Andrew Jackson

223

and fired two guns at him point blank but missed with both, had actually hit his target? What if John Wilkes Boothe had not been able to get into the theatre where Lincoln was seated? What if the man on the grassy knoll had his gun jam? Kennedy's murder was indeed a conspiracy, Owen, just as a side note. Trust me on that one, since I was there." Hade winked knowingly, before finishing. "The point is, the list of would-be assassins is longer then we will ever know. So, did I know there was the possibility that Petr would be involved in this? Yes. Did I worry about it much? No. Well, not about your friends anyway."

"You're a real stand-up guy, Hade," Owen said sarcastically.

"The bottom line is simple, Owen," Hade said, sounding irritated now. "Your friends are dead and you're alive. Sorry for that, but let's quit dwelling on it and move on, shall we? It's in the past and cannot be undone. Now, my plans, at least, have been completed successfully because here we're having our little chat at the Tumbleweed. Cole, on the other hand? Well, I can only assume that he had made a promise to Petr, and you don't break a promise to the Zhugravinsky family without paying the consequences. Of course, you don't turn down a job from Hade without there being consequences, either."

"So assuming that I buy all this, do you mean to kill me in the end?"

"I haven't decided yet, to be honest," Hade replied. "As I've said earlier, your fate is in your hands. Make the right decision and you very well could live to see another day."

"And what of your associate?"

"Well, I'm pretty sure Cole will die, either by my hand or Petr's or even yours, if the situation is right. But we're straying from the point again. He isn't the threat here anymore. Petr is. Petr hired Cole to kill you and your friends, and you're only alive because of me. Petr killed his family and he killed David Sumbawanga. He most likely thinks you're dead. Do you understand that? He already thinks he's free of you, Owen. This is the perfect opportunity for you to go in, find him, and kill him. This is your chance to avenge so many wrongs. This is your chance to do real good in the world. What does it matter who gave you the chance or what they gained from it? You have an opportunity to live happily ever after. And as you look into your grandchildren's eyes many years from now, you can decide then if you made the right choice or not. So what'll it be?"

Owen was silent for the longest time, wrestling with the implications. Hade was right. Petr had to be stopped. He was also right when he said that Owen could be the one to end his evil. But killing a bunch of zombies that were trying to kill you was one thing. Premeditating the murder of another human being, even one as evil as Petr, was quite another, and Owen's sense of right and wrong was a barrier that was extremely difficult for him to cross. In the end, the only choice he could make was the one that he finally did. Bowing his head, he almost silently said, "Yes."

"Good," Hade replied, all business. Reaching into his trench coat, he withdrew a smart phone. "Take this phone and go north," he stated, tossing the phone to Owen, who caught it with numb hands. "Take my truck. It's parked out behind the semi—the red Ford Ranger. The keys are in it. The problems that have been plaguing the world have made cell connections poor at best. But when you get close enough to Salt Lake City, you should be able to reach Alexis. And leave the phone on, Owen," he continued. "I'll call you when I know where Petr is. Once you've done what I request, this will all be over and you'll never have to see me again." Hade stood up and walked past Owen. As he walked by one zombie lying in his path, he leaned down and picked up his machete and slid it, bloodied and all, back into his boot. He then continued through the diner and, as he reached the shattered window, he paused and turned around. "One more thing, Owen," he added. "Before all else, be armed. There's a baseball bat in the back of the truck."

"A bat?" Owen asked slowly.

"Certainly," replied Hade with a smile. "You and I both know that you're not a gun person. I mean, really, what do you have with a gun? A quick squeeze of the trigger and your opponent is no more. No satisfaction of besting your opponent; just an empty spot and the lingering question—did the best man truly win? In a war where a battle is decided by killing more of the enemy than they can kill, guns are one thing. But this? This war between you and Petr should be settled without guns. This is as much about passion as it is about righting the wrongs. So what you need here is that good old *mano a mano*, man-to-man interaction. And don't worry, Owen. I have faith in you."

With that, Hade turned and stepped through the shattered window and disappeared into the darkness, leaving Owen alone.

The young man sighed deeply and looked around at the diner one final time, realizing the incredible magnitude of the horror that surrounded him. This was not a movie. It was not a video game. He found himself choking back the sobs as he surveyed the unbelievable carnage. Bodies lie strewn everywhere, beaten and torn savagely, some barely even recognizable as human. Clint and Chad lay where they had been killed, their blood slicking the floor and mixing with the blood of the others. He looked away quickly from their bodies, unable to process all the implications of what their lifeless forms meant.

They had come so far, had tried so hard to survive, and in just a moment they were both dead. Out of the recess of the dizzying memories, the thoughts swirled madly within his head. What was he to do now? Was he really going to do what Hade had requested? What about Alexis? Was Hade telling the truth? Was she waiting somewhere for him to save her?

Alexis. The name surged into his mind like a tsunami and overwhelmed his questions, putting them to rest once and for all. He had to get to Alexis. He had to save her. If it was the last thing he did, he had to make sure that she would survive. He would kill Petr and then rescue Alexis. He did not have much hope, but at least he had a direction. He would not forget his friends, but he had to save Alexis first. He steeled himself for what was to come, wiped some of the tears and blood off his face, and then climbed out of the building and walked to the truck.

Opening the door, he found himself suddenly thinking about Gideon and realized with cold clarity that he really did have a chance to further the greater good by getting rid of David Sumbawanga's killer. He got in and turned the ignition. Smiling grimly at the full gas gauge, he shifted it into gear and gunned it, spraying gravel as the truck shot toward the highway.

"I'm coming, Alexis," he said aloud, slamming the gas pedal to the floor.

CHAPTER 14

Salt Lake City, Utah: Alexis felt like she'd only been asleep for a few minutes when Father Dalacourt shook her awake. "Alexis," he whispered urgently. "Alexis, wake up."

"What's happening?" she asked, her voice slurred with exhaustion.

"There are people outside."

"People?" Alexis shot back, "Or more of those things?"

"I don't know. People, I think!" Dalacourt said as he helped her to her feet. "Come on." Together, they quickly ascended the stairs and hurried into the living room. McCain was standing next to the window, peering around the curtain. John and Stacia flanked the front door, backs to the wall. As Alexis and Dalacourt stepped into the room, John quickly motioned for them to stop, keep low, and stay quiet. They froze.

McCain spoke quietly, "I'm sure now, John. Two people; alive and moving from house-to-house. There are creatures out there, too. Looks like they might be looking for them."

"Do we help them?" Stacia whispered back.

"I don't know yet," her father replied. "They're checking the doors as they go. At least they're smart enough not to break a window and give themselves away."

"How close?" John asked.

"Still a couple houses down. Their pursuers are wandering and don't appear to be in any hurry." He paused, his face grim. "I still don't know how these things have tracked us so well."

"Will they make it here?"

"If they're careful," McCain replied.

"Should we signal them?" Alexis whispered from her position near the back of the living room.

"No," McCain answered, "too easy to give ourselves away."

"But they could be killed." Alexis said with conviction. She was tired of people dying. She was even more tired of being helpless to do anything about it.

The detective looked at her, a pained look on his face. "Look, I know how you're feeling," he said softly. "We'll take them in. They just have to get here."

It was quiet after that, only McCain speaking as he updated their position as they moved toward them. While it seemed an eternity waiting, it was really only five or six minutes before McCain motioned to Stacia. "Be ready to open the door and haul them in," he whispered urgently and then paused for several seconds before giving the command. "Now!"

The younger McCain quickly opened the door, her hands reaching out. She grasped the arm of the first one, dragging a young lady inside the door and immediately clamping a hand across her mouth to keep her from screaming, while John stepped out and quickly pulled the young man inside. John shoved the man behind him and quickly shut the door.

It had been open less than three seconds.

Stacia was face-to-face with the woman almost immediately. "Shhh!" she hushed, her hand still silencing the woman, who appeared completely terrified. "We're friends. We're here to help. Do you understand?"

The woman's eyes were wide and frightened, but logic kicked in and she nodded, though it did little to quell the wild look of fright on her face.

With a glance that said "stay silent," Stacia removed her hand.

"Father," McCain ordered quietly, "You and Alexis get them downstairs now."

Without a word, Dalacourt moved to the man and threw an arm around his shoulders, quickly guiding him out of the living room and toward the basement stairs, murmuring softly to him as they went. Alexis took her own place beside his companion and they followed. "You're safe now. You'll be all right," she whispered to the frightened woman.

The woman nodded rapidly and stumbled down the stairs beside Alexis, her breathing coming in rapid gasps. She was nearly frantic. Once in the basement, she buried her face against Alexis' chest and began to sob quietly. Her companion appeared to be faring much better and he moved immediately to her, gently taking her from Alexis' grasp and embracing her himself.

"Thanks," he whispered, a grateful look on his face. "I don't know how much longer we could have stayed away from those things."

"No thanks are necessary," the priest replied warmly. "I'm Father Michael Dalacourt. This young lady is Alexis Kennedy."

"Stephen," the man replied and then kissed his still sobbing companion on the top of her head. "This is my wife, Brandi."

"How did you end up here?" Dalacourt asked.

"We actually live nearby, seven or eight blocks away," Stephen replied. "Those things got into our neighbor's house and when we tried to help, they came after us. We've been running and hiding for hours now, trying to find someplace to hole up in until we can go back home."

"Maybe you should just stay with us," the priest offered. "As soon as it's light, we'll be heading out of town."

"Where?" Stephen asked, somewhat incredulously.

"Somewhere safer than this."

Stephen shook his head and then shared a quick look with his wife. "Nowhere out in the open is safe," he countered. "Best bet is to lay low and wait it out. As soon as we get the chance, we're going back to our place."

"Why?"

"Because I've got a lot more firepower back there," the man answered grimly, reaching behind his back and pulling a handgun from his waistband. It had been hidden under his shirt. "I almost wish we hadn't tried to help our neighbors," he added unhappily, looking at the weapon. "If we hadn't, we'd still be safe in our own home."

"Helping was the charitable thing to do, Stephen," the priest countered.

"I can respect your faith, Father," he said quietly, "but I don't share it. Especially not today. Not after what we've seen."

"I understand," Dalacourt said gently. "This has been a test of faith for everyone. But keep in mind that someone led you here."

The man looked thoughtful. "Maybe," he finally said.

"I'm going upstairs to check on things," Dalacourt added. "Will you be okay down here with Alexis?"

They both nodded and the priest hurried silently up the stairs.

"I realize what the priest is saying, but not everyone believes in God," Stephen said quietly after a few moments.

"And not everyone doesn't," Alexis added.

"I don't know," he said. "It's just hard to associate a zombie apocalypse with God. It makes more sense that this is all a biological catastrophe or something."

Alexis simply nodded, allowing the man his space.

"That's enough, Stephen," Brandi spoke up. Her voice was still shaky and her eyes were haunted, but she had composed herself remarkably well considering what she had been through. Looking at Alexis, she continued. "Have you found anyone else around? I mean anyone alive?"

Alexis shook her head sadly, her thoughts going back to Dakota, to the shelter, to everyone that had already been killed. "No," she answered sadly. "But for now, we're safe here."

"But for how long?" Stephen put in.

Brandi looked at her husband. "Maybe we should go then," she pleaded. "There have to be more people somewhere."

"Yeah, baby," he answered, then moved to embrace his wife again, comforting her. "We'll get out of here soon."

Alexis didn't know how to react, so she just remained quiet. She tried to imagine how it would feel to have Owen there, comforting her, and it almost brought her to tears. She longed for any word from him, any sign that would tell her he was alive and coming for her. As silence fell over the house and the minutes passed by, painfully slow, Alexis thought the stillness would test her nerves to their breaking point. She felt like she was just about to lose herself when she heard a hushed whisper from the top of the stairs. "Not a sound!" Dalacourt whispered down to them as loudly as he dared. At that moment, heavy footsteps sounded from somewhere outside, followed by a clumsy scratching on the front door. The doorknob rattled and Brandi sucked in a terrified breath and buried her face against her husband's shoulder.

Another moment of silence passed, followed by several loud thuds as someone or something hammered on the front door. They all held their breath.

Silence again.

It stretched.

Still nothing.

And then Alexis' cell phone began to ring, its musical tone knifing through the silence. There were collective gasps of dismay from both upstairs and down as Alexis grabbed for it, desperate to turn it off. Then she saw the name on the screen.

It was Owen.

"Owen!" she somehow managed to exclaim quietly.

"Shhh!" Brandi whispered urgently, her eyes wide with terror.

"Alexis, is that you?" Owen's voice sounded from the phone.

"Owen! Where are you?" Alexis pleaded, her voice quivering.

"I'm on I-15 North," Owen said. "Are you okay?"

"No," she replied, moving further back into the basement, hoping her voice wouldn't be heard by the things that hunted them.

"Where are you?"

"Somewhere near Millcreek, I think," she whispered. "Owen, you have to help us."

"I'm coming," he said quickly. "I'll be there as soon as I can."

"Owen, everyone's dead," she went on, fighting back the tears now.

"I know, Alexis," he answered somberly. "Clint, Luke, Chad…they're all dead, too. But I know who's behind it." The line crackled in and out for several seconds before Owen's voice came through again. "I'm going to end this, Alexis."

"Owen, what are you talking about?"

There was movement from upstairs and some hushed whispers. Something was happening.

"It's Petr," Owen said. "Petr killed Clint and Chad."

"Petr?" Alexis was dumbfounded, his statement completely throwing her into confusion.

"And I won't let him hurt you," he went on. The line burst into more static, but the connection held.

"Owen, stop," Alexis pleaded.

"I'm sorry, Alexis," he replied. "But this needs to be done. He killed my friends. I know where he's at and I'm going to do what needs to be done. I won't let him hurt you, too. As soon as this is taken care of, I'll come for you."

Alexis knew what his intentions were. "Owen," she said, her voice dropping. "You're not a killer. Don't do this. I need you here."

"Alexis, listen to me," Owen's voice came in strong again. "You have to trust me. This thing with Petr? It goes deep. He murdered Gideon's father, too."

Alexis felt her emotions well up. "No," she whispered.

"Yes," Owen countered. "I told you he was bad news, Alexis."

"Owen, don't do this," Alexis implored him, almost in shock now.

"I love you, Alexis."

"Oh, Owen. Don't..."

The call ended abruptly in a burst of static just as McCain's voice shouted from upstairs. "They made us!"

Stephen moved to the base of the stairs and looked up. Brandi pressed up against him in dread. From upstairs, they could hear McCain issuing directions. "Stacia, get everyone into the garage and into the car. We're going to have to make a run for it."

There was pounding from upstairs and Stephen whirled around and came face-to-face with Alexis. His features were grim, but there was no anger. He thrust his gun into her hand. "Here, take this," he whispered.

She looked at him in shock.

"I've got another," he continued, lifting up his shirt where she could see the butt of another handgun, this one in a concealed carry holster. "Look," he went on quickly. "If your faith won't stop a monster, a .45 slug will. Just take it."

Not wanting to argue, she accepted the weapon, one she recognized as a sub-compact Colt Defender, and carefully tucked it into her pants. If needed, she would have no problem using it, as her father had one just like it and the two of them had gone to the shooting range numerous times to fire it.

John came pounding down the stairs. "They're coming," he said urgently. "We must leave now!"

Stephen faced him and shook his head. "We're not going," he said, reaching out and pulling Brandi close.

"If they catch you…" John began, but Stephen waved him off.

"I like our chances better on foot," he said quickly. "Dawn is nearly here. We're going back home where we can defend ourselves."

John turned to Alexis, seeing the look of desperate worry on her face. He reached out and laid a hand on her shoulder. "What is it, Alexis?" he asked gravely.

"It's Owen," she replied, her eyes meeting his. "He's alive. But he's going after Petr."

"Petr?"

"He's a Russian student here in the States. I have him in a couple of my classes," she quickly explained. "Owen claims Petr killed his friends and is coming after me now. He's going after him first."

"How?" John's voice was urgent.

The young woman shook her head. "I don't know," she answered. "The call cut out."

"This is too early," John said cryptically, more to himself than anyone else. "I thought we had more time." He straightened quickly and looked at the others. "Come! We must leave now!"

"Stephen, we have to go!" Brandi's eyes were wild. She had nearly lost control.

The man looked at John. "When you bust out of here, they're going to chase after you," he said with certainty. "We'll circle back the other way and head home. They'll never even know we were here."

There was a loud bang against the front door, followed by the sound of glass breaking.

"Now!" McCain shouted, followed by a blast from his shotgun. Two more shots sounded in quick succession and he shouted again. "Get a move on!" he yelled.

They all rushed up the stairs, John and Alexis immediately headed through the doorway and into the garage where Stacia and Dalacourt were already in the SUV, while Stephen pulled his wife up the stairs to the next floor.

McCain fired one more shot through the shattered living room window, taking down another of the lumbering undead, then turned and hurried into the garage. A moment later, the SUV roared to life and blasted through the garage door, leaving a trail of debris and crushed bodies in its wake.

CHAPTER 15

Salt Lake City, Utah: Petr awoke to a throbbing pain in the back of his head. He opened his eyes and quickly shut them as light painfully attacked his senses. But this was different from the light that had blinded him the night before as he had sat, tied up and beaten. This was the light of the morning, pale and filtered as it was.

He opened his eyes again, this time slowly to soften the harshness of it, and after a few moments his vision had adjusted. The morning sun was dingy and dark, clouded by smoke, and the air smelled of burning wood, plastic, and worse. The sirens that had sounded throughout the night were now silent. Instead, the morning was punctuated by heavy gunfire and the periodic booming of big guns, making it obvious the military was still heavily involved in the insurrection. He wondered who was winning.

Petr stood up slowly and walked hesitantly over to the sofa where David lay dead, the man's aged hands crossed peacefully over his chest. His body was covered in blood, both from the wound to his back and the single shot Petr had fired into his heart. It was so much less than David deserved, to be left behind like this, but there was nothing else to be done.

Petr knelt beside him and placed his right hand on David's hands. He bowed his head in reverence. "I failed you, David," he began slowly, tears welling in his eyes. "I failed everyone. And I am so sorry." He paused a long while before continuing. "But I swear I won't fail you again," he said, his voice somewhat stronger. "I'll find your daughter in Tanzania and protect her. I swear it."

He stood up and looked down a final time. "You were a great man, Mr. Sumbawanga," he finished. "And you will be greatly missed."

He began walking toward the door when a chime sounded from

the nearby table. He walked over and saw the iPad sitting on the table next to the Glock. He looked at the handgun for a moment, considering what it had been used for. Then, ignoring it, he picked up the tablet. An image flashed on the screen, a single touch button with a video playback arrow. He tapped it and was not at all surprised at what he saw. It was Hade sitting amid the burned out and broken wreckage of what appeared to have once been a small diner, a large truck having blasted through the wall behind him.

"Wakey, wakey, Petr," came the overly cheerful salutation. "Privyet! I wanted to make sure you were doing well and that there were no ill effects from the sedative I gave you last night. If you're watching this, a message has already been sent to my phone, letting me know you survived. It also lets the driver of the car know you'll be down shortly. I wouldn't linger after finishing this, as you really don't want to miss your ride.

"Before you leave," Hade continued, "I want to let you know how badly I feel about what happened last night between you and David. But I believe fully that those who would have nothing to do with thorns must never attempt to gather flowers. If we're to take the world, there will be moments like these that we must learn to put behind us. You might not agree with me, and you certainly don't have to like it, but I think you learned some valuable lessons last night about who you were and what you are capable of. These are the times, Petr, when we're not afforded the luxury of second-guessing our decisions. We must act. Quickly. Decisively. As you did last night."

Hade's words did nothing to make him feel any better.

"There is one other thing, Petr," Hade said, changing gears. "As you prepare to proceed to your destination, you need to know there's a very good chance Owen DiConte will be there when you arrive. It's important to me that you do not harm him. If he's there, you're to escort him to the plateau and await Alexis. I know you have questions, but it will all make sense in time."

"Beyond that, I wish you the best of luck, Petr, in attaining all that you desire today. Don't forget who you are. Listen to your instincts, follow through with what you know, and you'll have everything you've ever dreamed of. Dosvidaniya, padruga," Hade said as the video message came to an end.

Petr tossed the tablet back to the table and shook his head angrily. The message, as with everything associated with Hade, was infuriatingly difficult to understand. He had no idea why Owen would be there and why he was so important to Hade's plans. He had no real problems with Owen other than the perceived competition for Alexis, but for him, that was not worth getting upset about. He would win that game any time it was played.

Confused and annoyed, Petr headed for the stairwell, pausing only to pick up David's mango tree walking stick. The wood was dark and Petr could see the bloody outline of a handprint on the smooth surface—David's handprint, David's blood. Hade had apologized for forcing Petr to kill his friend, but that didn't remove the hurt or ease the desire for vengeance. He silently swore to himself that somehow he would see David's blood avenged. He was unsure how or when it would happen, but he knew at some point he would make Hade hurt for what had happened to this man.

Taking a deep breath, he walked toward the doorway and then slowly down the stairs and into the Sky Bar. He wasn't at all surprised to find the bodies of Juke, Miguel, and Cappy scattered about the bar, their eyes open and staring, expressions of terror frozen on their dead faces. Their deaths had been particularly brutal. All three had had their throats ripped out as if an enraged animal had fallen upon them. Unsure if it was Hade or his undead army that were responsible, he was pleased to see they hadn't survived. It would save him the time of hunting them down later and killing them himself.

He continued through the bar and found the elevator, but it was still not operational. He proceeded to the stairs and descended the thirteen flights, reaching the bottom floor a short time later. The ground floor was a killing field. No one moved. No one was alive. Bodies were torn and broken, some of them hardly recognizable as human. The whole place reeked of death. Petr picked his way through the lobby, taking care to avoid bodies and pools of blood. He paused for a moment to listen and could still hear muffled gunfire, but his earlier question as to who was winning seemed to have been answered. Here at the Red Lion, it was clear who was in charge.

He pushed open the side door and stepped out into the parking lot. As promised, a car was indeed waiting for him, a black Lexus with heavily tinted windows. Through the windshield, he could barely make out the vague outline of a driver in the front seat. He thought briefly of Rene, whose body would be somewhere nearby, but he quickly buried his feelings and walked to the car. Without a word, he got into the backseat and the car pulled away, taking him toward whatever fate had been decreed for him. As he rode in silence, he realized that no matter what else happened today, one thing was guaranteed. His life would never be the same again.

CHAPTER 16

Park City, Utah: Windy Covington turned her Toyota onto the long gravel road and proceeded cautiously, her eyes scanning the fields on either side. The sky was dark, nearly black, as the storm closed in on the valley, and her windshield was spattered with intermittent raindrops. The drive had been relatively uneventful despite what she had been hearing on the few radio stations still broadcasting. The "conflict"—as some of the newscasters were calling it—was centered in major cities all over the world, one of which was Salt Lake City. The drive through the country had taken her through deserted rural areas between Park City and Salt Lake City, and she had seen absolutely no one. If people were around, they were barricaded in their homes, which was just as well. She wanted to find Owen and had no wish to deal with anyone else, be they living or the living dead.

She continued down the road, still alert for signs of danger. Several minutes later, her GPS announced she had arrived at her destination. She saw the barn right where Hade had said it would be, situated off of a short dirt lane. Rotting bales of hay were stacked up against two sides of the dilapidated, paint-peeled building, almost as if they were bracing the sagging wooden walls. She pulled her car into the lane and next to the barn. After a short while to calm herself, she got out. The air was still and smelled of smoke from the burning city, and, with the exception of an occasional birdcall and the distant neighing of some far-away horse, she heard nothing else.

"Owen?" she called out cautiously, stepping around the car and walking toward the open end of the barn.

Nothing.

Her body was tensed for trouble and her senses were alert as she walked into the shadows of the building and looked around. It was apparent the place had not been used in some time. Rusty, broken pieces of equipment were piled near walls, and lengths of chain and moldy twine hung on nails hammered into the walls. A thick layer of dust and dirt blown in from the fields lay everywhere, covering everything.

Almost everything.

It did not cover the fresh set of footprints in the grime ending near a ladder on the far wall that led up to the hayloft. At that moment, she knew instantly that she'd been set up. She whirled around to run, but before she could take a step, a heavy blow caught her on the back of the head, slamming her hard to the floor as her assailant dropped down on her from above. Stars exploded behind her eyes as she struggled to pull herself to her feet, knowing that to fail would mean death.

"Well, well, well," Cole Banyon said coldly, looking down at her. "Look who showed up, hoping to find her knight in shining armor!" He kicked her viciously in the ribs, smiling in satisfaction as he heard the snap of bone under the pointed toe of his cowboy boot.

"Cole," Windy cried out in pain, grabbing her side as she collapsed and rolled to her back. "Please..." she begged, fighting for breath.

"Please?" Cole mocked. "Please what? Please kill me quickly?" He grabbed her by the front of her shirt and hauled her roughly to her feet, causing her to gasp in pain as her broken rib shifted. "You're pathetic, Windy," he snapped and shoved her against the wall before he turned away in disgust.

Windy struggled to remain standing. Her lungs ached and her breath was hard to draw. If Hade had kept Cole from killing her at their apartment, it seemed as if all bets were off now. "Cole..." she struggled, her mind desperately seeking for a way out. "Why?"

He spun around, a wild look in his eyes. "Why?" he repeated, his face twisting with rage. "Because after all these years, I finally can!"

His fist pulled back to deliver a vicious punch to her face. Windy was ready this time, though, and she sidestepped the blow and lashed out with a punch of her own, catching him squarely in the jaw and snapping his head back. Pain roared through her body at the movement, however, and she lacked the strength to follow through with her attack. She could only stumble away, clutching her ribs in agony and praying she could reach her car before Cole recovered.

"Oh, boy," Cole said wickedly, spitting blood from his mouth as he quickly advanced on her. Surprised and bloodied by her quick strike, he wasn't hurt, but he was mad. He kicked his foot forward, tangling up her feet and sending her crashing to the floor in a scream of pain. "Feeling a bit feisty today, Windy?" he snarled as he reached down and wrapped his hand in her long hair. He savagely pulled her back to her feet again.

Windy's mind was a haze of agony as Cole slammed her back against the wall again. Red flecked her lips as she coughed up blood from a lung damaged by her broken ribs. "Please stop," she found herself begging. "All I...ever wanted..." she went on, but quickly trailed off, unable to finish.

"All you ever wanted?" Cole roared, staring at her through rage-filled eyes, his face close to hers. "Did you ever care about what I wanted, Windy? Did it ever cross your mind to think about me? What I aspired to? What my feelings were? No!"

"Cole," she pleaded, coughing up more blood. "I tried to help you."

"Help me?" he looked at her in amazement. "All you've ever done was hold me down!"

"No," she whispered. "I only wanted you back. I wanted... the Cole I fell in love with."

Cole threw back his head and laughed, a vicious hollow sound that cut the young woman to her soul. "Love," he finally spat. "What a useless emotion." He leaned close, clenching a fist in front of her face. "Love is dead, Windy. Power is what it's all about," he sneered and then grew calm, his face taking on an almost serene look. "I killed them, you know," he said, stating it as a simple fact and smiling as he did so. "Just like he told me to. I have to admit, it was easier than I thought it would be."

"Cole," she cried desperately, shaking her head.

"Oh, yes," he went on proudly, pantomiming with his hands as he explained. "A squeeze of the trigger; a slash of the knife. Easy work, good money. Power over the lives of others," he finished, clenching his fist again. "Just like the power I now have over you."

"Cole," she sobbed and choked. "You don't...understand."

"Oh, I understand perfectly," he said, walking across the barn floor. "I understand that I have you to thank for everything." He paused and kicked at a pile of junk near the far wall, as if looking for something. "I understand that you think it's okay for you to work for Hade and do all of those things he asked you to do, but I was never good enough."

"No," she gasped. "That's not...what I meant."

"It's exactly what you meant," he countered coldly. "It's all about power, Windy. At one time, you had it. Now, it's all mine and I've waited a long time for this."

"I'm...sorry," she choked. "I'm so sorry, Cole."

Cole closed his hand around an old wooden handle. Standing up, he looked at Windy, his face a mask of hatred. In his hands, he held an old rusty pitchfork. "Save it for God," he snarled, leveling the sharp tines at her and walking back toward her with savage purpose.

"Cole, no!" she screamed, but her plea fell on deaf ears. She could only watch in horror as he drove the pitchfork through her body with tremendous force. Her eyes flew open in shock as the rusty tines speared through her torso, imbedding themselves deeply into the wall behind her.

"That's power," Cole said icily, his voice devoid of emotion. Leaning forward, he grabbed her by the chin and forced her face up to look at him. "Remember this, Windy," he hissed, ignoring the stream of dark blood that ran out of her mouth and over his hand. "I was the one who took it all away from you." He released her chin and callously wiped his bloody hand on her shirt. "Owen is on his way," he said casually, looking at his watch. "Make sure you tell him 'hi' for me," he laughed wickedly, turning away from her, "if you live long enough."

Cole Banyon walked away, leaving her pinned to the wall, her life slowing draining away. Strangely, she felt little pain. Her lungs had been punctured and her legs were numb below her waist. As her lungs slowly filled up with blood and her breathing became labored, her mind wrapped itself around the fantasy of Owen coming to rescue her and delivering her from the life that she had lived. But her face quickly darkened as the shadow of Hade shredded her dream, sending it flying away in tiny wisps of smoke. No, she thought darkly as her vision began to dim. Hade would have never let it happen. She could not escape him and Owen could never save her. She couldn't free herself from Hade's web. Even now, as death took her, he still owned her.

Windy Covington would die.

But there would always be Hade.

And with that final thought, Windy was gone.

Owen turned the pickup off the blacktop and onto the country road, spraying gravel as he floored it. He knew the barn was close, and when he found it, he would find Petr and end this. Gritting his teeth in determination, he sped down the road. He saw the building and, as he drew near, he noticed a Toyota Camry parked out front. Adrenaline coursing through his veins, Owen pulled into the lane and skidded to a stop behind the Toyota. He got out and vaulted himself into the bed of the pickup truck. He grabbed the aluminum baseball bat and jumped back out, his face a mask of fury. "Petr!" he roared, ready to dispense the justice he knew was required.

He strode around the corner and into the barn and froze at what he saw.

"Windy," he whispered in horror. She was pinned to the wall by a rusty pitchfork that had been driven through her chest. Blood pooled in a large puddle in the dust at her feet. "Oh, no," he cried, dropping his weapon and rushing forward. Slipping his hand gently under her chin, he tenderly raised her head and looked at her beautiful face. Her eyes were still open, but they stared at him unseeing. She was dead. "No," he shouted, feeling a new wave of sorrow begin to feed the rage within him.

Ever so gently, he closed her eyes, then slipped his arm around her and gripped the pitchfork with his free hand. He pulled the pitchfork free, flung it to the side, and caught Windy around her waist. Effortlessly, he lifted her up and cradled her close. Then he knelt and gently placed her body on the floor. He took a moment to look at her face and realized that, even in death, she was beautiful. He reached out and wiped a single tear from the corner of her eye. He wanted to say something, anything—but he had no words. He just didn't know what to say anymore.

He stood up, feeling an icy resolve begin to descend upon him. Picking up the bat, he stalked out of the barn and back to the truck. Owen was done watching his friends die. He would find the murdering monster and kill him. And if anyone got in his way, he would kill them, too.

Owen DiConte had gone over the edge.

His face hard and his eyes set, he threw himself into the front seat of the truck. Starting it up, he shifted into gear and roared out of the dirt lane and onto the gravel road, back in the direction he had come. He was a half-mile from the turn-off when the phone Hade had given him rang. For a moment, he considered ignoring the call, but when it rang a second time, he answered it with a curse.

"What?" he snarled.

Hade's voice on the other end was calm and smooth. "Not quite what I was expecting," he said easily, "but it'll do."

"What do you want, Hade?" Owen went on angrily. "I'm kind of busy."

"Understandable," came the reply. "I thought you'd want to know my people intercepted a phone call. Apparently, a young lady has been killed at the location you were supposed to find Petr at. I'm told it wasn't Alexis. Another acquaintance of yours, perhaps?"

"I already know," Owen said quietly.

"Oh, then you've been to the barn."

"Been and left," Owen snapped.

"Well, good," Hade went on. "Then you're not that far from him. Listen closely, Owen, as you're only going to get one chance at this."

Hade gave Owen the directions needed to find his quarry. When he was finished, Owen knew exactly where he needed to go. He threw the phone on the floor without another word and stomped on the gas. The Ford roared down the road as the rain began to fall.

Owen was closing in.

CHAPTER 17

Salt Lake City, Utah: Tom McCain wrenched the wheel of the Ford Expedition to the left, cutting a path around a group of undead and running over a couple of stragglers. Just a short while ago, they'd blasted through the garage door of the house and into a cold, gray drizzle. It was morning. The sky was the dark gray of a coming storm and the rain had started. The creatures were everywhere. They'd surrounded the house and were breaking through windows and doors as McCain and the rest of them had piled in the vehicle. After leaving the house, their trek down the road had proven harrowing. McCain lost track of how many of the things he'd hit, and the front of the Expedition was cracked and dented and spattered with gore. Four blocks later, he was leaving the things behind.

"Where did they all come from?" he finally said through gritted teeth, his knuckles white on the steering wheel.

"And every one of them were coming right for us," Dalacourt added.

"They're trying to stop us," John replied. "At least it should provide Stephen and Brandi a safe exit."

"I hope so," McCain went on, taking a hard left and heading toward the highway that would take them up into the mountains. The rain was coming down harder now, but McCain did not seem to notice, pushing the car as fast as it would go.

"Why are they after us?" Alexis asked fearfully.

"Hard to say yet," John replied somewhat evasively.

But Alexis was not swayed. "John," she said, doing her best to keep her voice even. "There's something else going on here that you're not telling us."

"I know a great deal about what's happening," he replied slowly, picking his words carefully. "But I don't know everything. And much of what I know I cannot yet discuss. At least not at the moment."

"Why?" Dalacourt asked.

"He's being careful, nothing more," McCain interrupted, his eyes on the road. "Just trust him."

"I do," Dalacourt said. Somehow, he knew John would never purposefully mislead them, but he was desperate to know what was happening. "There must be a reason for all of this and, if you know what that is, I would hope you would share it with us."

"I understand," John replied wearily, as if he had been expecting this line of questions for some time. "For now, we're going to save Alexis' friend, Owen. That's as straight-forward as I can be for the moment."

Alexis started, her eyes going wide. "Owen? You know where he is?"

John nodded, his face hard. "He's being guided by the same force that is arrayed against us."

"Hang on," McCain shouted, swerving the big SUV down through a ditch to avoid an overturned milk truck blocking the entrance ramp to the highway. Their vehicle shot out of the ditch and hit the road hard, fishtailing dangerously before he got it back under control. A moment later, they were roaring down the highway again, the Expedition's big engine wide open. "How far, John?"

"Not far," was the reply. "We'll hit the mountains in a little while and eventually there'll be a big curve that heads upwards. We'll follow that as far as we're able."

"Roger that."

They traveled in silence, their thoughts on what awaited them. Alexis Kennedy did everything she could to focus. She did not know why John was suddenly so interested in helping Owen, but her heart was thrilled that Owen was alive and they were going to find him.

They passed a burned-out shell of a car on the side of the road, several broken bodies distinctly visible in the aftermath. She closed her eyes, her mind again seeing all the images of death and destruction she had witnessed in just the past twenty-four hours. She realized with a profound sadness that the burned and disfigured bodies in the car they had just passed did not repulse her like they should have. They were people! Dead people! A mother? A father? A child? She had seen so much death in such a short time that she'd already grown desensitized to the carnage.

Michael Dalacourt sat beside her, his own mind racing as he tried to decipher everything he knew or thought he knew about what was happening. He felt he was close to understanding, but the truth he sought remained elusive, just out of his reach. He knew John had them going into the mountains for a specific purpose, and that he and Alexis were somehow an important part of what was happening in the world. But what? He was but a lowly priest and Alexis was just a frightened college girl. What was the thread that joined them together?

Unlike Alexis, his own life was devoid of close relationships. He had nothing to go back on—nothing to indicate the strand that linked him to this battered little group. He'd dedicated himself to his God from an early age and left everything else by the wayside. The only pseudo-relationships he had with anyone outside of the car he was riding in were with his old mentor, Father Dunkirk, who had long since passed, and with Archbishop Francis De Solei.

De Solei. That name sent a chill through him like never before, and he couldn't dismiss the dream he'd had or John's telling words about his mentor. Even in all the chaos, he was still under orders to get to Los Angeles. Had that really been only a day ago? He'd had a choice then about going or staying with John, but that choice had been taken from him. He did not think De Solei would accept such a minor technicality as nearly being killed as an excuse for not following orders. If he lived through this, De Solei would punish him severely for his disobedience.

As his thoughts lingered over the past few days, all of the questions he had about recent events floated to the surface. Why did De Solei send him to the American Midwest and then command him go to Los Angeles? Did De Solei really expect him to make it to Los Angeles, or was this all part of some sort of elaborate plan to discredit him? His mind whirled about, trying to see behind the façade that was Archbishop Francis De Solei. If there was one thing he was certain about, it was that he no longer trusted his mentor.

"Curve coming up," McCain finally said, breaking the long silence. "Looks like we've got a welcoming committee, too."

As they all looked, they could see shadowy figures off to both sides of the road, moving with dogged purpose in the same direction they were going.

"They'll try to stop us," John said as more of the creatures appeared on the road in front of them. "They're drawn here as we are. Run them down, Tom. We cannot afford to be delayed."

McCain smiled grimly as he ran down half a dozen of them, before slamming on the brakes and sending the SUV into a sideways skid on the rain-slick highway. A tractor-trailer had jackknifed across both lanes of the highway, the trailer tires hanging over the ditch on one side and the tractor tilting into the ditch on the other. The ditches were too deep to navigate and there was no other way around it. The living dead were already closing in on them.

"We'll have to leg it!" McCain shouted, quickly throwing open his door as he grabbed the shotgun and jumped out. He brought the gun to bear on the nearest creature and blew a hole through its chest. On the other side of the vehicle, Stacia was out and moving as well, putting her makeshift staff to work with dizzying speed on those creatures nearest her.

John was out behind Stacia and, in a moment, he was locked in hand-to-hand combat with an advancing creature. As Alexis and Dalacourt exited the car, the rain began to fall harder.

"Over there!" John shouted over a peel of thunder as he quickly broke the creature's neck. "That low ridge! If we can gain the high ground, we might survive this!"

"Where are we going?" Alexis yelled, unable to see where he was pointing.

"Just follow me!" John started up the rocky slope. Stacia fell in beside him and McCain brought up the rear, alternately using his shotgun to either shoot or club at nearby creatures. At the same time, he herded Dalacourt and Alexis in front of him.

They moved up the slope, traversing the slippery rocks much easier than their recently-dead attackers. They soon reached the ridge and paused as John looked out over the expanse before them. In the dim light, he saw what he was looking for. "We're close," he called out.

McCain fired off a shot from his shotgun, blasting another oncoming creature in the shoulder and sending it skidding backwards on the rocks, where it took down several more pursuers as it fell. "Seven ten split," he remarked off-handedly. "Let's go, people," he said. "Those things will make it up here eventually. Even the really clumsy ones."

Without a word, they started from the ridge at a brisk jog and moved along the rocks as quickly as they dared in the pouring rain. The ridge widened and opened up onto a well-used path that wound itself up the mountainside. The rain had muddied it considerably and rivulets of water ran down little channels throughout.

"This path leads to a plateau that looks out over the valley. It's our destination," John said, but then he froze, his voice choked off. He closed his eyes tightly and brought a weathered hand to his forehead and pressed, trying to ward off the sudden feeling of something so purely evil, it filled his heart and soul with despair. It was a presence he had felt before, lifetimes ago—a presence he believed had long ago been purged from the earth. "Could it be?" he whispered.

In the driving rain, the others did not hear him, but all looked at him expectantly. Only McCain realized something was wrong. "What is it, John?" he asked.

The old man slowly opened his eyes, his features haunted. There was no doubt. His eyes went first to Alexis and then the priest. "Michael and Alexis," he said softly. "I want you to go. Now. The path is clear before you, but you must not stop for anything. Get to the top as quickly as possible. We will hold the lower path for you."

Alexis started to object, but John held up a warning hand. His voice was firm when he spoke. "Don't question, Alexis. Trust me and do what I say. You'll find Owen on the plateau. Now go!"

The look on John's face was so fierce that Alexis swallowed fearfully and stumbled back. Without another word, she turned and took hold of the priest's hand and started up the muddy path, pulling Father Dalacourt along.

John knew he didn't have the time to watch Alexis and Michael run, but he took the moment anyway. Fearing he had sent them to something much worse than death, he only wished he'd been allowed to prepare them better. It wasn't his choice to throw them in the deep end alone like this, but that did nothing to console him. He watched until they disappeared into the rain-driven darkness where the canyon trail met the rapidly descending clouds. The world needed them up there and he had to be down here. He'd long ago been shown the reason behind the first necessity and he had a pretty good idea now the reason for the second.

He turned back resolutely, ready to stand firm against anything that threatened the fate of what awaited the young people he had been charged to protect. Through sheets of heavily falling rain, he scanned the rows of the undead, calculating the best way to ensure they could give Alexis and Dalacourt enough time, but when his eyes reached the rear of their ranks, his worst fears were confirmed. A towering figure stood silent and unmoving behind the horde. Its presence swallowed light and hope like a black hole. John didn't recognize the physicality of the man—tall, dark, ageless. But the effect of that soul's presence was singular.

John knew him.

The spirit inhabiting that body had earned that presence. Years ago it walked the earth in a mortal form, performing unspeakable acts of evil. As his influence expanded, power concentrated within him until despair, fear, and hatred emanated from him so completely, it shriveled the hearts of any who stood against him, no matter how good or how courageous they believed themselves to be. Villages, then cities, and eventually entire civilizations succumbed and vanished under his evil sway and the machinations of the one that called him companion.

In time, John had met the demon on the battlefield and, after a cataclysmic struggle, he had destroyed him and sent his armies fleeing back into the shadows. He had thought the victory complete and assumed his vanquished foe was gone from the earth, never to return.

But that was then.

This was now.

Somehow, the evil creature lived again, and for the first time since he had finished his final sand painting, he feared that the greatness of his noble young friends would ultimately fail in this, their greatest test.

This was why John had been shown why he must stay behind. No matter what else happened today, this ancient spirit must not get past him to destroy Alexis and the others. Their struggle would be difficult enough against the one he knew was already waiting for them on the plateau.

"Friend of yours?" McCain asked quietly, his own eyes locked on the shadowy figure.

"You might say we go way back, Tom," John replied softly.

"Good enough for me," McCain said, hefting his shotgun. "Maybe it's time we had a proper introduction."

John looked warmly at the detective and his daughter and smiled. He'd seen generations of men come and go, but stronger companions he had seldom known. Maybe, just maybe, the three of them would prevail.

CHAPTER 18

Ferguson Canyon, Utah: Struggling to keep his anger and fear under control, Owen DiConte waited inside the cab of the red Ford Ranger as the rain outside came down in sheets. Just about every emotion he could possibly feel, from courage to remorse to anticipation to caution to excitement to pride to embarrassment, all swept through him in wave after wave. He was seriously beginning to question his dedication to following through on his promise to Hade when a black Lexus pulled into the gravel parking lot and came to a stop near his truck. The windows were tinted black and he could see nothing moving inside. But he knew who was in there, and he knew what he had to do.

Letting his fury take center stage, he hopped out of the truck and swung himself up into the pickup bed. His heart was racing. He had never been in a fight like this, and part of him was screaming inside about the insanity of it. Even worse, he knew what he was up against and that made his decision to fight even crazier. Petr was the son of a mafia lord who had experienced violence throughout his entire life. He was big, strong, and probably well-versed in many fighting disciplines. Owen was a college student who loved to climb mountains and play volleyball. One was a fighter, the other a dreamer.

But even a dreamer could fight when he had to.

He shielded his eyes from the pouring rain as his thoughts turned to all those he had lost, those who had been murdered by this man, those who were still threatened by him. His mind focused on Alexis. Whatever it took, he would make sure she was safe. He would make Petr pay. He would deliver justice once and for all and, whatever it took, he would end this. He picked up the metal baseball bat, jumped out of the truck, and waited, the bat resting lightly on his shoulder. The time for introspection came to an end as the rear door of the Lexus opened and out stepped the man Owen had been waiting for.

Petr Zhugravinsky stood facing Owen, some ten feet separating them. He immediately noted the baseball bat Owen carried and his right hand instinctively tightened on the mango tree staff that had once belonged to David, droplets of rain gleaming on the polished wood like diamonds. He nodded briefly toward Owen, hoping his instincts were wrong but knowing they were not, and he slowly took one step toward him.

"We are summoned, you and I," Petr said, his voice measured. "Up the trail, I'm told."

"You're not going anywhere," Owen said icily as he pulled a blood-spattered photograph from his pocket. He flipped it in Petr's direction and it fell to the mud in front of the Russian, landing face-up.

Petr glanced down to see an image of Alexis, with himself on one side and Owen and his friends on the other. It had been taken only a few short days ago at the charity basketball game for David's son, Gideon. "Where did you get that?" he asked, his eyes tracking Owen's every movement. He could feel the tension and knew the young man was ready to explode.

"Does it matter?" Owen challenged.

"It does," Petr snapped back. "That picture was supposed to come to me. How'd you get it?"

"I got it from the guy you hired to kill my friends!" Owen shouted and lunged forward, the baseball bat coming off his shoulder in a vicious swing toward Petr's head.

The Russian ducked and easily dodged the swing, bringing David's staff up at the same time to deflect the blow harmlessly to the side and force Owen off balance. As Owen's momentum took him past the Russian, Petr pivoted to face Owen again, the two men having switched places and once again standing opposite each other.

"Are you insane?" Petr snapped. "What is this all about?"

"Don't you dare tell me you don't know!" Owen shouted above a particularly violent crash of thunder. "You had my friends killed! I know what you are, Petr! I know what you want! And I'm not going to let you have it!"

"I swear on my father's grave," Petr shouted back, "I don't know what you're talking about!"

"You lie!" Owen roared and charged forward again, swinging the bat in another savage arc.

To Petr, the attack was again slow and predictable. With cat-like speed, he sidestepped the blow once more, this time swinging the walking stick up and catching Owen in the shoulder, pushing him further off his center. Owen stumbled past and Petr brought the blood-stained staff into a ready position before him.

"Enough!" he roared. "I don't want to hurt you!"

Owen pivoted quickly, his eyes glaring angrily at the Russian. He wiped the rain from his face with his free hand and lunged again, swinging low and trying to disguise his attack. Petr skipped backward along the side of Owen's truck to avoid having the bat shatter his shinbone and he caught hold of the truck's door handle as he did. Owen, unrelenting, rushed forward again, but at the last moment, Petr yanked the door open. It caught Owen in the solar plexus and drove the air from his lungs, dropping him to the muddy ground. Before Owen could struggle to his feet, Petr snapped the staff forward, catching Owen across the side of the head hard enough to stun him but not enough to do any serious damage. The blow sent Owen sprawling in the mud.

"I'm not going to fight you!" Petr shouted again, looking down on his opponent. He turned and pointed up the path. "I was told to head up with you to the plateau. I still intend to do that, with or without you. If you come to your senses, feel free to join me," he finished angrily. Petr turned his back and began trudging up the path, sparing not another glance at his opponent. It was his first mistake.

He'd just underestimated Owen DiConte.

Several minutes after Petr had disappeared into the pouring rain, Owen finally struggled to his feet as lightning flashed dangerously overhead. He paused to catch his breath, and a quick check of his body told him nothing was broken. His chest hurt and his jaw was sore, but all that had really done was make him angrier and focus a single thought in his mind.

He was going to kill Petr.

He picked up the bat and set off up the trail. The Russian might be a better fighter, but Owen was in great shape and these mountains were his home. He knew the rocks and the paths and the Russian didn't. The stamina that allowed him to climb sheer rock faces flooded his body as he loped along in the driving rain. He caught Petr at the top.

The canyon's river had swollen with the torrential rain, and the roar had silenced his approach. Petr had no idea of the danger he was in until it was too late. Sensing the attack at nearly the same moment it came, he started to spin to the right, bringing the staff around in anticipation of the blow he knew was coming. Owen had driven in from his left side, however, and the bat hammered cleanly into the Russian's back, sending Petr stumbling forward into the mud, David's staff flying from his hands.

Pain exploded through Petr's back and side and he heard the snap of bone as at least one of his ribs broke under the blow. Instinctively, he rolled to the side as he hit the ground, saving himself from Owen's follow-up swing that buried six inches of the end of the bat into the mud where his head had been only a moment before. Petr's reflexes took over, and although he was barely able to breathe, he kicked his leg forward, tangling up Owen's feet and throwing the enraged man to the ground. Petr rolled to his feet, twisting himself painfully into position, facing Owen once more.

Owen was on his feet immediately, facing the Russian, the bat lying on the ground just out of reach. But instead of lunging forward to attack the injured man, a hunch caused him to hold back, his body tense.

He guessed right.

Petr, his face a mask of pain and surprised fury, launched himself at Owen. But the Russian was slowed enough by his injury that Owen was able to catch the bull rush and hook his arms underneath Petr's. Using the Russian's momentum, he threw the man over in a classic Greco-Roman wrestling throw. Struggling on the slick path, both men went to the ground in a heap, but Owen twisted his body so he landed on top of Petr, driving the remaining breath out of him. Owen straddled his chest and immediately landed a nasty punch to the face, snapping Petr's head back into the muck and opening up a cut under one eye. "They were good men!" Owen yelled as he drew back and punched him again, this time catching him in the mouth, splitting his lips. "And you had them killed! Chad and Clint are dead because of you!"

"No…" Petr croaked, as he raised his arms to try and divert the blows to his head. Tasting blood, he knew he was in serious trouble.

"It could only have been you!" Owen roared as he drew back again, but this time the Russian struck first, driving stiffened fingers into the flesh just under Owen's ribcage. Pinching down with his thumb, he caught Owen's lower rib in an excruciating hold between his thumb and fingers. Owen practically screamed in agony and threw himself off Petr to escape the pain. Petr did not press the attack, instead rolling to his knees the other way, putting some distance between him and his opponent. "What...are you...doing?" he managed to cough, blood in his mouth.

"You killed them," Owen accused breathlessly, climbing back to his feet. "You killed Windy, too. What could she have possibly done to deserve to die like that?"

"Windy?" Petr was completely confused now. "Who's Windy?" he managed to stammer.

Owen wasn't listening and charged the Russian once more. Petr had found his center, though, and swung his leg out, his teeth gritted against the pain in his side. His leg swept Owen's leg from behind, driving the young man forward into the mud. He followed it up, snapping the edge of his hand down toward the back of Owen's neck, but his enemy was already moving, rolling out of the way, and the blow barely grazed Owen's cheek. Both men were back on their feet in moments, facing each other like gladiators who had no choice but to win or die.

"Enough of this!" Petr gasped. "I am not your enemy!"

"You took my friends from me," Owen spat. "I won't let you take Alexis, too."

Petr looked at him in shock. "Alexis?" he repeated. "I would never hurt Alexis!" he yelled. "I'm here to save her!"

The bloodlust was so strong now in Owen, that he literally could not hear the words coming out of Petr's mouth. Roaring, he drove in again, going low and letting his legs drive him up into Petr's gut. He caught the Russian solidly and lifted him, his legs propelling them both off the path until his enemy's body impacted with a nearby tree. The breath was again driven from the Russian's lungs and Owen fired off a succession of hard punches to the man's sides.

Petr groaned in agony as the blows landed, but he was far from beaten. With Owen's head lowered, Petr drove his elbow down, connecting with Owen's trapezius muscle just left of his spine. The effect was instantaneous, driving all strength from his attacker. Owen staggered backward, but Petr could not press his advantage and simply dropped to his knees, coughing and spitting blood with what little breath he could draw.

Owen's arm and shoulder were practically numb, but he was still on his feet. He glared hatefully at Petr, but the Russian appeared finished. His face twisted with rage, Owen walked over and picked up the metal bat. He turned back to Petr, just as the man was slowly climbing back to his feet, but it wouldn't matter. There was no way the Russian could avoid his fate this time. It was time to finish this. It was time to carry out justice. Stepping forward, he raised the bat high. It would be over with in a moment. So quick. So final.

So… wrong.

In that moment of truth, when one swift action was all it would take to end a man's life, Owen froze as the realization of what he was about to do struck him. What was he doing? Was he really ready to kill this man under some misguided notion that he was indeed judge, jury, and executioner? Where had he gotten that idea from? The answer was simple, and the truth of it chilled him to his soul.

It had been Hade.

All of it.

His features softened and he dropped his guard. "Petr," he began, his voice calm.

But this time it was Petr who wasn't listening. Instinct had taken over, and as his opponent showed weakness by hesitating, he drove his foot forward with all his remaining strength, slamming it into Owen's gut just beneath the sternum. As the young man staggered backward, doubling over in pain, Petr reached out and grabbed a handful of Owen's hair. He yanked his enemy's head up to face him, before lacing him across the jaw with a vicious elbow shot. Owen's legs turned to rubber and the bat dropped to the ground as Petr stepped to the side of him and drove a downward thrust kick right into the side of Owen's knee. There was a popping of cartilage and Owen found the breath to scream in pain as his knee collapsed from the blow and Petr shoved him violently back on the path.

The Russian staggered toward him, bruised and bleeding and ready to carry on the fight if he needed, but Owen was still, his eyes closed, rain splashing down on his face.

The pain in his damaged knee was excruciating, but his bloodlust was gone. Owen blew out a long breath and tried to push the agony to the back of his mind, but he could feel himself slipping in and out of blackness. A single thought rang clear in his mind. The rage was gone—the desire for vengeance had utterly vanished. "That hurt, Russian," was all he could say.

"I swear to you," Petr said quietly, never taking his eyes off the prone Owen. "I did not kill your friends."

Owen simply nodded, the fight within him gone. Peace flowed through him instead, reassuring and comforting. Owen had reclaimed himself. He had lost his battle with Petr, but he had won the fight for his soul.

A moment later, everything went black.

Alexis Kennedy broke into the clearing at a dead run, urged on by a nameless fear that told her she could not be late. As she reached the plateau and the scene before her opened up, she knew she was. A bloodied Petr stood tall in the driving rain, towering above the body of her beloved Owen who lay still, his placid face streaked with mud, his eyes closed.

Without hesitation, she drew the Colt Defender from the back of her jeans and pointed it directly at Petr. "Get away from him!" she screamed.

The Russian raised his head quickly at the sound of her voice. In the pouring rain it was hard at first to tell where it had come from, but he soon saw the figure before him, and at the same instant, he saw the gun pointing at him. He raised one hand above his head as if to surrender and used the other to wipe the rain and blood away from his eyes so he could see better. What he saw shocked him to his inner core.

"Alexis?" He stammered. "Alexis, it's me, Petr!"

"I said get away from Owen now!" Alexis yelled again, the gun never wavering.

Petr paused, completely unable to process what was happening. He should have been surprised to see Alexis act this way toward him, but not today. Nothing could surprise him anymore—not the murderous look in her eyes, not the gun pointing at him. He knew the look well and could see she held the gun firmly, a practiced marksman. With a resigned sigh, he shook his head. What was the use, he thought bitterly.

He considered trying to speak to her, but quickly discarded that idea. Clearly in her mind, he was the villain here, and why should that be a surprise to him, given his heritage? It no longer mattered what he did or how he explained himself, he would never escape his past. How had he ever convinced himself he could be free from his family and from what they stood for? He'd been a fool. He'd given up everything—and for what? To be standing upon a God-forsaken mountain in the driving rain, accused and convicted of crimes he'd never committed. It was a feeling of helplessness beyond anything he'd ever felt in his life.

"Alexis," Michael Dalacourt said as stumbled up beside her, still winded from their climb. "What are you doing?" he asked hesitantly, his eyes going from Alexis to the man she was pointing a gun at. "He's not one of them."

"No, he's worse than those mindless creatures," she replied, her eyes locked with the Russian's. "I said get away from him, Petr!" she shouted again. She took a step forward, the gun never wavering. "Back away or I swear, I'll kill you."

At that moment, things began to fall into place for the Russian. He did not doubt the sincerity of the look in Alexis' eyes. She fully meant to kill him no matter what he did. But the question was, why? And in a moment, he knew. It was her companion. He was the one using Alexis to further his cause; the one he must protect Alexis from. And it made perfect sense to him now. Of course Alexis would want to shoot him, spurred on by the words of this false priest and the fact that he now stood over Owen. An unconscious Owen. An Owen that looked...dead.

"This is all just a misunderstanding," he said loudly over the pouring rain. "If you shoot me, you'll shoot an innocent man."

"This doesn't look like a misunderstanding," Dalacourt said carefully.

"Please, Alexis," he said, ignoring the priest and fighting to keep his voice calm as he saw the way out of this unfolding mess—a way out for all of them. "Put the gun down and we can talk through this."

"Shut up, Petr! Just shut up!" she cried out. "Move, now, or I swear to God I'll shoot." Her voice cracked, overwhelmed with grief and confusion.

Petr backed away slowly, keeping his voice measured and calm. He knew from personal experience how hard it was to shoot someone who looked you in the eyes, and so he maintained eye contact with Alexis. She was on edge and one wrong move would destroy all their lives. "You. Priest," he directed his comments at the man. "You believe Owen is dead, but you're wrong. Both of you are. Check if you don't believe me."

Dalacourt paused, clearly unsettled. He looked at Petr and then turned his eyes to Alexis.

She nodded almost imperceptibly, but kept the weapon trained on the Russian.

Dalacourt took a deep breath and moved toward the prone young man, slowly curling around the line of fire until he reached him. He quickly knelt in the mud and felt for a pulse. It was there. It was strong. "He's alive," he said excitedly. "Just unconscious."

Relief flooding through her, she took a step towards Petr. "Why?" she asked him plainly.

Petr kept his hands raised. "It was self-defense. He was told lies about me, like you have been," he said. "He tried to kill me."

Confusion swirled within her and she took another step forward. She could feel the steel trigger pressed against her finger. The weight of the gun beckoned her—a quick squeeze of the trigger and the threat would be no more. She could go to Owen, they could be together again and everything would be perfect, as she had imagined it would be so many times in her mind. She took another step, but as she did her resolve began to waver. Tears coursed down her cheeks as she recalled her conversation with her friend Rebekkah only a handful of days ago. "You never know when it's going to be you who has to pull the trigger," Rebekkah had said. Had that statement been prophetic? Had her friend foretold this very moment in her life? Was this how it was all to end?

And then she heard it—Owen's voice penetrating the suffocating chaos that had engulfed her. "It's okay, Alex," she heard him say. "It's going to be okay."

As Owen struggled painfully to sit up, the flood of emotions Alexis had held at bay burst forth. She took several halting steps to reach Owen and then slumped to the ground in exhaustion, the gun falling from her hands. She threw her arms around his neck, her body shaking with sobs.

Dalacourt reached out and gently picked up the gun, tossing it off the path as if it was a poisonous snake. Petr, relief plain on his tired face, walked over to Owen and jammed the mango walking stick into the ground next to him. Holding tightly to Alexis, Owen looked up, his eyes uncertain. But Petr stood firm, his hand outstretched. "I'm sorry for what happened, Owen," he said. "But I swear I did not kill your friends."

Owen knew he spoke the truth. He reached up and accepted the Russian's hand. Grabbing hold of the stick with his other, and with Alexis and Petr both helping, he pulled himself steadily to his feet. Father Michael Dalacourt looked at them and allowed himself to smile. Three young people holding together a single wooden staff as if it was their guiding path, the bond that brought them together, that would point them in a direction in their lives that God would have them go. And suddenly it hit him.

"We are the kings," Michael Dalacourt whispered in awe as the revelation made itself known to him.

No one heard him.

"We are the kings," the young priest said louder, conviction beginning to fill his voice.

This time, all heads turned toward him.

"We are the kings!" he exclaimed again, looking around excitedly. "From the prophecy: 'And three kings shall rise up and stand upon the mountaintop. And they shall make war, one upon the other and the blood of their brother shall be spilled and they shall serve the anointed of the Beast, lest they humble themselves before God'." He finished and turned to look directly at Alexis. "It's the lost scriptures! We are the kings it speaks of!"

"What are you talking about?" Owen cut in, looking confused.

"It means we were brought up here to kill each other," Dalacourt answered confidently. "But we didn't. We survived. And that means the prophecy can't be fulfilled." He looked directly at Alexis and finished quietly. "We win."

Alexis let out a relieved smile and squeezed Owen's hand. "Father Dalacourt's right," she said to Owen. "I think it's over."

"Bravi, children!" a voice boomed out of the darkness, sounding like thunder itself.

As one, all four turned toward the voice. A huge man stood on the edge of the path, his long black coat flying open in the wind. Black shades hid his eyes, and his hair and beard ran with rainwater. He was smiling widely, white teeth gleaming, as he clapped his hands in mock applause.

"Hade," Owen and Petr both said in shocked unison.

"At your service," the tall man bowed.

Alexis, who had not yet seen this monstrosity before, knew instinctively this was the most dangerous foe she had faced since the chaos had struck. She stepped protectively in front of the injured Owen and glared at the man, wishing she still held the gun in her hand.

"Really, Alexis?" Hade said sarcastically. "You think you can bare your teeth and keep your dear Owen safe from me?" He chuckled deep in his chest. "I'm sure Dakota would have appreciated some of that heroism." Hade cocked his head inquisitively and gazed at her terrified features before he slowly bent down and picked up the gun Dalacourt had discarded. "Why, oh why, my dear girl, have you not exacted vengeance on this man, a vengeance so obviously deserved?"

Alexis barely shook her head, but did not answer. Nothing in her life had prepared her for the malice she felt in the huge man's presence, and she found herself petrified beyond reason.

"Here is a man responsible for so much heartache and death," Hade went on, swinging the gun around and waving it carelessly in Petr's direction. "He's a monster. He's killed many, Alexis. He's killed in Russia. He's killed here in America. He'll kill again, no matter where he is," Hade continued hypnotically, giving Petr a sly smile as he spoke. "There really is no other way. Justice must be served, Alexis, and the greater good must not be ignored. Will you not shoot him and right so many wrongs? Will you not shoot him and deliver justice for so many victims?" He paused and held out the Colt Defender, looking at her expectantly.

Thoughts twisted and tore through her mind as the spellbinding words of Hade washed over her. Should she have killed Petr? Had she made a mistake in not doing so? She looked to Owen, tears in her eyes and desperately in need of guidance. He was standing as best he could with the assistance of David's stick, yet he looked steadier than the rest of them. Owen said nothing, but his eyes expressed calm assurance and she knew what she had to do without him having to say it. She had broken through Hade's spell. She looked at the giant before her and said simply, "Not today."

Hade winked at her. "You know, I like you more every day, young lady!" He walked slowly around the four young people, coming to a stop in front of the priest. "I forget my manners sometimes, Michael. I apologize for not saying hello earlier. It truly has been too long." He paused for only a moment, looking at the priest's neck. "I see you have a few scars that are still healing. Sometimes we're straddled with outward manifestations of our inward sins. I think the good archbishop was almost as saddened as I was by your disobedience in seeking out Father Oliveira, but you've always been one to follow your own dictates."

Dalacourt, already bewildered, was caught completely off guard. How could this man possibly know about Father Oliveira? He wanted to reply, but nothing came out.

"Fair enough, I'll do the speaking for both of us," Hade said. "Let me start by saying thank you. I know it wasn't an easy task I laid before you, but you are a fine shepherd and you have guided my little sheep here as expected."

Dalacourt's eyes grew large as the other three turned to regard him suspiciously.

"You have to admit," Hade continued, baiting them expertly, "not just anyone could have lured Alexis up here. And without Alexis, I doubt we'd have Owen or Petr. And without all of you, it isn't really a party."

"Is this true?" Alexis asked hesitantly, suspicion in her voice as she stared at the priest.

"N...n...no," Dalacourt stammered in absolute shock. "I swear. I don't have any idea what he's talking about!" He turned back to Hade. "I don't even know who you are!"

"Why, Michael," Hade replied, leaning closer to the priest. "You really don't recognize me?" Hade's voice changed, growing slower and weaker and picking up just a hint of a Boston accent. A slow smile spread across his face. "Michael, recite Second Timothy 3:1-5."

Michael Dalacourt staggered back as the realization of the man's identity dawned upon him.

"Yes, Michael," Hade rumbled. "You knew me as Father Xavier Dunkirk, the man who helped raise you as a young boy after the senseless murder of your dear Aunt Helen. You, my dear Father, owe me everything."

Dalacourt could not speak. He could barely draw a breath. The man before him was indeed the former headmaster of the Catholic school he'd attended as a youth. It was Father Dunkirk who had set him on the path into the seminary and assured an eventual appointment at the Vatican under the continued tutelage of Francis De Solei.

"But," Dalacourt finally whispered, "you can't be him! You died when I turned twelve!"

"The day before, if I remember correctly," Hade answered mournfully, placing his hand on his heart. "Alas, you didn't need me anymore, and I had work elsewhere, so I entrusted you to my servant, Francis De Solei, who has apparently instructed you remarkably well in my absence."

"No," Dalacourt said again, shaking his head. His mind nearly broke as a series of doors opened up within and led him almost instantaneously through his past, a past that now looked like it had been meticulously orchestrated by someone else. He dropped slowly to his knees in the thick mud as the sick realization engulfed him.

"Yes, you recognize the truth, lad," Hade said, looking down at him. "But don't blame yourself. You've been mine from the moment of your birth. Everything you've ever thought or done has been orchestrated by me specifically to get you here, with them, for this moment."

Dalacourt shook his head, trying to find his center. He wasn't Hade's. He couldn't be Hade's! He was a man of God, even if someone else had directed him upon that path. "No," he finally said, lifting his eyes. Hade was wrong. In his heart, the young priest knew he was still his own man. Wiping the rain from his face, he made the sign of the cross as he spoke. "All of that might be true, but I serve God," he said defiantly, climbing to his feet as the strength of his convictions filled him. "You did not teach me to love God, Hade. And you will not take that love from me now. My faith is secure and I know that, while God remains, I will serve him to the end of my days. I serve God, Hade," he repeated. "Not you."

Hade raised his hands in a mocking gesture. "Testify!" he shouted, grinning. "You know, I almost feel ready to join the cause after that sermon, Father," he said. "Almost, mind you, but not quite.

"I think we all can agree Michael believes in his cause," Hade said, shifting his eyes to the Russian, "but I wonder what Petr believes in?" He looked at each of the group before him as he paced back and forth. "What do we know about Petr? I know he has a good heart somewhere inside that chest of his. And he has one of the sharpest minds you'll find," he continued. "If he could just learn how to control his emotions and focus his intellect, I daresay he could become one of the most powerful men on the planet. But history is littered with men who failed to live up to their full potential because they were never able to overcome their flaws." He turned back to the Russian. "With Petr here, it really starts and stops with his inability to make good decisions. You see, he makes bad decisions. Lots of bad decisions. And those bad decisions have consequences, don't they, boy," Hade laughed. "How many people have died in the last few days as a result of your bad choices?"

Petr just stood there, his face a stone wall. He had already gone down this road with Hade and knew from experience there was nothing he could say that would exonerate himself. And yet, he was still unprepared for how incredibly brutal Hade's mind games could be.

"Alexis, I'm wondering if you knew that Petr is responsible for the death of just about his entire family," Hade explained, glancing at the terrified girl. "Do you deny that, Petr?"

Petr lifted his chin. "It wasn't like that..." he said, painfully aware of the open stares of Owen and Alexis.

"Then there was Rene," Hade went on. "What a tragic ending to such a promising young life. Poor girl took a thirteen story express elevator to the pavement because Petr was too busy playing the action hero to worry about her." He smiled again. "How am I doing so far, Petr?"

The Russian said nothing.

"Then of course, Donovan ended up with a wooden chair leg driven through his heart, courtesy of you," Hade said.

"Donovan was already dead," Petr objected.

"Yes, yes, a technicality," Hade said thoughtfully and then looked at him, a sly grin coming to his face. "But you didn't just kill the undead on that rooftop, did you?"

"No," Petr warned, his voice deadly quiet. "Not here. Not in front of Alexis."

"I think I'll make the decisions about what I tell Alexis or not," Hade replied. "She deserves to know about your poor decisions concerning David, an innocent father unnecessarily swept up by the tide of chaos that consumed the city. She should know you led David into a dangerous situation on the roof of a hotel, which ultimately resulted in his demise." Hade smirked. "You never even gave him a chance, Petr. Admit it."

"Stop," Petr objected, his eyes haunted, stricken with a pain that reached deep into his soul. "Please, I beg of you."

"I'm sorry, Petr," Hade countered. "I think she has the right to know that one of her suitors is the man who put a gun to David's chest and pulled the trigger. It was you who killed David Livingston Sumbawanga. Do you deny this?"

Petr could say nothing, his eyes focused on Alexis. He was not surprised to see she was looking at him with undisguised hatred.

"Is he telling the truth, Petr?" she asked. "Did you kill David?"

Petr looked at her for the longest time and then finally nodded his head. "Yes," he answered, "but I had no choice. I did it out of mercy."

"Are we rethinking our decision not to kill Petr, Alexis?" Hade asked Alexis, holding out the pistol to her. "It's not too late, you know. You would be avenging a terrible crime and preventing countless others in the future." He paused, looking hard at the girl. But she refused to be baited and looked away from the big man.

"No?" he asked. He continued on, not expecting her to answer. "Well, I'm nothing if I'm not accommodating," he said. "Let me know if you have need of the Colt at any time and I'll be happy to oblige."

"He was dying, Alexis," Petr explained hurriedly, looking hard at her. "He begged me to end his life in a way that would keep his body from being taken over. He asked me to take care of his daughter, Chuike, and I said I would." He looked at Hade and then back to Alexis. "It was the worst thing I've ever done in my life, but I did it out of compassion, Alexis. I'm not a bad man," he trailed off.

"None of us believe we are," Hade agreed knowingly. "Still, if a dark cloud follows you everywhere you go, is that not enough to suggest that you are the cause of the storm? Your hands are covered with blood, Petr, by those you have killed and by those who have died because of your actions. I'm more worried about dear Chuike having Petr protect her than if he was just to leave her alone."

Hade turned to face Alexis and bared his teeth in a wide smile. "I'm sure at this moment you're feeling a sense of betrayal, aren't you? Maybe even righteous indignation? Perhaps this would be a perfect time to remember 'She that is without sin among you, let her cast the first stone'," Hade said slyly. "Oh, how I wish Petr was the only one here responsible for the deaths of those he cared deeply about. Unfortunately, our young Alexis here has decided to give Petr a run for his money."

"What are you talking about?" she asked, her eyes showing the confusion churning within her at Hade's accusations.

"Well, I didn't want to bring this up, especially in front of you, Owen," he said, looking at the young man. "But it seems Petr has this strange fascination with Alexis, thinking she's some sort of a muse for him to take as his own," he explained. "I suppose there's something romantic about that, although what it is, I haven't the foggiest idea. But Petr is mistaken, as I can tell you all the muses I've ever met are decent enough creatures who would never hurt anyone, let alone purposefully put them in harm's way." He looked back to Alexis and addressed his next comment to her, a knowing smile on his face. "How many people have died under your care in the last twenty-four hours, Alexis?"

Alexis' world stopped. She tried to piece together an answer, but the faces of all the people she had seen die, flooded through her mind. "No one," she managed to stammer, not even managing to convince herself.

Hade could only smile. "Oh, we both know that isn't true," he said. "Just for kicks, let's look at your recent history and see what it tells us. You watched as Libby was hit by a car. You hid in a bedroom while Emily had her throat slashed while trying to protect you. You allowed Gen and Todd to drive off to their ultimate deaths. Then you left Libby, Sally, and countless others to die at the shelter while you escaped. And, just a short while ago, you left your friends at the bottom of the mountain to face an entire army of undead, led by Death itself, just so you could reunite with your Owen." He looked closer at her. "Am I missing anything, dear girl?"

Alexis choked back the sobs that threatened to overcome her.

"But all that pales to your worst sin, does it not?" he went on. "You made a promise to a little girl, Alexis," Hade said knowingly, his voice dripping venom. "You promised her you'd protect her. And what did you do? You allowed Dakota to be killed by her own mother."

"It wasn't like that…"

Hade leaned closer. "A perfect, innocent little girl," he said, his voice almost a whisper. "Does your word mean nothing to you, Alexis? Or are you what you appear to be—a manipulative, scheming, selfish, cold-blooded, heartless witch?"

Alexis snapped and lashed out with her hand, slapping Hade hard across the face. Tears glistened in her eyes, and the amount of pain that tore at her was beyond anything she had ever felt. "What would you know about giving your word to protect anyone?" she seethed. Her body shook with renewed sobs and she turned away.

An odd look flashed across Hade's face, but it was gone in a moment. "You know nothing of sacrifice, Alexis," he growled, reaching up and stroking his cheek where she had slapped him. It was the only indication he gave that she had struck him. "Perhaps someday, you'll see what true sacrifice is all about. Perhaps someday, you'll know what it means to keep…your…word," he finished, purposefully dragging out the last three words of his charge.

He straightened and placed his hands behind his back, assuming a thoughtful pose. "You have a great deal of growing up to do, girl," he said after a few moments, "but to do that you need to know what kind of person you are. You might be different from Petr and Michael, but not the way you think," he said, turning and locking his gaze on the Russian again. "If I gave Petr here the task of walking a little old blind lady across a busy street, he would do so. But he would see danger in every car, in every pair of eyes that strayed their way. He would act without thought and remove those threats. But in the meantime, our poor little old blind lady would walk right into the path of the very bus that Petr was supposed to have protected her from."

He switched to the priest. "And if our good Father Dalacourt was given the same charge, he would believe he was following God's command but would become so wrapped up in his own concerns, he would walk her right in front of the bus and kill her as well. And while that would be terribly sad, it's not evil, is it, Alexis?"

He turned his gaze back on the shattered girl. "No, not evil at all," he repeated. "But you, I think, would see Owen across the street and you would push that sweet, dear innocent old lady right into the path of the bus and to an eternal slumber, just so you could be with your man." He smiled, a look of absolute malice. "What we can gather from this is that, while the woman dies in all three scenarios, only one of you would do this for your benefit. Only one of you is evil enough to kill anyone who gets in your path, just so you can get what you want." At that, he shrugged. "It isn't the best metaphor I've ever used, but I think it makes my point."

"Enough," Owen said, his voice strong. "I have heard enough."

"Have you now?" Hade asked, turning his full gaze on him. "I wonder, what would you do in that situation, Owen? What would the white knight do if he was tasked to help the little old lady to cross the street?"

"You're twisting events to suit your own purposes," Owen replied. "I won't play along."

Hade ignored him. "Tell me, lad," he pressed. "If you, the good Samaritan in our story, were helping the little old lady across the street and an out-of-control bus came barreling down the road out of nowhere, what would you do? What if you had only enough time to jump out of the way or push her out of the way and get run down yourself? Her life or yours, Owen. What would it be?"

"I told you, I won't play your game, Hade," he said with conviction.

"Ah, but that's where you're wrong, Owen," Hade countered. "You're playing my game right now, and just because you think you aren't giving me an answer, doesn't mean you aren't. In fact, you're telling me more then you care to know."

"Fine," Owen relented. "I'll give you your answer. I would save her!" He looked at Petr, Dalacourt, and Alexis. They were soaked to the skin, shivering, beaten, lost. But they could still win. "We all would," Owen said, his voice defiant.

"I think we've been over that, and I'm pretty sure no one else would, Owen. All of you are weak," Hade said. "You lack conviction. You lack sacrifice. God should bless me for destroying you."

"We'll beat you, Hade," Dalacourt spoke up. The big man looked at him in surprise but let the priest continue. "You're right, Hade. We are weak individually, but together we are strong. The scriptures tell us, 'And though a man might prevail against one who is alone, two will withstand him—a threefold cord is not quickly broken'."

"Ecclesiastes 4:12," Hade answered knowingly. "Nice touch, and you are correct, of course, that a threefold cord is indeed difficult to slice through. But why even try? Would you try to cut through a blacksmith's puzzle? Of course not. You study it, maneuver the parts, and simply pull them apart. Separating the rope of a threefold cord is beyond easy if you know where the ends of the cords are, and trust me, I know where the ends of your cords are. I've completely unraveled your threefold cord before your very eyes.

"You see, John sent you up here alone," Hade continued. "He sent you up here to go toe-to-toe against the greatest force the world has ever known. He likely assured you of victory if you would remain righteous, faithful, and strong. Am I right?" he asked, looking at each of them in turn.

"Your silence speaks volumes," the man went on. "But I put to you that there is more to life than this, my young friends. There is knowledge and patience and understanding. And there is Hade. And Hade has unraveled you and shown you for what you are. Hade has won," he crossed his arms across his massive chest. "And you have lost."

"No," Owen declared boldly, leaning heavily on David's walking cane. "You've unraveled nothing, Hade. You're the one who doesn't understand what's happening here. We won't serve you. The four of us will stand together. We'll beat you."

"Four?" Hade questioned, feigning a look of exaggerated shock. "Did I hear you right, Owen? Did you just say four?"

Owen stopped, thinking furiously, wondering what Hade was playing at now.

"I could have sworn I distinctly heard you say four," Hade went on. "I've read a lot on this subject over the years, and I don't ever remember the number four showing up anywhere. I'm familiar with a different number, though. Quote me that scripture John gave you, Father," he commanded without looking at Dalacourt, his voice deadly. "Just the middle part, if you would be so kind."

Dalacourt looked at Alexis, then Owen, and finally to Petr before he answered. "'And three kings shall rise up and stand upon the mountaintop. And they shall make war, one upon the other and the blood of their brother shall be spilled and they shall serve the anointed of the Beast, lest they humble themselves before God.'" The priest took a deep breath, steadying himself. "We have not made war, Hade. So the prophecy remains unfulfilled," the priest said, emboldened by the knowledge that they had held firm in the face of overwhelming adversity. "Owen is correct. You lose."

Hade's laughter came from deep within and lasted for some time. "God help you, Michael," he finally said. "So faithful, so sure, and so lacking for information! You should have paid more attention in math class. The scripture states the three shall serve the anointed of the Beast. You think you were here to show me your strength, and you did," Hade went on. "I congratulate you. And one of you has shown me more strength than the others. One of you I'm now sure will never serve me, which means I've found the three who ultimately will."

Hade's voice grew cold and he raised the gun before him. "Unfortunately, this means it's time to say good-bye to one of you."

Hade walked forward and placed the muzzle of the Colt Defender between Petr's eyes. The Russian did not flinch. "One of these kings is not like the other," Hade began to sing the popular Sesame Street tune, doing so off-key. He swung the weapon so it was pointed at Dalacourt, who closed his eyes in anticipation. "One of these kings just doesn't belong," he sang on, shifting his aim to Alexis. She shrank back from him in terror.

Hade then pointed the weapon at Owen's chest and smiled.

"Go to hell," Owen said through clenched teeth.

"You first, dear boy," the demon before him said quietly. "You first."

And Hade pulled the trigger.

RISEN

CHAPTER 19

Ferguson Canyon, Utah…One Year Later: Alexis Kennedy knelt beside the edge of the rocky path and ran her hand lightly across the swath of bright red Indian Paintbrush wildflowers growing there. To her, they were a stark reminder that exactly a year ago, the only red she saw was blood.

She'd been waiting with somewhat dreaded anticipation for this day for weeks, and now that she was here, she was not in any hurry to reach the top. The flowers had drawn her close and, as she breathed in their scent, her eyes glimpsed a piece of wood lying nearly buried beneath the wildflower patch. Reaching out, she touched it, then grasped it and drew it forth. Her breath caught in her throat as she recognized it immediately.

It was a piece of wood, long and polished to a dark hue, crafted of a mango tree that had once given up a branch to serve as a walking stick to a man who had become her friend in the short time she had known him. It had been David Livingston Sumbawanga's, before he died in the chaos last year with so many others. How it remained here untouched, for so long, Alexis had no idea. She let her eyes examine the staff and she felt a sense of sadness as she regarded the polished wood and David's handprint on it, somehow burned into the wood by his blood.

She stood up, holding the staff before her. Somehow, it was fitting that she would discover such a personal treasure on the day she returned to this hallowed spot. With a sad smile, she took a deep breath and looked up the rocky trail that would take her to the plateau. Today, there would be no hurry. Today, she had much to think about, and the walk up the peaceful path would help her sort through the chaos that still churned within her mind.

The sun was sinking into late afternoon, yet it was still warm and a few birds off in the distance were singing just softly enough for her to hear. The song offered a bit of comfort to her troubled soul, but her mind quickly drifted back to her purpose. She scanned the landscape around her again and noted how different this spot was from a year ago, when the rain and the mud had swallowed so much of her life. That visit had been one of loss. She was nervous what this visit might bring.

Gathering her emotions, she began to walk, leaning on David's walking stick not because she needed to, but because it gave her comfort. Eventually, she reached the end of the path and walked out onto the rocky plateau. She closed her eyes and paused to breathe in the clean mountain air before settling herself into a cross-legged position on the rocky outcropping that overlooked Ferguson Canyon. She laid the wooden staff gently on the rocks beside her and let herself relax in the warm breeze blowing in from the south.

The air up here was clean, much better than what blanketed the valley floor below. She looked out over the valley and sadness filled her heart. A year ago, the Salt Lake valley had been lush and verdant from a wet winter, green and full of promise. That was right before the horror that had been unleashed upon the world. Today, it was different. It was as if nature had recoiled at the devastation that humanity had wrought upon itself, and it had withdrawn like a turtle hiding in its shell. After the terrifying carnage last spring, it had been one of the driest summers and winters in recorded history, and any grass that had been there the year before was now long gone.

The great city, like so many others across the globe, had survived the terrible calamities, but not without deep and savage wounds. Large sections were still darkened and burned over, and despite a year of almost constant construction, the city still looked withered and diseased. Sadly, she knew there were too many scars for the city to ever heal completely. Too many thousands had died and too many thousands more were still missing and would likely never be found. Her closest friends Libby and Gen and the little girl Dakota were included among the former. Her family was among the latter. All of it added considerably to her sense of loss. She was alone in the world, which was why she was here today.

Sighing, she blinked back the tears and again fought the daily battle to control the desperate sense of loneliness that always threatened to consume her. This place she was in, this unmarked memorial to all she once had, was known to many as the Everlasting Hills. Perhaps the grandeur that inspired its name was what had attracted Owen DiConte to them in the beginning. Owen had always appeared everlasting to Alexis, like the mountains that stood as silent sentinels around her. They had survived. Owen, though, was gone. And with that stark reminder of all she had lost, she curled up tightly on the warm stone under her and cried.

Eventually the tears slowed and, with the sun now considerably lower on the horizon, Alexis wearily sat up. She had known this journey to the plateau would be difficult, but she'd been unprepared for the rawness of her pain. She had cried long and hard for Owen when Hade had murdered him a year ago, but then she'd buried her emotions deep as the tumultuous year following that horrific event had unwound.

Now, back up on the mountain and away from the painful rebirth of Salt Lake City, her soul had been laid bare. She sat on the very spot where Owen had died in her arms that stormy afternoon, his lifeblood rapidly draining away from him. She had told him she loved him, that she loved him more than anyone ever could, even as death claimed him with its cold embrace. She relived his murder in stark, soul-cleansing clarity, and in doing so, her own spiritual wounds were reopened and the pain poured forth as quickly as his blood had.

In time, the pain lessened and a sense of determination settled in. Drying her eyes, she watched the setting sun touch off blazes of color around the few clouds in the sky.

The time had come.

"Hello, Owen," she began tentatively, speaking softly as if he was there and their faces were nearly touching. "It's me, Alexis." She paused for a while before continuing. "I've stayed away for so long..." she trailed off again and fought to keep her composure. "I need to talk to you, Owen," she finally said, her voice stronger as she placed her hands flat on the still-warm rock. "I have so much I want to say."

A soft breeze blew across her skin, drying the last of her tears, and she managed a sad smile, wanting to believe it was Owen's way of telling her to be strong.

After another long pause, she continued. "I can hardly believe a year has gone by, Owen. It's been so lonely without you. It still seems like a terrible nightmare, and often I believe I'll wake up and it'll all be over. But it's real, isn't it?" she stated softly, her voice breaking again. "I miss you, Owen. I miss everything about you. And there's so much I wish I'd been able to tell you before you left me."

She was silent again, fresh tears rolling down her cheeks. She thought again about Owen's death and the deaths of those she cared so much about. As the past year had unfolded, she had devised a system within her mind where the vivid memories of loved ones dying roared through her psyche like a tornado and then immediately roared back out again. She soaked it all in, the sounds, the smells, the sight, the touch. She let it surround her and nearly consume her, but just before it did, she let it surge back out. It resulted in a moment of soul-wrenching pain, but it was her way of remembering without letting the terrible sadness consume her. It was her way of surviving. With a shudder, she tightened her resolve and, when she spoke again, her voice was slightly stronger.

"It's so hard sometimes," she said softly, looking out over the wounded city. "I still visit you in the cemetery every week, but it's so cold and lifeless there and when I talk to you, I'm not sure you can hear me." She waited again for the answering breeze, and when she felt its warmth caress her cheek, she went on. "For so long, I've wanted to come back here, but it's been so hard. I've always been afraid you wouldn't be here." She paused again, sending her soul as far as it could reach up into the skies, seeking for his answering touch. "But I know you're here, Owen," she whispered. "I can feel your presence."

She watched the sun sink lower, the shadows of evening growing longer. She was in no hurry to leave yet. Owen was here. She could feel his presence in the rocks and the trees that surrounded her; his essence was on the breeze that lovingly caressed her.

"You know, I still remember when you brought me up here for the first time," she finally said, bending her mind to happier times. "I remember watching you climb the path, watching your excitement at being in this place. It was a way for me to see what you were made of. It was a way for me to see you as yourself."

Alexis laughed softly at that, the happy memory of that day clear and vivid in her mind. "I know I was just another friend of yours, 'one of the guys', sitting on this rock next to you while you enjoyed the sunset. But for me, it was so much more." She smiled again and ran her hand through the soft mane of her hair, brushing it from her face. "I saw who you truly were and I understood you in a way I've never understood anyone before or since. It was actually up here I realized that I loved you. I just wish it hadn't taken me so long to let you know."

The wind blew softly, ruffling her silken hair. She knew that he was there with her. She was silent again, focusing her attention on the sun's rays. They lit up the barren mountainside behind her as the glowing orb began its descent into the hills beyond. She thought how Owen might have been inwardly disappointed at this sunset. It was harsh and blinding, casting the parched trees and scrub grass in a base relief of ebbing life. It was so unlike the night she had sat with him up above the world and secretly dreamed of their bright future together. Still, she knew that Owen would have found something worthwhile to say about it and he would have found joy in the sunset no matter the message. That was just the way he was, and that was why she had loved him so.

"The world has changed, Owen," she said, taking her eyes from the horizon and looking back down at the rock. In her mind's eye, she could see Owen's blood covering it and her mood darkened. "It's a different world, and I don't know if I'm ready for what's expected of me," she continued, thinking back to John's words, to the immense responsibility placed on the shoulders of her and two others. It was something she'd continued to struggle with throughout the past year because it was also the reason Owen was dead. Three kings, not four, Hade had said before brutally murdering her beloved.

"I need you, Owen. I feel so lost. You used to dream of being the white knight in shining armor," she said, a haunted smile gracing her beautiful face. "I could really use rescuing right now." She trailed off again, letting her feelings sort themselves out. "But you're not here to rescue me," she finished, her voice dropping to a sad whisper. "No one is."

Once more, she closed her eyes tightly against the overwhelming surge of sorrow, of anger, of hopelessness that threatened to pull her down into the depths and drown her. But the Alexis of today was not the Alexis of yesterday and once more she fought and mastered the tumult within her soul. With a deep breath, she opened her eyes and continued to watch the sun sink even lower on the horizon. In a few minutes, the top edge of the mountains would cut into the perfect circle of the sun as the afternoon deepened into dusk.

She watched a pair of swallows zigzag across the darkening sky and breathed deeply, catching the slight scent of pine and wildflowers on the evening breeze. The sun began to dip behind the mountains as a cloud drifted in front of the reddening orb, casting deep shadows across the wounded city below. She knew her time with Owen was coming to a close and that, once again, he was going to be taken from her up on this hill. Only this time she was going to say her good-bye properly.

"I love you, Owen," Alexis said again, her voice stronger. "And I miss you so much. I wish you were here with me. Someone once said that however far the stream flows, it never forgets its source. I want you to know wherever I have to go in my life, I will never forget my source. You are my source, Owen, and I'll always take you with me. I'll always look to you for guidance when I'm lost."

Alexis paused for the last time that night, knowing Owen was listening, hoping he knew her heart. As the clouds slipped away from the sun and touched the peaks of the Oquirrhs, the mountains connected to the heavens. The setting sun cast a shadow that marched down the slopes of the Oquirrhs, and Alexis silently watched it walk across the valley and to the foot of the mountains where she sat. Slowly, the shadow ascended the Wasatch and finally reached out to her, shrouding her feet and then slowly enveloping her body. To her surprise, the shadow spread over her with a glowing warmth that she was unprepared for. Sunset usually spread its cooling blanket over the valley, as if to tuck it in for the night, the warmth and glow of the day turning to darkness and solitude. Tonight, however, it felt as if the air was swirling and alive. It surrounded her and willed her not to withdraw and disappear from the world, but to arise and go forth to find her destiny. She closed her eyes and basked in the warm caress of the wind, feeling Owen's spirit embrace her, filling her with life like she had never felt before. It was a moment in time she could live in forever.

The shadow continued to march on and the warmth eventually faded. The breeze shifted direction and this time, it was cool on her skin. Alexis opened her eyes.

"Thank you, Owen," she said softly. "I will always love you."

Alexis Kennedy arose from her perch upon the rocky plateau and gently picked up her new walking stick. As darkness claimed the mountainside, she began her slow and careful decent back down the path, leaving behind the place that had ripped her world apart and had now given her the first bit of thread she needed to stitch it back together. She had come to find Owen in the Everlasting Hills, but she had done much more than that. She had found herself.

INTERREGNUM: ONE YEAR LATER

Ground Zero, London, England: Contrary to popular belief, the bomb that had destroyed London was not detonated by terrorists, despite the eventual claims of more than a dozen different such groups, all of them eager to claim responsibility and glorify whatever god or cause they were attached to. The bomb had been a powerful and creative combination of nuclear and chemical explosives, leaving a large section of London and the surrounding area uninhabitable for years to come.

The bomb had gone off just above the ground, but scientists had determined that, at up to one hundred kilotons, coupled with the flat terrain and lack of tall buildings on the west side of the city, nearly three hundred thousand people had been killed within the first twenty four hours. Over the next two months, a poisonous cloud had spread throughout the area, and over a million more had died of radiation poisoning. Over the past year, another million deaths throughout England and Western Europe had been directly attributed to the resulting fallout, and future deaths by cancer and disease were immeasurable.

But Krypteia had not detonated the bomb for the destruction of life, although that was certainly a positive outcome for them, as it did much to solidify their control over the world through fear and chaos. The real purpose of the bomb was to actually bring about life. More specifically, it was designed to bring about one life. For a year, the unique poisons in the air and the ground had been feeding its flesh, while the spirits of Satan's minions had been feeding its mind. Now, almost twelve months from the moment the bomb had exploded, that life was nearly complete.

Imprisoned deep underground in a concrete bunker built

specifically to allow the poisons to surround it, the creature had seethed and festered, growing stronger and more horrible as each day passed. It was nearly ready to be set loose upon the world. It only required someone to release it.

High above it on the surface of the earth, a single figure stood. Cloaked in black, the figure was virtually invisible in the deep of the night. Only two glowing points of red light could be seen glimmering in the darkness, but there was no living thing within miles.

"Quis est thy nomen? Quod is refero, sententia, Meus nomen est Legio: pro nos es plures," the figure spoke Latin clearly, reciting the Bible's fifth chapter of Mark, the ninth verse—"And he asked him, 'What is thy name?' And he answered, saying, 'My name is Legion: for we are many'." Its timeless voice was dry and cracked, as if echoing over eternity from the very pits of hell itself. It stood upon the spot for another moment before vanishing into the darkness, sinking into the ground like a wraith, its voice speaking English this time, whispering one final warning into the black night.

"The time has come."

וודגמרא

Death Valley, California: The ancient Indian crouched down on the sand-blasted rock and stared out over the California desert. It was mid-afternoon and the desert heat was at its worst, weaving shimmering curtains over the landscape wherever one looked. But the old man ignored the heat, his mind solely occupied with the coming task.

A year he had spent in solitude, preparing for the inevitable, and he knew now it was finally upon him. It was upon the world.

Reaching down, he picked up a handful of sand and let it sift through his fingers, watching the finer particles whip away on the hot desert wind. He wondered how many would be swept away by the coming of this second, more powerful maelstrom. Humanity had survived the first wave. More importantly, the chosen three, the kings spoken of in ancient and hidden scripture, had overcome all odds and defeated Hade's gambit. It had been an outcome that was never certain until those final fateful moments on the mountain.

But John knew the victory, while important, was by no means the end of the war. In fact, it was only the beginning. Everything that had happened last year had been carefully orchestrated by an enemy mankind could not even begin to comprehend, and the chaos of last year was only the opening salvo in this, the final conflict. This next round would test them all far beyond anything they had experienced.

Shaking his head sadly, John slowly and painfully rose to his feet, his knees and legs creaking more than ever. He was tired. He was battered. And hope was fading. But as long as he breathed, he would not give up. None of them could. With a sigh born from a journey thousands of years old, he slowly started down the windblown mountain path.

It was time to join the battle once more.

וודגממרא

New York City, New York: Tom McCain listened to his coins clink through the inside of the battered machine before they released the door catch. Pulling the rusty door open, he reached inside and pulled out a copy of the *New York Times*.

He winced slightly as a sharp pain lanced through his shoulder, and he paused to rotate it slowly, trying to loosen the injured muscle. It had taken him almost a year for most of his wounds from the battle on the mountain to heal, but it was certainly better than the alternative. He was still surprised that he, Stacia, and John had survived that onslaught of undead, but he hadn't prepared his entire life for that moment to fail when it mattered most. He coughed twice to clear his throat of the dirty New York City air and looked at the headline splashed across the front page of the paper.

> "ISRAEL SEALS BORDERS"—Tel Aviv, Israel: Israel's Prime Minister today put the country's military forces on full alert and sealed all of the country's borders. Travel in and out of Israel has been forbidden and there's no word yet on what the country plans to do with visiting foreigners and dignitaries. The rest of the world is loudly expressing its outrage. "It's hard to understand," stated one Washington senator. "Israel suffered little of what we or any other country suffered during the tragedy of last year. And now, when the rest of the world could use their help, they have withdrawn from all of us."

McCain stopped reading and looked around, snorting derisively. "You can hardly blame them," he chuckled bitterly. "Who would want this?"

New York City functioned today—barely. After the holocaust of last year, it had taken more than a month to get the electrical grid back online. The transit system was finally back up, not more than three months ago. Buses and trains were running on limited schedules and routes, but at least people were moving again. The hardcopy Times had been printing again for only the past few weeks, coming out every few days or so. That was the only way he would take his news. The events of last year had sent "Big Brother" into overdrive and McCain had no intention of doing anything—even something as innocuous as signing up to get an online newspaper—to allow anyone the slightest chance to pinpoint his location.

The Big Apple itself had been hit hard when the world had gone crazy and now, a year later, the city was not much better. Nearly a third of the city's eight million people had been killed, were missing, or had moved away after that horrible week. Today, many burned-out buildings still stood throughout the city, some with skeletal frames, others with blackened and broken windows and doorways that hid people who were better off remaining hidden.

McCain could always feel their eyes on him when he walked the streets. Many people had said the world was moving toward becoming a better place today than it was a year ago, but he knew that was a crock. He saw it every day, felt it in the presences he knew existed in the dark, saw it in the decaying refuse piled along deserted streets. The world was not a better place—it was nowhere near it. And, if the rest of the world was anything like New York City, the world had a long way to go. He could hardly fault the people of Israel for not wanting anything to do with it anymore.

Tom McCain tucked the paper under his arm and patted the gun bulge under his jacket reassuringly. Hoping he might get through a day in this diseased city without having to use it, he headed down the street to meet his daughter for breakfast.

וודגמרא

Tel Aviv, Israel: Rebekkah Kassem set her steaming mug of coffee down and spread the morning newspaper out on her kitchen table. It had been years since she held a newspaper in her hands, and although she knew she could read the same article online, she couldn't resist picking up a copy of *Haaretz* earlier that morning during her monthly shopping trip.

Maybe it was the headline and the way it stood out, pointing toward darker times and further upheaval in the world. Mankind was a master at self-destruction and had a very short memory. How quickly they forgot the wars of the past, the terror in recent years, and the worldwide catastrophes of last year. How quickly they were ready to start a new war once the old one was over. The headline immediately jumped out at her, confirming that the more things changed, the more they stayed the same.

"BRAZILIAN PRESIDENT CONDEMNS ISRAEL"—Brasilia, Brazil: Newly-inaugurated Brazilian President Jose Maria Wilson Nunes da Silva dos Santos made his first public comments to the world and delivered a scathing rebuke aimed at Israel, even as he pledged the full support of his country to those hardest hit by the calamities of the last year. President Wilson stated, "As a country, we were fortunate to be spared from the greater part of the horrors that swept the world last year. To the United States, Russia, Australia, and to all of our allies in general, we the people of Brazil publically pledge our aid and our resources in the colossal task of rebuilding. We refuse to follow the lead of nations such as Israel, who would turn their back on those in need."

The story was full of more saber rattling and posturing, the age old nationalistic saga of positioning one's own country as the savior of the world and the next country as the devil. The young Israeli woman shook her head and smiled. She picked up her cup of coffee to take a sip of the bitter liquid. "If they only knew," she thought.

וודגמרא

Brasilia, Brazil: President Wilson, as he identified himself these days, for it was simply too much to use his full name, walked briskly into his office and paused. He closed his eyes, savoring the moment, and breathed in deeply the smell of power. For as long as he could remember, the former Brazilian soccer star had aspired to this. Now it was finally his. The power, the fame, the perks—oh, there were so many perks associated with being the leader of one of the most powerful countries still standing.

And it was all his.

He brushed a tiny piece of lint from his dark blue Armani suit and walked to his desk. Large and crafted of beautiful mahogany to his exact specifications, it was the perfect representation of who he was. As he seated himself into his luxurious black leather executive chair and ran a hand lovingly across the polished surface of his desk, there was a sharp knock at his door.

"Come," he said immediately, having no worries of some secret assassin ready to do him harm. He had annihilated his competition in the recent election and believed he had no enemies. Besides, one of his first duties as president was to award the contract for upgrading the security of his building to Legio Securities Inc., a subsidiary of the company he owed so much of his personal progression to.

The door opened and he was greeted smartly by his top aide. "Good morning, Mr. President," Enrique Araiza said cheerfully, walking into the room. He had a stack of various colored folders in one hand and an iPad in the other. "I trust you had a restful night?"

"I slept like a baby, Enrique," Wilson replied with a sly smile. "And why not? I now lead perhaps the most powerful nation in the world."

It did not hurt his position that, prior to the run up to the election, his predecessor had seized the opportunities afforded to him by the rampant chaos in the world to invade neighboring Venezuela and take control of its rich oil fields. The invasion had been swift, decisive, and surprisingly easy. Fortunately for Wilson, any good press that the invasion received for the former president was offset by the breaking news a week before election day of widespread corruption throughout his administration, as well as claims that the president had a sixteen year old Argentinian mistress. When put together with Wilson's natural charisma and widespread connections, he had jumped in the polls from 19% to 57% almost overnight and rocketed easily to the presidency the next week, where he found himself in charge of one of the few countries still standing strong after the problems of the past year. It had been a perfect storm, and Wilson had reaped the benefits more than anyone else in the world.

"Indeed," Enrique replied as he returned the man's smile and handed the tablet to the president. "I thought you might find this interesting, sir."

Wilson laid it on his desk, taking smug satisfaction in noticing it was dwarfed by the immense size of the desktop. Yes, power was a heady potion, and Wilson would be a profound imbiber. Looking down at the screen, the headline immediately caught his eye.

"CHURCH NAMES NEW POPE"—Los Angeles, CA: The Catholic church last night officially named its new pope, putting to rest any further speculation over the leadership of the church. Former Archbishop Francis De Solei solemnly accepted the mantle in a ceremony that was a surprise to no one. With the Vatican destroyed in last year's tragic explosion and most of the church leadership, including the previous pope and fifty-seven of the one hundred and sixty-four cardinals, killed in the atrocities, Pope De Solei has been the de facto administrator of the church ever since. He was given unprecedented emergency power during the *sede vacante* by the remaining members of the College of Cardinals to direct its operation from the magnificent Cathedral of Our Lady of the Angels in Los Angeles, and has used that power to restore the church to heights of power and influence not seen for centuries. In a surprise appearance and announcement this morning, De Solei made it clear there would be sweeping changes within the church and in the world itself, to prepare for what he insisted would be 'the Second Coming of Christ, himself'."

President Wilson looked up at his aide, sharing the man's knowing smile. "Good thing we're of the church, Enrique," Wilson said as he reached for the phone and dialed a number.

וודגמרא

Cainsville, Missouri: A tired-looking man slumped into his chair at the back end of the bar and with a sigh, reached into a threadbare shirt pocket. Pulling out a battered pack of cigarettes, he shook out the last of them, one that had already been half-smoked and was bent crookedly near the filter. Putting it in his mouth, he patted and checked his other pockets in vain for a match, before gently tucking the butt back into the pack as if it was his most treasured possession.

"Need a light, Father?" a nearby voice asked.

Michael Dalacourt looked up and watched the kindly owner of the small bar and grill walk over to him. It was mid-day, two in the afternoon, and there were no other patrons in the place. Usually, the crowd didn't start arriving until shortly after five, when most of the remaining population of the tiny town got off work. "Can't figure out where my matches went," Dalacourt replied absently. "Thought I had a whole book of 'em."

"Here," Gus Olaffson said softly, tossing a new book down on the table in front of him. "You look tired, Father," the heavy-set man went on, still insisting on calling him "Father" despite the fact Dalacourt had long ago discarded his collar as well as any notion that God even existed. "Want a bite to eat?"

"Not today, Gus," he replied helplessly. "No money."

"It's on me," Gus went on, ignoring him. "I insist."

Dalacourt shrugged, but was inwardly grateful. He was not used to such kindness. Most people shunned him, or did worse if they were in foul moods, which seemed to be in abundance these days. He'd shown up in the little town two months ago, broken down and drunk. Gus' was the first place he'd stumbled into and, instead of throwing him out as was normally the case, Gus had given the broken man a hot meal and a place to rest from his wanderings.

The next day, sober but with another hangover, Dalacourt had thanked Gus by doing some odd jobs for him, and their relationship had been born. When Gus needed some work around the restaurant done, Dalacourt would do it, making a little money to survive.

Gus laid a newspaper down on the table. "Here, have a read, Father," he went on. "I'm done with it. Nothing but bad news anymore and, without any football or baseball in the world, I don't even know why I pick up the thing." He turned to head back to the kitchen. "Give me a few minutes and I'll be back with some bacon and eggs," he said as he walked away.

"Thanks, Gus," Dalacourt mumbled appreciatively and then picked up the paper. The headlines sent his head into a spin.

"LOS ANGELES THE NEW VATICAN?"—Los Angeles, CA: Parting with tradition has been a hallmark of the newly-appointed Pope of the Church, even in the short time he has been at its head. From maintaining his own name to actually striking the Catholic name from church doctrine, Pope De Solei has declared that Los Angeles, California, will be the new seat of the One Church. "As the final days loom before us, we must be able to move quickly and decisively in all that the church does," he said in last evening's worldwide broadcast. "The Vatican is gone. We must accept that. The terrible calamities and catastrophes of the past year have tried us all; have changed the very fabric of reality that encompasses humanity. Since then, I have directed God's church from Los Angeles and, for the very same reason I have remade God's church into the One Church for the entire world, I have decided to remake our location here as the new Vatican. The clock moves toward midnight and we must move with it. We must bring all God's children to us. We must prepare each and every one of you to receive Christ's glory through this, God's Church."

Michael Dalacourt, former priest of the Catholic church, former protégé of Francis De Solei, former creation of the monster Hade, laid the paper down. With shaking hands, he pulled the bent cigarette back out of the pack in his pocket, lit it with a match from the matchbook Gus had given him, and then took a long drag.

"Oh, my Lord God in heaven," he said quietly for the first time in nearly a year.

וודגמרא

Los Angeles, California: Bowing deeply, the young serving maid excused herself from his presence and silently left the spacious dining room. As she passed through the large double doors, a man pushed past her, giving her a cursory glance as he did. She was a pretty one, he thought. He would still have to get used to having female servants in the church's most holy house, but he was inwardly pleased with the change.

"Good morning, your Holiness," Cardinal Viandre said as he pushed those thoughts to the side and stepped into the personal dining room of the Holy Father himself. He knelt down on his left knee and waited for the Pope to acknowledge him. After a lengthy pause, the Pope finally held out his hand for the Cardinal to kiss his ring.

"Good morning, Vigo," Pope De Solei replied grandly, looking over the breakfast the maid had just brought to him. Three different kinds of eggs, trays of bacon and sausages, toasted breads, sliced fruits, and a large plate of expensive pastries—it was a breakfast fit for a king.

And why not? Pope De Solei was the most powerful man in the world. Sure, countries still had their secular leaders, but most deferred to the power of the church now and that power was Francis De Solei.

He picked up a piece of bacon and took a bite, then placed the remainder on a large empty plate nearby. He would finish his entire meal in the same fashion, eating single bites of what he wanted. The rest would be disposed of. It was considered blasphemous for anyone else to partake of his food.

"What news of the world?" he asked serenely, selecting a maple-cooked sausage link for his next sampling.

"Wonderful news indeed, your Holiness," the man replied happily, placing a copy of the *Los Angeles Times* in front of him. Another example of the conspicuous consumerism of the new Pope was his insistence on having at least one major newspaper from each nation delivered daily to his office, although he rarely, if ever, bothered to pick any of them up to read. "This can only portend magnificent things for the church."

Pope De Solei looked at the headline.

"SEPARATION OF CHURCH AND STATE STRUCK DOWN"—Washington, D.C.: In a stunning blow to the centuries-old tradition of separation of Church and State, the United States Supreme Court today announced their decision in U.S. v. Buxton that the federal government can align itself with an organized church to form a national religion. Chief Justice Emma T. Hendricks, in her majority opinion, wrote, "The First Amendment clearly says 'Congress shall make no law respecting an establishment of religion, or prohibiting the free exercise thereof.' Since our inception, Americans have accepted this to mean complete separation of church and state, but nowhere is that stated in this amendment, nor in any other part of the Constitution. As long as Congress makes no law that would result in a loss of life, liberty or property as a result of establishing a connection with a national church, there is nothing in the Constitution that would preclude such an event from happening." Secretary of Defense Anne Banyon, speaking on behalf of President Abrea, said that the Executive Office was fully behind this decision and would work diligently to ensure the new interpretation of the Constitution was upheld. Harvard Professor of Government, Christopher Tonash, however, was extremely critical of this decision, saying it's an "informal amendment" that would give too much power to the leadership of religious groups in the country. There is a short list of possible religions that would meet the requirements for being named the new, national religion, but most experts agree that none are positioned as well as the One Church led by Pope De Solei.

Pope De Solei placed the paper on the table and smiled. "Absolutely phenomenal news," he said easily. "It appears the old maxim that in desperate times men turn to God remains true in our day, as well."

"Indeed, your Holiness," Cardinal Viandre said, smiling himself. He knew how powerful Pope De Solei already was, and this would be a beautiful jewel in his glorious crown. Vigo Viandre held no illusions as to what this meant for him personally as he had no problem at all riding the man's coattails. He was perfectly content to sample the luxuries, the power, and the prestige, from behind the new Pope's shadow. "And your next step?"

"I believe the time has come to have a voice in world government," Pope De Solei answered. He reached over to a small desk stand next to his breakfast chair and picked up a piece of paper. Handing it to his subordinate, he went on. "The people on this list are to be immediately contacted and brought to Los Angeles post-haste. I expect every one of them in my office in forty-eight hours." He paused for a second. "And let's extend an invitation to our revered professor from Harvard. I believe he could use some enlightenment as well."

"Yes, your Excellency," Cardinal Viandre replied and hurried out.

After he left, Pope De Solei went back to his meal, a smile on his face. Things were indeed progressing as planned.

וודגמרא

Ujiji, Tanzania: The heavily-bearded man, a newspaper folded and tucked under his left arm, pushed open the front door of his home and walked out onto the small screen-enclosed porch. It was mid-morning, but the African sun was already baking the parched landscape. Still, he preferred the airy heat of the outdoors to the stifling heat of the indoors, so he spent much of his time outside of the house.

With a sad smile, he gazed, as he did every morning, at the mango tree still growing in the front yard and he thought of happier times, times when the world was still not yet savagely insane. Petr Zhugravinsky had experienced much of that insanity, and had lost much in the process. One of those losses had been the venerable David Sumbawanga, and not a day went by when Petr wondered if he might not have done something differently on that hotel roof last year and saved the man from his fate.

But the past was engraved on the stone tablets of time, and Petr could no more change it than he could change the color of the sun or the sky. David was dead, along with so many others. Petr had honored David's final request to come to Africa to find the man's daughter. He had done so, had imparted the sad news of his passing to the young woman, and then stayed in Africa as her protector. Chuike had grieved for her father as she grieved for her brother, but life is for the living, and so six months later she had gotten married as originally planned, with Petr standing in David's place during the ceremony.

Afterward, Petr continued to stay in David's home, preferring the solitude and the relative peace he found in the small village. He'd not run to Africa as much as he'd run from America. Hade had wanted him to go back to Russia, to take his place beside his brother, and then he had set him up to be murdered by Alexis for reasons he still did not understand. Beaten, bitter, and carrying an anger that threatened to poison his soul, he had long ago abandoned his dreams of making his mark in literary history. Today, it was all about survival, and part of that survival was making himself invisible to the eyes of the word. He sat down heavily and then opened up his Russian newspaper and glanced at the headline.

"NEW RUSSIAN PRESIDENT PROMISES SWEEPING CHANGES"—Moscow, Russia: In a stunning election upset, political idealist and hardliner Nikolai Zhugravinsky narrowly defeated incumbent president Viktor Dubrovski for the presidency and the leadership of the country. While Dubrovski's camp immediately called for a recount vote, alleging rampant voter fraud, President Zhugravinsky was confident the vote would stand. "The people have spoken!" he made clear in his victory speech. "The world has spoken! I swear that as president, I will make certain Mother Russia stands tall with her brothers and sisters of the United States, Brazil, and all other God-fearing countries around the world!"

Petr shook his head in helpless anger and tossed the paper to the floor beside his chair. A year ago, the thought of a bloodthirsty son of a Russian mafia family becoming the president of Russia was absolutely preposterous. But Petr knew better. Hade had foretold Nikolai's improbable rise to power, had even picked Petr to be his brother's keeper, but after everything that had happened on the mountain, Petr had refused and instead come to Africa to honor the memory and the plea of David Sumbawanga. Sometimes he wondered if Hade even knew where he was, but those thoughts never lasted long. Hade knew. Hade knew everything. And Petr knew it was only a matter of time before he would see the man walking up the path to his front door.

With a sigh, Petr leaned back in his chair and waited.

וודגמרא

Moscow, Russia: Nikolai Zhugravinsky stood in front of the huge bulletproof window of his new office and looked down into the streets of Moscow. His streets, he smiled to himself. His city. His country. Almost his world. Indeed, all that had been promised to him was now his. Hade had not lied, had in fact completely predicted the outcome of the election. And now, Nikolai had the power he'd always dreamed of.

"Mr. President," a voice sounded behind him, causing him to turn slightly to eye the man entering his spacious office. Neither of the hulking bodyguards standing on either side of the door moved, as the man was well known to everyone in the building.

"You have my itinerary for the day, Vanya?" he asked the newcomer.

Vanya Kasianenko had long been Nikolai's closest confident and was now his new head of security. He was the cousin Nikolai had collaborated with to eliminate his family and begin his incredible rise to power and, as such, Nikolai trusted him implicitly. He nodded and sauntered over to the desk, tossing a newspaper down, followed by a sheet of paper. "I do, Mr. President," he replied, "along with today's news. Our satellites are not all completely back online, so you'll have to make due with a regular newspaper again, I'm afraid."

"Ah, technology," Nikolai laughed. "When shall we make the trains run on time, I wonder?"

Vanya smiled, but did not answer the question. "You have an easy morning, sir. You have a conference call with President Wilson at nine a.m. and then your flight leaves for Los Angeles, California, at ten-thirty. President Abrea of the United States will have a VIP caravan waiting to take you to the Cathedral of Our Lady of the Angels. He'll meet you there."

"Security?"

"Nothing to worry about, Mr. President," Vanya answered easily. "I've checked it all the way to the Pope's office and we have men on site now. All is taken care of."

"Excellent," the new president of Russia said with a smile, seating himself at his large desk. Picking up the *Wall Street Journal* Vanya had brought him, he glanced at the headline.

"STOCK MARKET SURGES TO NEW YEAR HIGH"—
New York City, New York: Almost wholly on the
strength of Legio Industries, the stock market
surged to a record high for the year at the closing
bell yesterday, topping six thousand for the first
time since the crash associated with last year's
world-spanning catastrophes. Even with
continuing political and religious unrest, tech and
medical stocks, especially stock from those
companies owned under the umbrella of Legio
Industries, continue to power global trade. Many
analysts are quick to point out the recent stock
surges could also be attributed to the various
power vacuums around the world being filled,
from newly inaugurated presidents to the newly
named Pope De Solei of the One Church."

Nikolai smiled and laid the paper down. "We're on track, Vanya,"
he said with a smirk. "We're part of the elite—power brokers who will
control the destiny of the world. From nothing we came, and now the
world bows at our feet."

"It has been some journey," the other man agreed.

"Yes, it has, Vanya. But in truth, we're only just beginning."

וודגמרא

Monterey, California: Callithrix Aurita "Marmoset" Williams sat
alone, engulfed in the incredibly over-priced executive leather chair at
the head of the giant slate black boardroom table, his eyes distant, his
brain deep in thought. His left hand tracked idly back and forth across
the table, slowing every time it came to the crack that had nearly split

the table in half. The fracture had appeared over a year ago on the same day that a sizable number of board members had met untimely accidents. Marmoset was smart enough to recognize the hidden message in that, even if he had no idea who had sent the message. The board of directors had been nearly halved, the survivors had voted unanimously to back Victor Legio's ridiculous plan, and shortly thereafter, Legio himself had disappeared. Then the world had turned upside down in a cataclysmic series of events that had changed the fabric of mankind's very reality.

But true to Victor's word, Legio Industries had emerged from the chaos stronger than ever, and Marmoset had found himself president of the company. To say he'd been stunned would be a pitiful understatement, particularly since he'd never personally lobbied for anything like it. Marmoset had never considered himself as anything more than a behind-the-scenes player.

But someone else had viewed him as much more, and now he was the third richest man in the world and the head of the most powerful corporation ever to exist. And yet, even after a year in charge, he was no closer to understanding why.

Absentmindedly, he muttered the phrase, "Screen up," and an image of the Legio Industries corporate logo immediately appeared in the air before him. Holographics were a wonderful thing and Marmoset headed up the foremost company in developing such technologies. "Search financial news," he continued. "Keywords: Legio, acquisitions, recent."

It took the immensely powerful computer that controlled the holographic display less than a second to pull from the cloud every recent article on Legio Industries' acquisitions. By swiping his finger through the air, Marmoset scrolled through the top fifty articles as he did every night, keeping an eye on the growth of his company. As always, some of those acquisitions were from his own brilliant business mind, created by him and approved by him. Others were simply there, created and driven by someone else, but all of them bearing his approval.

Marmoset shivered at the thought and shook his head. "Personal file," he said quietly. The acquisition data on the screen vanished and was replaced with a file tree of Marmoset's personal database. "Document: Directive. Access: voiceprint match," he said, his voice dropping lower.

The computer worked for another second before the words, "Voice Recognition Approved," shimmered in the air before him. A moment later, a scan of the letter he'd requested appeared. It was a letter he'd received shortly after chaos had smashed through the world and, in the year since, he'd read it countless times. He still marveled at the words.

> Dear Mr. Williams,
> Though it goes against my nature, I shall attempt to be brief. Victor Legio is no longer with the company. Legio Industries is mine. In due time, you will be unanimously elected to the position of CEO. Use your newfound power to grow Legio Industries as you see fit, while understanding I will be doing the same—in your name, of course. Use your newfound wealth to fund a well-deserved and extravagant, but quiet, lifestyle. If you do as I ask, I'll have no need to contact you for quite some time. If you disappoint me, you'll meet me much sooner than you wish, and I can promise it will be a fairly unpleasant encounter.
> Audentes fortuna iuvat—fortune favors the bold, Mr. Williams. But it does not favor the curious. I trust my

meaning is clear. Your path is laid plainly before you. Follow it. Enjoy it. But don't forget you are beholden to me in all things.

Until we meet,

I am Hade

Marmoset stared at the words and shivered again. For the past year, his life had been more than he could have ever imagined. He'd obeyed Hade's directive to the letter—acting for the betterment of the corporation and himself, and never so much as even uttering the name Hade. Today, richer than most, more powerful than all, there was nothing in this world he couldn't have; no hunger, lust, or desire he couldn't slake.

But things always change.

With a sigh, Marmoset looked up to the ceiling and, although he knew there was nothing there, he could feel the Sword of Damocles hanging heavily over his head. He knew it hung by a thread and he wondered if that was how Victor Legio had felt. He wondered if his end would be the same, or if the sword would fall on another instead. Looking down, he tried unsuccessfully to slow his heart rate as he unclenched his right fist and looked at the crumpled pink Post-it Note he had found on his desk not more than an hour ago. Still shaking, he slowly smoothed it out and again looked at the words that had been written on it.

"I think the time has come to finally meet, Mr. Williams."

It was signed "Hade".

ןודגמרא

Tishomingo, Oklahoma: The huge man placed his box of cigars on the counter, then picked up a copy of the *National Enquirer* and laid it down with the cigars. "Fine evening, isn't it?" he asked the smallish, balding and visibly shaking man behind the cash register. He towered over the proprietor of the little convenience store and his voice was deep, sounding like thunder rolling ahead of a great storm.

"Yeah, I suppose," the storeowner stammered, glancing past the man and out the window into the darkness, as if wishing he could be anywhere else but standing before this monster. Outside, darkness had come two hours ago, bringing with it a summer storm that promised to be a wild one. In the distance, he could hear the low rumble of thunder, and the occasional flashes of lightning had been slowly growing closer over the past hour.

The customer offered him a wide smile and leaned forward, white teeth flashing. "Do you read the National Enquirer?" he asked amicably, not noticing or caring about the effect he was having on the little man.

Summoning up all of his courage, the man shook his head and wrinkled his nose.

"Well, you should," the huge man said, tapping a well-manicured fingernail on the headline across the top of the front page. The nail was long and filed to a point and clicked on the countertop. "It could save your life."

"VAMPIRE KILLS FAMILY IN BUTTE, MONTANA! Read the gruesome story of how the Polk family was brutally murdered! See the shocking photos of proof that vampires do indeed walk among us! All inside!"

The storeowner shook his head again, this time in derision. "I don't read that garbage," he replied sourly. "Ever since last year, there's no story too wild for 'em to print. But people still buy 'em, so they keep printin' 'em."

"Do you believe in zombies?" the customer asked, changing the subject to one he knew everyone could relate to these days.

"Well, anyone should by now, after what happened last year," the clerk replied.

"Then why not believe in vampires?"

The storeowner was silent at first and then, in dawning horror, he stared at the man.

Hade tossed a one-hundred dollar bill on the counter and held the man's gaze. "Keep the change, my good man," Hade said casually, still smiling and making a show of tapping a long fingernail against an even longer canine. "Go buy yourself some wooden stakes."

Coming Soon...

FERRYMAN

THE THIRD SEAL OF
THE KRYPTEIA CONSPIRACY

As the world edges ever closer to the end of times, the ancient prophecies of the Book of Revelation continue to come true in devastating ways never before imagined.

Through it all, the race is on to find a long-lost relic that might very well swing the balance toward the forces of evil. As horrifying creatures from the underworld rise up to terrorize the faithful, the enigmatic Hade once again pits himself against the beleaguered "Kings" of prophecy in a contest for their very souls. But the Ferryman has his own secrets and his own motivations…and in time, the fate of the world may hang on who and what he truly is.

www.ingramcontent.com/pod-product-compliance
Lightning Source LLC
Chambersburg PA
CBHW051138030726
47504CB00004B/927